THE RENEGADES

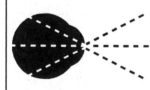

This Large Print Book carries the
Seal of Approval of N.A.V.H.

THE RENEGADES

T. JEFFERSON PARKER

THORNDIKE PRESS
A part of Gale, Cengage Learning

GALE
CENGAGE Learning

Detroit • New York • San Francisco • New Haven, Conn • Waterville, Maine • London

LIBRARY OF CONGRESS CATALOGING-IN-PUBLICATION DATA

Parker, T. Jefferson.
    The renegades / by T. Jefferson Parker.
        p. cm. — (Thorndike Press large print basic)
    ISBN-13: 978-1-4104-1274-4 (alk. paper)
    ISBN-10: 1-4104-1274-1 (alk. paper)
    1. Police—California—Los Angeles County—Fiction. 2. Police murders—Fiction. 3. Los Angeles County (Calif.)—Fiction.
    4. Large type books. I. Title.
    PS3566.A6863R46 2009b
    8137prime;.54—dc22   2008041882

Published in 2009 by arrangement with Dutton, a member of Penguin Group (USA) Inc.

Printed in the United States of America
1 2 3 4 5 6 7 12 11 10 09 08

For my father and mother,
Robert and Caroline,
who put bread on our table
and stories in our heads.
Thank you.

1

Hood got partnered up with Terry Laws that night, another swing shift in the desert, another hundred-and-fifty miles of motion on asphalt, another Crown Victoria Law Enforcement Interceptor that would feel like home.

They walked to the motor yard without talking. Hood was tall and lanky and Laws had a weight lifter's body that made his jacket tight across his shoulders. Various sections of the lot were marked by signs bearing the names of fallen deputies, and there were other sections awaiting names.

Hood logged the mileage and checked the tires for pressure and wear while Terry checked the fluid levels. The Los Angeles Sheriff's Department patrol fleet was old and worn, so they had to check even the obvious. Two days ago the LASD Lancaster station had lost another prowl car engine, over 260K miles on it, finally succumbing just half a mile short of the yard with a clanging metallic death rattle. The deputy had pushed it to the curb and called a tow.

Hood drove. He bounced the car from the yard onto the boulevard and felt the comforting sense of motion that connected him with last night's motion, which connected him with the motion of the night before, and of the week and the months before that. Motion ruled. He believed that it might lead him to what he was looking for. It had to do with a woman who had died, and a piece of something in him, perhaps soul, that had gone missing.

It was windy and getting dark, and the desert cold was sharp and weightless as a razor blade. A tumbleweed skipped across Avenue J. The overhead traffic light at Division Street shivered on its cables. Snow was coming and Hood had not yet seen snow in this desert.

He drove and watched and listened as Terry talked about his young daughters — basketball players, good students. Terry's friends called him Mr. Wonderful because he was two-time L.A. Sheriff's Department bodybuilding champion, a devoted father, and a Toys for Tots warrior each Christmas season. He had a heroic chin and an open face and a quick smile. He'd made a high-profile arrest on a double homicide almost two years back, which gave him good mojo in the department. He was thirty-nine, ten years older than Hood. Hood had patrolled with Laws before and had thought that something was eating the big man, but Hood believed there was something eating most of us.

They drove north on Division, east on Avenue I past the fairgrounds. Tuesday nights in winter were slow.

Hood's world was the Antelope Valley, north of L.A. The valley is the new frontier, the final part of the county to be heavily developed. It is high desert, ferociously hot and cold, and dry. The cities are booming but not quite prosperous. Thousands of the homes are new. They're affordable. The cities have nice names, like Palmdale and Rosamond and Pearblossom and Quartz Hill. There were no antelope in the Antelope Valley until the twentieth century, when some were released so the valley could live up to its name, a California thing, to dream big and fill in the details later. Beyond the Antelope Valley is the vast Mojave Desert.

"What do you make of AV after six months?" asked Laws.

"I like that you can see so far."

"Yeah, you get the wide open spaces. It's

not for everybody. You'll like the snow."

Antelope Valley was in fact the Siberia of the Sheriff's Department, but Hood had asked to be transferred here after some trouble in L.A. He wanted to forget and not be seen. He had been a Bulldog-in-training — LASD homicide — for about four weeks but it didn't work out. Then, he had talked to Internal Affairs about a superior he mistook for an honest man, and who was soon to stand trial for eight felonies. Hood would be called as a witness by the prosecution, which he dreaded.

They got coffee and continued out Avenue I, made the loop around Eastside Park. On the western horizon the last yellow strip of day flattened under the black weight of night. Hood looked out at the new walled neighborhoods stretching for miles, tract upon tract, houses huddled roof-to-roof like they were trying to beat the cold. Hood had thought that he would like Siberia and he did. He was a Bakersfield boy, used to open land, heat and wind, fast cars and good music.

"I hate these Housing Authority raids," said Terry. "They make me feel like a hired thug."

"Me, too," said Hood. At roll call they'd been told to expect an early shift assign-

10

ment to assist L.A. County Housing Authority at the Legacy in east Lancaster. The Legacy was Section 8, federally subsidized housing. When the owners had a problem with tenants they went to the Housing Authority, but HA officials had no real authority at all — they were not armed, could not make arrests or serve warrants. Tenants were not even required to allow them into their home. But HA could request assistance from LASD deputies, and fear opens doors. Hood resented these assignments, which played out by class and race: the owners and renters, the landed and the poor, white and black.

Dispatch called a drunk and disorderly out at the Orbit Lounge and a west side cruiser rolled on it. Hood had quickly learned that the AV is flight country — from Edwards Air Force Base and Yeager and the Right Stuff to the Stealth Skunkworks to the huge commercial aircraft plants that once flourished here. He knew that most of that work was done elsewhere now, but the bars still had names like the Orbit or the Firing Range or the Barrier.

"I feel action on tap tonight, Charlie. That's good. You know Mouse Washington? You seen him? Big, Eight Tray Crip, built like a Hummer? Lives with his mom and a

11

bunch of pit bulls in a Section 8? He beat the piss out of two Bloods right outside the mall yesterday. Two of his dogs held them, deep puncture wounds all up and down their legs. One of 'em's still in the hospital."

Hood, in his six short months up here in the desert, had seen that the gangs were thriving. There had been another killing just last week, a seventeen-year-old clicked up with 18th, standing on a street corner waving a big foam "New Homes" sign shaped like an arrow. Hood had learned that these people were called "human directionals" by the developers who hired them, but most people just called them sign wavers. He'd also noted that some of them got really good at it — twirls and aerials and behind-the-back NBA stuff. They could entertain you at a stoplight. But when the Blood gun car had passed by, the human directional with the "New Homes" sign had six bullets in him and he died later in a hospital.

"Speaking of dog bites," said Laws. He unbuttoned his long-sleeved uniform shirt and showed Hood his left forearm, discolored and punctured, but healing. "That's what I got for helping a guy out." He turned on the dome light for a moment and looked at the wound as if it were a mystery he hadn't yet solved.

"Dog have shots?"

"Yeah. Don't worry, I'm not going rabid on you."

They pulled into the Legacy housing development. Big homes, two stories, peaked roofs with dormers and faux shutters on the windows. The tract was ten years old and some of the houses already looked like they should be condemned. The desert ages buildings and people twice as fast as anywhere else.

Fourteen-eleven Storybook had a dead brown lawn, weeds eating through the driveway concrete and a broken window patched with plywood against the cold. There were signs of effort, too: a couple of shiny kids' bikes up by the porch and a bird feeder swinging from a lemon tree in the middle of the dead grass, and a bed of wind-lashed rosebushes by the garage.

A Housing Authority van was parked in the driveway, two men standing by the driver's door. Hood and Laws pulled up to the curb opposite and parked just short of a peppertree thrashing in the wind. Hood heard the crunch and rattle of peppercorns when he stepped out of the car and crossed the street.

The Housing Authority investigators were Strummer and Fernandez, both mid-forties, both wearing jeans and athletic shoes, Los Angeles County Housing Authority windbreakers and baseball caps. Strummer had lank blond hair and a long nose. Fernandez, who held a clipboard, was slope-shouldered and short.

Strummer explained that they'd heard complaints of marijuana use and loud music, and rumors that the boys living here had broken into a neighboring home, stolen a flat-screen plasma HDTV and put the family's Chihuahua in the freezer before they left. The dog was almost dead when the family found it, but it had survived. Nobody had filed a complaint with the Sheriff's Department.

"Single mom, Jacquilla Roberts," said Strummer. "Sons sixteen and eighteen, down with the Southside Crips. Two young ones. She's got a boyfriend, of course — a Lynwood felon who smelled the easy pickings up here in the desert. He's not supposed to live here but he mostly does. Fine citizens all."

"We'll see what we see," said Hood.

He and Laws followed the investigators up the walk. The porch light was on.

"If you guys draw some iron we've got a better chance of being invited in," said Strummer.

14

"Draw your own iron," said Laws.

"Would if I could."

"That's exactly why nobody will give you a gun."

"I'm trying to do my job."

"Then do it."

Strummer banged hard on the front door and waited. Then he banged again.

A woman's voice asked who it was and Strummer told her to open the goddamned door.

She was a tall black, strongly built and angry. Hood guessed upper thirties. She had on white warm-ups and white athletic socks and a white sweatshirt. Her hair was straightened and pulled back from a handsome face. She looked at each one of the men with an unhurried hostility.

"I don't have to let you in."

"We've had reports of drug use and loud music," said Strummer. "We want to talk to you and your sons."

"Come back with a warrant."

"We have the cops instead," said Fernandez. "These are Deputies Laws and Hood. We have no warrant because we don't wish to arrest you. We simply want to assess your status under Section Eight. We'll be back with the paper tomorrow, or we can get this interview out of the way now."

She shook her head and pushed open the door. The house was warm inside and smelled of fried fish and vinegar and mentholated tobacco. By the time Jacquilla Roberts had shut the door, Strummer was marching into the heart of the house, followed by Fernandez.

"They can't do that," she said, watching them walk into her kitchen. "I know they can't."

"They can't come in if you don't invite them," said Laws. "But once inside they can do a plain-sight search."

She glowered at Laws.

"Are your sons home?" asked Hood.

"Two young ones are upstairs watching the TV. Two older ones are out I don't know where. I got home from the plant about half an hour ago. I barely had time to get my long pants and work shoes off and you show up. That story about the dog in the freezer ain't true. Everyone talking about it. My older ones have some problematic behavior at times but they don't go puttin' no dogs in freezers."

"Tell the housing guys," said Laws.

"*Authority.* They have no *authority* over me."

"Don't aggravate them," said Hood. "They can make your life miserable."

16

He and Laws followed her down a short hallway and past the stairs. Two boys watched in silence from the shadows on the landing. Hood nodded at them and he heard the wind whistle against the house outside.

The kitchen opened to the dining room. There were pans and dishes in the sink and cut flowers on the counter and big boxes of kids' cereal and a jar of instant coffee under the cupboards. A pile of newspapers by a red trash can. A stainless steel bowl of dry cat food and a matching one of water. Hood saw that things were messy but not dirty.

Strummer was using a blue pen to poke around in a big red glass ashtray on the counter by the flowers.

Fernandez was looking down into a big fake-snakeskin purse that sat slumped and open on the dining room table. He pulled a hardpack of Kools from the purse, tilted open the top and looked inside as he shook it. "We heard some boys broke in one block over, on Shady Lane, and ripped off a big-screen and put this dog —"

"You heard bullshit, mister."

"Good weed isn't cheap," announced Strummer. "Maybe these boys — whoever they were — broke in, looking for some money to buy more of this."

17

He held up the pen, which wasn't a pen at all but a mechanical pencil, the kind with the clamp at the end to hold the lead. Or to grasp something. In this case, a small black roach.

Jacquilla looked at Hood, then at Strummer. "It ain't mine."

"But it's here," said Strummer. "And our drug policy is zero tolerance. That really does mean *zero.* This is enough to get you evicted. Fifty percent of our investigations result in evictions, Ms. Roberts. Fifty."

"It ain't *mine.* Mister, I got friends come here, maybe party sometimes. I got two older ones that might get into some trouble now and then. I admit. But *that* ain't mine and *I'm* who signed the Section Eight papers to live here and I am *not* going back to South Central on account of what is not mine."

"Let's get out of here," said Laws. "There's no profit in this."

The wind kicked up and flailed at the walls.

"How many kids you have?" asked Strummer.

"Four."

"By how many men?"

She glared at him and said nothing.

"Where are your two older sons?"

18

"They gone to get take-out. I don't feel like cooking again tonight, not after eight hours on the PCB line."

Fernandez looked at his clipboard. "Keenan and Kelvin. We need to see their rooms."

The youngsters scattered as the four men started up the stairs. A door slammed and there was laughter behind it. The room shared by the older boys was hot and cramped and smelled like bleach and cigarette smoke. There was a twin bed along one wall and a sleeping pad and bag along another. A closet stood open, mounds of clothing piled on the floor, more hanging. An old Zenith TV sat on the floor in a corner, with labyrinths of wires leading to a DVD player and a satellite receiver and an Xbox. The carpet was dirty and strewn with games on CD. From amid the sea of plastic game boxes rose a push-up bench with two hundred pounds on the barbell. Strong boys, thought Hood. The walls had posters of Suge Knight and Tupac, Mary Blige and Ludacris, Snipes as Blade, Smith as Ali, and the old Death Row Records logo with the masked guy strapped into the electric chair.

Fernandez went to the closet, leaned in and sniffed at something. Jacquilla stared at him.

"Keenan and Kelvin drive to get the take-out?" asked Strummer. "Or did they walk?"

"They took my car, soon as I got home."

"An hour and a half to get take-out?"

She tried to glare again at Strummer, but Hood saw something go out of her. "It might be late."

"Yeah, I'll bet it might be," said Strummer. "You don't even know where they are, do you?"

"Out there. In the wind."

Strummer shook his head and sighed. "We'll be in touch. Come on, Al. I've seen enough."

Laws and Hood thanked Jacquilla on their way out and she slammed the door behind them. Strummer gunned the van down Storybook.

"Idiots," said Laws.

Hood let himself into the cruiser. As Laws settled in, Hood looked out at the swaying peppertree and wondered how long Keenan and Kelvin would be out tonight. Terry closed his door.

Hood turned the key and got nothing.

It felt like a dead battery.

"Let's take a look," said Laws.

Hood was feeling for the Interceptor's hood release when he saw the windswept swaying of the peppertree become a different kind of motion — something thicker, concentrated and purposeful.

Someone coming.

Someone stopping in front of the car, on Laws's side.

Black man. Detroit Tigers hoodie. Sunglasses, red bandana worn pirate style, shiny black gloves. Vaguely familiar. And an M249 SAW machine gun pointed at Laws.

Hood was reaching for his weapon when the machine gun rattled and the windshield shattered and Laws screamed. Hood shouldered open the door and rolled into the street as the bullets whapped into metal and flesh. Then he heard a metallic clang and a pause in the volley so he rose into a shooter's crouch just as another spray of bullets cracked into the door right in front of him and something hot hit his face. He scrambled around the back of the car and came up again with his sidearm in both hands but the shooter was already midair, vaulting a fence into someone's backyard. Behind the shooter Hood saw a house light go on and a face in the window and he held fire, cursing as he ran around to the driver's side of the cruiser.

He pulled Terry flat to the seat and felt his neck for a pulse. Nothing. A car engine came to life one block over. Hood looked

21

down at Terry's ragged body then grabbed the radio handset and called in the officer down.

Then he broke out the shotgun and ran to the street corner, just fifty yards away. But the car was gone and there was only wind whistling against a light pole, and the lights coming on in the houses, and the deafening report of his heart.

Hood ran back to the cruiser and hit the flashers. He stood looking down at Laws, then covered him with his duty jacket. He made a promise. The cold hit his back and he felt the sharp pain in his right cheek. He wiped away the blood and looked in the sideview mirror and saw the dark shard of metal, or perhaps lead, hooked into his skin.

By then the residents were gathering in the street, wrapped in jackets and robes. Hood told them a deputy had been shot to death and the gunman was still out there, go back inside and stay safe. A few of them did this, but most of them stood staring at the bullet-riddled radio car as if hypnotized by the flashing lights. Hood saw the steam coming from their mouths and noses and he kept them away from the car and his dead partner, shivering as he waited for help.

2

Hood tried to talk to the homicide detectives at the scene, but two men emerged from the darkness, badged the dicks and said they were part of the Internal Affairs "shoot unit" and this was theirs.

The detectives cursed and the IA men cursed back. But the bald black IA man in a sharp suit guided Hood away from the detectives and the other, a white man in a beaten bomber jacket, fell in behind them. Half a block down the street, in a dark patch midway between two street lamps, a black plainwrap Mercury waited by the curb.

Sharp Suit got into the driver's seat and Bomber held open the rear driver's side door. In the faint dome light Hood saw a big craggy-faced man with a graying buzz cut and round, wire-rimmed glasses. Late fifties, high mileage, thought Hood. He wore cowboy boots and jeans and a white shirt with a leather vest.

"I'm Warren," he said. "Get in."

Hood sat and Bomber shut the door then went around and got in the front passenger seat.

No one spoke until they were out on Twentieth Street, headed toward Edwards Air Force Base. The air conditioner was turned up high and Hood felt his muscles shuddering against the cold. He thought of his duty jacket, soon to be riding away in the coroner's van with Terry.

"Talk to me," said Warren. His voice was rough and low. He set a small recorder on the seat and turned it on.

It took Hood twenty minutes. By then they were north of the city limits, paralleling the base on Avenue E. Through the cold air Hood could still smell the faint sweet odor of coming snow. The Joshua trees flickered in the wind.

"Describe the shooter again. Carefully. Everything about him."

"Black male, six feet tall, medium-to-slender build. Sunglasses and a red bandana worn pirate style. His face was narrow, not wide. His nose and mouth were unremarkable. His skin was very dark. His hoodie was black with the Detroit Tigers logo on it. He used a M249 squad assault weapon. He fired it right-handed, with the butt jammed

24

into his middle and his left hand pushing down on the stock to keep the muzzle down. I recognized the gunner's stance from my months in Iraq. Then he was gone. He could have been sixteen years old or forty. I'd guess young, by how easily he jumped the fence."

Warren nodded but Hood saw that he was looking past him. "Not bad, Hood, for a guy with a machine gun firing at him."

"I think it jammed."

"God and his mysterious ways?"

"I don't know anything about God. But my life was on his finger and I don't know why I'm alive."

"Tell me if you get any ideas about that."

"Yes, sir."

"How long have you been up here in the desert?"

"Six months."

"L.A. Internal Affairs speaks highly of you. I think highly of them. Some of them."

"That's good to hear."

Bomber turned and looked at me, then back at the road.

"Do you know who I am?"

"No, sir. IA is all I know."

They turned south on 110th Street, back toward Lancaster.

"What did you promise Laws, Hood?"

asked Warren. "Before he died."

"He was dead by time I could form a thought."

"Then what did you promise him when you saw he was dead?"

"That I'd find who killed him."

"Do you believe that, Hood?"

"Without question."

"Good. You are assigned to this case as an officer of Internal Affairs. The fewer who know that, the better for everyone. Your superiors will be advised and tomorrow someone will e-mail you an IA charge number for your time card."

Hood thought about this. From his tours in Iraq assigned to NCIS he knew what it was to be hated. And not just by the enemy, but by his own men. "Mr. Warren, I don't want to work for Internal Affairs."

"You made a promise and this is the only way for you to keep it."

"You have more experienced investigators."

"None with his partner's blood on his shirt."

Someone in front pushed a button, and an overhead light came on. Hood looked at the front of his winter-weight wool-blend shirt and at his shield and he knew it was more blood than could have come from the shrapnel still caught in his cheek.

"I respect what you did in L.A.," said Warren.

"The last thing I wanted to do was take down a fellow deputy."

"It was unavoidable for anyone with a functioning moral compass. Hood, I want you with us. I want you watching the watchers, protecting the protectors. There's no higher calling in law enforcement — you will learn this with time. I'll have Laws's package on your desk tomorrow morning."

"I don't have a desk," said Hood.

"You do now. It's at the prison. In a place we unjokingly call the Hole. Report to the warden's office at seven a.m. His secretary is named Yolanda."

Hood watched the dark desert march past the windows, sand blowing upon sand, Joshua trees stiff against the wind.

"You can say no, Hood. But you can only say it once, and that time is now."

Hood was not a planner. He was a man of the present, used to following his heart, which had gotten him mixed results.

"I'm in."

"Know the target and you'll find the shooter. They meet — beach and wave. I want you to bring me the beach. Bring me Terry Laws. Bring me everything he ever

27

did at this department. He's ours. He's mine."

IA dropped Hood off at the substation, where two of the homicide detectives were waiting at the main entrance. One was big and white and the other was big and black.

"I'm Craig Orr and this is Oliver Bentley," said big white. "We've got lots of questions and a fresh pot on."

"Lead the way, Bulldogs." Hood used the nickname for LASD homicide because he'd worked with them in L.A. for a few weeks, and he had wanted badly to be a Bulldog.

"Want to clean up that face, Hood? Looks nasty."

"Later."

Sitting in a small conference room he told them what happened, then told them again. Orr used a digital recorder and Bentley wrote notes. The coffee was bad and they drank a lot of it.

"So," said Orr. "Did Warren just recruit you to IA?"

"I'm on Terry."

"Thanks for being square with us," said Orr. "We all have jobs to do."

Bentley looked at Hood for a beat then tapped his fingers on the desk. "Someone cut the battery cables in your cruiser while you and Terry were with Roberts. The door was jimmied to get to the hood latch."

An hour later Hood put on a canvas jacket with a blanket lining and buttoned it all the way up and got in his old Camaro and drove back to the Legacy development.

It was two in the morning. The investigators were gone and the bullet-riddled cruiser had been towed away. The yellow crime scene tape had torn loose from the pepper-tree and now it flapped in the wind like it was trying to escape.

Hood circled the area with his flashlight. He picked up a few of the shards of windshield safety glass and rubbed their edges with his thumb, then dropped them into a jacket pocket. He could see where the crime scene investigators had dug into the asphalt to retrieve bullets and bullet fragments.

He shined the light up into the peppertree and watched the loose branches swaying in and out of the beam. He walked across the front yard to the fence that the shooter had so easily cleared, counting his steps: ten. Then he ran the light up the fence, then along the top, wondering if the man might have snagged something on the rough wood. If he had, the investigators had found it first.

He drove around the block to where he'd

heard the car start up, and he sat there a minute with the windows down and the heater turned up high.

At home Hood showered and dressed his wound and scrolled through the LASD enforcement-only Gangfire site. He could picture the familiar face he was looking for, and now, after the great slow settling of his adrenaline, the name came to him. He was an Antelope Valley Blood named Londell Dwayne.

Hood had shaken him down a few times and Dwayne was unpredictable. Once he ran. Once he smiled and offered Hood a Kool. Once he told Hood that if his johnson was big as his ears then Hood must have happy ladies. Hood had told him his ears were nothing compared to his johnson and Londell liked that. On that occasion, Dwayne had been wearing a Detroit Tigers hoodie.

Hood looked at the picture of Dwayne and a chill registered across his shoulders. He wrote down Dwayne's numbers on a small notebook he carried in his pocket.

Hood thought. L.A. County has fifty thousand gangsters, he knew, and over two hundred clicks. The killer's red bandana meant a Blood affiliation, but sometimes shooters fly enemy colors to mislead witnesses and to implicate rivals.

He looked at Keenan Roberts's picture and saw that he was not the shooter. Kelvin wasn't either. They were too big and too heavy. And it was hard for Hood to imagine either of them getting their hands on a weapon like the M249 SAW. He had seen their destructive talents in Anbar. A properly working SAW throws a thousand rounds a minute.

He went outside to the deck and looked out at his Silver Lake neighborhood. When Hood requested a transfer to the desert he had kept this apartment in L.A. because he liked the city, and because it gave him another hour of driving time each way, to and from the substation in Lancaster.

Hood smelled rain. He fingered the sharp pieces of safety glass still in his jacket pocket and for the hundredth time that night he wondered why Terry Laws had been murdered.

It wasn't done in the heat of the moment. It was an execution. An execution of a sheriff's deputy known to his friends as Mr. Wonderful.

Beach and wave.

Then he wondered something else for the hundredth time that night. Had the executioner let him live, or had his M249 jammed? They jammed in Iraq all the time from age and dust — it was an untrusted weapon.

If the gun had jammed then he was lucky.

If the shooter had let him live, why?

The only explanation he could come up with was that Londell Dwayne — or whoever was hidden behind the sunglasses and the bandana — had wanted to be seen.

He'd wanted a witness to tell his tale.

3

"Listen and don't interrupt. I invited you here to tell you a story. It's about a friend of mine we called Mr. Wonderful, and the things that happened to him and why they had to happen to him. Your friend Hood plays a role in this story, too. But it's bigger than both of them. It's about chaos and opportunity."

We're sitting in La Cage, a rooftop cigar bar on Sunset, which puts us at eye level with a billboard of two enormous models posed in a pouty stare-down. Their bodies are painted a gold that glitters in the up-turned lights. It's an ad for a scent that both men and women can wear and sure enough, you can't tell if these people are male or female or what. They're teenagers, just like the boy sitting across from me, though he looks older than they do.

His brow creases skeptically and he looks around as if someone could hear, but we've got this corner of the rooftop to ourselves. He leans toward me. I have his undivided attention. Terry Laws is big news in L.A. Everybody knows what happened to him, or thinks they do. The boy across from me starts to say something but I shake my head and put a finger to my lips.

"Picture a desert night in the Antelope Valley, August, two years ago. I'll help you get started, my friend — it's black and hot and windy. The tumbleweeds roll and the Joshua trees look like crucified thieves. Terry Laws and I are on patrol out of Lancaster substation, northern L.A. County. The wind bumps the cruiser, moves it around a little. The sand hisses against the windows and you can't see a single star. And that's when we spot the van, parked on the Avenue M off-ramp, halfway between L.A. and nowhere. Right where the tipster said he'd seen it. When I open the door of the cruiser, the wind tries to rip it off, and it takes me both hands to slam it closed before I pop my holster strap and follow Terry to the van. I'm whistling something because that's what I do when a situation gets tight. Helps settle the nerves, okay? Even walking up to the van I see it's all wrong — windows open, windshield smeared, lift gate up. Up close, there it is, two men inside shot dead, all sand and blood, sure, we check for life but it's fucking pointless and we both know it. All this had happened minutes ago. Not hours, minutes —"

"The Baja Cartel couriers, Lopes and Vasquez. This was all in the papers, Draper."

"We didn't know who they were. We call it in and wait for the crime scene people and the coroner and the dicks. We set up the detour cones then close the ramp. Hardly any cars using that exit in the middle of the desert at two a.m. An hour later the dicks and sergeants don't need us anymore so it's back in the cruiser to finish our shift. Not long after that we see the truck, a red Chevy half-ton, just like the caller said, and he'd gotten most of the plate right, so we flash the truck at the ruins off the Pearblossom Highway, where the utopia used to be.

"The tipster said he'd seen an older red pickup truck speeding away from the Avenue M off-ramp where the van was parked. We figure there's a good chance that the guy in the truck did the shooting. But the truck driver plays good citizen and pulls right over when we flash him. He parks by the river-rock columns of the old Llano commune. Terry and I get out and put a few yards between us. We both have our flashlights up and our hands on our gun butts.

"The driver gives Terry his license but he looks high, tweak city, shaggy hair and a beard and a black T-shirt. I can see blood spray on his upper left arm and when Laws gives me a look I know he sees it, too. The inside of the Chevy stinks like ammonia, you know, meth sweat. Terry orders him to get out of the vehicle. When he steps out I see he's about six foot seven or eight — Laws was six-two and this guy made him look small. He's looking at us like he wants to eat us.

— I haven't done nothing wrong tonight, he says.

— For a whole night, says Laws, congratulations.

"Then Terry hands me the guy's license. Shay Eichrodt, thirty-four, six-eight, three hundred. I'm going to run it for warrants just as soon as we get this guy cuffed and stuffed.

"I look in the truck bed and see four suitcases, the big rolling kind, all lying flat. Like this guy's headed to the airport for a vacation, right? Terry tells Eichrodt to turn around and put his hands on the truck and spread his legs. Eichrodt turns around. He sways and loses his balance and I can see he's not just high, but drunk, too. Son of a bitch falls down to his knees then groans and pitches over facedown in the dirt, prones himself right out for us. Terry takes a wrist restraint and goes to lock him but Eichrodt kicks Terry's shins and knocks him ass over flashlight. Eichrodt is up, fast as a cat, and I'm drawn and yelling but he and Terry are already going at it and there's no way I can fire so I holster up and draw my baton and jump right into the fun. I hit him hard on the knee so he picked me up and threw me against the cruiser. I weigh one-eighty, and none of it's fat, but he threw me like I was a doll. Even Eichrodt wasn't strong enough to lift all of Terry and his muscles off the ground, but I could see them in the cruiser lights, Terry with the baton and Eichrodt with his fists, bludgeoning each other like a couple of giants in combat. So I charged back just like I had good sense, working his legs and knees before he could hit or kick or throw me. But that bastard just wouldn't fall. He was a bloody mess. So were we. For a minute I thought he was going to win.

"When Terry hit Eichrodt over the head with his baton for probably the tenth time, Eichrodt went down hard and he didn't move.

— He looks dead, says Terry.

— He's breathing, I say. He's alive.

"We cuff him with two pairs of restraints on his wrists and two on his ankles. Then Terry and I check our wounds. Terry's got a deep cut over his eye and a torn ear, and his jaw is swelling up like it's broken. I have a cut lip and a swollen eye, and my forehead has a lump the size of a baseball from hitting the car. But we're okay, none of it is that serious. Terry calls in. I kneel down by Eichrodt and check the restraints and I watch the cars going past just a few yards away on the highway, and it dawns on me how close I've just come to getting killed by this guy."

I pause for a moment and sip my tequila. The boy drinks beer. I relight my cigar then pass the lighter to him and he relights his. Down on the Sunset Strip the sidewalks are busy with people. The cars move slowly. Taillights twinkle and brake lights flash. A million hearts, a million hustles.

"I read the papers, Coleman," he says. He yawns. Like a lot of teenagers, he is eager to be unimpressed. "You and Laws found a handgun and forty-eight hundred dollars in a toolbox in the truck. You found brass that matched the gun, and the bullets that killed the couriers. That would have nailed

38

Eichrodt in court but he never made it to trial."

"Correct."

I watch the parade on Sunset. The cops have pulled over a black Suburban and I think of all the black Suburbans I saw in Jacumba, where I grew up. Jacumba squats at the Mexican border down east of San Diego. No man's land. Suburbans are the vehicle of choice for soccer moms and Mexican drug traffickers, and there were no soccer moms in Jacumba.

"I've already told you one thing that didn't make the papers," I say. And I'm sure he knows what it is.

"The suitcases," he says.

"Yes."

"Well, what was inside? What did you do with them? How come they didn't make the news?"

"Before I answer that, I want to tell you something. It's something that the young don't understand. It's the most important thing I've learned so far and I want to give it to you now. Listen: things in life only happen at two speeds — fast, or not at all. That's why you need to know what you want. Because when you know what you want, you'll be able to see the difference between chaos and opportunity. They're

39

twins. People mistake one for the other all the time. You get about half a minute to decide what you're looking at. Maybe less. Then you have to make a choice."

"So what was in the suitcases?"

The boy is staring at me now. I'm about to tell him something that I've never told another person, something damning and dangerous and unretractable. I'm going to do it because I see big potential in this young man. He's gifted by history and inspired by his blood. I think he's what I'm looking for.

I curl a finger at him. He leans in and I whisper in his ear.

"The couriers' money, Mexico bound. Four suitcases. Three hundred forty-seven thousand and eight hundred dollars."

He sits back and his brow furrows again and he looks out the window then returns his gaze to me. He wants to smile but he doesn't want to be caught smiling. Love has a face. So do fear and envy and surprise and every emotion under the sun. His face is joy.

"Incredible."

"Not really."

"You and Laws took it."

"Did we?"

"You had to. It's the whole point of the

story — chaos turning into opportunity."

"I'm glad you understand that. Because this is where the story begins to get interesting. Another beer and another cigar?"

"Oh, yes."

I nod to the waitress and she nods back.

4

Yolanda led Hood down a hallway in the rear of the admin building of the Mira Loma Detention Facility, then down a flight of stairs half-hidden behind some vending machines. The door to the IA room had no window, just a plastic shield with the numerals 204 on it. There was no electronic card entry. She opened the door with a bright new key and placed the key in his hand.

Inside, the office was small and cold. Four cubicles shared an empty common area. The carpet was sea green. There was one window in the office, vertical, narrow and fortified with chicken wire. Through it Hood saw the concrete retaining wall for the basement level, and above the wall was a peekaboo view of the west prison grounds, the twenty-foot chain-link fences topped by razor wire, and the sun-bleached gun towers.

Hood looked at the neat, impersonal cubicles.

"This is your station," she said. She had a pleasant face and bony hands.

Hood's cubicle was smaller than a prison cell. Yolanda gave him one of her cards, with a county number handwritten on the back for charging long distance calls on this, the state line. The phone on the desk was black and heavy and had a curled cord and looked Hood's age. Terry Laws's package — department slang for a personnel record — sat squarely in the middle of Hood's new world.

"The state watches every penny," said Yolanda. "So please turn off the lights when you leave. The thermostat is centrally controlled so there's no use trying to turn up the heat."

"No heat."

"There is heat. But it's unavailable."

On the way out she flicked the lights off, then on again. When the door swung shut behind her, the lock clicked loudly.

Hood soon discovered that Terry Laws had been a solid deputy. He'd played football and graduated from Long Beach State at twenty-three, one year after the L.A. riots. A year later he'd completed training at the

L.A. Sheriff's Academy, and begun his sworn duty at the Twin Towers jail in Los Angeles.

Laws had worked his way up to deputy III, leaving the jail after two years for patrol, then warrants, then back to patrol. His base salary was $4,445 a month. He'd been cited for distinguished service for resuscitating a child after a swimming pool accident. He was LASD bodybuilding champion in 2001, when he was thirty-one, and again the next year.

He had never been cited for excessive use of force and his number of citizens' complaints was average. He'd fired his weapon only once on duty, at a fleeing assault suspect who had fired at him. Both had missed.

He and his partner, Coleman Draper, had arrested the killer of two *narcotrafficantes* back in the summer of 2007. Hood remembered that story. The murderer was an Aryan Brotherhood head-cracker named Shay Eichrodt. He was later committed to Atascadero State Hospital. Both Laws and Draper had been commended for making the arrest.

Laws had married at twenty-four, had a daughter a year later, and another a year after that. He divorced at age thirty-four and asked to be transferred from L.A. to the desert substation in Lancaster. Just like me, thought Hood. Why the desert? Hood wondered if Laws liked the miles, the motion, the flat, wide-open land, the twisted Joshua trees and the hot orange sunsets. Hood read that Laws had remarried eighteen months ago. For the last four holiday seasons Laws had helped run the sheriff's Toys for Tots program.

Hood looked at the pictures. Laws's department mug showed a square-jawed man with wavy dark hair and a forthright smile. There was a picture of him receiving a bodybuilding trophy, the sleeves of his sport jacket taut with muscle. The *Daily News* photographed him with two other LASD deputies, all wearing elf caps and standing behind three large boxes overflowing with new toys.

Hood saw that he would have been forty years old in June.

He remembered what Laws had said the night before, about helping the Housing Authority shake down Jacquilla Roberts: *There's no profit in this.*

He remembered the sound of bullets going through Terry Laws's award-winning body.

He left a message for one of Terry's

45

regular partners, saying he wanted to talk with him.

He called another regular partner, the reserve deputy Coleman Draper, who answered on the third ring. Hood told him who he was and what he wanted. Draper said that Terry Laws was one of the finest human beings he'd ever known and there was no time like the present to talk about him, especially if it involved breakfast and would help them find the dirtbag who'd killed him.

The snow started just as Hood left the prison parking lot. It materialized out of an endless silver gray cloud that looked to be no more than a hundred feet off the ground. He stood for a minute and let the light, dry flakes fall around him. They were cold on his neck but on his hot punctured cheek they were soothing. The snow settled on the spikes of the Joshua trees, rimming them with white. The storm followed him down Highway 14 but at Agua Dulce turned to rain that roared heavily upon the cruiser roof.

Hood met Draper in Santa Clarita, between Lancaster and L.A. Draper was average height, wiry, with a clean-shaven face and white hair cut short in the back with a wavy forelock in front. Hood guessed him at roughly his own age — late twenties. Draper had a sly smile and a spark in his gray eyes. His handshake was strong and his clothes were expensive.

He told Hood that he owned a German car garage down in Venice, lived right around the corner. Hood saw that Draper's hands were clean.

"Right," said Draper. "I don't do the work anymore. Seven years of that is enough. I'm just the manicured boss now."

Draper smiled at the waitress and ordered the works omelet, extra cheese, with a side of biscuits and gravy.

Hood was agnostic about reservists. He knew that some of them were good people, trying to help, getting a little buzz off the danger. But he also knew that some had a little-dog complex and that some were bullies. Some were rich and some were poor. Whatever they were, Hood knew, once approved, they got a gun, a badge and one dollar a year to work a minimum of five hours a week. Some of them worked full-time for that one dollar a year.

"Terry was a cool guy," said Draper. "He brought in his VW one day, said he'd heard good things about my shop. We did a valve job for him and Terry and I hit it off. A few months later he brought me into the Reserves. That was four years ago — '05. We rode as partners. But we were friends. Good friends."

Hood watched as Draper looked out the window. Draper blinked twice, quickly, and sighed. "Black dude in Blood red is what I heard. An M249 SAW machine gun."

Hood nodded.

"How many shots did Terry take?"

"Many."

Draper looked at him. "Murder a deputy? That's a prestige initiation. Fuckin' animals."

"Any threats against Terry?" asked Hood.

Draper nodded. "Well, he'd popped his share of punks and gangsters. Aryans, black gangstas, Mexican, *Eme,* MS-13. They all threaten. Even the drunk desert rats threaten. The Antelope Valley, what do you expect? Nothing but the usual trash from those people."

"How about a Blood with a grudge?"

"We busted a guy named Londell Dwayne a month ago — grand theft auto. That's what it looked like to us, anyway. Turned out to be his girlfriend's sister's boyfriend's ride. Something like that. By the time we got to the bottom of it, Londell had spent forty-eight in jail. He's a big mouth. They

48

might have roughed him up some. Not a happy punk. He's clicked up with the Antelope Valley Bloods and they've got ties to L.A. because most of them came from South Central."

At Dwayne's name, a jolt of adrenaline went through Hood.

"After the bust Terry tried to help out with Londell's dog — a pit bull, of course. The dog ended up lost and Londell blamed him. Londell is a hothead. He's got no self-control. But I don't know if he could do something like this."

"The shooter looked like Londell," said Hood.

"Be careful. He was packing a twenty-five auto when we rousted him."

The waitress brought more coffee. Hood looked out at the slowing rain and the drenched oleander that ringed the parking lot.

"It looked planned," he said.

"It sounds planned."

"Talk to me, Coleman."

While they ate, Draper told Laws that Terry was an easygoing man, big on fitness and small on 'tude. Smart. Generous, willing to work hard. One of the good guys.

Hood asked for the downside. Draper thought for a minute, then said Terry didn't have enough ego to stand up to some people. He said Terry was happy to show his good side, like being in shape and helping with the Toys for Tots thing, but wanted to hide the fact that he was prone to drinking and depression. Who wouldn't?

Draper said Terry's ex-wife was a bitch but Terry's two teenaged daughters were good girls who adored him. His second wife was a divorcee, a cute young peach with a taste for nice things.

"He picked the wrong women without fail," said Draper. "That was a true talent, and a running joke of ours. But he was loyal to them, to a fault."

Draper looked out at the rain and blinked twice again and Hood saw the moisture come to his eyes. Then his eyes became dry and still.

"What can I do?" he asked.

"Names and l.k.a.'s of black gangsters he'd rousted or busted."

"I'll have them to you by noon. I'd look at Londell. Tell him I said hi. How are you holding up, Deputy Hood?"

"I can't believe what happened."

Draper was nodding. "How'd you get mixed up in IA?"

"They came to me. You know, I'm doing this for Terry."

"If you go back to patrol, let's ride sometime, Charlie. I can learn from you."

"Judging from history I'm due back on patrol in about three weeks."

Draper smiled. "I heard about all that. You nailed a bad cop. That was a good thing."

Hood drank the last of his coffee and got out his wallet. "Draper, how come you do this? You make a dollar a year putting your life on the line. It could have been you sitting next to Laws."

Draper stared at Hood. "Deputy Hood, I wish I *was* sitting next to Terry. I mean no disrespect. Law enforcement is something I feel strongly about. My father was a reserve deputy. His father was a real one. In Jacumba, down by the border."

"Rough country."

"The roughest in the world."

Hood called Orr and told him what he'd learned about the bad blood between Terry Laws and Londell Dwayne, and that Londell looked enough like the shooter to warrant a knock-and-talk.

An hour later he met Orr and Bentley in the parking lot of Londell Dwayne's apartment in Palmdale. The storm had blown through but the sky was dark and shifting. A few inches of fresh white snow lay everywhere. There were snowcapped tumbleweeds piled up against a sign that said "The Oasis — Now Renting." Londell's crib was upstairs.

Hood popped the snap on his hip holster and followed the Bulldogs up the concrete steps. Their weight vibrated the metal staircase, and the snowflakes on the railing wobbled and fell. The front windows of Londell's place were blacked out with tinfoil and Hood heard a bass line throbbing inside. Bentley timed his knocks between the beats.

The door opened and the music got louder and Londell stood eye-to-eye in front of them. He was a slender man, no shirt, heavy bling, shorts below his knees and clean white K-SWISS ankle-highs. Hood watched him focus on the badge that Bentley held up. His eyes were deep brown in the middle and yellow outside. He looked at Bentley, then Orr, then Hood. Hood's nerves rippled — goddamn if Londell didn't look like the shooter. Facial type. Body shape. Posture.

"Bentley," said Dwayne. "The whitest nigga in Antelope Valley."

"We'd like to talk to you," said Bentley.

"So talk to me."

"You'll have more privacy inside."

"None of you is coming in here without no paper."

"You know Terry Laws, the deputy," said Bentley.

"I know he's room temperature."

"What else do you know?"

"I know he busted my ass for something I didn't do, and he stole my dog and lost her. Her name is Delilah if you see her. She's running loose somewhere in this world."

"Were you there when Deputy Laws was shot?"

"Naw, *man.*"

"Yeah, man. We've got a witness who says the shooter looked a lot like you. He picked your picture right out."

"I was here with Latrenya." He turned back to the room. "Lattie, get over here and tell these guys the truth they want to hear."

She appeared beside him, a tall woman with cornrows and hoop earrings. She was older and bigger than Londell. "We were right here. My sister, too. We heard about that killing this morning. We don't know nothing about it. Nothing."

"There," said Dwayne. "Can you handle that much truth?"

"You were here all night?" asked Orr.

"Whole night except out for pizza at Little Caesar's at seven o'clock sharp. Me and Latrenya and Tawna and Anton, right here where I currently stand."

"They don't have nothing on you, Lonnie. They acting like they do but they don't."

"You heard the woman," said Londell.

"Give them Tawna's number," she said. "Let 'em talk to her. I'm going to write it down."

She was back a moment later with a matchbook. Londell snatched it away from her and gave it to Bentley.

"See this? This a Pep Boys matchbook and these are the Pep Boys. When you're done confirming my innocence with the phone number on it, you can poke little holes in their crotches and pull the matches through from the back. Make you laugh. You muthas need to laugh more. I can tell by the looks on your faces."

The door slammed.

The three deputies stood in the parking lot. The snow-frosted tumbleweeds tried to climb the "Now Renting" sign while Orr called the number and put the phone on speaker.

A polite and soft-spoken girl named Tawna Harris told him she was Latrenya's sister, and that she and her friend Anton had been with her and Londell from Monday evening around six until just after midnight: TV and King Cobras and Little Caesars and more beer and TV. She said that was the whole truth and nothing but.

Orr asked her a few questions, tried to get a contradiction, but couldn't. He finally thanked her and punched off.

The Bulldogs drove away. Hood watched them. He wanted to be a Bulldog himself someday but he'd had his shot in L.A. and now it was gone.

He drove off, too, then circled back around and parked across the street and down half a block from the entrance of the Oasis. He could see the front door and the foil-covered windows.

Half an hour later Londell bounced down the stairs. He'd put on a clean white T-shirt and a pair of shades. He drove a sun-faded Chevrolet Impala to a 7-Eleven.

Hood followed and parked across the street and watched. Londell came out of the store a minute later with a case of beer and a bag of something, flipped off Hood and got back into his car.

So Hood drove to the Little Caesars. The girl behind the counter said she had just talked to two detectives about Londell Dwayne and she'd tell him the same thing she told them: She worked the six-to-midnight last night, she didn't ever take a break except for the ladies' room, and she didn't ever see Londell and his ugly dog and ugly Detroit hoodie and his stuck-up girlfriend, Latrenya, never once, and she paid attention to every person who walked into that place because it was the most boring job in the world and you had to do something to make the time pass. And Londell was gonna make a move on Tawna, she promised Hood that.

5

Draper made himself a martini and carried it to his tiny Venice backyard and looked up through the bowing telephone lines at the cool, clear sky. The storm had passed and the stars looked polished. Music played from somewhere as it always did.

His shoes were quiet on the concrete as he crossed the old driveway and punched the code for the wooden gate. He walked thirty feet down the Amalfi Street sidewalk then into the parking lot of Prestige German Auto. He let himself into the small building, deactivated the alarm system, then walked through the short dark hallway past his office and into the garage. The familiar smells of gasoline and oil and steel and rubber all greeted him. He turned on the overhead fluorescents and saw the five bays, each with a German car either racked up or straddling a repair pit. He sipped the drink and turned off the lights.

Back in his office he reviewed the last few days of business on the computer. His manager, Heinz, had run a tight, fast ship. Draper liked Germans because they were dogged enough to grapple with the complex cars so proudly overengineered by their countrymen, and intelligent enough to prevail. They were honest with the customers — *und here are ze old Bilsteins vee-took off* — and therefore honest with him. He paid them well. Prestige German had grossed almost twenty thousand dollars in the last week, which after payroll, overhead, and insurance would land thirty-five hundred dollars in Draper's pocket.

He locked up and reset the alarm and called Alexia as he walked home.

"I'm back," he said.

"Are you all right?"

"Everything is okay."

"Now I'm happy. I've missed you. I only breathe properly when you're here."

"I'll be home in an hour."

"I'll be waiting, Coleman. I've missed you very much. And Brittany misses you very much, too."

He packed his clothes — mostly dirty — and stopped at the Mexican market for cut flowers, a bottle of the sweet Riesling that Alexia loved, and a sugary churro for the girl.

Half an hour later Draper pulled into the garage of his Azusa home. Alexia stood in the doorway to the house, backlit by the warm light from the kitchen. She was petite and perfectly proportioned and her black hair shone like that of a groomed racehorse.

Draper stood there with the roses in his hand, just looking at her. She wore a new white dress with red piping, and a red belt and heels, which were beautiful against her young brown skin. He hadn't seen her in a week and his heart beat hard as she came down the steps into the garage and opened her arms to him. He hugged her and pressed his nose against her luminous, fragrant hair.

"I'll help you with your luggage," she said.

"It can wait."

Alexia brushed his lips with hers then moved away from Draper, and together they looked through the open door into the house, where two-year-old Brittany waddled toward them. She was a pudgy miniature of her mother, sporting a pink satin dress and pink sneakers.

"She has a new dress for you, too."

"I'm the luckiest man alive."

Draper had first seen Alexia almost two years ago, exhausted and dirty and sick, carrying her baby daughter across a dusty lot up near Palmdale. She was cutting through the lot on a 109-degree day, Draper had noted, to save a few steps on her way to the bus stop. He couldn't take his eyes off her. His mind had instantly filled with possibilities, many of which had since been made real.

"Are you okay, Cole?"

"Now I am."

He handed Alexia the roses then lifted Brittany by the waist and shifted her to the crook of his arm and they all went into the house.

After dinner Draper's cell phone rang and he checked the caller ID before answering. He walked into the spare bedroom and closed the door. It was Hood, asking more questions about Londell Dwayne and his dog and Terry Laws.

Draper told him what he knew, then returned to the neat little dining room.

He looked at Alexia. Brittany smiled and drooled and banged her pacifier on the table.

"What happened, Cole?"

"A man I work with was shot and killed last night. The shooter got away. That was someone official, with questions."

She stood behind him and kneaded his

shoulders and neck with her small strong hands. Coleman hung his head and wiped a small tear from his eye. He kept wondering what Terry had told Laurel. Nothing? Everything?

"I'm sorry, Cole. I am so sorry for you."

"I'm all right now."

"When will you have to go away again? No. I'm sorry. I didn't mean to ask that. I know. I'm very sorry."

Alexia's small knowledge of him bordered the vast, willed expanse of her ignorance of him. To Draper it was better than trust.

"A little to the left. Yes. There."

6

Prosecutor Ariel Reed met Hood in the lobby of the downtown District Attorney building. They had talked on the phone several times but had never met. She was petite and fair-skinned, with dark hair squared off just above the eyes and just below her chin. Her shoulders were straight. She was about Hood's age and she walked fast. She led him down a hallway and into her office and began talking as she closed the door.

"We don't go easy on bad cops," she said. "The jury's been impaneled and we're ready to rock. We're on the trial docket for week after next, Superior Courtroom Eight — the honorable William Mabry. I'm going to call you as a witness, which means you'll need to be available."

"I'll be available."

The defendant was a Sheriff's Department deputy that Hood had helped bust last year in L.A. He had been running a stolen goods racket out of a Long Beach warehouse. The DA had charged him with ten felony counts of grand theft, and buying and selling stolen property. He was looking at eight to ten years.

Ariel gave Hood a level gaze. Her eyes were hazel. She tapped something onto her computer keyboard.

"I forgot to offer you coffee," she said.

"No, thank you."

"I go too fast sometimes."

"I forget to tie my shoes sometimes," he said.

"Our caseload is heavy. To think about it directly is to court insanity. But you detectives know all about that."

"Insanity."

Her smile was thrifty and brief. "Caseload."

"Okay, then."

She gave him another flat gaze. "Deputy Hood, what I want from you in court is two things. One is the straight story of what you saw in the Long Beach warehouse. I've got your reports here and they're very clear and detailed. I'll let you describe the stolen property. I'll also want a little emotion to show through. Sometimes it's hard to get a jury to care about merchandise. This L.A.

sheriff's deputy had eight hundred *thousand* dollars' worth of stolen goods. I want our jury to know what that looked like. What it felt like to see it."

Hood remembered exactly what it felt like to see it. He remembered standing in the warehouse the day IA made the arrest. It was a large, high-ceilinged room full of shelves of pallets containing new electronics, computers and peripherals, building materials, liquor, soft drinks, furniture, tools, toys, clothing — just about anything Hood could imagine. It was all new stuff, most still in the shrink-wrap, and it was stacked almost to the ceiling. It was barely organized. There were rolling platforms and electric forklifts to move it all.

"It looked like a madman's fantasy Christmas," Hood said. "It was impressive, the sheer volume."

She was nodding. "Good."

She looked at her monitor, then back at Hood. "Now, the defense will introduce into evidence the letter written to you by Allison Murrieta, telling you where to find the warehouse. I need to know why she wrote you that letter."

"We knew each other from a related case," said Hood. "She thought she was doing me a favor by handing me a dirty cop."

"The defense will try to link you to her."

"That won't be hard."

"In order to impugn your character, suggest that you were a dirty cop, too — consorting with a criminal."

"I'll tell the truth."

Reed paused and looked at Hood. "Then you've got nothing to worry about."

He could feel her gaze as he looked around her office. Her workstation was more than unusual. The walls were painted a pale gold. She had a very handsome desk of bird's-eye maple, not county-issue. The file cabinets behind her were finished in flame red enamel. On a sidewall were three framed photographs, staggered on a diagonal from high to low. They weren't easy to see from where Hood sat, but he could make out the general images. The top one was of a dragster doing a wheel stand off the start line. Below it was a photograph of a dragster with flames blasting from the exhaust pipes. Below that was another photograph of a red-and-gold dragster waiting at the Christmas tree. The top photo was in black-and-white. Three generations of dragsters, he thought. But he couldn't keep his mind on dragsters.

"I wish you could get him on murder-for-hire."

Reed looked at him sharply. "I can't prove murder-for-hire. Allison is dead. The guy who was supposed to kill her is dead. It's Shakespearean. What can I do with a cast like that, Deputy?"

"Okay."

She smiled. "I'm going to throw him in the slammer for a decade. Is that good enough for you?"

"I'll help."

"Tell me about the letter from Murrieta. I need to understand why she wrote it, and why she gave it to you."

Hood steered through the rough seas of memory, but he told her.

A few minutes later Ariel walked him outside. The day was cool and bright and the palm fronds shimmered in the sunlight. She put on dark glasses.

At First Street they stopped and faced each other. "A Blood with a machine gun on full auto? Close range?"

"Yes."

"You're a walking miracle."

"I'm not sure what I am."

"What do you mean?"

"The gun either jammed or the shooter let me live. Either option makes me kind of nervous."

"Do you miss the city?" she asked.

"I still live here."

"Thanks for making the long drive down."

She offered her hand. It was smooth and cool in Hood's own.

"If I can ever return the favor, let me know," she said. "I helped on Shay Eichrodt's preliminary hearing, so I got to know Terry Laws a little. Maybe there's something I can contribute. Anyway, I've got the Eichrodt file if you think it might help."

"It would."

"I know you're working it for IA. Jim Warren is a good and trusted friend of mine. Don't worry. He has me under an oath of secrecy."

She took off her sunglasses and gave Hood the same forthright hazel stare she'd given him in her office. At twenty-nine, Hood was inexpert at reading the unspoken language of women. Ariel put the shades back on and joined the flow of humanity on First Street.

7

"So we pull up to the U.S. Customs booth in TJ. It's the Friday after we arrested Eichrodt. Laws and I look out the window to where U.S. soil ends and the concept of guilty until proven innocent begins. We're making the leap. We've got 347 grand *packed* into two suitcases in the trunk and Laws is scared shitless. I tell him to relax, exhale dude, we're going to be okay.

"Homeland Security stops us, little black guy, looks like Sammy Davis, Jr. He looks at our LASD ID cards and our badges, wants to know why we're going to Mexico and I tell him to fish in Baja. A two-day trip, I say. He looks at our beat-up faces, wants to know where we're staying, and I tell them the Rosarito Beach Hotel. We've got three clear plastic tubs of fishing gear in the backseat, and six short, thick big-game rods in the storage space the Beemer has for golf clubs or skis. One of the tubs has some very expensive new saltwater reels. Sammy pokes at it and moves it around but he doesn't open it. Then he wishes us good luck.

"Next, the Mexicans ask us the same lame questions. I answer them in Spanish. There are three young Federales leaning against the booth, guys not much older than you, and they stare through us like we're not there —"

"Did you badge them, too?"

"One hundred percent not, my man. Cops mean guns and nothing terrifies Mexican officials more than guns. Guns can end up in the hands of unhappy citizens, and Mexico has plenty of those. Guns are the *only* thing that scares Mexican officials. Illegal drugs? Hell, bring them in, move them north. Drug cash? Sure, everyone wants American dollars. But guns in Mexico are another story.

"They wave us through. TJ's a pit but I love that toll road and all the little cities on the coast — Rosarito, Puerto Nuevo, Cantamar, El Descanso, La Fonda, Bajamar. Burning trash and tires, smells like heaven to me. At El Sauzal we turn east on Highway 3. Three miles from the turnoff we spot the dirt road with the pipe-rail gate across it. It's exactly where Herredia's L.A. lieutenant told us it would be —"

"Hector Avalos."

"Don't interrupt. So we both get out of the car and stand in the hot dust and wait. A few minutes later I hear a vehicle up the road. Two men materialize from the darkness. They simply *appear.* They're in camo fatigues and they've got machine guns. They unlock and open the gate and signal us through. Once on the other side I see an armored Humvee like the ones in Iraq, and we follow it — five miles of washboard trying to jar our fillings out of our teeth, and ruts that must lead all the way to the gates of hell. I don't know how the M5 handled it, but it did.

— I don't like this, says Terry.

— Keep your cool and a hand on your gun, I tell him.

— This was all supposed to go smoothly.

— For Mexico this *is* smoothly.

"Two men on the road direct us, waving like an airport crew to get the M5 across a wooden bridge, down a steep sandy hill then back up to a wide turnout where the road ends. Past the turnout is a ten-foot-high concrete-block wall. There's rebar poking up through the top and a gun tower behind it.

— Amazing, says Laws, the fucking criminals have protection like this.

70

— I think you'll be more impressed later, I tell him.

— If they don't kill us.

— They won't kill us, I say. We're American cops. Herredia will recognize a good deal when he sees one.

"In the dash lights I see Terry's face, still puffy and bruised from the arrest scuffle with Shay Eichrodt. He looks deeply uneasy. Then the wall itself opens. A whole section of it swings open to let us through. Laws cranes his neck around for a look at it as we drive in.

— It just opens, like a magic castle or something, Terry says. Like in a movie.

"Then four more machine-gunners appear on the road, one with his hand up, and suddenly this blinding beam of white light scorches into my car. I hear rapping on my window and get out. I tell Terry to get out. I'm half-blinded by the tower light and I feel hands on me, down and up, front and back, son of a bitch is muttering in Spanish to his friends but I can't quite hear him. My ribs are killing me from Eichrodt but I won't flinch, it's a matter of honor. The guy takes the nine from my hip holster and the thirty-eight derringer from my boot. He takes the twenty-two-caliber eight-shot Smith from the pocket of my Abboud

71

blazer, and the thumb-action folding knife from the pocket of my jeans. He takes my goddamned car keys.

"They pop the trunk and scuttle up to it with their weapons aimed into it, like they expect something to escape. Terry's standing staunch against the pat-down while they strip his weapons away. I start whistling because it helps me think. I understand one thing at this point: we are absolutely at the mercy of Herredia now. There is no accountability here; all it will take is a mere nod and Terry and I will be tortured and executed and never found. *Ever.* But I've seen these kind of people and this kind of lawless power before in Jacumba, when I was a boy, and I find it comforting. I can't say why. I understand it. It's simple, physical, predictable. I remind myself that there's life and there's death and you must choose life at all cost.

"Then we're back in the Beemer, following the Humvee down a much better dirt road; it's graded and graveled, with the lights of what must be Herredia's compound way back in the hills. I see an irrigated pasture with cattle, what looks like a driving range, and an airstrip. How's your beer, son?"

"I'm ready for another."

I get the woman's attention and she comes over and we order two more drinks. I call an excellent sushi bar down the boulevard and order a large plate of sashimi delivered. The traffic down on Sunset is getting heavier now, more of the republic cruising for sex, drugs and rock and roll. I light my cigar again, roll it in the heavy butane flame and draw the smoke into my mouth, send some down into my lungs, then exhale a blue gray cloud into the L.A. night.

I see the boy studying me. I pass him the lighter and he proceeds with the same ritual. When he starts to say something I cut him off.

"The wall around Herredia's compound was eight feet high, stone and concrete. I drive through a varnished wooden gate, still following the Humvee. Two more machine guns wait inside. I see the words El Dorado built onto the gate in wrought iron, the letters raised and connected like the letters of a cattle brand. I remember reading the poem as a kid.

"The home is a plaster-and-beam Spanish-style hacienda, hunkered low and flat beneath a canopy of palms. I see a bunch of smaller outbuildings up on the hillside to the west. Near the east side of the house there's a grove of thatched *pala-*

pas that glow, lit from the below. Pale blue reflections of water move on the undersides of the roofs. And I think: swimming pool and hacienda and driving range and airstrip and a hundred head of cattle and a small army — Herredia is doing all right in his rustic little office here in Baja.

"Then the Hummer driver points to a parking place outlined by jagged desert boulders. I park and we get out and face another goddamned gunman, this one an old man dressed in peasant clothes, with a head of wild white hair and a black eye patch. He's got a combat-shortened automatic shotgun on a strap over one shoulder and it's pointed at me. I lean into my car and pull out the plastic tub of new saltwater fishing reels. I tell him that we have brought gifts for Mister Herredia. He looks across at Laws, standing on the other side of the car, and tells him to get the luggage from the trunk. Terry does what he's told. Then the old man jabs the gun toward the outbuildings and I lead the way up a gravel path. At each of the first two buildings the old man barks *andale* and I don't break stride. I note that the moon is in the northwest now and I can smell the pasture and the cattle. The third building we come to is squat and square, with faint light coming through bright blankets hung over the windows. The door is cracked open. I look back at the old man and he motions me forward. I crunch up the path, nudge the door open with my foot and step inside. Pavers on the floor. Bare white walls. A black chandelier. The smell of cigars. A big iron desk, looks like something salvaged from a shipyard or railroad scrap, set on caissons made of tree trunks. I hear Terry and the old man come in behind me."

"Is it really Herr —"

"Herredia sits behind the desk with a fifty-caliber Desert Eagle in his hands and his eyes locked on my face. I bow and set the plastic tub down on the floor beside me. Then I take each of Terry's suitcases by their handles and roll them over next to the box. I'm winging this by now, son. Believe me. But I've got a beginning.

— I have journeyed long, I say to Herredia, whistling a song, in search of El Dorado.

— In the poem he sings the song.

— I forget words but I never forget a tune.

— I forget nothing. Explain this spectacle.

— My name is Coleman Draper. This man is Terry Laws. We came to offer our respect and ask your favor. We brought gifts.

"Herredia's gaze goes to the plastic box.

75

He's a big man, thick and wide, with curly black hair and a round, clean shaven face. His eyebrows are bushy and slant upward toward each other, which gives him a soulful, suffering look. His nickname is *El Tigre,* and there's some truth in it — he looks like a big lazy cat but you know he can turn it on when he wants to. He's wearing a white guayabera and a gold watch. Forty-six years old, I know. What else do I know? That he runs the North Baja Cartel to the tune of an estimated half million dollars a week profit. And murders his enemies often and theatrically. And donates millions of dollars to Mexican politicians, law enforcement and military personnel, at all levels. That he's influenced state elections in Nayarit and Sinaloa and Baja California for over a decade. And lost two brothers, a wife and two children to the drug wars. That he loves deep-sea fishing and American fast food. The fishing and fast food I learned from Avalos in L.A. Herredia stares at me and then, in a soft voice, asks me to show him the gifts. So I kneel and pry the plastic lid from the tub and set it aside. I pull out a box and open it.

— I say: This is the new Accurate Platinum TwinDrag. The ball bearings are impregnated with Teflon, it's got anti-reverse dogs and a removable spool stud. You can't overheat these things, no matter how fast they're screaming out line. And they're beautiful. This one is the ATD-130, rigged with a thousand yards of one hundred-thirty pound monofilament. For large tuna and marlin.

"I look into Herredia's deep-set black eyes. I hold the open reel box in both hands, placed it on the iron desk near the *patrón,* then step back to the plastic tub and lift out another box.

—We also brought you Daiwa's new Tana-com Bull TB100 power-assist reel, I say. It's sleek and powerful, nothing like commercial winches or those add-on contraptions. It's powerful. It comes with a power cord and a battery clip. It will save your strength, believe me. I thought at first that these power-assist reels were for fags but I'm telling you, if you're looking to drop a thousand feet of line and get it back up again, you might like the electric help. Let me know what you think.

"Herredia's eyebrows lower into a glower. His face goes from pensive to implosive. I step forward and set the Daiwa next to the Accurate, then return to my box of goodies.

— You'll recognize this, I tell him — the Penn International V 80VSW, rigged with fifteen hundred yards of two-hundred-pound test. It's considered a classic because it really is a classic. I'm partial to these reels, I say.

"Then I set it on his desk and go back to the tub."

"What's he thinking?" asks the boy. He blows a plume of smoke into the air.

"How can I know? Where to shoot me with the Eagle? Where to fish the Penn? Reading Herredia is like trying to read an Olmec head. So I continue.

— Mr. Herredia, I say, we also brought this Shimano Stella FA rigged up with one hundred and seventy yards of fourteen-pound test. Just a little goof-off reel, but the slow oscillation lays down line straight and fast, and the magnesium frame weighs hardly anything. Waterproof gasket, natural wool washers for low start-up inertia. Plus, I like the name, *Stella.* I knew a Stella once and she was tons of fun.

"I smile and set the box on the desk beside the others. Herredia trades hands with the Desert Eagle and picks up the Accurate, and starts turning its platinum-hued solid-block aluminum frame in the light of the chandelier. There's seven thousand dollars' worth of stuff on the desk in front of him. Then Herredia sets down the Accurate and picks up the Daiwa. He has sportsman's hands, dark and weathered on the tops and pale on the bottoms. I wait.

— I own all of these things, he says. All of them, except this electric reel.

— Then give them to your friends, I say. Or to your church. They're tokens of respect.

— But what else do you have for me?

"I reach into my shirt pocket. The Desert Eagle finds my center. So I show both my hands, then very slowly deploy two fingers into my shirt pocket. I bring out the small envelope. Inside is a card. The envelope has a cartoon hamburger with a smiling face on it.

— I know you like these restaurants, Mr. Herredia. There are plenty of them here in Mexico. You can load these cards in different currencies now — it's a new thing. So this one is loaded with fifty thousand pesos. The new third-pound Angus Thunder is good, if you haven't tried it yet.

"I step forward and waggle the gift card and set it on top of one of the reel boxes.

— Don't tell me you have one of these, too, I joke.

"So Herredia holds the huge pistol on my chest, and pulls the trigger. The action of the Desert Eagle is tremendously loud, and

I hear every machined part click and clunk into place until the hammer drives the firing pin into the empty cylinder. Terry hits the deck and the old man points the shotgun at him, cackling. Herredia is smiling so I smile back.

— No, I don't own one of those, he says.

— And that's not all, I say.

"I help Terry up and feel the trembling in his hand. I ask him to wheel the suitcases over and put them on the big desk. He rolls them over and has trouble getting the retractable handles back down. He's beyond nervous now, he's just plain scared. When he gets them on the desk in front of Herredia he unzips them and folds open the tops. Herredia looks into them, then back up at Terry, then at me.

— We recovered this two days ago at a crime scene near Lancaster, I tell him. We arrested the man who killed your friends. He was armed. There was a struggle, which came out in our favor. But it didn't seem right that your hard-earned money should sit in a property room in Los Angeles so we brought it back to you. It's all there, except for seventy-two hundred dollars. Two pounds of *your* five-dollar bills were found in the killer's vehicle and therefore booked as evidence. Another pound was left behind in the luggage to form a evidentiary link from the suspect to the couriers. Not one dollar more has been lost. We weighed it. Twice. There are three hundred and forty-seven thousand, eight hundred dollars.

"So, Herredia sits back and watches me from behind that heavy brow. I turn to see the old man puffing on a cigar, the shotgun across his lap.

— What do you want? asks Herredia.

— We want to be your couriers, sir, I tell him. We want to make this drive every Friday night, and deliver your money to you. We've got our own vehicles and guns, uniforms and badges, and our contacts, as necessary. We are American law enforcement officers in good standing. All we ask is to be treated with respect and to be paid four-and-a-half points. I suspect that's a point-and-a-half higher than your former employees made, but they were obviously not competent. Look how well they protected what belongs to you. We, as you see, are extremely competent. We're worth the extra pay, for punctuality, dependability and the security of having your assets handled by sworn law enforcement professionals.

— You murdered them and took my money.

— We arrested the murderer and he'll be convicted in a court of law.

"Herredia nods. I note a thin shaving of white around *El Tigre*'s big black irises. I wonder what it means. He raises his right hand and points at us, then circles the finger in the air.

"We turn clockwise, in the direction of Herredia's finger. I listen for the sound of the Desert Eagle being lifted and aimed, and know that if I hear it, it will be the last sound I'll ever hear. I keep turning — walls, windows, the old man with the stub of the cigar in his mouth and both hands on the shotgun. When I come full circle I meet *El Tigre*'s eyes again and I see something light and new in them.

— I will pay you four points, says Herredia. You will deal only with Avalos in Los Angeles. I will calculate the points and pay you here, in Mexico. Avalos will always know exactly what you have when you leave L.A. If you are ever short or late, your lives are over. If you bring someone else into my world, your lives are over. If you ever speak my name to anyone but Avalos, your lives are over.

"I take a deep breath and nod solemnly. I've just closed a deal that will earn each of us around seven-plus grand a week for

#2   05-15-2016 1:41PM
Item(s) checked out to Zinzi, Pasquale

TITLE: Corrupted [large print]
BARCODE: 3365640018596
DUE DATE: 06-12-16

TITLE: The renegades [large print]
BARCODE: 3365604932791
DUE DATE: 06-12-16

Boca Raton Public Library (561-393-7852)
Find us on Facebook!

eight hours of work. That's thirty grand a month, tax free, month after month after month. And if things go the way I figure, if Herredia's bloody cartel continues to prevail in the wars, and its market share of the U.S. craving for drugs continues to rise, the paycheck will only get bigger and bigger. I look at Laws. He's pale, but he's smiling.

"Then Herredia stands, and in one motion he tosses the Daiwa power-assist reel into the air over my head and shoots it with the Desert Eagle. The sound wave alone almost knocks me over. Bits of something metallic rain down on my head. There are holes in the ceiling. My ears are roaring but through it I can hear Herredia laughing, and the old man laughing behind him.

— You bring me a reel for fags! yells Herredia.

"Laws's face is bruised and his eyes are wide but I can see that he's deliriously relieved, almost happy. Herredia slides the fifty-caliber revolver into a holster on his belt, and points to the door."

The boy looks at me with a skeptical frown. He says nothing for a few moments, then he shakes his head and the frown melts into a smile.

"Sweet," he says. "Thirty a month for a

Mexican holiday once a week."

"Depending on what you consider a holiday."

"You've got rocks, Coleman. And luck."

"We stayed for dinner that night," I say. "Herredia insisted. The old man joined us. His name was Felipe. The dining room in the house was nothing like Herredia's office. The walls were adobe brick, with exposed beams of Douglas fir running the span of the ceiling. The floor was walnut, spar-varnished to a thick resinous glow. The window casements were walnut, too, and during the dinner they stood open for the warm Baja air. It was the best Mexican food I've ever had — ceviche tostados and chile rellenos and carnitas and bowls of pico de gallo.

"We drank California wine and Mexican tequilas. After dinner we went to the poolside cabana where four young women were waiting. They were beautiful and expensively dressed, relaxed and eager for conversation.

"When I woke up late the next morning, my companion brought me strong *café con leche* and a copy of the *Los Angeles Times*. Her name was Meghan, a California girl. She missed Redondo Beach. My ears were still ringing from the Desert Eagle. But I saw that I had died and gone to heaven, and

I couldn't wait to do it again and again and again."

8

Laurel Laws opened the door of her San Fernando home that morning and Hood held up his shield. She looked at it while Hood looked at her: a twenty-something blonde in a black satin robe over long black pajamas tucked into shearling boots against the cold. She held a big mug of coffee. Her fingers were slender and her diamond was large. Standing beside her was a black pit bull with a dinged face.

Hood followed her down the foyer, past a living room and a dining room. The home was ranch-style, open and light, with cool olive walls, trimmed with crisp white moldings, and pale maple floors. The paint and flooring looked new. There were paintings on the walls and wooden shutters on the windows. The dog stayed on her left, nails clicking on the hardwood floors. Laurel said the dog had been rescued by Terry, and his name was Blanco.

The kitchen itself was a darker green, and the appliances were all new and white. An interior wall was partially demolished, the drywall stripped off and the studs exposed.

"Remodels never end," she said.

She pushed a button on an elaborate contraption that ground and brewed and dispensed for Hood a cup of very good coffee.

They sat in a sunny breakfast room. She said Terry was a beautiful man, inside and out, and that her heart was fully broken. They'd been introduced by friends. At that time, she'd been divorced for two years from an abusive producer. Terry and his first wife had divorced two years before she met him.

"You know why divorce is so expensive, don't you?" she asked.

"No, I don't."

"Because it's *worth* it."

Now, after eight months of married happiness with Terry, and finally closing on this little piece of paradise, she had to start over.

"The house is just the house," she said. "Come out here."

She and Blanco led Hood outside and Laurel showed him the stable and the barn and the arena and the hot walker. It wasn't a large property, she said, just over a half acre, but it was zoned for horses and horses were what she needed. They'd only lived here for six months. It was a foreclosure. They had purchased it for nine hundred thousand dollars and it had already been appraised at a million one. Thank God, Terry had taken out a mortgage protection policy that would pay off 100 percent of the loan now that he was dead. She said that although she worked part-time at the Valley Equestrian Center, she didn't make enough to pay the mortgage and live on.

Hood saw that there were two horses, a mare and a gelding. Laurel gave them carrots and kissed them. "My children," she said to them. Hood felt invisible. Laurel took a call on her cell phone and walked away and Hood looked at the horses and remembered riding with his father through the rough Bakersfield farmland — the heat and the dust, the oil pumpers and dirt roads, the spring surrounded by willows and cottonwoods — and the happiness this often gave him. Laurel snapped her phone shut and walked back over and told Hood she had to go.

He followed her back toward the house and asked her if Terry had been afraid or worried, if he had had threats or money problems. No, she said, Terry was a simple man, and a good one. He asked her if Terry had been drinking more than usual and she said he never had more than two drinks a night — he was *so* into fitness. Hood asked her if Terry was happy and Laurel stopped and looked at him.

"He was happy."

"Did he mention the name Londell Dwayne?"

"Yes, of course. Terry arrested him then tried to take care of the man's dog while he was in jail. The dog bit Terry and got away and Londell blamed him for the dog getting lost."

"Did Terry say that Londell had threatened him?"

"Londell *did* threaten him."

She gave Hood the names and numbers of Terry's banker and doctor, and the last three months of telephone bills for their home number and for Terry's cell.

Driving out, Hood noted the late-model Range Rover and the silver Mercedes Kompressor convertible and the red F-250 extended cab with the camper shell.

He thought it was odd that Laurel had not asked any questions about Terry. Not one.

Adam Grimm was the personal banking

consultant who had worked with Mr. and Mrs. Laws. The branch was on San Fernando Boulevard. Hood identified himself and offered Grimm an LASD department number to verify his assignment to the murder of Deputy Laws. Grimm made the call and asked a few questions, hung up. Then he tapped at his computer keyboard, adjusted the monitor, and looked at Hood.

"Terry and Laurel Laws did a lot of business with us," he said. "They have two savings accounts, two checking accounts and a first mortgage with us. They have a stock portfolio offered through this bank, two IRAs and a Keogh. They have a line of credit and two credit cards issued through us. What do you want to know?"

He gave Hood the savings and checking account balances — and Hood saw that they were all in line with the earnings of a sheriff's deputy and a part-time equestrian center employee.

He saw, too, that the stock portfolio had been opened a year ago for fifty thousand dollars and was now worth fifty-one thousand, and that the retirement accounts had been rolled over and were in line with earnings. The line of credit was untouched and neither credit card had ever carried a balance.

"They are . . . I mean, he was a very scrupulous client," said Grimm. "They watched their money closely."

"Why two savings accounts? Why two checking accounts?"

"That's not uncommon, Deputy Hood. Autonomy. Independence. The accounts were held jointly, so either one could get balances, make transfers, write checks."

"Did any of those accounts apply to an investment property, or a business?"

"No. They are personal accounts."

Hood asked for the balance on the home mortgage and Grimm clicked away on the keyboard. It took a while. When he said three hundred thousand dollars, Hood was intrigued.

"Mrs. Laws told me they bought their place for nine hundred thousand dollars," he said. "So they came up with six hundred thousand dollars down."

Grimm tapped again, found the loan history, and nodded. "Six hundred and fifteen thousand."

"On a combined income of under a hundred grand a year."

"Yes."

"Did they close an account to get that money?"

"Not one of ours."

"Sell a property?"

He tapped and tapped more. He apologized for the slow computer. He stared at the screen.

"Yes. Mrs. Laws sold a town home in Studio City. She realized two hundred thousand dollars from the sale, it says here on the loan apps."

"Leaving four hundred fifteen thousand to go for the down."

"Correct."

"Did Terry sell a property also?"

"No. He was renting."

Grimm frowned at the screen as if it were misleading him. "There's a photocopy of the down payment check. It's drawn on the Pearblossom Credit Union, and signed by Terry Laws. Maybe there was an inheritance involved, or some other instrument."

"Is there a copy of Terry's ten-forty with the loan application?"

"Yes. I'm sorry I can't show it to you or divulge any information from it. Federal, you know."

"If I were to see it, would it explain to me where he got four hundred and fifteen thousand dollars?"

"If you were to see it, it would explain nothing of the kind. But you will not see it here in my office."

"Thank you," said Hood.

The Pearblossom Credit Union was new, small and neat. The vice president was a slender brunette named Carla Vise. Framed pictures of a cat faced out from her desk. Through her office window Hood could see a vacant lot filled with twisted Joshua trees and Spanish dagger. Hundreds of plastic shopping bags flapped and pressed against the windward side of a chain-link fence. The day was cool and bright.

Carla offered Hood jelly beans from a plastic bowl and he took a few to be polite. She eyed him over a pair of reading glasses as he asked her what she knew about Mr. Laws's down payment on his home. She told Hood that Terry Laws was one of her favorite customers, and that she couldn't believe that he had been murdered, right here in Lancaster. She excused herself, then came back a moment later with a thick green file folder. She dabbed an eye with a wadded pink tissue.

"Yes, he wrote the down payment check on his personal account here," said Carla. She opened the folder and started fanning through the pages. "High Country Escrow."

"Do you know where he got the six hundred and fifteen thousand dollars?"

She was already nodding. "Two hundred thousand dollars is what they made when they sold Laurel's place in Studio City. And the balance came from Mr. Laws's trust."

Hood's nerves stirred. "This is the first I've heard about a trust."

"Oh really? Build a Dream? He started it in the summer of 2007, a charitable trust. It raises money for Southern California children living below the poverty line. Terry raised a lot of that money from the Sheriff's Department — rank-and-file donations. You law enforcement people are generous. I think it's because you see so much poverty and crime. I'm surprised you haven't heard of it."

"So you handle this trust?"

"We have the trust account. I opened it for him. And Mr. Laws transferred four hundred thousand dollars from his charitable trust to his checking account the day before he made the down payment on his home. He got a good deal on the place, I might add. I was actually the one who told him about it. We had foreclosed and we sold low, as lenders sometimes do."

Hood was impressed that Terry Laws had raised at least four hundred grand for poor children in less than a year and a half. It was about six times his annual salary as a deputy.

"Isn't it unusual for someone to withdraw a large amount of money from a trust, then deposit it in a personal account?"

"He drew it as salary, according to the terms of the trust."

"He paid himself."

"As sole trustee he could do whatever he wanted. But to be honest — yes. It was unusual. I told him it was unusual. He was sitting right there in the same chair that you are. In uniform. And he told me that he was raising money much faster than he thought he would. Most of it was done online, he said, but the deputies were also setting up tables in front of supermarkets, giving out information and taking donations. The trust was just really taking off. But he needed a home — he was throwing away his rent money. Terry said the four-hundred-plus thousand dollars wouldn't take much time to replenish. And he said that he and Mrs. Laws had already arranged a charitable re-maindered trust that would deed their home to Build a Dream upon their deaths. And of course, by then it would be many times more valuable than four hundred thousand. He was good to his word about replenishing Build a Dream. The very next week . . ."

She went to her computer now and tapped away at the keyboard. "Yes. He deposited seven thousand, seven hundred and twenty dollars, back into Build a Dream. And the week after that, another seven thousand, two hundred. And so on. Always a Monday, unless we were closed. The trust stood at one hundred and forty thousand dollars the day that Mr. Laws died. He made a deposit the day before."

Hood did the math and figured the trust should have been up to $180,000. He wondered if forty of it might have found its way into the Laws's never-ending remodel.

"Always cash?"

"Yes."

"Did you report the deposits?"

"No, sir. The legal limit is ten thousand — we must report anything higher. Below that is perfectly legal."

She tried to muster a frank look for Hood, but then she dropped her gaze to the desktop for a long moment. "And to be honest yes, I wondered at the amounts, their size and frequency, and the fact that they were never over ten thousand. I wondered if something . . . not right was going on. But I didn't wonder long. Terry was the law. And I very much wanted to believe in the children's trust, established by a cop, and supported by law enforcement throughout California. When I looked at Deputy Laws, it was easy to believe. His . . . well, everything about him said honesty and goodness. I saw him in the paper with the elf cap on at Christmas. And I thought, well, if he overpays himself with funds he's raised, okay. It's temporary. He's earned it. He deserves a nice home and it will go into the trust someday. He's upholding the law and bringing in money for the poor. Now he's dead."

She was still staring down at her desk. She dabbed her eyes again.

Hood believed her rationalizations, especially when he factored in the thirty-something thousand per month that Build a Dream was bringing in to Carla Vise's small credit union. It was easy for Carla to believe in Terry Laws. It was profitable, too.

Four hundred grand in less than a year and a half, thought Hood. "When did Laws create Build a Dream?"

She flipped through the file, still not looking at Hood. "He opened the account on August 13 of 2007, with two hundred dollars. His next contribution was on Monday, August 27, for seven thousand and thirty dollars."

"Then once a week thereafter?"

"Yes. Every week."

"Look at me. You know you should have reported him."

"I broke no law."

"The world dies a little when good people do nothing."

She nodded and looked down while Hood set his card on her desk and walked out.

Sitting in his car, Hood thought back to August of 2007. He had been riding patrol in Section I, down in south L.A., glad to be out of Iraq.

While Terry Laws was riding patrol up here in the desert, making his first big deposit in the charitable trust he had just created.

After that, seven thousand dollars plus change fell out of his pockets every week, straight into Build a Dream. And when the trust amounted to just over four hundred thousand dollars he paid it to himself and put it down on a horse property in the valley.

Hood looked up to see Carla Vise coming across the parking lot toward him. She had her arms crossed against the chilling afternoon breeze. He lowered the window and she leaned in and looked at him with tearful, angry eyes.

"The day he opened the savings account

98

for his new charitable trust, Terry Laws was happy and smiling. Light came from him. He looked like he could carry the world on those big shoulders of his. But two weeks later, when he made that first big deposit, he was pale and he wouldn't look at me. His face was bruised. He had stitches. I asked him if he was okay and he said he'd made a difficult arrest. But it wasn't the arrest, because he never got over it. The bruises and stitches went away but he never got his light back. He never looked at me the same. His posture was not the same. I don't know if other people noticed. I don't know if his oblivious and condescending wife even noticed. But I noticed every single thing about Terry Laws, Deputy Hood. He was a different man."

Hood thought for a moment. He believed that people could be changed immediately and irrevocably by what they chose to do. The mark of true foolishness was to ignore this fact.

"I was swayed by my own foolish heart," said Carla. "It's the story of my life."

"It's everyone's."

Hood drove back to the prison wondering about Terry Laws. The Terry Laws he had known was neither radiant nor haunted. He was a nice guy but Hood had always thought

Laws was trying too hard. He was vain about his muscles and proud of his smile. But he had the decency to take sides against the Housing Authority on behalf of Jacquilla Roberts and her imperfect sons.

Again, Hood remembered what Laws had said that night. *There's no profit in this.* He wasn't sure why it stuck in his head. Maybe the odd application of the word "profit" to a routine citizen interview.

He wondered what had changed Terry Laws. When he got to the Hole he let himself in with his shiny new key, turned on the lights and took Laws's package from the locked desk drawer.

Hood knew that on August 13 Laws had opened his trust with two hundred humble dollars. He was happy and strong. He had the light.

But less than two weeks later, when he brought that first big cash deposit for the trust, he looked battered and tormented. If you saw him as clearly as Carla Vise had, thought Hood, it was clear that Terry Laws had died a little.

Hood saw that two things had happened in between.

One: Laws and Draper had arrested Shay Eichrodt — the kind of high-profile, get-a-killer-off-the-street arrest that any cop would love to make. An arrest that mattered, protected people.

And two: Laws had come up with seven grand in cash.

Hood stared out the window at the prison, the razor wire, the cold blue Antelope Valley sky. The sky and the wind and cold reminded him of Anbar. When he thought of Iraq his mind resisted and his heart became heavy.

Next Hood spent some time on the search engines, but couldn't come up with Terry Laws's Build a Dream Foundation. There were plenty of Build a Dreams, but none were charities raising money for poor children in Southern California. He could find no number through Information, no listing in the Antelope Valley phone books, no one at the Antelope Valley Chamber of Commerce or Rotary who had ever heard of it. He called some of his deputy friends and not a single one of them had heard of it, either.

Hood called Ariel Reed. Then he drove south to LASD headquarters in Monterey Park, and signed out the Lopes/Vasquez murder book from Records.

9

"The tip came from an anonymous caller," she said. "It was made from a pay phone in Lancaster a little after two in the morning. Poor quality — wind and road noise. He said there was a shooting on Avenue M at the highway. Said a guy with a gun drove off in a red pickup truck. He'd gotten partial plates. He gave those to the nine-one-one operator then hung up. I heard the recording. Mexican accent. He sounded drunk."

Hood looked up from his notebook and bumped into Ariel's frank gaze.

"Laws and Draper were first responders," she said. "Both victims were gunshot to the head, both dead on scene. The deputies sealed it off and gave the detectives what they needed. By three-thirty they were back in the cruiser, finishing out the graveyard shift. And lo, the maybe-drunk tipper got the partials right. At four-twenty Laws spotted a red Chevy pickup westbound on the Pearblossom Highway. They saw some of the right numbers, pulled it over. It was right there where the ruins of Llano del Rio are — you know, the old socialist utopia. Anyway, no utopia that night, just a bloody battle."

Ariel's office had a view to the west. It was evening and the old DA building was hushed. The sun had rolled off the horizon but there was still a tint of red in the blue black sky. The lights of L.A. flickered below. Hood thought of his view from the Hole.

"It was violent," he said.

Ariel nodded and flipped through the file. "Shay Eichrodt, age thirty-four, six-eight, three hundred pounds. A felon, Aryan Brother, later determined to be very high on crystal meth and alcohol. Laws ordered him out of the vehicle. Eichrodt complied. But instead of shutting the door he collapsed in a heap on the road shoulder. They went to cuff him and he came up fighting. He punched and kicked and blocked their blows for several minutes — he had some martial arts and he was strong as a bear. They struck him approximately forty times before he went down and they finally got him cuffed."

Ariel handed Hood the Sheriff's Department photographs of Eichrodt, Laws and Draper shortly after the arrest.

Eichrodt was an immense, unconscious and bloody pulp. Laws and Draper were cut, bruised and bleeding, too, but it was nothing by comparison.

"Some of the blows were glancing," said the prosecutor. "Some were not. The head shots took eighty stitches to close. Eichrodt had a severe concussion, a fractured cheek, fractured shin, two fractured hands, a broken forearm and four ribs. Your Citizen's Oversight Board took thirty days to investigate that arrest, and they decided it was reasonable use of force. There wasn't much public or media reaction — no video was shot, Eichrodt had attacked the deputies, Eichrodt was a white racist felon. He had few friends or family to stir things up with the press. He had just gunned down two *Eme*-protected drug runners in very cold blood, and taken their money. It took your detectives less than a week to flesh it out. Which was about the same amount of time that Judge Arthur Suarez took — two months later — to rule that Eichrodt was unable to assist in his own defense. Suarez committed the suspect to Atascadero State Hospital for an indefinite period of time. Eichrodt has been there for almost nineteen months."

"How's he doing?"

"Slightly improved."

Hood wondered if Laws's arrest injuries might have been worse than they appeared. He was glad to have the name of Terry's doctor, courtesy of Laurel.

Hood looked up at the photographs of the race cars on Ariel Reed's wall.

"Three generations," she said. "Grandma Ruthann on top in black-and-white. That was 1955. My mother, Belinda, in the middle in 1980. Me on the bottom last year. I ran a 6.95 at 202 miles an hour and got ninth overall. That was the NHRA sportsman class Top Alcohol Dragster. I don't have the reactions to become a pro, and I won't dedicate the time it would take. I do it for fun. And I like the idea that you enjoy what your ancestors enjoyed."

"It must be really something to go that fast and not leave the ground," said Hood.

"There's nothing like it."

"Do you get dizzy, or disoriented?"

"Disoriented at times, not dizzy."

"What does it feel like when you see the light go green and push the pedal down?"

"You go before the light goes green. By a fraction of a second. You anticipate."

"Well, okay, then how does it feel?"

"There really is nothing like it. So I can't say, it's like this or like that."

"But I asked you how it feels."

"First you asked what it feels *like*. Then you asked how it feels."

"Way to split that atom."

"I'm possibly too good at splitting atoms."

"I still want to know how it feels to blast off the starting line."

"It's by far the most exhilarating feeling on Earth. You're humbled by the power, and it makes you godlike at the same time. You are helpless but in control of your fate. I highly recommend it."

Reed smiled. It was the thrifty smile that Hood had seen before, not an expansive one. It made her nose wrinkle. There was something like play in it, and a touch of malice, too. It was the same one she had given Hood when she talked of throwing the crooked captain in prison for ten years.

Hood smiled back. "Terry had an interesting financial situation."

"Money problems?"

"The opposite of money problems."

She gave him the hazel stare.

Hood told her about Build a Dream and the cash donations allegedly raised by LASD deputies and deposited by Terry every Monday for two years, the down payment he took for himself, the admiring credit union employee who believed Terry Laws's lie because she wanted to.

"What lie?"

"I've never heard of Build a Dream. None of the people I work with have, either. I rode with Terry half a dozen times but he never once mentioned Build a Dream. It's not in the search engines. It's not in any listing of charities that I could find. It only exists on paper and it's taking in thirty grand a month in cash."

Ariel was looking out the window now, her elbows on the desk and her chin resting on her hands.

"Was he a trust funder?"

"No. No inheritance, no lottery score, no smart investments that went big. I'm not finding any of that."

"Did he make any big arrests? I mean big assets recovered?"

"If he did, I haven't found it yet."

"Well, there's the obvious: drugs, gambling, loan-sharking and prostitution. They're still the cash crops of our society. There's robbery for the desperate and vending machines for the organized. A deputy rubs up against all of that."

"He never worked narcotics or vice. He was a patrolman. He was in that car forty-eight hours a week, doing overtime, earning his sixty-five a year. If you patrol five or six shifts a week when do you have time to earn seven grand on the side?"

"On your day off," she said.

"That's an interesting idea."

"I was half joking."

"The other half interests me." Hood made a note to look more closely at Terry's time cards.

"Private security?" she asked.

"Even a posh security gig two days a week wouldn't net him seven thousand bucks."

Hood made more notes. He kept coming back to the idea that Terry couldn't be earning seven grand a week on the side while driving forty-eight hours on patrol. But he was.

"Tell me about Eichrodt's preliminary hearing," he said.

"We laid out the evidence we'd bring to trial. Truly overwhelming. Both victims' blood was on a jacket in Eichrodt's truck. We found a Taurus nine in the big locking toolbox in the bed of the truck. It fired the four bullets that killed Vasquez and Lopes. Eichrodt had collected the brass and tossed it in with the weapon. His fingerprints were all over them. He had forty-eight hundred in cash hidden down in the bottom of the toolbox. And we had the anonymous witness who put the shooter in the red truck.

"Eichrodt's PD claimed that Eichrodt was unable to assist in his own defense and Suarez said okay, we'll see, put him on. So, for about two hours, Eichrodt sat in a wheelchair at the defense table and tried to answer questions. He knew his name. He was able to name his father and mother. He wasn't sure what country he was in, but he did say 'California' when asked what state he lived in. His long-term memory was spotty, but his short-term was practically nonexistent. He wasn't sure what kind of facility he was in, couldn't remember anything about his arrest, couldn't explain his presence in the courtroom. Couldn't remember a van, two dead men or four plus grand. The PD was furious. He said someone should sue the living daylights out of the County of L.A. for what they had done to this man. Suarez took testimony from three doctors — a neurologist, a GP and a psychiatrist. Suarez thought about it for three days, then ten-seventied Eichrodt to Atascadero pending recovery enough to stand trial."

"Why didn't someone sue the county?" Hood asked.

Ariel nodded. "The ACLU considered,

but the homicide evidence stopped them. If our case would have been wobbly, they might have filed, but even the ACLU doesn't want to spend its resources on a double murderer. And, like I said, Eichrodt had few friends and family. There was literally nobody interested in going through a long and expensive lawsuit on his behalf."

"What's his medical prognosis?"

"The swelling damaged his brain. The craniectomy did little apparent good. The chances of meaningful recovery are slim, according to the doctors at Atascadero."

Hood thought that if there was a definition of aloneness it was Shay Eichrodt. Even Shay Eichrodt had been taken away from Shay Eichrodt. The louder truth was that he'd brought this down on himself, thought Hood. We make our own luck. Character is fate. All that.

As a deputy Hood saw things from Laws's and Draper's side. A violent arrest is a cop nightmare. But there was one thing Hood saw that he would have done differently: he would have waited for backup. Laws should have, too. Draper was not even a true deputy, but a successful businessman acting as a reservist for one dollar a year and a chance to experience the thrill of law enforcement. Their opponent was large, strong, probably high on meth, and had very likely just committed a crime that would get him an LWOP or a death sentence. They should have known better.

"Why didn't Laws wait for backup?"

"He never called for backup. He said he wanted the homicide collar for himself and his partner. The suspect was being co-operative by pulling over and turning off his engine. Then everything happened too fast. Laws admitted it was pure pride and pure foolishness to go after Eichrodt without backup."

"He was right."

"His pride. His physique. Foolish, but I can see it."

Hood saw it, too: Mr. Wonderful.

"What can you tell me about the men that Eichrodt murdered?"

"Bad guys with *Eme* ties, probably working for the North Baja Cartel. That's Carlos Herredia and company. Both men were U.S. citizens. East side *vatos.* Johnny Vasquez and Angel Lopes."

"Doing what, parked early in the morning in the middle of the desert?"

"Good question. Waiting for someone? Waiting for Eichrodt? We don't know. Your helo spotted luggage strewn on a dirt road about two miles from the murder scene. The dead men's prints were all over it. At one time that luggage almost certainly contained seventy-two hundred dollars in pressed five-dollars bills. Eichrodt had forty-eight hundred of it in a plastic bag in his toolbox. There was another twenty-four hundred down in one of the suitcases left by the road, in a zipping plastic pouch for toiletries or wet items. Apparently he'd missed it."

Ariel showed Hood pictures of the van and the dead men and the luggage thrown into the desert.

"You guys have more pictures," she said. "The lead detective was Dave Freeman. He worked hard. Brought us a very strong case."

Hood noted the name. Freeman was big on the LASD softball team. When Hood looked up from his notepad, he caught Ariel Reed looking at him.

Hood smiled and looked out at the city — office lights and streetlights and headlights and taillights and brake lights and traffic lights all sparkling in the cool wake of the storm. The eternal parade. He thought how death can be so slight, barely registering, just a small event that is momentarily considered before we march on. He shifted his gaze and saw Ariel's reflection in the glass, looking at his reflection. They held each other's image.

"I'm racing out at Pomona a week from Saturday," she said to the glass. "Get yourself a pit pass and I'll sign a picture for you."

Hood smiled and nodded, then they broke the moment and stood.

10

Hood drove around L.A. for a few hours, listening to music, James McMurtry and the Heartless Bastards, hard guitars and hard lyrics, country music less by way of Nashville than Hood's own beloved Bakersfield. He liked to drive and look. He liked to see. Hood's uncorrected vision was twenty/ten, a rare blessing, he knew.

All of this driving had started six months ago, on the night that Allison Murrieta had died. Later that night, he had felt something inside him escape. It felt physical, not spiritual or sentimental, but a tactile object taking leave of its place, like a leaf detaching from a tree or a bird flying off a branch. He had weighed himself and found he'd lost a pound and a half according to his bathroom scale. Then he went for a drive, trying to figure out what it was that had left him, and that drive had never really ended.

Hood stopped at the Voodoo up on Sunset

because Erin McKenna was set to perform with her band, the Cheater Slicks. It was nice seeing her name on the marquee. She played guitar and keyboards and sang and wrote the songs. She was an acquaintance of Hood's, but mainly he wanted to see her boyfriend, Bradley Jones. Jones was seventeen and headed for trouble and proud of it. Erin was nineteen. They were in love. Hood thought of them as children. And he thought he should help them with their lives because Allison Murrieta was Bradley Jones's mother.

The Voodoo was dark and muffled, the walls tacked with black carpet, the acoustics good. Hood entered the percussive darkness. Erin was onstage with her band, skin pale, eyes blue, and her straight red hair shining in the overhead floods. She was startlingly beautiful and her voice was strong but delicate, like glass.

Hood saw that Bradley had a table off to the side, with his usual gang of two. The two men were older than Bradley, but Hood knew that Bradley led the gang because he had the brains and the gumption and what LASD Human Resources would call "leadership qualities." One of the men was a car thief and the other a document forger, and Hood knew that they both had dealt in computer fraud and stolen goods. Both had done time. They were sharp dressers and fast talkers and they attracted desirable, acquisitive women.

Hood took a stool at the bar. Bradley saw but didn't acknowledge him. Instead, he signaled the cocktail waitress for three more. Hood knew he had a fake ID, courtesy of one of the creeps at his table, but Hood also knew that Bradley didn't have to use it very often. He was six feet tall, weighed probably one-eighty, wore his hair long and a neatly trimmed goatee, like Robin Hood or a poet. He loved clothes and wore them well. Allison had adored Bradley and he had adored her back. Hood understood that Bradley would never fully forgive him for being with Bradley's mother in the days before she died. Things could have unfolded differently, and Hood believed that he owed the boy something.

Hood got a beer and swiveled on his bar stool and watched Erin sing an X cover. Bradley stared at him from across the room. Months ago Hood had seen that there was something genuinely wild in Bradley, something not always controlled. He was emotional and reckless and occasionally violent. Like his mother.

When the song was over Erin looked out

and smiled at Hood, then Bradley ambled over and took a stool beside him.

"The long arm of the law," he said.

"She sounds great tonight."

"She sounds great every night. They charge cops extra to get in?"

"Watch it or I'll tell them you're still a child. How's tricks, Bradley?"

"Fifteen units, all A's and B's. Solid units. No wood shop. No auto shop. No criminal psychology or whatever it was that you studied."

Erin moved to the piano and the Cheaters started in on one of her songs that Hood had heard before. It was about a junkie walking on the water at Malibu and Hood thought it was funny and haunting.

Allison had told Hood that Bradley had a high IQ. His arrogance was high also. Hood knew that last year, as a high school junior down in Valley Center, Bradley had played varsity football, starting both ways, and maintained a 4.25 GPA by not studying and cutting class often. When his mother died he left Valley Center and came to L.A. Two months ago he told Hood that he'd quit high school and enrolled at Cal State L.A., taking five solids, and joined the football team for off-season workouts.

"Funny," Hood said. "Because Cal State

L.A. told me there was no Bradley Jones enrolled there."

"Long Beach, Hood. I transferred."

"I talked to Long Beach, too. And eleven other colleges and junior colleges. You don't attend any of them, in case you were wondering."

"Buy you a beer?"

"I'll buy my own."

Bradley motioned to the bartender and two beers arrived, lime wedges on the side. "I'm taking some time off from school, Hood. But I've got a job at the hapkido studio where Mom used to work out. I'm a first *dan* black belt, so I drill the kids and keep the books and answer the phone."

"Okay."

"What do you mean, okay?"

"You can submit that Sheriff's Department application when you're nineteen and a half. That gives you two years to get some college. Don't waste them."

"Yeah, yeah, yeah."

"Sheriff's is a good gig. You'd start at forty-nine a year once you're sworn. With your grades and sports, and a letter from me —"

"You've told me a million times."

"I'm trying to keep your bratty white ass out of trouble."

"I don't want your help. I'm cool. Kick is cool."

What Bradley meant by this, Hood knew, was that he had not yet killed the boy who killed his mother. He had told Hood that someday, he would. The shooter's name was Deon Miller and his street name was Kick. He was a sixteen-year-old Southside Compton Crip when he shot Allison during an armed robbery last year.

A few weeks later Bradley told Hood he was going to kill Kick. Hood believed him. The look on his face and the tone of his voice were unmistakable and true.

So Hood had come to see Bradley as a rope: vengeance pulling him one way, and the Los Angeles Sheriff's Department — Deputy Charles Robert Hood — pulling him the other.

"And Kick is cool?"

Bradley looked at him, then shrugged and squeezed the lime into his beer. "When Kick stops kicking, you'll know."

"Don't do it. I understand why you want to, but don't."

"You cannot and do not understand."

"I loved her, too."

"You didn't even deserve to touch her."

"Maybe that's true but if you kill Kick it's going to change you and everything about your life."

"Exactly."

After the song the Cheater Slicks took a break and Erin came over. Bradley gave her his stool then walked back to his table without a word to her or Hood.

"He's chipper tonight," she said.

"You sound terrific. I love that walk on water song."

"Thanks. I quit smoking. Kinda worried it would wreck my voice but so far so good."

"You okay?"

"Why wouldn't I be?"

Hood nodded toward Bradley.

"He hasn't said a word about Kick lately. That worries me. Usually, you know, he's always mumbling something or other about what he has to do."

"Has to do."

"Yeah, has to. I'm surprised he's contained it as well as he has."

"The college thing was all bullshit."

"I told him he wouldn't fool you. He's looking over here. He's got the look. I should go."

Hood listened to the whole next set. Bradley didn't look his way again. Two beautifully dressed women joined Bradley and his friends at their table.

Hood drove L.A. for a couple of hours,

then home to Silver Lake. It was almost two a.m. His apartment was cold. He didn't sleep well but he looked forward to the drive back up to Lancaster the next day for eight more hours of patrol through Antelope Valley.

11

The first Friday night after the death of Terry Laws, Draper went alone to collect Herredia's money. He felt conspicuous and friendless and reminded himself not to let it show. He also reminded himself that without Terry, he would now be taking home twice the pay.

As he drove through Cudahy, Draper wondered again if Terry had told Laurel what they had done, and what they were doing. Or maybe some part of it. Terry had always denied having said anything to his wife, but this question was an itch that Draper couldn't scratch. It angered him that he couldn't put it to rest, deal with it effectively like he dealt with everything else. But now, heading into the dark labyrinth of Hector Avalos, he felt even more anxious. Certainly Laurel had talked to Hood by now. And yet, Hood hadn't come back to him with more questions about Terry — so maybe Laurel had no idea what her husband was doing.

It was okay.

It was going to be okay.

Draper was dressed in street clothes and beside him on the seat of the Cayenne was his leather briefcase.

As usual, Hector Avalos's gunmen watched him drive down the Cudahy side street. As usual, more pistoleros stoically escorted his car down the alley and through a vehicle port and into the warehouse. When he was inside, they watched him get out of the car before leaving him alone to navigate the maze of darkened rooms and hallways that formed the south end of the big building.

At the final door, in what had become a Friday night ritual, Draper knocked fists with Rocky, Hector's number two man and his most trusted bodyguard. They talked for a minute in the Spanglish they were both comfortable with. Rocky was a small knot of muscle with a web of tattoos that started on the back of his head and spread across his back and shoulders and down his arms. Rocky knew some of the 'manos that Draper had grown up with in Jacumba, clever desert drug runners who could evade law enforcement by using the vast network of dirt roads and caves and tunnels and hidden bridges that surrounded Jacumba on both sides of the border. They talked a moment about what happened to Terry Laws. A look passed between them that was hard and silent and mutual, then they knocked fists again. Draper rapped sharply three times on the door, waited a beat, then knocked two more.

"I hear the secret knock," he heard Avalos holler. "Enter. Enter!"

Draper pushed through the heavy metal door and into Avalos's dogfighting arena.

It was a big room with high ceilings and exposed girders and beams. Now it was only partially lit. Built onto one wall was an elevated "luxury" box with sliding glass doors through which to view the action. Draper could see Hector sitting inside where he always sat, watching TV. Camilla, his wife, sat next to him. Light from the TV played off the glass in arrhythmic flashes.

Draper waved and headed toward the stairs that led up to the box. He could smell the spilled alcohol and the bleach used to clean the floor of the pit when the fights were over.

Draper entered the box, shook Hector's hand, and nodded to Camilla. The couple sat on a red leather couch that faced the fighting pit. The television was on the floor.

There was a bar in the rear of the box, a refrigerator, a privacy screen and a bed. There were two recliners, also facing the pit, and a half a dozen extra bar stools that could be brought up close to the sliding glass doors for unfettered viewing of the action below. Four large rolling suitcases stood along the glass, handles up and ready to go. Draper sat in a lumpy plaid rocking chair across the coffee table from Hector and Camilla and set the briefcase on the floor beside him.

Avalos was big and bald and clean shaven except for a great brushy mustache that he grew long. He looked Confucian. Beneath his eyes were five small tattooed teardrops — each one representing a murder he'd committed. He wore a crisp Pendleton. He had a cheerless face and his eyes were dark and calculating. He was drinking gin and *tamarindo* from a big red plastic tumbler.

Camilla was a *nalgona* — a big-butted woman — and strong, her long black hair curled into ringlets that bounced like tree-bound snakes. Her face was pale and her lips were black. She sat on the sofa beside her husband, one hand resting high on this thigh.

"What happened to Terry?" asked Avalos. "The newspapers don't have nothing."

"A Blood gunned him down."

"While he was working, man? In his uniform and they do that?"

"That's what happened."

"That's like TJ, man, like TJ."

"It was Lancaster."

"But you weren't there."

"I was off that night."

Draper saw the implication and ignored it. Avalos was a world-class suspecter of people, borderline if not clinically paranoid.

"Terrible, man, terrible," said Avalos. He took a long draw of the gin. When drunk, Avalos became thoughtful, then inward, then unpredictable. "I lose my friends. You lose your friend. It's an evil business that we're in."

"Who are you going to share your money with now?" asked Camilla.

"How about nobody?" asked Draper.

"*El Tigre* will force you to have another partner," said Avalos. "He will tell you who it will be. He can't put his property in danger, not for you or nobody."

"We'll be talking about that," said Draper. "How did we do this week?"

"Yes, yes, very good."

As always Avalos offered him a drink, and as always Draper refused it, alluding to the task at hand. Draper took the wad from his jacket pocket and put it on the coffee table in front of Avalos. One thousand dollars — his weekly tribute, payable from the four points he earned the week before. It was this money — and Hector's unshakable suspicion that his former couriers were cheating him — that had opened the door into the North Baja Cartel for Draper.

Camilla examined a black fingernail then set her hand back on Hector's thigh.

Draper looked through the sliding glass door. The fight pit stood in the center of the room. It had a concrete floor, and walls made of three-quarter-inch plywood panels painted red, yellow or green. It was ringed on three sides by gymnasium bleachers. Long pairs of fluorescent lights hung by chains from the ceiling. There were no windows. Industrial floor fans, turned off now, were stacked behind the bleachers to help cool the bloodthirsty crowds that packed the room once a month.

"Then I'll do my job and be going," said Draper.

"Yes, yes," said Avalos. He was an impatient man, who thought that saying things twice, quickly, saved time.

Draper took his briefcase over and set it on the bar. He brought out the digital scale and set it on the bar top and tapped the on and reset buttons. Then he brought over the suitcases two at a time and unzipped them and lifted the stacks of bills and went to the other side of the bar. He worked off the thick rubber bands and began weighing them.

Camilla sat on a stool and watched. She was drinking through a straw from a large red plastic tumbler like Hector's and Draper could smell the bourbon wafting out from it. She always wore a different cocktail dress and tonight's involved claret velvet and black lace. Her perfume was sensual and strong. There was a small CD player on the bar and Camilla put on some *corridos* — tales of brave and handsome traffickers and the dull-witted police who can never catch them. She hummed along.

Draper ignored her. He knew she hated being ignored and he truly enjoyed this part of his job. He whistled quietly to himself while he worked and marveled at the simple math that could only have been created by a loving God:

A pound of fives contained 480 bills worth $2,400.

A pound of twenties contained 480 bills worth $9,600.

A pound of hundreds contained 480 bills worth $48,000.

He weighed each bundle twice but the scale was fast and accurate. A few minutes later, stacked up on the bar and waiting to be photographed were two pounds of hundreds, six pounds of fifties, twenty pounds of twenties and five pounds of fives.

Draper didn't need a calculator to know that he was looking at $444,000, the best week he had ever had. His four points would be $17,760 and it would be in his pocket just a few hours from now. He missed Terry, but what a blessing, not to have to share it. He flipped on the vacuum packer to let it warm up.

Camilla gave him a frankly craven smile and Draper smiled back.

"Camilla," he said. "This reminds me of the time I went to church and the preacher said that God and Jesus want us in heaven with them. They *want* us there. And they always get what they want because they're God and Jesus, right? I remember thinking: this world is a place of beauty and forgiveness. It made me deeply happy to be alive. Deeply. I feel that way now."

"You're all screwed up, Coleman," she said. "This is not what Jesus is about."

"You both shut up," said Hector. "What did you get, Draper, what did you get?"

"Four-forty-four."

"Then you make sure it gets to El Dorado, or you get to eat your own *cojones* for dinner tonight. Okay?"

"Yes, Hector, I've been very clear on that from the beginning. You're always eager to feed me my own balls."

Draper got a small camera from his briefcase and photographed the slabs of cash. He checked the vacuum packer to make sure it was loaded with the continuous-roll bags. Then he went to work. The machine was called the GameSaver Turbo. It could seal fifty bundles without overheating. Draper loved the machine, the efficiency of it, the eagerness with which it packaged his bills.

When he was done he packed them into the four suitcases and threw in the cheap thrift-store rags to realistically fill out the luggage.

"You tell Carlos business is good," said Camilla.

"I won't have to."

"Do his women still entertain you?"

"They're good women."

"They're whores."

Hector and Camilla and Rocky helped him get the luggage down to the Cayenne.

"You always have different cars," Hector said.

"I borrow them from friends. I vary them because Customs officials remember cars and plates, but not faces." And it helped that he could always pluck well-maintained specimens from his Prestige customers, fudging the odometer numbers, no harm done.

"I didn't know an honest policeman made so much money," said Avalos with a smile. "Drive safely. Click it or ticket."

"Yes," said Draper.

Hector handed his empty red tumbler to Rocky. "Re-fill, man. Pronto, pronto."

Herredia was most pleased by his thirty-three-pound haul of U.S. cash. He sat behind his big steel desk at El Dorado and sipped a very dark tequila. The suitcases were flat on the floor and the vacuum-packed bundles were stacked neatly by the scale on the desk.

Herredia looked at Draper and his thick eyebrows lifted up and away from each other and he looked soulful. "To this crazy life, Coleman."

"Yes," said Draper, holding up an invisible shot glass.

The old man, Felipe, sat where he always did, but he had propped his shotgun against the wall behind him rather than holding it

131

on his lap, a gesture that suggested trust.

"I was very surprised to hear about Terry," said Herredia.

"So was I. I still can't believe it."

"A black American gangster?"

"That's what a witness saw."

Draper felt the weight of Herredia's attention.

"I'm sad," said Herredia. "I admired him. But I believe he was becoming dangerous. You know this."

Draper nodded and looked down at his hands.

"But, twice as much for you," said Herredia.

"Yes."

"You are not pleased?" asked Herredia.

"Twice as much pleases me."

"But you do not drink. You do not talk to me."

"The drive was long tonight."

"You have your bed and your whore."

"I have a real woman in my life," said Draper.

Herredia looked puzzled, but he nodded as if he understood.

"And I'm going to drive home tonight," said Draper. "I mean no disrespect, Carlos."

Draper guessed that Herredia was taking in well over two million a month now.

Draper knew that the *Eme* faction led by Avalos was the primary collector of Herredia's money, taking it from the hundreds of street gangsters who sold product, and paid obeisance and taxes. But Herredia had other arrangements, too. The drug world was filled with secret allegiances — some very old and others very new, such as Draper's and Laws's sudden and dramatic entrance as Herredia's new couriers. It was a world in flux. Loyalties shifted. Allies became enemies. Friends became dead. The cartels were as complicated as the Vatican.

And Draper had always believed that disorder was opportunity.

"Con permisso," he said, rising slowly and taking two steps toward Herredia's desk. He folded his hands in front of him and looked first into Herredia's now glowering face, then to the flagstones on the floor.

"Sir, I think —"

"You think I'm going to force you to take another partner."

"That is another —"

"Silence, *gringo.* And listen to the sound of my good news. You have my trust and respect. You have your gun and your badge if you need them. In two years you have never been late or short. You have never given me reason to worry. So I say this to

133

you: you will continue to work for me, alone, as you wish."

Draper bowed. "Your trust means very much to me. But —"

"And you will take five points, not four, on all of what you deliver."

Draper was truly flabbergasted so it wasn't hard to portray it. "It's hard to speak."

"This is probably because I am interrupting you. Tell me now, Coleman, what you are trying to say."

"Avalos is cheating you."

Draper heard the old man shift behind him, the soft clink of the shotgun leaving the wall.

"I have trouble hearing sometimes," said Herredia.

"Avalos is cheating you."

"You prove this."

"I can't. But Rocky can. He's seen it. Rocky is afraid that when you find out you'll have him killed along with Hector and Camilla. I told him I would try to keep that from happening."

"How much does Hector cheat me?"

"Approximately two points every week. Camilla takes it before the bills are stacked and pressed and weighed. A few hundred here, a few hundred there, from many different people. Rocky said she's proud of her defiance. She doesn't bother to hide her thievery. But Hector never sees her do it, so he can tell himself there is nothing to see. So he can tell us all there is nothing to see."

The old blackness had come back to Herredia's eyes. It was like shades being drawn on a window for the enactment of secrets inside.

A moment later Herredia rattled off a series of commands in Mexican Spanish bristling with obscenities. Draper had trouble making out the rapid phrases that involved a series of names he had never heard.

The old man listened, his face dark and wrinkled as a peach pit, his hair long and white, then he vanished.

"You will spend the night here and we will talk, Coleman. Tonight I want to talk."

Draper was surprised to see the sadness in Herredia's eyes.

In the black of early morning, Draper idled at the United States Customs booth in San Ysidro. He offered his badge holder and Sheriff's Department ID and answered the usual questions: two days, friends at La Fonda, purchases of two bottles Santo Tomas table wine and a silver bracelet inlaid with turquoise. These items, supplied by

135

one of Herredia's jolly cooks, sat in pasteboard boxes on the seat beside him. His fishing gear was piled in the back. His dollars were vacuum-wrapped and fitted into a bumper cavity.

"How many times a year do you cross this border?" asked the official.

"Six or eight," said Draper. "I've never counted."

"What do you do?"

"I fish."

"For what?"

"Snapper. Bass. Jack. Tuna, if I'm lucky."

The Customs man peered into the back. Draper saw the second Customs official appear at the passenger-side window and he rolled it down.

The inspector swung open the rear door and pulled one of the boxes across the seat and rummaged through it. He slammed the door and went around to the back of the vehicle and Draper popped the hatchback for him. In the rearview Draper watched the man paw through his fishing gear.

"Slow night?" he called back.

No answer. He knew these idiots wouldn't find anything; even the dogs of secondary inspection would have a tough time with the vacuum-packed bills.

Then the hatchback slammed and the

man to his left waved him through.

"Proceed, Deputy Draper."

He drove the speed limit north on Interstate 5, but his mind was filled with Herredia's proposal, its details and possibilities, its potential consequences.

When he hit Solana Beach he called Alexia. She answered on the first ring.

"I've been called," he said. "I'm very sorry."

He heard the breath catch in her throat. Then she whispered, "Coleman, I love you."

"I'll come back to you and Brittany, alive and soon. You have my solemn promise."

"I will pray and wait. And when you come back I will be alive again."

"I'll be alive again, too, Alexia."

He clicked off and dialed Juliet in Laguna. He got her machine, said her name and waited.

"Coleman?"

"I'm home."

"I don't know why I do this."

"Yes, you do. I'll be there in less than an hour."

She didn't bother to get out of bed. He showered in the darkness and slipped in beside her. She pretended to be asleep, then vaguely receptive, then she greedily took Draper and fled to that place he couldn't

see or name, a place all hers, located somewhere behind or beyond her tightly closed
eyes.

12

Hood's phone rang early the next morning, not long after he'd let himself into the Hole.

"Latrenya changed her story," said Bentley. "Now she says Londell was gone all night — business down in South Central. She didn't see him until morning. She said she lied to us because Londell threatened to kill her if she told the truth. She got Tawna and Anton in on the plot, too. But Londell beat up Latrenya on an unrelated matter — something about her gaining weight. ER called us. Latrenya wouldn't press charges but we sent two uniforms over to arrest Londell. He Maced them. Now he's in the wind and he looks a little better for Terry's murder. We're searching Londell's Oasis pad in ten minutes. You are cordially invited."

Hood, Bentley and Orr crammed into the small outer office of the Oasis manager, Sanjay. Sanjay was a young Indian man who smoked eagerly and said he wanted no trouble. He said Londell Dwayne was rude but always paid his rent, though never on time. And he played his music loud.

The men climbed the wobbly stairs and walked single file to the front door of Dwayne's apartment. It was quiet now — no Londell and no Latrenya and no music. Orr knocked. Hood noted that the foil on the window had been tattered by the last storm.

Sanjay stomped out his cigarette then unlocked the front door. When the lock disengaged Bentley gently but firmly moved the manager back and away and told him to stay outside for now.

With his sport coat open and one hand on the butt of his automatic, Bentley turned the knob and pushed open the door. "Sheriffs," he called out. "We're coming in."

The place was small and smelled of reefer and bacon. The carpet was dirty and there were yellow stains on the popcorn ceiling. The kitchen sink was piled with dishes and the refrigerator hummed loudly. There was a counter between the kitchen and the living room and on it were dinner plates with old food on them, and plenty of King Cobra empties.

Orr slipped down the hallway with his

weapon drawn and went into a bedroom. Hood walked past him, gun at his side, went into the next room and flicked on the light.

It was a small room, with small windows up high. It was cold and it reminded Hood of the Hole. There was a mattress on the floor in one corner, with some sheets and blankets wadded up on top. There were dirty clothes in another corner. Hood spotted a Detroit Tigers hoodie. Down deeper in the pile were two red bandanas. Hood saw that one of them had been worn pirate-style, rolled on one edge and knotted, with a loose flap on top. He set them on the floor next to the black sweatshirt.

There was a chest slouching against one wall, drawers hanging open. On top of it were two empty cigarette hardpacks, four gun magazines and a blackened hash pipe. The closet doors hung askew but Hood got one open enough to see in: a few wire hangers, a few shirts, some beaten sneakers on the floor.

Hood went through the dresser looking for black gloves but didn't find any. There was nothing under the bed. He stood looking down at the Detroit sweatshirt and the bandanas.

Then he heard Orr's voice from the other

bedroom. *"Gentlemen, we have something here."*

The room was close and crowded by a king bed. The mattress had been swiveled out from the springs. Bentley and Orr stood in the cramped space between the bed and the closet. Hood joined them and looked down on the M249 SAW set into a crude cutout in the box spring. The mesh material had been cut open and a yard-long section of one of the slats had been broken out. The gun was jammed into the space. Orr replaced the flap that was cut in the cover material, hiding the weapon, then lifted it open again.

"Dead man," he said.

13

By late morning Hood was standing on the Avenue M off-ramp of Highway 14, where Johnny Vasquez and Angel Lopes had been shot to death. The day was cool and the breeze came and went like a doubt.

He balanced Freeman's murder book on his left arm and used the crime scene drawings and photographs to find where the van had been parked. Now there was nothing but sand and gravel.

According to Laws's report, the van engine and lights had been off when they got there.

Detective Freeman had guessed the temperature at eighty degrees, and he wrote that the night was clear and windy. The moon was new on the twelfth of August, four days earlier, so there wasn't much moonlight.

Hood flipped forward: in the impound yard the next day the van started up and idled without a problem. The tires were good. The gas tank was full. There was a second mention of the flats of strawberries found in the back of the van and the basket of them spilled up front.

Deeper in the book Hood found that Vasquez and Lopes both lived in Lancaster.

So, he thought: two men, mid-level bangers with an *Eme* blessing, thought to be working for the North Baja Cartel, heading south around two in the morning, seventy-two hundred in pressed five-dollar bills stashed in two suitcases.

He talked into his recorder: "Why two big suitcases for only seventy-two hundred dollars? Why such a small amount pressed and stacked?"

He found the crime scene photographs of the two pieces of luggage thrown into the desert. The clothes were strewn across the road. A lot of clothes. It looked like a table at a rummage sale. Hood wondered how those clothes could fit back into the two bags, large as they were.

Again to the recorder: "How so much clothing into two suitcases?"

Then he walked a slow circle around the place where the van had stopped.

Another question for the recorder: "Why did they pull over and stop on the off-ramp? Illegal, plain sight, no car trouble."

He set the murder book on the hood of his car and found the ballistics pages, which established the shooter's positions through angles-of-entry drawings and victim body positions. All four shots had been fired through the passenger-side window. Eichrodt had used a Taurus nine-millimeter automatic — a budget gun, unregistered. He'd shot Angel Lopes, the man closest to him, first. Lopes had crumpled and turned partially away when the second shot struck him in the right temple. Meanwhile, Vasquez was apparently trying to get out. The first shot hit the back of his head, the second entered through the right ear.

Hood compared the line-of-fire sketches with the crime scene photographs. It all made sense. Through all the gore and ugliness emerged a clear picture.

"But these were *Eme* runners," he told the voice recorder. "Where were their weapons? Why didn't they use them? Were they surprised? Did they know Eichrodt? Were they expecting him?"

He found photographs of the guns that had been recovered from the van. There were two, both within easy reach. But neither man had so much as gotten a hand on a weapon, in spite of the shooter at their window.

Hood carried the book back to where the van had been parked.

It was hard for him to imagine that these guys had been surprised, unless they were both very drunk or exhausted. He found their autopsy reports and checked blood alcohol. None at all. They had both ingested amphetamines in moderate amounts. A long night ahead, he thought. A long drive? They were chemically enhanced. Were they surprised by a six-foot eight, three-hundred-pound gunman as they sat exposed on an off-ramp, windows down in the heat? There was no place at all for Eichrodt to hide. The night was dark, but a jackrabbit couldn't have hidden where Hood now stood.

No. They weren't surprised, he thought. They just didn't react. Why?

Freeman had concluded that Eichrodt and the two couriers did not know each other. Freeman had asked that same question that Hood was asking: why hadn't they reacted? And he never answered it.

Hood leafed through the murder book, prospecting. He looked at the graphics and read the words and let his mind wander as his hands turned the pages.

A few minutes later he was struck by another anomaly. It was looking back at him from an evidence photograph of the brass

146

casings that had been found in Eichrodt's truck. It took Hood a long quiet minute of staring to find it. The casings had been tossed into the same locking toolbox where the gun and money had been found. There were four of them. They were heavily smeared with blood. He pictured the scene, the order of shooting, the distances to the targets. He pictured Eichrodt collecting his casings. And it made no sense that the brass would be heavily smeared. Touched with blood? Sure, he thought. Dotted with blowback from Lopes, the closer victim, to Eichrodt's fingers? Possibly. But all four casings, smeared heavily? No.

So he turned to the lab reports and found what he expected: the fingerprints lifted from all four casings were Eichrodt's. But he couldn't find anything about the blood itself. Whose was it? And, more importantly, why was there so *much* of it?

He sat in his car with the windows down in the cool desert breeze. It took him a while to get through to the crime lab technician who had lifted the prints from the casings. Keith Franks spoke in a soft, high-pitched voice that sounded young. He told Hood that the prints had come off the brass clearly and cleanly. They were Eichrodt's. He said he hadn't run the blood on the casings because his superior said there was no reason to — Eichrodt's prints and Lopes's blood were on the Taurus nine-millimeter and that was all the DA needed. It was beyond reasonable doubt that Eichrodt had fired the gun. And of course, the lab was overloaded with work.

Hood flipped to the photographs of the Taurus and saw that it, too, was heavily marked by blood. There was a misting on the muzzle, as you'd expect — Mr. Lopes again. But down on the handle and the trigger and the trigger guard the smears were heavier. There was no positive identification on the lower, heavier traces.

"I want you to type the blood on the casings," he said. "And on the handle, trigger, and guard of the Taurus."

"Detective, the case is closed."

"I'll get the DA to reopen it."

"You know they won't. It was an open-and-shut case."

"Then how come Vasquez and Lopes used two big pieces of luggage for only seven grand plus change? How did they get all those clothes and the money into two bags? Why did they pull over in the middle of the desert in the middle of the night, then park in plain sight? Why didn't they defend themselves? How come Eichrodt's brass was

148

thick with blood? And his gun? There's too much. The blood is wrong and you know it."

For a moment Hood thought Franks had hung up on him. The cool breeze hissed against the phone and he turned his back to it.

"What's your name, again?" Franks asked.

"Charlie Hood. I'm young, like you, and we need to help each other because we're the future. At least that's what they say."

Franks went quiet for a long moment. "I'm sixty-four years old. Give me your numbers."

14

A few minutes later Hood parked off the
Pearblossom Highway where Laws and
Draper had battled Shay Eichrodt beside
the ruins of the Llano del Rio utopia. The
stone columns of the old assembly hall rose
from the hard ground. The highway was
bleached pale gray by the sun and there was
a raven blown by the wind onto the nearest
Joshua tree, outstretched wings and body
crucified on the long spines.

He walked the area where Eichrodt's truck
had been pulled over. Big rigs thundered
down the highway and he could feel their
vibrations in his chest.

Hood sat on an old river-rock wall and
read Laws's arrest report. Laws wrote in the
plodding, jargon-heavy style of most cops:

> . . . at approx. 4:20 a.m. we observed a
> pickup truck, red, with plate numbers
> partially matching . . . the apparently

150

unconscious suspect then suddenly extended one leg, which caused me to lose
balance and fall . . . the suspect appeared
to be under the influence of a stimulant . . .
the suspect was eventually subdued . . .

Hood imagined the bloody fight between
two strong men with batons, and one huge
and very strong man who had just taken
two lives, jacked up on crystal meth and
fighting for his own.

After reading the report, he wondered if
that brutal fight had taken something out of
Terry Laws, the thing that Carla Vise said
had vanished and never returned, even after
the stitches were removed and the bruises
healed.

Hood left the murder book on the wall
and walked among the Llano del Rio ruins.
He'd read about this socialist utopia in
school. He had always liked stories that
began with good intentions, then became
complicated. The utopia was founded in
1914 and it survived three years. There were
pear orchards and alfalfa fields and a modern dairy — all made possible by a clever
irrigation system that distributed water from
the snow-fed Llano del Rio. The utopians
grew 90 percent of the food they needed.
There were workshops for canning fruit,

151

cobbling shoes, cleaning clothes and cutting hair. A Montessori school sprouted up, Southern California's first. All this was done by cooperation — no one made money. Detailed drawings for the Llano of the future depicted a city of ten thousand people living in craftsman-style apartments with shared laundry and kitchen facilities, surrounded by a road that would double as a drag strip for car races. There would even be grandstands for viewing. Being a car guy, Hood had always liked the racing idea. He wondered what Ariel Reed would think of it. But Llano lost its credit and water rights, and its leaders began to fight. They got no help from powerful Angelenos made uneasy by Llano's goofy success. Hood looked at it now: no sign or historical marker, just a ruin that the desert bums and migrant workers sometimes used for a temporary shelter in this relentlessly hostile desert.

Looking at these ruins, Hood thought about the utopian ideals of shared labor and shared prosperity. He thought about Terry Laws using the ideals of charity to feather his own impressive nest. The settlers of Llano were partially done in by their own squabbling and the distrust of others. Terry Laws was done in by a man with a machine gun who wanted something that Terry had.

But before that, something good in him had already died — just as Carla Vise had observed.

Hood wondered if it wasn't the arrest at all, but something else that had changed Terry Laws forever. Something he did. Something Mr. Wonderful couldn't live with. Something that earned him seven to eight grand a month and cost him his soul.

On his way back to the prison, Hood called an acquaintance in narco and asked him why some drug money was weighed, pressed and stacked, and some wasn't.

"Transport," he said. "Big cash takes too much time to count and too much space to pack, so they weigh and press it." His name was Askew and he'd worked narcotics for his entire career, starting as a baby-faced twenty-two-year-old posing undercover as a high school student/dealer.

"The big dollars go to Mexico," he said. "Before 9/11 they'd fly it across from Phoenix or San Diego or L.A. After that, airline security got a lot tougher, so now they just drive it in. About a million dollars a day — three hundred and fifty sweet million a year. U.S. Customs intercepts maybe two percent of it. Mexican Customs welcomes it. Even the Colombian money goes

153

through Mexico."

"What's big enough for a run south?"

"Who knows? Say a hundred grand."

"What about seventy-two hundred?"

He laughed. "No."

"How often?"

"Different cartels, different schedules, different routes. They have to change things up. But at least once a week. Couriers make good money but the price of being late or short is extremely high. You know — wives, children, that kind of high."

"North Baja Cartel," said Hood. "What's an average weekly run?"

"Oh, big stuff. Three, maybe four hundred grand. Since the Arellanos, it's been Herredia all the way. Are you looking at Vasquez and Lopes?"

"The book's on the seat beside me."

"Why?"

"Let's come back to that," Hood said.

"Don't tell me you have problems with Eichrodt."

Hood thought about that a moment. "I'm starting to."

"You know why? Because he wasn't *enough.* Tweaker, loser. Vasquez and Lopes were pros. They knew what they were doing. They should have made short work of Shay Eichrodt."

"Talk to me, Lieutenant," said Hood.

"I think they were starting a run that night. The evidence was there — they were high on amphetamines for the drive. They were armed. They'd hidden cash — weighed and pressed — in suitcases full of clothes. They had a full tank of gas and they were heading south. None of this mattered to the DA, who got fingerprints, blood, stolen cash, and an Aryan Brother with the murder gun. Pretty good chance that Eichrodt did the shooting, but I don't think he was alone. I didn't make any waves. I'm narco, you know? Let the Bulldogs and the lawyers do their thing. But if I'm right, you've got an accomplice and three hundred something grand unaccounted for. Maybe less; maybe more. What's your interest, Charlie? Your turn to make nice."

"Laws busted Eichrodt. I'm looking for enemies."

Hood didn't say that he'd also been looking for a way that Terry Laws could have gotten his hands on a few hundred grand, and had just found one.

He got an idea.

Back in the hole, Hood turned on the lights. In the cold cubicle he put one stack of Terry Laws's time cards on his desk, and another on the desk that Warren had used. The stack on Hood's desk were pre-arrest and the cards on Warren's desk were post-arrest.

Hood examined Terry's pre-arrest time cards and looked for patterns. He looked for anomalies. He saw his breath condense.

He found nothing.

But at Warren's desk now, looking through the post-arrest time cards, Hood found a pattern: Terry had not worked a Friday in twenty straight months.

Hood remembered that Terry always made his Build a Dream contributions on Mondays unless the bank was closed.

Fridays, Terry had all day to work a second job, thought Hood. Three days later, he deposited his earnings from it.

After work Hood drove to a Museum Store in an L.A. mall and found what he had seen there last holiday season, an giant-sized plastic H2O molecule. It sat on a stand that housed two AAA batteries and when you turned it on, the hydrogen and oxygen atoms careened through clear plastic tubing and changed colors. It was recommended for ages seven and up. Hood bought it and some batteries and had them wrapped. He also bought a card with a close-up picture of a Ferrari grille, and wrote in it: *A week from Saturday is a long way off. Will it get here quicker if I drive fast? CH.*

Ariel wasn't in her office but Hood and his Sheriff's badge convinced the lobby guard to deliver it upstairs to her.

He drove L.A. for a few hours before heading home.

15

The late dinner arrives and we eat in silence. I can tell that the boy is trying to process my story without seeming to. More than that, he's trying to process *me.* But you know how important it is for the young to be cool. I order another round of drinks. He's plenty high by now and working hard not to show it. He downs the miso soup, eats his way through ten slabs of wild-caught salmon, downs a bowl of rice drenched in soy sauce. Nothing left on his plate so he relights his second cigar.

"So, Laws and I have a nice arrangement," I say. "We're talking roughly seven grand a week each. We drive a few hours to get what we need. We weigh and package it. We drive a few more hours to deliver it. Then we party down with Herredia. Months go by, but trouble is coming. Trouble always comes. Something is going wrong with Terry. The Mexicans have a word for it, *gu-*

#2 05-11-2017 1:25PM
Item(s) checked out to p1194964.

TITLE: The renegades [large print]
BARCODE: 33656049327 91
DUE DATE: 06-08-17

Boca Raton Public Library (561-393-7852)
Like us on Facebook!

sano, which means worm, but it also means something inside a person that is eating them. So, what is it? What's eating him?"

I look at the boy and he's studying me hard. He puffs the cigar and blows out the smoke but I can tell his full attention is on me and the question before him.

"I can't know," he says. "Because you've left something out of the story. You haven't given me all the information."

"What have I left out?"

"Things don't add up with your story about the couriers and Eichrodt. How can a stoned tweaker execute two *veteranos,* two tough-ass cartel runners? I don't see why the couriers pulled over that night and parked on the off-ramp. They were right out in the open. Where were their guns? How could Eichrodt possibly disguise himself as anything but a three-hundred-pound man? Did they know him? The papers never said that. And something else that bothers me — how did you and Laws get so lucky that night? How did you find the van and the truck so easily? How come some other unit didn't find at least one of them before you did? And also, why didn't you call for backup when you pulled over Eichrodt? He was cooperative. That doesn't make a bit of sense to me. And also, what about this

159

tipster? How come he sees everything and calls it all in, but won't give his name? That's very convenient. I don't trust him. I think he's involved in a big way."

"You think like a cop."

"It's just common sense."

I understand that I've come to a cross-roads. I've only met with this boy a few times over a few weeks, but we've already arrived at a moment of truth. Only truth can support the great weight of the future.

As I said before, I almost believe in him. I think he has what I'm looking for. One man can accomplish much, but two men? Then three, then more? The sky is the limit. It takes a team. There were some forward-thinking deputies at my department back in the eighties. They gave themselves names and they got respect. There were the Renegades and the Vikings and the Saxons and the Reapers. They understood the power of working together. I've never met one of them. But I can tell you that they had the right idea.

I lean in close and lower my voice.

"Actually, when we first see the van, it's headed southbound on Highway Fourteen near Avenue M. We flash it. At this point, Lopes and Vasquez are very much alive and well."

He looks at me with an expression I've never seen on him. Time passes before he speaks. "Oh, man."

"Oh, man is right, son. Do you want me to go on? You can say no but it has to be now. In life there are no retractions and in this story there will be none either. Once it is told, it is told."

"Yes. Go on."

"You're sure? I'm offering you a way out."

"I need to know."

"You cannot unhear."

"I want to hear."

I lean in close and I whisper. "Good. Terry goes to the driver's side and I take the passenger side. The couriers roll down their windows. We talk. They're eating strawberries out of a basket on the console between them. In the back of the van there are shapes covered by blankets. Flats of strawberries holding them down. We know what is under those blankets. I shoot Vasquez. Terry is supposed to shoot Lopes but Terry can't pull the trigger. So I do. I give them both the new look. We take the money. I can't explain to you the thrill of killing two criminals and driving away in a law enforcement vehicle with their money in the trunk. It's the essence of life as I know it. I call in the tip and we arrange some things for evidence. Then we drive out Pearblossom Highway and wait for Shay Eichrodt to come home from the bars."

He can't hide the shock. He also looks disappointed, confused and afraid. It's a storm of emotions and I can read every one of them. He looks as if he's witnessed something that has changed his life.

Which, of course, he has.

His face looks older now. He can't see it but I can. "So," he says.

"So."

"Really."

"Yes."

"I don't know what to think or say."

"It's been thought and said before."

"Except that I . . . face a similar situation."

"Of course you do."

"Where I will have to decide."

"Yes. And I want to hear all about it. It's a complex circumstance. There is little simplicity in any life worth living."

There's a long silence while we vet each other's confession.

"Why did you tell me?" he asks.

"I chose you. And you needed to know what's required. It's the difference between being a boy and being a man. Do you want to hear the rest of the story? There's so much more to tell."

"But why did you choose me?"

"Because of who you are."

He sits back and sips his beer. "I want to hear more."

16

The next morning Draper ran north on Laguna's Main Beach with Juliet beside him. The winter sky was gray, and out by Rockpile he saw a pelican tuck its wings and drop into the green wind-chopped water. A moment later the bird bobbed to the surface and raised its head and a fish tail disappeared down its beak. The waves were small and orderly.

Juliet was older than him by two years, thirty-one, but she had no trouble keeping up with him. He pulled up closer to her and she looked at him flatly, as if he were either a slight annoyance or of minor interest — he couldn't guess which. All he knew for sure was that he was both the personification of, and a remedy for, Juliet's self-loathing.

She was brown-skinned and brown-eyed and her body was strong and smooth. Her hair was blond and she wore it with impudent unstyle. Her smile was rare and subtle. She was beautiful. Draper had been with her for a year, and before that with two other women in Laguna very much like her, ever since he came north from Jacumba ten years ago. To Draper she was a type easily attracted by pretty, forgiving little beach towns — women of great outward beauty and physical health that disguised serious inner damage.

"It's nice to be home with you," he said. "It makes my heart glad."

She ignored him.

They ran up the ramp to Heisler Park and Draper saw that the rosebushes were beginning to bud out. Then up Cliff to Coast Highway north, across at Crescent, down PCH past the galleries and across again to Main Beach and all the way down to Juliet's place at the Royale.

Draper opened the door and stepped inside. Her condo had a big picture window that looked out at black rock formations and the cold green ocean journeying far to meet the sky. They had furnished it beautifully. There was still a fire going against the morning chill. They made love in the shower and Juliet scratched his thigh hard enough to draw blood. Later she made a show of cleaning the scratch and putting on a dressing then they dozed on a blanket in front of the fire. Later they went out to lunch and sat by the fire there, too. They sat close and spoke in near whispers, their heads touching lightly. Draper loved the smell of her hair.

"How's work?" he asked.

"It's work."

She was a hostess in one of Laguna's good restaurants, which kept her busy three nights a week and brought in enough money for clothes and cosmetics. She also worked part-time at the Laguna Club, a day-care center, because she liked children, and volunteered part-time at the animal shelter because she liked dogs.

"Everything went well," he said.

"You know that means nothing to me. You've made it mean nothing to me."

"It was my only condition."

"I'm thinking about Aspen."

"I can tell."

"I feel as if I'm a shadow here. I have no face. I think I need a change of scenery."

Aspen, thought Draper. She wouldn't last a week of winter.

"Get me another lemon drop," she said.

Draper ordered another drink for each of them and they ate lunch and watched the people on the sidewalk and the eucalyptus trees shimmering outside city hall.

"It didn't work, Coleman."

"I didn't think so."

"I don't see why it doesn't work."

"It will, Juliet."

"I'm tired of it not."

"I'm sorry, too."

"Maybe another doctor. I have a name."

"Here, I brought this for you," he said.

Draper pulled the lab report from his jacket pocket. "This says that I'm a fertile little mongrel."

She took the slip, looked at the checked boxes and the numbers, handed it back. "But I've done my part, too, Cole."

"They said patience. When everything is right, it happens."

"Three months and nothing."

"It's going to happen for us."

"If it's me, we can use another woman's," she said.

"It isn't you," he said. "I want it to be ours."

Draper was functionally sterile. It was a rare condition that he had been born with. But he knew how much she wanted his child so he'd created the favorable lab report for her, based on forms he found on-line, checking the right boxes and filling in hormone levels and sperm count based on

Wikipedia information, signing a doctor's name with convincing haste and sloppiness. He wanted no more children to provide for — Brittany was enough — but he wanted Juliet to be happy.

"Maybe it's not meant to be," she said.

Juliet was godless as a lizard but believed life to be scripted, something that Draper found odd.

"Have faith," he said.

"I want to be normal, like everyone else," she said. "I want things to be easy and natural. For you, too, Cole. You don't want it all to end, either. I know that."

"No, I don't."

In fact it bothered him not at all that it would end with him. Draper was the end of his family line. Being the last of his kind gave him broad and sometimes terrible liberties. He thought, if he bothered to think of such things at all, that the world would actually be better off without people like him.

"We can be phoenix people," she said. "We can rise out of the ashes and become beautiful and strong, even when the odds are against us."

"You're already beautiful and strong and I'm proud to be with you."

She sighed into his ear and gently kissed

his cheek.

In the Fiori store Draper bought a four-foot-tall ceramic vase, a stunning piece with rich blues and bright yellows and a luminous glaze.

He handed her the receipt and hefted the big piece over his shoulder and they wandered down Coast Highway to Splashes where Draper sat the vase beside them in the bar and they ordered drinks and watched the waves.

"I think I'll have more than one," she said.

"You have whatever you want."

Draper took her hand and turned it up and gave her a wildly optimistic palm reading, as he often did. It was rich in children and dogs, all with preposterous names.

They talked about a sailboat painting she'd seen at the Pacific Edge Gallery, how good it would look in the media room. Draper registered concern over the $7,500 price tag.

He got her to gossip about her restaurant coworkers, and tell him about the great puppies that came to the shelter this past week, then he guided her into talking about her childhood. She was comfortable there. It was the only truly happy time of her life. It was mostly in San Bernardino, humble but fun. She had friends, and a swimming pool in the tract home where she lived with her wild older sister and mom and stepdad, and there were dogs, and long walks to the 7-Eleven for snacks and pop. She could talk on for hours about those times.

But Juliet's childhood stopped abruptly at age fifteen, when one of her stepfather's handsome friends had convinced her, not absolutely against her will, to do bad things. It had gone on awhile. There were female problems and a late-term procedure with complications. After that came the chaos, the pills, the men, the purposeful overdose that just barely failed. Finally came the rebirth of Juliet in Laguna. She had told Draper this dark tale only once, and he had held her hand while the tears spilled out of her.

Draper ordered another drink for each of them then went off on a chipper monologue about his own childhood in Jacumba — his family's restaurant; his little brother, Ron, whom he had loved and protected from rougher boys; his cute sister, Roxanne; dogs and friends; hitting a grand slam on the frosh-soph baseball team. He told her about the heat and the dust, and the drug runners and human traffickers who used the complex of roads and trails and caves and tunnels and gullies and canyons to transport

170

their products to the north. He told her of the car chases and the spectacular wrecks and even about Mikey Castro, gunned down just like a thirties gangster as he walked from his shiny clean Suburban toward the Draper family's restaurant — Amigos.

She squeezed Draper's hand in high surprise as he told her this tale, though she'd heard it before. She had empathy and it led to genuine emotions and Draper liked this quality in her.

Like Juliet's childhood, Draper's had a sudden ending when he was also just fifteen years old. A propane line had broken while the Draper family slept on a very cold night, and when the accumulated gas hit the pilot light of the oven, the explosion killed Coleman's parents, his brother and his sister. Draper had been sleeping out in the barn with the horses and dogs. The explosion had blown fireplace bricks through the barn wall. He had never forgiven himself for surviving. Several times, though, he had asked Juliet to hear the story and forgive him. *Please tell me I'm forgiven,* he would whisper. It was the deepest, darkest jewel he could offer her.

So when the river of Draper's memories approached the great black dam that marked its boundary, he became quiet and looked out at the waves. Juliet worked herself closer to him and ran her fingers through his soft blond forelock.

"Be my phoenix," she whispered.

"I'll be that."

"And I'll be yours. Take me home. Fill me up."

Draper paid and hefted the vase onto his shoulder and they walked slowly down the beach.

Inside he set it on the hearth as Juliet unbuttoned her blouse then took him in her arms and kissed him.

The next morning Draper drove down to Jacumba. He passed through the remote-controlled gate and parked in front of his old family home, which had been long rebuilt since the catastrophic fire. It was bigger now, and Draper had had the propane heating system completely replaced by electric.

The old barn that had saved his life was still there. Draper walked over and slid open the door and stepped inside. He stood for a moment, enjoying the smell that never changed and the images flickering in his memory.

He closed the barn door behind him and headed for the house. He'd sold the property a few years back to Israel Castro, which was almost like selling it to a brother or sister. Better, in some ways.

Israel now came through the front door and gave Draper a big hug, slapping him on the back.

Inside he poured cold beers as Draper set the duffel stuffed with cash on the kitchen counter.

They drank to health and Draper piled the vacuum-packed bundles of cash on the granite.

"Fifteen thousand," he said.

Israel produced a checkbook from a drawer and wrote a check on the East County Tile & Stone account for $8,450 to Prestige German Auto and another for $6,550 to Coleman Draper.

Draper wrote a check from Prestige German Auto to Castro Commercial Management for $2,535 and another for $3,875, which were mortgage payments on two of the four Jacumba investment properties that Israel had shown and sold him.

They exchanged checks, then clinked their beer bottles together again. Thanks to Israel's numerous capacities — most of them legitimate — he could launder Draper's cold hard cash with just a few strokes of the pen. Israel owned a construction

materials business, was a commercial property landlord and manager, a real estate
agent, a mortgage originator, a credit union
board member and a notary. He did business in both the United States and Mexico,
most of it along the half-lawless strip of
borderland where he and Draper had grown
up. He also helped transport large quanti-
ties of heroin and cocaine into California,
but not nearly as often as he used to. It was
too risky — a young man's work. His goal
was to be 100 percent legit by the time he
was thirty years old, and it looked as if he
might make it.

"Let's go see how Jacumba looks today,"
said Israel. "You'll like the progress on the
hacienda."

They took Israel's trick black Denali, the
big tires kicking up dust as they rode
through town. Jacumba was poor and parts
were nearly squalid, but to Draper it was
simply where he had grown up. The fact
that it had changed little was a comforting
reminder of how far he had traveled from
here.

They passed Amigos restaurant, which
Draper had purchased five years ago, then
closed, gutted, remodeled and reopened.
The lunch business looked brisk. Draper
looked at the sign that he had commis-

sioned. It featured two happy men with big mustaches, arms around each other's shoulders, smiling and brandishing cartoonishly large pistols.

"Oh, the new waitress," said Israel, pain in his voice. *"Miranda."*

"And how is your child bride?"

"Glory be to Gloria. She's in Puerto Vallarta with the kids. I behave. I look but don't touch."

As they rumbled out a rutted dirt road headed east, Coleman thought back to when they were ten years old and Israel's father Mikey was shot down outside Amigos. He and Israel had watched it happen. Coleman would never forget how clean Mikey's Suburban was. In Jacumba no vehicle stayed clean overnight and when Mikey pulled up across the street from Amigos Coleman knew that it had just been washed. Mikey was wearing new creased jeans and a blue cowboy shirt and snakeskin boots and a black Resistol. Ten seconds later a black Chevy 1500 rolled by and stopped and when it rolled on again Mikey was just a tattered rag on the street. His hat blew into the gutter. Israel's mother had left his father years before, so at Coleman's insistence the Draper family had taken in the boy. Three years later he moved in with a gang of traffickers living across the border in the Mexican half of Jacumba, called Jacume. Israel was drawn to a pretty girl and some very easy money helping the mules and coyotes navigate the bleak desert border. He was fast, strong and fearless. He'd married Gloria at sixteen, with the full permission of her *narcotrafficante* father. After the tragic death of his family, Draper had joined Israel over in Jacume.

Now they came to Draper's hacienda east of town, just a mile from the border. Draper had named it Rancho Las Palmas. The parcel was fifty acres, mostly just dry rolling hills, but part of it was thickly wooded with manzanita and some oak, and there was a glade with a spring where Draper had seen deer and mountain lion.

Thanks to Israel and his labor connections south of the border, the structures were going up under budget and ahead of schedule. There was a main house built of concrete and iron and river rock, a wooden barn, a five-car garage with an apartment over it, and three guest cottages. The swimming pool was excavated and framed, and as Draper approached he saw that the masons were making the artificial rocks that would form an overhang and waterfall. Draper craved water and the idea of water, and his four wells were dug deep into the bountiful aquifer and ready to be plumbed for service. Dozens of Canary Island palms, still in their big wooden boxes, were positioned around the site for planting. There were queens and kings and sagos and blues, too, and a bounty of palms that Draper couldn't even identify.

"In six months you'll have one of the best properties in East County," said Israel. "It'll be magnificent. Ten years from now, when you sell it, it will be worth five times what you paid for it. Between your wells and your spring, you'll never have to buy one pint of water. You'll be self-sustaining."

"You don't have to sell me on it," said Draper.

"And shade. You'll always have the shade of the palms."

They walked over to a grove of seven Canary Island palms. Draper put his hand on the big wooden box and looked up at the stunning symmetry of the fronds emanating from the center.

"Let's go see your old house. I'm in a sentimental mood."

"Yes, we should see it. It's been years for you, hasn't it?"

"Two at least."

Using a series of perilously rutted roads

and a short dark tunnel, Castro delivered them to the other side of the border fifteen minutes later. They traveled unseen by the law but were duly noted by the cartel lookouts and the human smugglers dug into the rocky hillsides with their powerful spotting scopes. These men and boys communicated by walkie-talkies because cell phones wouldn't work down here. They scurried back and forth across the border with impunity, sometimes hourly, like fleas hopping from one part of a dog to another.

The old Castro family home was still large and rambling. It was freshly painted, white with pale green trim. Draper had lived there for the three years following the death of his family thanks to an influential Castro uncle who was rarely ever there.

As the Denali idled at the gated driveway, Draper looked at his old home and thought of the great dusty freedom of life in Jacume. There were hours out-of-doors, making trails and paths and tunnels and learning how they connected to the bustling warren of trails and paths and tunnels that already existed. There were motorcycles and ATVs and dune buggies and, of course, SUVs. There were moonless runs and flashlit sprints and elaborate distractions involving flares and even dynamite — all to throw off the DEA and the Baja Police and the Border Patrol and the sheriffs and the cops. There was easy cash and there were easy drugs and easy girls.

After the death of his parents and brother and sister, Draper had felt like a rocket launched into space. All things were blurred and indefinable by his senses. He was speeding, barely controllable, totally unstoppable. For the first time in his life he felt truly free and truly happy.

"I need a man," he said. "Someone who can pull a trigger."

"Jacumba and Jacume are still full of them."

"No one close to you."

"Oh?"

"You know. A onetime job. Someone slender, but don't give me a boy."

"I do know. Well, that's another thing."

"There's five thousand for the work and five thousand when the work is done."

"When?"

"Friday. I need him in L.A. by afternoon. I'll have everything he needs. Tell him that someone will bring him back here later that night."

Draper took the thick square of folded hundreds from the rear pocket of his jeans and gave it to Israel.

"I'll get a man for you," said Israel.

"To Amigos," said Draper. "I'm starved."

"I can introduce you to Miranda."

"I'd like that."

He pulled onto Laurel Laws's horse property just before sunset. Standing on her porch he neatened his necktie, then knocked.

A moment later he heard movement behind the door and he looked at the spy hole.

"Coleman?"

"Yes. I'm sorry to just come over unannounced."

The door opened and Laurel stood before him. Her face was puffy and her hair was a mess and her blouse was wrinkled. Draper bowed.

"Well . . . ," she said and stepped back into the foyer.

Draper entered and pursed his lips solemnly and gave her a brief, formal hug. He handed her a sympathy bouquet.

"I'm so sorry, Laurel," he said. "He's all I can think about."

"Me, too. It's sinking in. Thank you for your calls."

"Is there anything I can do?"

She looked around the foyer and back into the living room as if searching for a chore or project. "Well, oh, no."

"Anything at all, Laurel."

"I'm fine, really. Come in."

"I won't stay long. I'm sorry I didn't call. Right up until I knocked on your door I was telling myself I'd turn around and call later."

"It's okay. I wasn't doing much."

They sat in the darkened living room, Laurel at one end of a leather nail-head sofa and Draper across the room in what he assumed was his partner's favorite recliner. This usurpation pleased him in a way that had nothing to do with the reason for his visit. Draper told her a little about his grief, then he began praising Terry in a soft voice, telling Laurel some anecdotes from their years together. Draper had never become close to Laurel because he and Terry socialized less and less after he was married, but there was still a broad bond between them and Draper felt its natural weight and comfort as he talked. The flowers lay on a coffee table in front of her and the distant glimmer of a street lamp came through the window to land on the plastic wrapper and prompt the faint colors of the lilies.

"What about you, Laurel? Are you handling it?"

She was quiet for a moment. Draper was

surprised that she was this thoughtful. And he was more surprised as he listened to her words.

"I always wanted nice things and I always thought I was happy. I wanted a man who was impressive and controllable. I told myself that what I got in life was because of my taste and personality. When I married Terry I thought I would finally have it all. Then, when he died, I realized I have almost nothing. Our life is gone. It's very strange, but — and maybe this happens all the time — but I love him more now than when he was alive. I just miss him, so much. I never even got to tell him good-bye. When it's so sudden . . ."

Draper said nothing, just let the darkness absorb her tears. His instinct was to go to her.

A while later he spoke again. He told her about losing his parents and brother and sister to fire, how this childhood event had replaced the boy he was with a new, strange one he didn't know very well at first. He'd felt the same vast loss, he said, and for many years — even now, actually — the thing he wanted most was to be able to say good-bye to them.

There was another long silence.

"Have they told you anything about who

did it?" he asked.

"Two detectives came out and I talked to them. Bentley was one of them. Then, later, another one — Hood or something. He was Terry's partner that night. They asked questions, over and over. They were interested in Wayne, or Dwayne or . . . you know, the one with the dog."

"I know the detectives. How many times have they come out to talk?"

"The two of them, twice. The other guy, just that once."

"Hood is part of Internal Affairs. They police the police. Was he respectful?"

"I don't know what he was. He didn't say much. He looked a lot. At our things. I was out of it. I was weak and angry at Terry for leaving me. Nothing had sunk in yet."

"Hood probably focused on Terry's state of mind."

"Yes. He asked if Terry was happy."

"I know the answer to that."

She said nothing. Draper sensed that she was looking at him.

"Laurel, I know Terry was happy. But I also felt that he was troubled by something that he'd done."

"Oh?"

"I'm sorry to be vague. But he seemed different to me after that big bust we made, the one where we took down the biker."

"He was different. Yes. I don't know why. I thought it was our money situation, him wanting to make me happy with a horse property. But it worked out. We did a charitable remaindered trust, buying then donating this home to Build a Dream."

"Maybe that's all it was. Maybe I was wrong about him being haunted by something he'd done."

"I honestly don't think so. Terry was a Boy Scout. I mean that in a good way. He'd even found Jesus. That surprised me. It came out of nowhere but I don't think it was because something was haunting him."

"Did Hood ask if Terry might be worried about something he'd done?"

"No. He didn't."

"He didn't suggest that Terry was hiding something from us?"

"No."

"Because Internal Affairs can be prying and judgmental. And just plain wrong. That's why I'm concerned."

Draper felt relief begin to flow in him. After another respectful silence he stood and Laurel stood and he bowed to her again.

"If Hood comes back, it's probably best if you don't tell him I was here. He's been questioning me about Terry's behavior, looking for something that isn't there. He may want another crack at you."

"No," she said. "I won't tell him we talked."

"If there's anything I can do," he said. "Anything. I want to honor him any way I can. Terry was my friend, and you are, too."

He was back in Laguna by dinnertime. Juliet greeted him with her studied nonchalance. Her hair was wet and combed back and she was wearing a green satin robe snugly tied. Draper stood there with the dozen red roses he'd purchased at the same time as the sympathy bouquet for Laurel. Then he kissed her lightly on the lips and took the flowers to the kitchen. He cut the stems and placed the flowers in a heavy crystal vase. He added water then walked around the kitchen island and set the vase on the dining room table and adjusted the arrangement. Then he pulled out a chair and turned it around and sat down facing her.

"Come here," he said.

She stood in front of him and Draper brought her closer and parted the robe without untying it. He kissed her and heard her breath catch. Salt and perfume, her ass cool in his hands, her fingers in his hair.

"I got us a very good Brunello," she whispered. "And reservations at nine."

When he looked up her eyes were closed and she was smiling.

17

Atascadero State Hospital for the criminally insane sits in the coastal hills of California, midway between L.A. and San Francisco. It is one of the largest mental hospitals in the world.

The surrounding countryside is rolling hills and oak glens and pastures. Smooth tan and sudden green. Hood saw horses and cattle. The March day was cool but the sun came through the oaks and lit the grass in pools of soft light. He was driving his '86 IROC Camaro. The car had a stiff ride but Hood loved it anyway. He had once heard the Camaro described as a workingman's muscle car. That's me, he thought.

He parked outside the administration building. The trees were bare and the buildings seemed industrial and secretive. The hospital looked like a prison trying to smile.

Hood found his way to Unit 8, where prisoners are treated when they're judged incompetent to stand trial. They're called PC 1370s. The goal of Atascadero is to protect, evaluate and treat the 1370s so they can return to the courts and understand what's expected of them. If the patient shows no progress, he'll be transferred to a smaller hospital, where protection and maintenance are the goals and recovery is not expected.

Dr. Able Rosen was an older man, dusty and gentle. He wore a sloping corduroy coat with shiny spots at the elbows and a Jerry Garcia necktie.

"We'll do another evaluation in June," he said. "And if Shay hasn't shown measurable progress, we'll have to transfer him. Our philosophy is recovery. We're a hospital, not a correctional facility."

"Can he talk?"

"In fact, we've seen some improvement in his short-term memory and his speech. His speech center was damaged by the swelling caused by the beating. Brain cells do not regenerate but the compensatory powers of the brain are prodigious. His ability to retrieve memories and form sentences to communicate information is, unfortunately, still limited."

"Is he violent?"

"He had one violent incident here. We try

our best to provide a norm of nonviolence. He will be restrained. We have a special facility for this kind of visit."

Dr. Rosen tapped his fingers on the desk. "What do you hope to accomplish?"

"I want to hear about his arrest and his crimes."

"Surely you've read the reports and court records."

"He couldn't say much back then and I don't expect him to be talkative now. I just want to hear what he says and how he says it."

"Why?"

"There are some facts about the arrest, and about Mr. Eichrodt's crimes, that don't make sense to me. It's very possible that some areas were overlooked."

"Areas?"

"I believe that a large amount of money is unaccounted for. It's possible that Shay hid it before his arrest."

Dr. Rosen raised his eyebrows. "How large?"

"Three hundred grand. Give or take some."

"Drug money?"

Hood nodded.

"Have you been in contact with Ariel

Reed, of the L.A. District Attorney's office?"

"We've talked."

"She was knowledgeable and rational. I also thought she was very . . . humane. For a prosecutor. That came out wrong."

"I understand."

"I was impressed by her. She might help you."

"Dr. Rosen, thank you for letting me visit. I'll be happy to tell you what I learn, if I learn anything at all."

He looked at Hood oddly, as if not understanding what he meant. "I hope you're not disappointed, Deputy. Shay has been a challenge for us all."

In the Unit 8 visitation center Hood was searched, and surrendered his wallet, badge, keys, change, digital recorder and penknife.

He was then led downstairs to a narrow hallway. The orderly unlocked a door and stood back so he could enter.

The room was small. It had a wooden chair and a stainless steel table. One wall was a thick plate of clear plastic, with a round speaker grille about mouth level. A small video camera was fastened to the ceiling behind Hood. On the other side of the plastic window was an identical room, as if a reflection of the one that he was in.

Eichrodt was ushered in by two big men in navy scrubs. He wore a pale blue jumpsuit and slip-on canvas shoes. His hands were cuffed behind him and secured by a waist restraint. He wore ankle irons. He was nearly a head taller than his handlers, and much heavier. His head and face were shaved and his skin was white and his eyes were brown, with a distant glitter. A tattooed serpent's head stared out from the hollow beneath his larynx.

The orderlies backed out of the room and Hood heard the lock clank into place.

Eichrodt sat and stared at him.

"Thanks for seeing me," Hood said.

He kept staring. Some time went by.

"The deputy who arrested you, the big one — he was murdered last week. A gangsta shot him down. I'm one of the investigators."

Eichrodt's lips parted. He inhaled. He tried to say something but no sound came forth. He exhaled, and tried again. "Strong."

"Yes. Terry Laws was strong."

Again, Eichrodt's lips parted and he seemed to be concentrating on controlling his breathing. It looked like he was waiting for just the right moment to begin forming a sound.

"They used. Clubs."

"You put up quite a fight."

Eichrodt looked at Hood for a long time. Hood saw blankness. If there were wheels turning, they were turning slowly. Something on the wall caught Eichrodt's attention and he fixed his gaze on it, but Hood saw nothing. So he looked at the thick plastic window between them, the scratches and dull sheen, and thought about the thin line between the sane and the mad, and the way that line can vanish so quickly.

Then Eichrodt shifted and turned and squinted at him and his breathing accelerated. Wheels turning, Hood could see it. Eichrodt opened his mouth and in the tension of his neck and jaw Hood saw the great effort it took for him to raise a memory and say something about it.

"No. Reason."

"No reason for what?"

"For the thing I told you about. The word went away from me just now."

"Clubs?"

"Yes. No reason for clubs."

"You're a big man, Shay. They were afraid of you. When you swept the deputy, Draper, off his feet, they knew you had tricked them. So they used force."

He lowered his gaze. His mouth fell open again and his lips moved but no sound came out. He shook his head very slowly — bewildered, stymied, disbelieving — it was hard for Hood to tell what he was feeling. Then he inhaled very deeply, as before, and looked up, eyes narrow, mouth open, lips moving.

"There was no . . ."

"No what, Shay?"

"No . . . *shit,* the word again. The words go away when I go to say them."

"No fight?"

"No! There was no . . ."

Eichrodt jumped out of his seat, raised his face to the ceiling and roared. Hood stood. Eichrodt banged his forehead against the window. Up that close Hood could see that his teeth were man-made, large and very white.

He tried again. "No reason . . ."

He looked down at Hood, growled, then shook his head violently and banged it against the window again.

Then Hood got it.

"No reason *for* the fight," he said.

He stared at Hood for a long beat, then very slowly nodded. His mouth hung open and he slumped back into the chair. Again Hood could see the wheels of Shay Eichrodt's mind slow. Again he turned to the wall and stared. Minutes passed and Hood waited. He believed that Eichrodt wanted him to wait.

"Cuffed. Then clubs."

"Cuffed, then clubs? What, you were cuffed when they beat you?"

He nodded again.

"That's not in the transcript," Hood said. "Did you tell your lawyer that?"

Eichrodt stared off at nothing for a moment. Then at Hood. "I couldn't remember that, back then. It comes back. The words come back. The worst is when I have a memory but no words to describe it. But I used to have the words."

"You had no memory, then."

He shook his head, looking down at the steel counter before him. It took Hood a minute to fully absorb what Eichrodt was claiming. Of course it was his word against that of a sworn deputy and a sworn reserve, Hood thought. And Eichrodt could be faking a memory, and lying.

Then Hood realized something.

"Shay, did you hide some money?"

Eichrodt stared at him with a blankness that looked eternal. But then he blinked and frowned and his dramatically refurbished mouth hung open again and Hood could see him straining to get at another memory.

"There was no money."

"You took money from the men in the van. Vasquez and Lopes. You had four thousand in the toolbox of your truck. But they were carrying more, weren't they?"

His breath came fast again and he struggled to slow it down, inhaling and exhaling as he stared at Hood.

"No van. No men except cops. No money."

"You never saw a van, or Vasquez and Lopes, or any money?"

He looked at Hood with fury. *"No."*

Hood remembered the court transcript. Eichrodt had been unable to remember a van, or murder victims, or money.

But now, Hood realized, he was saying that he never *saw* them.

Hood sat for a moment, listening to the restless thump of his heart. He took a deep breath and told it to slow down but it didn't.

He had the black thought that Laws and Draper had killed the two couriers and taken the real money. Eichrodt was the fall guy. All they had to do was cuff him, beat him back into the dark ages of his own consciousness, plant some evidence and cover the rest in their official report.

It would account for Laws and Draper not calling backup.

It would account for Vasquez and Lopes

pulling over on the shoulder of the off-ramp, right out in the open — they'd seen the law enforcement car behind them and done what anybody would do.

It would account for the fact that they had not drawn the weapons that were so closely at hand.

It would account for Terry Laws's sudden fortune.

It would account for the something that had died inside him after the arrest.

"Shay, do you understand that if you tell this story to your doctors, and to the court, that you can be tried for murder?"

He looked at Hood blankly. Then his expression changed to curiosity. He smiled at me with his large, perfectly white teeth.

"Let them."

Hood had just come back upstairs when Dr. Rosen pulled him back into his office.

Rosen closed the door behind them, but he didn't sit. His expression was intense and his words came fast. "I'm very encouraged by what I saw. He broke through to things he couldn't recall — right before our eyes. It's very unusual. We rarely see such recovery after so long a time. I've never seen anything quite like this."

"I don't know what I expected, but it

wasn't that," Hood said.

The doctor looked at him. "That's a big accusation he's making."

"You don't know how big."

"Do you hope he's lying?"

"What does my hope have to do with anything?"

"No. I apologize." He went to his desk and sat. "I'm tempted to move the evaluation up to next week. I want to run a CAT scan and an MRI. See what's really going on in that brain of his."

"I'd like to know, too."

"It would be a capital case, wouldn't it? Wouldn't he be eligible for a death penalty?"

"Very eligible."

"Did you believe what he said?"

"I believe that he did."

The doctor nodded. "Truth can be a powerful weapon. But first you have to find it."

Hood was half an hour down the road to L.A. when Keith Franks called.

"The heavy blood on the casings didn't come from Vasquez or Lopes. It was Eichrodt's. So was the blood on the grip, the trigger, and the guard of the murder gun."

Hood tried to speculate why Eichrodt was bleeding so generously as he gunned down the couriers and picked up the brass. He couldn't make the scene play right, because Eichrodt's bleeding came later, at the hands of Draper and Laws. But there was one way it could make sense: the murder weapon never touched Eichrodt's hands until after he'd been knocked unconscious by two LASD deputies.

"What do you think?" asked Franks.

"I'm afraid to think what I think."

Hood called Warren before he made L.A. and asked him to get Coleman Draper's package.

And a copy of the anonymous 911 call reporting the red pickup truck leaving the murder scene.

Warren told him to consider it done.

18

Hood got to the Pomona Raceway early, bought a pit pass and walked down among the dragsters and the drivers and the crews. It was Saturday and more rain was on the way. The air smelled of burnt racing fuel from the early elimination runs. Hood liked the smell, the unmistakable scent of power and speed and internal combustion.

The event was sponsored by DRAW — the Drag Racing Association of Women — and its purpose was to raise money to help people hurt in drag races at a track.

The pit was congested with brilliantly painted dragsters and funny cars. The hoods were propped up so people could appreciate the lavishly chromed engines. The drivers and mechanics were dressed in the same bright colors as their cars. They answered questions and let themselves be photographed. During lulls Hood heard them talking with quiet specificity about what needed to be done to their cars before the racing began.

Ariel Reed stood with a group of fans, autographing photos and programs. She was wearing red leathers with gold trim and her hair was pulled back in a ponytail. Her car stood behind her, a sleek red AA alcohol dragster with a mountainous engine. A teenaged boy stared at her while she signed a photo, then he croaked his thanks and stood there smiling at her. She looked up at Hood and winked then went back to signing.

He joined the little crowd around her and listened as she related dragster facts: top fuel diggers can put out over 6,000 horse, hit 330 miles per hour and cover a quarter mile in less than five seconds. She said that a vehicle going 200 miles per hour as it crosses the starting line will lose to a top fuel dragster starting from a dead stop at the same time. She said that the noise outputs have been measured at 3.9 on the Richter scale and the G force exerted on the driver is enough to detach her retina.

Someone asked about fuel efficiency and Ariel said she got over five hundred feet per gallon out of this puppy.

Someone asked if she was afraid when she raced and she said don't be silly, she was too scared to be afraid.

A few minutes later the fans had drifted away to the next car.

"I love my molecule. It's on my desk at work. I can split atoms anytime I want!"

"You're very welcome."

"Thanks for coming.

"I like the drags."

"You're a fan?"

"Since I was a kid. Dad would drive us down from Bakersfield."

"I learned here. Raced for the first time when I was eighteen. Ran twelve seconds in a borrowed Dodge. How's our friend Shay Eichrodt?"

She looked at Hood with her level, opinionless gaze. He thought it would have been unsettling from across a poker table.

"Better," he said. "The doctor was surprised."

"So we may be trying him for murder after all."

"You might be.

She shrugged. "Stick around after the race and I'll buy you a beer."

Hood got a good seat, up top in the bleachers with a touch of sunshine on his back. The northern sky had darkened more and the Pomona foothills were green. The first two drivers rode their cars to the start line, gunned their engines into ear-shocking roars of rpm and took their burnouts to heat the tires and make them sticky. Then the racers lined up for the real thing. The Christmas tree lit up yellow and red. The sound of gunning nitro engines was thunderous. The cars growled like beasts that knew they were about to be unleashed for just a few seconds. Then the bottom lights went green and the world roared with torque and fury. The dragsters shot forward. Hood watched the bodies shudder and the tires dig for traction in the blast of speed. One second they were coming at him, then they were racing away. He saw how close the drivers were to losing control but how skillfully they maintained it. Then the roar lessened and the parachutes blew into shape behind the cars and the finish line light gave victory to the winner. The crowd clapped and cheered but the totaled response of thirty thousand spectators was little more than a gesture compared to the spectacle of sound and motion that Hood had just witnessed.

Hood thought of his family, lined up shoulder-to-shoulder on these same bleachers, soft drinks in their hands and plugs in their ears while the top fuel eliminators and funny cars rocketed past. He was five. They would stay with an uncle in Pasadena and make the drive to Pomona for the races. Hood loved then what he loved now: the smell of the fuel and the sound of the engines and the impossible velocity shaped by human skill into a straight line. And he had always liked the way you could get a pit pass and meet the drivers and the crew and see the cars up close.

Ariel was matched up against Walt Bledsoe in the fifth race. Bledsoe's AA methane rail was black and cobalt blue — a stallion with major attitude. According to Hood's program Bledsoe was tenth in the states in the NHRA Sportsman Top Alcohol Dragster Class. Ariel was forty-first. When her red and gold rail came onto the launching pad burping fire and smoke Hood was impressed and proud. He looked down at her in the cockpit, harnessed in, her helmet soon to be pushed back against the seat in an explosion of power. The two rivals did their burnouts, jockeying and bellowing at each other. Then they rumbled up to the starting line and the lights on the Christmas tree illuminated downward.

Flames belched from the chrome pipes and the dragsters were off. Both drivers were a little eager on the throttle and Hood saw the faint rise of their front ends, then the corrections — a shimmy as weight moved downward — followed by a surge of speed and a howling sprint to the finish line. The parachutes deployed and filled and the finish light gave the win to Bledsoe: 215 mph in 6.64 seconds.

Hood stood and clapped as Ariel guided her car off the track. She won her next race and lost her last. By then it was dark and the starless sky above was heavy with the gathering storm.

Hood found her in the pit, helping get the car onto its trailer behind a big silver pickup truck. Her crew of three ignored him. When the dragster was fastened down Ariel shook hands with each one then the crew climbed into the truck and eased it out of the pit and toward the exit. She watched the truck and trailer amble slowly into the darkness.

"Didn't exactly set any records," she said.

"You've got a steady foot, young lady."

She leaned into the bed of a shiny black El Camino and brought two beers from a cooler.

"Let's walk," she said.

The pit was almost empty of fans now but Ariel stopped and talked with a few other drivers. They congratulated each other with easy fraternity.

Then Hood and Ariel walked down the track, beers in hand, she in one lane and he in the other. The lights were still on above the bleachers and the safety railing shone softly.

"My mom and grandmother raced," she said. "And my daddy and granddad — that'd be Bill and Frank. Frank died eight years ago but Dad's still going strong."

"My dad's got Alzheimer's."

"I'm sorry for that."

"It's just a fact."

Ariel sipped her beer, then reached out the bottle and tapped it against the finish light stanchion.

"It's a family thing. Generation after generation, speeding down the track. But I'll let you in on a little secret — I don't care if I win or not. I don't do it for history. I do it because it thrills me."

"To thrills," said Hood. They touched bottles.

Some time passed and Hood sensed that Ariel was brooding in her silence.

"You think thrills are a sign of immaturity," she said. "Because you were a soldier. Because you enforce the law on the street. Because your partner got shot to death right in front of you."

"Nothing about you is immature, Ms. Reed."

"I said you think thrills are overrated."

"You don't know what I think."

"Then tell me."

"I like it that you put bad guys in jail. I like it that you drag race. I like your smile."

She pulled the band off her ponytail and shook out her hair. "I'm wound tight as a golf ball, Charlie."

"I know."

"Doesn't that make you want to walk away?"

"It makes me wonder what makes you tick."

"You found out what made Allison Murrieta tick. An armed robber."

"Thrills," Hood said. "Gain. Fame. Vengeance. History. It was complicated."

"There must be something in the thrill seeker that attracts you."

"She loved fast cars, like you do."

"It's not really my business, but you and her were about all the DA's office talked about for most of that week."

They walked into the grandstands and up the rows of empty seats. When they got to the top it started to rain and Hood could hear the patter on the sunscreen over their heads. The drops came faster and heavier and the racetrack looked like it was coming to a boil. They sat and looked out at the track and watched the rain slant down through the lights.

"Bakersfield. You like the music, deputy?"

"I wish they'd make more of it. I got just about all of it they ever recorded. They put out a Bill Woods 'Live at the Blackboard' in '03. Red Simpson, Don Rich. Great CD."

"I wish I could play an instrument. I've got no discernable talent for anything. Except maybe for splitting atoms, as you pointed out."

"It was kind of a compliment."

"I took it as one."

"Wish I had another beer," she said.

"Me, too."

"Long walk back to the cooler in this rain."

"Let's watch it for a minute."

"While you tell me about Shay Eichrodt."

He told her what he'd seen and heard. Ariel listened without interrupting, her expression dark.

"You really think Laws and Draper cuffed him and beat him?" she asked.

"Possibly."

"I very highly doubt it."

"I can go one uglier."

"They killed Vasquez and Lopes and took their money, which explains Terry Laws's sudden fortune."

"That and a whole lot more," he said.

Hood looked out at the rain.

"All you have is the very questionable word of a brain-damaged felon who can face a death sentence if he's convicted," said Ariel.

"In some simple-ass way, that's why I think he's telling the truth."

"If a jury doesn't, the state can execute him."

"Yes, it can," said Hood. "But what's he supposed to do? Shut up and stay in a mental hospital the rest of his life?"

The rain roared against the shade roof above them. Hood watched the water pour off the racetrack lights, little waterfalls bent south by the wind of the storm.

"What's all that mean to a Blood gangsta machine-gunning Terry Laws one night?" asked Ariel.

"I don't know what it means."

"What have the homicide guys come up with?"

"Londell Dwayne. He looks right. He'd threatened Terry. We talked to him but his alibi fell apart pretty quick. Next thing, Londell maced two detectives and blew into the wind."

They sat for a long while without saying a word. The rain got heavier then it slowed. Hood held her hand as they went down the wet steps and across the track to the pit.

They got into her El Camino and she gave Hood a ride to the parking lot.

"Nice Camaro," she said. "Glasspacks and fat soft tires. Maybe you're not immune to thrills after all."

"I'm really not."

She pushed the car into park and took Hood's face in both her hands and kissed him and he kissed her back.

"Nice," she said. "Very nice. Thank you. That's a dumb thing to say."

"Thank you. There."

Hood got out of the El Camino and shut the door. Ariel gunned the engine and looked at him for a long moment, then smiled. Suddenly the El Camino burned away and slid into a big screaming one-eighty on the wet asphalt, back tires throwing up rooster tails of water, which brought her right back to where she'd started. Her window came down.

"Call me later."

19

In the Hole's early chill Hood unlocked the center drawer of his desk. The CD was there — a recording of the anonymous tipper. And so was Coleman Draper's package from HR, both promised by Warren.

He listened to the recording. It was just as Ariel had described it — hissing with wind noise, barely audible, a drunk sounding man with an accent. Hood knew that spectrographic voice prints were not allowed as evidence in California state courts but he was still hoping that the recording would be clear enough to tell him something about the caller. Now he doubted it.

This was disappointing, but what Hood really wanted was a basic understanding of Coleman Draper.

First he scanned through Draper's package, which was surprisingly light, even for a reservist. Hood went straight to the money, looking for signs of Draper's cut of the courier cash, which had sent Terry Laws into the charitable trust scam. Draper's bank was First West, and at the time of his "hire" four years ago by LASD, he had a savings account with $5,890 in it, and a money market savings account of $15,433, a stock portfolio valued at $12,740, and a SEP IRA with $8,500 in it. He was making reasonable payments on a home in Venice Beach, with a purchase price of $939,000. He owned a late-model Audi valued at $40,000. His last year's income from Prestige German was $82,000.

Hood's computer led him to newspaper accounts and government sites and the usual personal sites and pages. His law enforcement status got him into state and county information that a normal civilian cannot access.

He read patiently.

Coleman Marcus Draper was born on December 12, 1980, to Gerald and Mary Draper, formerly Coleman. That made him about three months younger than Hood was.

Gerald and Mary briefly made the news in 1990 when a local man named Mike Castro was gunned down outside their restaurant in Jacumba in 1990. They said he was a regular customer and a nice guy.

The restaurant was called Amigos. According to unnamed sources, Castro was a suspected smuggler of drugs and human beings.

Coleman attended San Diego County public schools and graduated from Campo High School in 1998. He was oldest of three children — his sister, Roxanne, was twelve and his brother, Ron, was ten when an explosion rocked the Draper home in Jacumba.

Hood read from the digitized *San Diego Union-Tribune* of February 5, 1995:

FOUR PERISH IN JACUMBA BLAZE

Four members of a Jacumba family were killed early yesterday morning when their home exploded into fire.

A minor and a neighbor who was spending the night survived the blast but authorities are withholding both names pending further notifications.

One firefighter suffered smoke inhalation but was treated at the scene.

A San Diego County Fire Department spokesman said the apparent cause of the fire was a propane gas leak but the fire is still under investigation.

The fire broke out in the early morning hours when the family was sleeping. It is believed that the victims died of asphyxiation while they slept.

Liquid propane turns to an odorless gas at normal pressure and is usually mixed with a strong odor-causing compound in case of leaks. Flames rapidly engulfed the wood-sided home.

A county fire crew extinguished the fire after a one-hour battle. No neighboring structures were damaged.

Jacumba is a small town of less than 1,000 on the U.S.–Mexican border in East County.

George Bryan, a neighbor, said the family were lifelong residents of the quiet border town and were well liked. He said that his dogs woke him up barking in the early morning but the house had not yet begun to burn. He said "it sounded like a bomb went off" shortly before four a.m. when the house exploded.

Hood studied the page-one photograph of the Draper home after the fire — blackened and skeletal, nearly roofless, windows and doors blasted out by the firefighters' hoses.

A follow-up story the next day identified the four victims, and the survivor, Coleman Draper, 15. His friend, Israel Castro, was on the property at the time of the fire, and was unhurt.

The boys were friends and sophomores at Campo High. They had been sleeping in the barn with the family dogs, something that they had done several times in the past, especially on cold nights. The *Union-Tribune* said the temperature in Jacumba that night got down to thirty-seven degrees.

There was a picture of young Coleman sitting on a blue sleeping bag on a bed of hay in the Draper barn with two Jack Russell terriers and two Labrador retrievers nearby. He looked to Hood much like the Coleman Draper he'd had breakfast with just a few short days ago — slender-faced, serious, a curl of white hair on his forehead. In the picture he had a blank look on his face and though he was looking at the camera his eyes seemed to be focused on something else.

Two days later a county fire department spokesman said that the cause of the fire was a faulty propane coupling on a hot water heater located in the hallway.

"The gas leaks into the home and if the people are asleep they might not awaken to the smell," he said. "When the accumulated gas hits a pilot flame or any kind of spark, it explodes. Even static electricity can ignite a gas-filled room."

Hood saw that one month later there was a *Union-Tribune* article about the friends Coleman Draper and Israel Castro. It pictured the two boys outside the barn, dogs present again.

The article said that five years ago the Draper family had taken in then-ten-year-old Israel Castro after his father was murdered by suspected drug cartel gunmen. Three years after that, Israel had left the Draper home and moved in with relatives living across the border fence dividing Jacumba of the United States from Jacume of Mexico.

Now, in what the writer called a reversal of fortune, fifteen-year old Coleman was going to move in with Israel's extended family in Jacume. It would be temporary. He would finish his education at Campo High. It was an example of good international relations.

And, as far as Hood could determine, it was the last time Coleman Draper was mentioned in the *Union-Tribune.*

A decade later, Israel Castro's name appeared twice more, both in connection with water-rights issues and his businesses, East County Tile & Stone, and Castro Commercial Management.

Hood looked out the narrow window of

his prison room and saw the morning sun reflected on the razor wire of the eastern cell block. The storm had passed and the high desert was damp, clear and cold.

He wondered how Coleman had gotten along in Jacume, if Coleman had been allowed to bring his dogs, if Draper and Israel Castro were still friends.

And he wondered what the San Diego County Health and Human Services case worker had thought of young Coleman running off to live with a friend in a smuggler's hive like Jacume.

But most of all Hood wondered if the fire investigators could explain why the propane coupler had leaked abundantly on February 4, but apparently not before.

Three hours later he was sitting across a desk from Teresa Acuna, head of the Child Welfare Service in National City. She had handled the Coleman Draper family-to-family living arrangement back in 1995.

"We had grant money to seed that program," she said. She was black-haired and heavyset, early forties. "There had been some success in Ohio. The idea was to make it easier for the families of children who were friends to become foster caregivers. We wanted continuity, familiarity, cohesion. In

Coleman's case, this was complicated by the fact that Israel Castro's extended family was living in Mexico. We'd never tried anything like that before, so we opened talks with the Baja Norte Bureau of Social Services. At first they said it would be impossible. Then they said it wouldn't be a problem. That kind of wavering is not as unusual as it sounds, in a place where graft, corruption and dishonesty abound."

"Jacume."

"Jacumba. East County. North Baja. The entire border, really. It's a paradise of iniquity out there."

"Baja Norte Social Services changed its mind?"

"Yes. With no explanation. The Castro family was influential and I assumed that they were behind it. When I say family, I mean it loosely. I personally traveled to Jacume to see the home that Coleman had been invited into. It was neat and clean and large and had a free and open feeling to it. Although there were only an aunt and an uncle of Israel's present that day, I knew from my Jacumba sources that the home was actually shared by three married couples and usually filled with children — cousins, friends, friends-of-friends. There were frequent guests. The uncle was a

217

landowner in the Santo Tomas Valley. He grew grapes and owned a large winery. He had government connections in Mexico City. There was a taint of prison in that line of the Castros — not the uncle, but the uncle's uncle. This was not talked about."

"Why did you let the boy into this paradise of iniquity?"

"A good question. I wrestled with it. The good was that he would be with the family of his friend. He would be in a stable environment, and he would have at least some sense of continuity to his life. He would be on the other side of the same city he'd grown up in, as it were. The downside was obvious. What swayed me finally was Coleman himself. He was an exceptionally likable boy — intelligent and well mannered and calm. He seemed emotionally strong and capable, even though he was stunned by the sudden death of his family. I believed that he would have a good life with his friends in Jacume. I believed in him."

Teresa Acuna sat back and folded her hands in her lap. "I interviewed Coleman when he turned sixteen, and again when he turned seventeen, and once more before his eighteenth birthday. He seemed happy. His grades were good and his citizenship was good. He played baseball. He had a group of friends."

"When was the last time you saw him?"

She tapped her keyboard, waited and tapped again. "That last interview was November of '98. He was getting ready to move up to L.A. He said he was tired of Jacume. He wanted to be a car mechanic. I told him that good, honest car mechanics were hard to find, and that he could do well at that. He said he wasn't sure about the honest part, but he was a joker."

Hood told her that he was doing a background check on Coleman because he was a person of interest in an ongoing investigation. He said he was sorry that he couldn't tell her more but gave her a card with his cell and landline numbers.

"If he contacts you I'd like this conversation kept confidential."

"I understand. You will want to talk to Lloyd Sallis. He investigated the fire. We had different views."

"I have an appointment with him in half an hour."

Fire department investigator Lloyd Sallis had retired and now lived in San Diego. He was a large man with thick gray hair and a deeply lined face. His home was dark and the couches were slouching and he apologized to Hood for his housekeeping. He was a widower, he said, and didn't mind a little dust.

He offered Hood a bourbon then told him to sit outside on the patio. He came back with a plastic grocery bag and two drinks and sat across from Hood. The sun was warm in the early afternoon. The backyard trees bristled with hummingbird feeders, and the birds sped from feeder to feeder, squabbled over territory, vanished into the sky like bullets then hummed back into the yard to start it all over again. A calico cat nosed the plastic bag then jumped into Sallis's lap.

"I helped put out that Jacumba fire," he said. "And when it was out enough to get in, I helped get the bodies onto stretchers. That was grim business, especially the two children. They were just ten and twelve. It looked like they'd asphyxiated on the gas, then been burned post-mortem. When the coroner's report came in, it confirmed that scenario."

Sallis pet the cat slowly with a big gnarled hand. He clinked the ice in his glass and looked at it but didn't drink.

"I talked to the first responders and got the narrative. When the place cooled off enough for me to start poking around, I took my time, went slow, took plenty of pictures. It was an older home, stick built, wood siding, a wood shake roof. No sprinkler system inside, no smoke alarms. It had been in the Draper family for twenty years, no changes of ownership or remodeling, so they were out of code."

"And a cold night," said Hood.

"Yes. Thirty-seven degrees that morning. The heater thermostat was set at sixty-two. It was a typical propane setup, with a hundred-gallon tank about fifty feet from the house and an underground line. The line came up in the laundry room for the clothes dryer and heater, then branched out to the kitchen, then to the hot water heater, which was located in a hallway closet."

Lloyd Sallis sipped his bourbon, then sipped it again. His eyes had a distant look to them, reminding Hood of fifteen-year old Coleman Draper's in the newspaper photograph. The hummingbirds shot around the yard from feeder to feeder. Hood heard the cat purring.

"The line was brass, schedule C, to code, installed by a licensed plumber. The coupler was functional but it was loose. It was a standard gas line coupler, with two sets of opposing threads so you need two wrenches to tighten and loosen them. Well, here, you can see in the pictures."

Lloyd set down his glass and picked up the grocery bag. The cat heard the rustle of the plastic sack and it sprang off and hustled away with its ears back. Lloyd watched the cat with gentle amusement and Hood had the thought that he used to do that to his wife. Lloyd pulled out a thick deck of photographs.

"I always shot digital and film back then," he said. "Didn't trust the digital to be there when I needed it. When I retired I made it a point to take these home with me."

"Why?"

He looked at Hood but the distance in his eyes was gone. "Because I thought that someday a detective might sit across from me and ask questions about that fire. Move your chair over here next to mine. I can point out some things."

There were pictures of the crew battling the flames, the big hoses blasting water against the house. There were shots of what remained of each room. Then there were dozens of close-ups: burned appliances, beds, electronics. The bodies were charred badly. Their positions and postures suggested that they died in sleep, not in struggle. Only the daughter had somehow gotten out of her bed. She was on the floor beside it.

"She woke up from the gas long enough to climb out of bed," said Sallis. "Apparently that took all her energy. Looks like she fell back asleep when she hit the floor. Later, I got the propane company delivery receipts and I figured up roughly how much gas was in that tank before it started leaking. I came up with about forty gallons. Well, the tank was empty by the time the fire crew shut the valve off."

"Forty gallons."

"Give or take ten. You know that the gallons are liquid gallons, right? When the liquid is released to atmospheric pressure it expands as a gas. So forty liquid gallons under pressure can fill a volume many times greater when it enters a house."

"Enough gas to asphyxiate four people?"

"More than enough. Much more."

Hood looked at the pictures of the coupler. Sallis had done a good job with the camera — there were wider shots, tight-in and close-ups, all shot from different angles. The details in the closer shots were good and well lit: the dull brown brass tubing, the cross-hatching at both ends of the coupler where it could be loosened or tightened, the glint of brass where the cross-hatching had been disturbed.

"There's fresh brass exposed on the coupler," Hood said.

"You're damned right there is."

"Not you guys?"

"We didn't touch that thing until long after these pictures were taken."

"What did you make of that, Lloyd?"

"My first thought was the father. Gerald Draper, age forty-eight. Owned a local restaurant. He had a DUI when he was in his twenties, an assault and battery from a bar fight when he was in his thirties, but other than that he was clean. The San Diego Sheriffs did some background on the mother, too — Mary. She looked okay. Nobody had reported any domestic problems. The neighbors all said that the Drapers were normal, more or less happy. They ran a decent restaurant. So."

"So you looked at Coleman, the survivor. And his buddy, Israel Castro."

"Castro struck me as a fairly honest kid. I didn't feel any meanness in him, nothing out of balance. Ballsy, sure. Arrogant, yes. Headed for trouble, likely. But to my eyes, Coleman was strange. He should have been in some kind of emotional shock, but I could not detect anything like shock. He was calm, lucid, never expanded or changed his story. He was controlled. He cried once

224

and I swear it looked like an act to me. I had the feeling the first time I saw him, the first time I walked into the room where he was waiting, that he had prepared himself for that moment. I did not like or trust him. The sheriff's investigators and the social workers had the opposite impression. They found him to be sensitive, communicative and helpful."

"What did the detectives say about the coupler?"

"They said the fresh brass on the cross-hatching could have been exposed up to a year earlier. It takes that long for brass to discolor when it's kept out of the sunlight like that coupler was. At least that's what the FBI told them. I said if that was true why didn't the damned house blow up a year earlier and they said well, because it didn't. They weren't eager for my help. They thought I was being overly suspicious of the boy."

"Did you ask Coleman about that coupling?"

"Yes, I did. His response was interesting. He didn't pretend to not understand what I was leading up to. He didn't even give me a puzzled look, or a surprised look, not for one moment. All he said was that if he'd killed his family he would have used something to keep the coupler from being scratched by the wrench teeth — an old T-shirt, or a cloth."

"Did you tell the investigators that, too?"

"Yes, yes. They were satisfied that the leak was an accident and the disturbed brass could have happened months ago. They found no motive for anyone to have loosened the connection. Coleman's insurance benefit was modest and he wouldn't get it for three years anyway. Case closed, a tragic accident. And then Coleman went off to live with Castro in Jacume. Why are you here?"

"I can't discuss that."

"That's what I was always supposed to say, too."

Sallis picked up his bourbon off the patio. They were sitting side by side, facing the backyard and the late afternoon sun and the trees with hummingbird feeders rocking slightly in the breeze. Hood thought of his father spending his declining days in an assisted living facility. His Alzheimer's had come on almost suddenly, and it had progressed quickly. Two years ago he was present, owned his memories, had a future. Now he drifted aimlessly, like a boat without a rudder. His memory and his imagination were almost impossible to disentangle, and the concept of tomorrow seemed to have escaped him. He could not recognize Hood's mother — his wife of nearly five decades — or any of his five children. When Hood looked at him he saw himself, and this terrified him.

"An LASD deputy was murdered earlier this month," he said.

"Terry Laws. Lancaster."

"I got the nod from IA to look at him, see if there was some good reason why a deputy would get gunned down in cold blood. Well, I found out some interesting things about Terry Laws. He had a lot more money than he was supposed to have. Cash money — seven or eight grand a month coming in from somewhere. I still don't know if it came from a hole in the ground or if he was earning it as he went. I'm doing the same thing you did with the burned-out house in Jacumba. I'm asking questions, doing the legwork. And I'm coming up with a bad arrest by Laws, a large amount of missing drug money and a dead-cold murder of two cartel couriers. And guess who keeps coming up?"

"Coleman Draper."

"He's a reservist. Gun, badge and a dollar a year to play cops and robbers. He and Laws arrested the suspect in the courier killings, but they beat his brains so bad the court sent him to a mental hospital. When the bust started looking bad I started looking at Draper. That brought me to Child Welfare Services, who thinks Coleman was a charming and innocent boy, and to you, who has a different story to tell."

"I saw the way he talked to those people," said Sallis. "Very different from how he talked to me. He told them what they wanted to hear. Have you ever come across a dog that doesn't like you? Somebody's pet, a family dog, loves everyone around him but you? He wants to chew your balls off and you know it and he knows it, too. That's how it was with Coleman. First I thought it was me — like he knew something about me, or I gave off some smell only he could detect. Then I thought, naw, it isn't me. It's him."

The cat came walking across the patio and jumped into Sallis's lap.

"Well, you got the cat fooled," said Hood.

"Israel Castro still lives in Jacumba, last I heard. Bought the old Draper house. He's a mover out in East County. Big fish, little pond. But his name comes up now and then. I don't know. Maybe he could help."

"I don't want Coleman to know I'm looking."

"Oh, yes, of course not."

"Why would he kill his entire family?"

"I thought about that a lot. Talked to some people. It happens occasionally, extremely disturbed children — almost always a young male adolescent, almost always by fire. The doctors say these boys have a psychotic break. Sometimes there's a family history of mental illness. Sometimes it seems to come out of nowhere. There's usually problems with the parents and siblings. They're usually isolated boys, loners. They pee the bed and torture animals, really. On a PET scan, their brains give off different charges than normal people, different levels of activity. They become paranoid schizophrenics, hallucinators, pyromaniacs. I'm no doctor but I didn't see that in Coleman Draper. I saw a boy with blackness in him. Cruelty. Malice. Those words don't accurately describe what I saw. But I don't know any words that do."

"Can I take a couple of those pictures?"

"Take the whole bag. I told my story. I'm done with it now."

Hood parked down the street from the former Draper home in Jacumba. The new house was modern and proud and looked nothing like the burning hulk in the newspaper picture of fourteen years ago. A skinny boy clanged down the street past Hood's car, rolling a hubcap in front of him with a stick. There was a chain-link fence around the property and an electric gate. There were cottonwood trees in the front but they were leafless and still. The boy guided the hubcap around the corner ahead of Hood and was gone.

Hood cruised by Amigos restaurant. It looked quiet but it was late afternoon by then, between lunch and dinner.

He drove around Jacumba the same way he drove around L.A. — attentive and curious but not looking for anything particular. The town was sullen and bleak, Hood thought, even for a person who enjoyed the desert and its rough land and hard weather and tough people. Hood saw a Border Patrol SUV spitting up gravel on a dirt road. He saw a Homeland Security jeep parked off in the brush. Two dust-covered Suburbans with blacked-out windows made their way along a ridgeline. Above them five vultures glided in a ragged circle. High above the birds a helicopter hovered, a tiny black spider fixed in a vast blue web. An older, low-slung Impala came toward Hood, bling swinging from the rearview mirror, catching sunlight, the four men inside staring at him as they rolled past. Two boys on quads sped along an invisible trail on a very steep hillside. Smugglers of the future, Hood thought, getting the lay of the land. He heard a familiar clanging sound and saw the skinny boy guiding his hubcap along another dusty street.

He pulled onto a sandy shoulder and made a U-turn but an oncoming black SUV veered into the middle of the road, pulled broadside and stopped. Another one pulled up behind him. The men who spilled from them carried automatic weapons and combat shotguns and they were dressed in helmets and tan desert camo. They surrounded the Camaro before Hood could open the door.

He got out with his hands up, to the metallic ring of safeties coming off and slides being racked. Neither SUV had visible emblems, just black paint and bodies bristling with antennae.

A stocky man with a drum-fed combat shotgun strode toward Hood, gun pointed at his middle. He came closer than Hood thought he would, then stopped.

"United States Department of Homeland Security, Southwest Border Detachment, Patrol Unit Sergeant Dan Sims. Who the fuck are you?"

Hood told him.

"Deputy Hood, I want you to lower one hand very slowly and show me your shield."

Hood handed him the badge and holder. Sims read it then studied him.

"What are you doing here?"

"Background. The Terry Laws case."

Hood could see he'd never heard of Terry Laws, which is what he was hoping.

"Finding what you need?"

"I don't know yet."

"Nice IROC."

"Thank you. It's an '86."

"Watch yourself around here. On the border, anything that can go wrong does go wrong."

He handed Hood back his shield.

Hood drove around Jacumba for a little while longer, then aimed his nice IROC north for L.A.

20

Of course the boy wants to hear more of the story but his reasons are different now. His face is different now, too. A man's face looks back at me through the smoke-laced darkness. The change is small but the difference is everything.

"Move forward to May of last year," I say. "We're heading south on I-5 for Mexico with three hundred thirty-eight thousand dollars in the trunk of the car. We've made a run every Friday for nine months. Seven grand a week. Sometimes more, sometimes a little less. Out of nowhere, Terry tells me he's met someone. He's been divorced for a couple of years, doing okay with the ladies. But this new one is everything he's ever dreamed of in a woman. She has unbelievable legs. Terry Laws is drinking from his stainless steel flask. He's been hitting it since Cudahy and if tonight is like the last several Friday nights, he'll fill it up again in

Orange County and be done with the whole damned bottle by the time we hit El Dorado.

— Good for you, I say.

— *Laurel,* says Terry.

— There's a coffee place on this next street, I say to Terry. You can tell me all about Laurel.

"So I park the car at the Coffee Stop in San Ysidro. Laws wobbles as he gets out of the car. We sit at a window table to see the car and make sure nobody fucks with the money. The night is hot and Laws takes off his jacket, and of course everybody in the coffee bar looks at him, Mr. Wonderful, with a shoulder holster and a forty-cal autoloader inside it.

— I made Laurel laugh on our first date, he tells me. I did my Arnold, and my Jack, and my George Bush. She was dying the whole time.

— Divorced?

— Yeah. A wannabe movie guy.

— Children?

— No, man. She's only twenty-five. Says she's going to wait on that.

— What about you, Terry? You want more?"

— I got my girls. That's enough for me.

But you know, if Laurel and I really hook up . . .

"Laws looks at me and I can see the eagerness in his eyes, the need to please her. I see the childlike happiness that will be so brittle and easily dashed by Laurel. And I see delamination. It started that night out on Avenue M nine months ago. I smell it on Terry's breath.

"The moon is nearly full and I steer the car along the toll road south of Tijuana. The black-and-white bars of the highway divider blur by. I blast past a big rig on its way south. Laws's bottle is empty and he's gone quiet on me. I think that just a few months ago that one flask full would have lasted him all the way to Herredia's compound. Now Terry's head is back on the rest and he's gazing out the window and thinking God knows what.

— Terry, I worry about you. You're drinking more.

— What do you mean? I'm in really good shape.

— I know you're working out more, too. But a man who drinks a lot isn't balanced. I need you to be balanced.

— You need me period. We're partners.

— Be real careful what you say to this Laurel person.

— I think I'm in love with this Laurel person.

— Then be extra careful, okay? It's easy to say things you shouldn't when you're in love.

— It's just that . . .

— Just what? Tell me, Terry. I'm your partner in all this.

— Man, he says, I thought I had it all put away, you know? All contained. Every day I'd lift more weight, do more reps. Every day it seemed a little further away. Not so real. Then these dreams. And this thing where my heart speeds up and it feels like it's coming up in my throat, and my whole shirt gets soaked in sweat in about half a second. And I can't hardly even breathe. Man, it feels like I'm being electrocuted or something. Lethally injected. I don't know.

— It's anxiety, Terry, I say. There are good drugs for that. Keep you locked down tight.

— That's what I need, Coleman. Everything locked down tight. But with Laurel? When I'm with her? Nothing needs to be locked down. I'm Terry and I can make her laugh. I feel open and free, instead of like I'm carrying around a giant black mountain inside me.

— Forgive yourself, Terry. Forgive and forget.

— I'm sorry. I try. But I can't forget you blowing those guys' brains all over the windshield. And the damned strawberries flying everywhere. It just will not go away.

— I've forgotten the details, actually.

— Not me. I remember you making the tip call with your head out the window, faking like a drunk Mexican. I still hear your voice in my dreams. And remember that black eye you gave me? It never healed up all the way. It's still swollen. Just a little, but I can tell. There are reminders everywhere.

— Well, if it's any consolation, the three stitches they took on my eyebrow are still puffy and sore. That was one helluva punch, Terry.

— What a scene, two friends beating on each other so they can frame a dude they just clubbed half to death.

— We're blood brothers, Terry.

— Blood something. Let me ask you a serious question. And I mean this, because I've been thinking about it a lot.

— Okay.

— If you had it to do all over again, would you do it?

I look at the man/boy sitting across from me here in the cigar bar, and I can tell he's nearly hypnotized by the story, the beer, the smoke, the tremendous weight of what he's having to learn. He is changing. He is ripening.

"I can tell you, at that moment, my heart fell," I say. "Sometimes the deep animal stupidity of Terry Laws surprised me. This was one of those times.

— Terry, take the seven grand a week for driving a few hours. Cheer up.

— I wonder.

— You can't afford wonder. Wonder is for children. Have you told Laurel what we did or what we're doing?

— Hell. No.

— What am I supposed to do if you tell Laurel?

— What do you mean by that?

— *Have you told anyone?*

— No.

— Terry, let me break this off for you real simple: keep your goddamned mouth shut.

"That's what I would have told him," says the boy.

"After re-weighing the bills and drinking and dinner we went out for a swim. It's late and warm. Terry is spectacularly drunk. He approaches one of the women, trips and falls into the swimming pool. He struggles comically, flailing the water, spitting and screaming that he can't swim. The women laugh at the performance. It sure beats the Jack imitation he did at dinner. But I watch and see that he's floundering not closer to the edge but closer to the middle of the pool. And he's getting less and less breath. His voice sounds to me like pure panic. All of a sudden the women go quiet and Herredia takes my arm.

— I don't know what to do with him, Herredia says quietly.

— He needs direction, I say. I'll take care of it.

— Do you know what is wrong with him?

— He's developing a conscience.

— A man like this is dangerous. We can let him remain where he is and we will never have to worry about him again. The desert is made for secrets.

"I look to the pool and Laws is a tangle of hair and shirt and muscles and bubbles now, a storm percolating mostly beneath the surface. I pick up the skimmer and telescope the handle all the way and when Terry's gasping head comes up for what looks like the last time, I whack him. His hands fly up and clutch the basket. I pull him across the water, hand over hand. Laws grabs the side of the pool deck and he vomits water and gags and coughs and vomits again. I throw down the skimmer and walk back to my casita. I lie awake all night because no matter how I look at it, I keep seeing that this is the beginning of the end of everything we worked for."

21

Draper gave Hood a pleased nod when the patrol teams were announced, and Hood nodded back. When the roll call was over the deputies broke into their usual talk and bluster and headed out.

It was another cold night in Antelope Valley and for Hood it felt good to be back in uniform. He had had his duty jacket cleaned and he zipped it up as they walked across the lot under the names of the fallen deputies. Hood looked up and saw the stars were bright and close.

"It'll be good to ride with you," said Draper.

"This one's for Terry," said Hood.

"I thought you were looking at him for IA."

"I was. Not much to see. He was clean, but that's not news to you."

"Terry clean? He shined. So you're back on patrol?"

"Just once in a while. I like the overtime and the driving."

They got coffee at a Lancaster convenience store, then cruised town. The colder the desert, the slower the night, and tonight was slow motion.

"I heard you guys found an M249 SAW at Londell's," said Draper.

"Hidden in the box spring."

Draper shook his head. "But why would he use it on Terry?"

"If we could find him he might tell us."

"Wily little shit. He'll be with a woman. He's always with a woman."

"We've got Latrenya and Tawna covered. They blew his alibi."

Hood drove a slow and indirect route to Jacquilla Roberts's home in the Legacy development. When they passed the place where Terry Laws had been murdered, Draper stared at it.

"I patroled here the next night," he said. "The street was clean from the rain and it was like nothing bad had happened."

Hood U-turned at the end of the street and started back. He parked in front of the Roberts home.

"He came from behind that tree?" asked Draper.

"Fast."

"So you, what?"

"I put my right hand on my sidearm and my left hand on the door handle and pretty much fell out of the car."

Draper looked at Hood, then back out the window. "Did you fire?"

"No. The windshield shattered and I couldn't see to shoot. By the time I hit the street and came up, he was strafing the roof, waiting for my head to show. Then he was gone, over that fence back there. The fence lines up with a bedroom window. He was fast."

"I heard he fired a hundred and thirty-three rounds."

"That gun will deliver a thousand rounds a minute if you let it. It was over before I really knew what was happening."

"I'm not saying you should have taken a shot," said Draper. "I didn't mean it that way."

"I didn't take it that way, either."

"I was angry when I heard. I loved that guy. This is a job, you know. You shouldn't have to die for it."

No, you shouldn't, thought Hood. He looked out at the perfect stars. Build a dream on them.

When Hood looked back Draper was shaking his head. "I wonder why he didn't take you out, too."

"I've been thinking about that."

"Maybe he wanted you to see him."

"Why?"

Draper shrugged. "Initiation? Maybe he wanted someone left to tell his badass tale. Someone to witness his mighty deed."

"I think so, too," Hood said. "But that's only part of it."

"What's the other part?"

Hood looked out to the peppertree and remembered the motion that at first seemed to be wind in the branches, then the emergence of the dark killer with the D on his hoodie and a machine gun.

"I wonder if he wanted me to see the wrong thing."

"What do you mean, wrong?"

"Something apparent but not true."

"Like what, Hood?"

"I don't know yet."

"What could have been not true? A guy with a SAW gunned down Terry. What you saw was pretty damned true."

Hood looked out the window. He looked at the tree. He looked at the fence and the house.

"My money is on Londell," said Draper. "My money was on him early. Now that they've found the SAW in his bed, well, maybe it belonged to one of his girlfriends. Or maybe he was just keeping it for a homie. But I think he killed Terry with it. Londell's just dumb enough to kill someone over a dog."

Later, after three passes down the freeway, Hood drifted off at Avenue M and drove past the place where Lopes and Vasquez had been executed, then took the avenue west.

"Pretty slow out here," said Draper. "I like it when there's calls."

"How come you like the action?"

"Don't know, just grew up liking it."

"Jacumba."

"Jacumba," he said. "It's a little border town, down in San Diego County. Most people call it miserable but I liked it. I like open country with not a lot of people."

"Why'd you move to L.A.?"

"Business opportunity. Women. Jacumba didn't have much of either."

He told Hood about his family's restaurant, and growing up in the dusty border streets, and the wall they built to separate Jacumba from Jacume, and watching the good guys chase the creeps all over the hillsides day and night, and the bodies and the jettisoned drugs and guns. He told Hood about Mike Castro getting gunned down in front of him and Israel.

"It was the Wild West, but with AK-47s," said Draper.

"Brothers, sisters?" Hood asked.

Draper looked at him. "One of each, both younger. Roxanne and Ron."

Hood waited for more and got none. Draper sat still and Hood sensed that he was deep in thought as he looked out the window. Hood told him about his own brothers and sisters, all older, and how his early memories of them always involve them getting into cars and driving away. How he disliked saying goodbye. Hood said that his siblings kept in touch but were not close, although a dependable loyalty ran through them all.

He picked up the Pearblossom Highway and meandered east. It is a winding and often dangerous little highway during the day, but that night it was quiet and Hood could see the headlights coming well out ahead.

"Terry and I made the Eichrodt pinch right up there," said Draper. "Those are the Llano ruins. Llano was a utopia. That's funny, isn't it? A utopia out here in the middle of the goddamned desert. You can see how successful it was."

Hood U-turned and drove back to the Llano ruins and pulled over. In the headlight beam he could see the foundation of the old meeting hall, a chimney, a partial river-rock wall.

"You guys spotted the plates?"

"Anonymous tipper," said Draper. "He only had four of the seven numbers right, but the order was there. It was a three-series plate — a beat-up old Chevy pickup. God-damned Eichrodt driving around at four in the morning with a tool chest full of stolen money and a murder weapon and brass. Looking for God knows what, somebody else to kill and rob, I guess. Man, he put up a fight. It was almost exactly here, where we're parked right now. He beat us up pretty good until we got the batons going. Either one of us, alone? He would have killed us. Even Terry. He made Terry look small. Eichrodt couldn't wait to get violent. He played possum on us then took Terry down with a sweep. He was high on meth. Terry got a concussion and I don't even remember how many stitches. I got three on my right eyebrow and three in my lip."

"And he never stood trial."

"Naw. Loony bin. If they'd kept him longer on that two-eleven back in '03, maybe he wouldn't have been running around killing people."

247

Hood eased the cruiser into a wide circle. In the headlights he saw the ruins become desert then the desert become highway.

"Go to the Avenue M exit," said Draper. "I'll show you where the van was."

A few minutes later they were parked on the Avenue M off-ramp, halfway down. Draper pointed through the windshield.

"There. Pulled off, parked right out in the open. From twenty feet away I could see the blood on the windows in my flashlight beam. It was hot that night. Windy. Spooky. Check it out."

Draper got out and shut the door. He walked toward where the van had been parked, then turned and looked at Hood. Hood shut off the engine and climbed out and crunched across the shoulder. Draper pointed with his flashlight beam.

"The front was pointed just a little south, not quite squared up with the road," he said. "I could never figure how two hoods got jumped by a six-eight monster right out in the open, nighttime or not. But then, that's not my job to figure those things out. Eichrodt must have fired from the passenger side because both guys fell the other way."

"That was good luck, you finding the van then finding the shooter."

"Yep."

"People told me that Terry wasn't the same after that night."

Draper turned off his flashlight. "He thought he was Mr. Wonderful, then got the shit kicked out of him."

"Something more than that. They said something inside him changed. He lost something."

"Who said that?"

"People."

Draper was quiet for a long moment.

"People yap too much about things they don't know," he said. "To me he was the same guy. Maybe a little more serious. Maybe not quite so light. How do you stay light after that? He was still Terry Laws, man. That's who he was."

They stood for a moment in the darkness. Hood could hear a big rig out on Highway 14, heading south fast. The ground vibrated as it thundered by. He zipped his jacket up a little higher and jammed his hands into the pockets.

"Hood, I don't think this little trip down memory lane was an accident."

"I'm still looking at Terry."

"Then keep looking. But you don't have to sneak around with me. I'm on your side. Or at least I want to be."

"Thanks, Coleman."

"That's the trouble with IA," he said. "It's not really your job to look. It's your job to find. And if you look long enough you'll find something, even if you have to invent it. Otherwise you haven't done your job."

"No invention here, Draper."

"Good. Because I don't want anybody talking trash about my partner."

They rode out the shift talking about what single cops always talk about — work, sports, cars and women. Hood told him he'd be finished with IA when he was done with Terry. And after that, maybe he'd get another chance at the Bulldogs.

Draper said he'd love to work homicide but reservists were out of their league in that game. He was volunteering two shifts a week now, sometimes three. He told Hood he'd also been doing some recruiting things for the LASD — fairs, campus career days, things like that. He said he was a people person. He said he thought that getting the right people was the key to good law enforcement.

Draper told Hood about a girlfriend in Azusa and another one in Laguna. He said he'd like to settle down and have a family. Maybe even two, or three. He smiled. He was twenty-nine now, thought it was just about time for all that. He was only working one or two days a week at Prestige, just keeping the books and doing payroll and purchasing, and "keeping the Germans in Beck's." He had a small apartment building in Bell that was bringing in steady money.

They pulled over a drunk driver around midnight, their one arrest. She was too drunk to stand up on her own. By the time they booked the shift was up and they clocked off. They shook hands in the vehicle lot and Draper walked away toward a well-kept but older black BMW M5.

Hood opened the trunk of the cruiser and pretended to be checking the contents.

When Draper's car growled down the street and out of sight, Hood climbed back into the car and retrieved the voice recorder from under the seat.

22

The next evening Draper steered his black M5 down a Cudahy side street. He looked out at the troubled city, a city eaten alive by corruption and gangs and drugs. It was now spottily patrolled by the Maywood PD, which was contracted to fill the shoes of the recently fired Los Angeles Sheriff's Department. But Draper knew that it was really Cudahy's mayor — and Hector and Camilla Avalos — who ran the place. More or less together, thought Draper, in wicked harmony.

It was Friday, and Israel Castro's gunman sat beside him. He was slender, with calm eyes and a recently barbered head of thick black hair. He was younger than Draper had wanted but now he was stuck with him. Draper had given him a stolen stainless steel Smith .357 Magnum revolver and the kid had thumbed open the cylinder, spun the loads and slapped it back into the frame.

Just like a gunslinger, Draper had said. The boy had smiled and jammed the gun into the waistband of his Wranglers. He had beautiful teeth.

Now the gun was still in the boy's pants and the boy was in the car with him and, as usual, Avalos's sullen gunmen coalesced on the dark Cudahy streets to direct the car into the sprawling, shabby lair.

Friday night, thought Draper. There's life and there's death.

"Victorio, I ask you once again to keep your mouth shut," said Draper. "You are Herredia's man. You are loyal to Herredia. You are only with me because he has ordered you to be with me. You are to be my new partner."

"*Sí.* Yes."

"Do not show me respect. Avalos doesn't respect me and you must not respect me either."

"I no respect."

"Kill him only when I tell you to. Only then. I will say it with a look, not with words. You must understand this perfectly and do it perfectly. Then the other five thousand will be yours."

"*Sí.* Herredia has *gueras putas?*"

"I have no idea if he has blond whores."

One pistolero directed them through the

253

sliding metal door and into the warehouse. Another waved them through the vast dark space. The big M5 engine grumbled and Draper could hear the sound magnified by the walls around them and see the dust rising in the beams of his headlights.

Two more gunmen waited for him at the far, weakly lit end. When Draper and Victorio got out they were frisked and their weapons were taken away. Draper saw that Victorio had been hiding a fat black-handled switchblade in one boot and a one-shot derringer in the other. Victorio gave the men a contemptuous stare as they confiscated his things, and he gave one to Draper, too.

Then one of the men pushed open a heavy metal door and led them out to a courtyard, down a pathway worn in the near dead grass, and into a large metal building. The second pistolero brought up the rear. Draper walked and looked at the old tables and benches, the rows of industrial overhead lights. He had always thought of this big room as a former machine shop, or perhaps an ancient assembly line. Then they all stepped into the groaning old elevator that would take them down two stories and into the warren of rooms that was Avalos's headquarters, and of course, the dogfighting arena.

Draper stared straight at the floor as the elevator lowered. No one spoke. When the car rumbled to a stop another one of Avalos's men slid open the door for them. Draper stepped out and was surprised to hear the two gunmen getting out behind him. They usually rode back up and he never saw them again until after the weighing and pressing and packaging.

He turned and looked at one of them. The gunman was a *culiche* — old-school Sinaloan — creased Wranglers and ostrich boots and a white yoked cowboy shirt. He reminded Draper of Victorio, and Draper conceded that if Ostrich Boots and Victorio knew each other then this was likely his own last day among the living.

"Extra security tonight," he said.

"Rocky says."

"Rocky should know," said Draper.

Ostrich Boots spoke rapid Spanish to Victorio, who looked bitterly at Draper before he answered. Draper only caught a few of their words: *Los Mochis, Tijuana, El Patrón* and, of course, *gueras putas.*

They walked through the room with mullioned windows and the one that smelled of creosote, then down the hallway with the high ceiling trailing cobwebs. Draper wondered how many years they had been there, lifeless shreds swaying in the currents.

Then they came to the entrance of the sanctum and Ostrich Boots knocked on the door.

Rocky opened it and the gunmen folded back into the shadows. Draper heard their steps diminishing, then a door clanging shut and there was only silence.

They stepped inside without speaking and Rocky led them to a small room that contained apparently empty beer kegs and a large, carnival-style popcorn maker with the image of a clown etched onto the glass. Draper introduced Victorio to Rocky. Rocky seemed to stare straight through the boy as he listened to his name and the way he spoke. Then Rocky told him to take off his shirt. Victorio stood bony and half-naked as Rocky handed him the neatly folded *guayabera* shirt and told him to put it on. It was crisp and white and hung loose, cut for tropical heat. Then Rocky handed Victorio the stainless steel revolver that had with seeming magic transmigrated from Draper to Victorio to the distant gunmen to Rocky and now back to Victorio again. Victorio accepted the gun with a small nod and then the weapon vanished under his shirt. Draper saw that Victorio was so slenderly built he could have concealed a sleeping bag under the *guayabera.*

"No existan balas capaces de matar nues-tras suenas," said Rocky.

There are no bullets that can kill our dreams, thought Draper.

Rocky led them from the small room to the entrance of the fighting arena. He used two keys to open the scarred and dented steel door. His hands were steady. The welds were still shiny on the newly added lock flange.

Draper stepped in and saw the familiar fight pit, and the seats raised up around it on three sides, and the glass-walled box where Hector Avalos paced, not slowing as he looked across the arena at his closest lieutenant, his gringo cop courier, and Herredia's new boy.

Draper climbed the stairs to the suite. He smelled spilled beer and cigarette smoke and the underscents of blood, shit and fear. Avalos pulled him in for a punishing hug and Draper could feel his power, drunk and unsteady as he was. Avalos had never so much as touched Draper, who wondered at the increased security and Avalos's sudden affection. Avalos crushed half of Draper's air out of him and pushed him away, his teardrop tattoos riding the wrinkles of a crooked smile.

Avalos stood back, ignoring Rocky but regarding young Victorio. He walked around the boy like a man assessing a horse.

"*Culiche,* man?" Avalos asked.

"Yes."

"Herredia's top-of-the-line best?"

"Yes."

"Do you speak more than one word of English?"

"Yes."

"Fuck, you're only a child. A child. Would you like a drink of reposado, my boy?"

Victorio nodded and Avalos went behind the bar and poured four shot glasses of the tequila. He carried one to Victorio and held onto one for himself, jerking his head for Draper and Rocky to get their own.

Draper noted that the luggage was in its usual place by the bar, four rolling bags with their handles upright as always, as if skycaps were about to race in and claim them.

"Where is Camilla?" asked Draper. The crude dogfighting arena seemed even more charmless without Camilla, whose strongly perfumed, expensively dressed, snake-haired, big-butted presence Draper had always looked forward to. It was a shame. Business was often a shame.

"Shopping. Shopping! Why do you ask?"

"Simple good manners."

"Nothing good is simple."

"Fire is good and simple."

"Fire! Who cares about fire?"

Avalos dropped into his recliner and Rocky stood by the sliding glass door that could be opened to let in the cries of the crowd and the snarling of the fighting dogs and the waft of various smoking substances on fight nights. Draper and Victorio got the couch across from Avalos. Avalos brought a pipe and a small glass jar from the cigar box on the coffee table and jiggled a rock into the blackened bowl. He used a lighter in the shape of a miniature flamethrower to heat the rock. Then he reached out and handed the pipe to Victorio.

The boy took a huge hit and coughed hard and gagged, then his body shuddered and he handed the works back to Avalos.

Avalos burned the rock again and sipped the smoke, then looked at Draper and proffered the pipe.

"No thank you. I enjoy having brain cells."

Avalos looked at Rocky but proffered nothing.

"Show Victorio the cash," said Avalos. "Show him the scales and the vacuum sealer. Show him how we do our part of *El Tigre*'s business here in beautiful Southern California."

Draper rolled one of the suitcases to the bar, flipped it over and unzipped the main compartment and hefted the loose bundles of bills to the bar top. He turned on and reset the digital scale, making sure the plate surface was clean and properly affixed. He turned on the vacuum sealer to give it plenty of time to warm up, and made sure there were plenty of bags. He waited for Rocky's phone to ring but it didn't.

Victorio hovered and watched. He seemed both alert and disinterested and Draper wondered at his fine acting skills. He was playing his part well.

Rocky stood unmoving with his back to the sliding glass door, arms crossed, seemingly caught in the net of his own tattoos.

Avalos stood and lumbered drunkenly to the bar.

"In the beginning there was loyalty," he said to Victorio.

"Yes."

"This is no place for selfishness. The selfish will rot. You can ask Señor Coleman about that on your long drive south."

Victorio looked at Draper with eagerness on his face. Draper looked back down and adjusted the bag feed on the sealer and whistled quietly.

"Look at me," said Avalos. "Do you believe in the father and the son and the holy ghost?"

"Yes, *mucho.*"

"You're not a citizen of the United States."

"I have good papers."

"You're not the kind of man who should be traveling across the border. You look suspicious, even to me. You look guilty. You look like the unholy ghost."

Draper looked up at Avalos and saw the drunk belligerence in the man.

Rocky's cell phone rang.

Avalos showed no reaction. "There are dollars for us all," he said to Victorio. "Week after week, and year after year, more and more. But only for the loyal."

Rocky held the phone to his ear for a moment, then lowered it. "There are no problems," he said.

Draper looked at Victorio with something new in his eyes.

"What problems would there be?" asked Avalos. "I said what problems?"

The revolver was almost touching Avalos's stomach when the first shot scorched through him and shattered the sliding glass door behind him. His knees collapsed and Victorio shot him twice more in the chest and when Avalos slumped over, Victorio tried to put a bullet in his head but the gun clicked loudly, then again and again.

Victorio looked up in confusion. Rocky blew him through the window with two deafening blasts from a sawed-off ten-gauge and the heavy steel shot carried Victorio out into midair, then he descended in a bright shower of glass and landed dead faceup in the fighting pit.

Draper pushed Avalos with his toe and a lifeless arm flopped to the bloody carpet.

In Draper's mind, time did something funny — it stuttered or snagged or maybe just jiggled a little. Then it was right again.

"We did it," he said.

"We'll burn in hell for it, but that's a while from now."

"Camilla?"

"We have no idea where she is."

"That's a good thing. I'm happy to be in business with you, Rocky. We will prosper."

In silence they finished the weighing and the sealing, then they began packing the bundles of cash back into the suitcases with some old clothes. Draper looked once at Avalos and once at Victorio, mainly to be sure there were no miraculous recoveries in progress. But he enjoyed the insult, too, the disrespect of working so close to the dead that he could smell their blood.

One of Avalos's gunmen came into the

arena when they were almost finished packing the cash. He looked into the fight pit then climbed the stairs and looked at Avalos and the money and the men.

"Can I get a drink?" he asked.

"The bar is open," said Rocky. "I'll have a beer."

A few minutes later another trusted Avalos lieutenant came in, and he did almost exactly what the first had done — he stopped and looked at the young Sinaloan in the middle of the fighting pit, then he came up the stairs and looked down at his old boss with amazement and disgust.

"Get him a drink," Rocky said to the first.

Then another man came, then another.

By the time the last suitcase was packed and the equipment was put away, four more former Avalos soldiers had made their way up into the suite. Roughly half of Avalos's top men, thought Draper. The smart half. The half that chose life at all cost. He knew he'd never see the others or Camilla again and that was the way it had always been and always would be.

Rocky poured drinks and handed one to each of his men. "The killer from Sinaloa murdered Hector," he said. "So I closed his eyes. This is the truth. Tell everyone you know. Coleman and I will make the delivery

263

to *El Tigre* tonight. You'll clean up this mess. Make sure that Hector will be found so we can have a good funeral. Make sure the others are not."

23

Hood picked up a Friday graveyard patrol shift for some OT but mainly just to drive. It was a solo run and the minutes dragged but the hours flew.

After clocking off shift at five-fifty Saturday morning he drove his Camaro up to Bakersfield and stood awhile by Allison Murrieta's grave. It was her birthday and she would have been thirty-three. Hood reflected that she had had big appetites and never apologized for them. These were largely why she was no longer among the living. But he hadn't come here to analyze her or to affix blame, only to pay respect and to remember the way she carried herself through this world. He could still taste her breath.

When he was done he drove back to L.A.

Sunday morning at six Hood's old boss on the Bulldogs called. His name was Bill Marlon and he was still running the homicide show out of LASD headquarters in Monterey Park.

"Charlie, get yourself to Fifth and San Pedro."

"Skid Row."

"ASAP."

"What's this about?"

"Your old friend Kick."

Hood made it quickly in the light Sunday morning traffic. He drove into the shadows of the downtown buildings, made his way into the forbidding darkness of Skid Row. To Hood this was the worst of L.A., a twenty-four/seven bazaar of drug use and narcotics deals and prostitution, often conducted in Porta Potties set up for the homeless, who gathered here for services. He knew it was one of the only places in Southern California where rival gangs could be found buying and selling drugs side by side, violence suspended for the fast dollars. There was heroin on Broadway, crack on Fifth at Crocker or Main. Addicts, dealers, hookers, hustlers, gangsters, the homeless, the hopeless, the insane. All here, thought Hood, the devil's arcade. Or a fifty-square-block party, if your idea of a party is crack and sex in a Porta Potti.

He found a place off San Pedro to park.

Up ahead near the intersection of Fifth he could see three LAPD Central Division units with their lights flashing, a coroner's van, a Fire and Rescue truck and a couple of unmarked police and sheriff units.

When he got near the corner he saw two men wheeling a shrouded body into the back of the coroner's van. A small, ragged crowd had gathered. Marlon was talking to two LAPD sergeants. He thanked them and pulled Hood aside and they stood in the doorway of a shabby office building that was closed on Sundays.

"That's Kick with the body snatchers," said Marlon. "Deon Miller. He was walking down Fifth, apparently alone. A black Silverado pickup stopped beside him, the driver got out and shotgunned him. All of this according to the one witness, a Guatemalan dishwasher who rents a room with friends on Los Angeles Street. He was on his way to work."

Hood watched the coroner's van roll away, no lights or sirens for this vehicle, just death on wheels. "Did the dishwasher get a look at the driver?"

"White or light Hispanic male, tall. He wore a cowboy hat and dark bandana over his face. Boots and jeans. A long black coat. The hat was black, of course."

Pretty much what Bradley Jones would wear to avenge his mother's death, Hood thought.

Marlon took a small digital camera from a pouch on his belt and fiddled with it for a moment before handing it to Hood. On the viewer the pictures of Kick were sharp in the faint first light of morning. He lay center-shot on the sidewalk, faceup in a pool of blood.

"Anyway, Hood, I remember what Bradley Jones told us. I remembered that you believed him. I thought you felt some responsibility to him because of what happened. Maybe it wasn't him but I figured you'd want to see this."

Hood handed his camera back. "He said he was going to do it."

Marlon looked out at the LAPD cruisers on street. "You going to tell these guys?"

"I'll talk to him first."

"So you're in touch?"

"I can find him."

"Maybe you should do that."

"Since when do you answer LAPD calls?" Hood asked.

"I drive sometimes at night," Marlon said. "I look at things and listen to the law enforcement scanner. I can't sleep. A possible one-eighty-seven always gets my blood moving."

"I do that some nights, too."

"You're too young for that, Charlie," Marlon said with a smile. "Get yourself another pretty girl. Make yourself tired. How are you liking the desert?"

"I like the desert."

"And IA?"

"I'd rather be back with the Bulldogs."

"There may be a time for that. I worked with Warren way back when. He's okay."

"I'm glad to hear that from you."

"You know his story?"

"None of it."

Hood looked at the bloodstained sidewalk. By now the sun was up but Skid Row was still shrouded in winter shadows. A few blocks away, Parker Center, the police headquarters, caught the early sunlight like a shrine.

They talked to the dishwasher for a few minutes and learned a few more things. He said the black truck had approached and departed slowly. No hurry. The shotgun was long, not sawed off. The shooter raised it to his shoulder and aimed, like a hunter. It had been hard to make things out in the dark, with only the streetlights to see by. The dishwasher was afraid that he would be shot next, but the gunman tipped his hat

269

and got back into the truck.

Tipped his hat, Hood thought: pure Bradley.

"Let's drive, Charlie. I'll tell you about Jim Warren."

Hood moved his Camaro to a pay lot. Marlon drove his Yukon, just a few months old, the interior still smelling new and the police band scanner under the dash turned low.

"You've heard of the Renegades?" he asked.

"Tattooed deputies out of the old Lynwood station."

"Gung-ho white guys," said Marlon. "They had big attitudes, thought they ruled the known world. They got tattoos of six-guns on the inside of their ankles, with 'Renegades' written underneath like barbed wire. This was '89, when you were what, nine or ten years old? Those were rough years in the ghetto stations, and Lynwood was right in the middle of South Central. Lots of racial tension between white deputies and black citizens, Gorillas in the Mist and all that kind of thing. Warren was the founding member. The Renegades were his."

Hood looked at his old boss. "Yeah," said Marlon. "You wouldn't think of that with what he's doing now. Back then, Warren swore they were good deputies, total professionals, the good guys. He said the tattoos were just a way of showing solidarity — like a Marine Corps tattoo. He said it wasn't about power or race, it was only about being a good cop in a bad place. A lot of the Lynwood deputies wanted to be invited in. They really wanted that revolver and the word 'Renegades' tattooed on their ankles."

"There were the Vikings and the Reapers and the Saxons, too," Hood said.

"The Renegades were the first and the toughest. It finally came down to Warren and the sheriff himself, meeting for an hour behind closed doors. When the meeting was over, the Renegades were allowed to continue on with the membership and the tats. That went for all the clicks. The sheriff washed his hands, said he didn't approve of them, but the deputies had a constitutional right to assemble in that way. Then came Roland Gauss."

Hood knew of him, as did every LASD deputy. Roland Gauss was the infamous Renegade who staged a series of "drug raids," in which he and two other deputies, all in uniform, busted known drug dealers, took their cash and product, and sold the dope themselves.

"When Gauss got caught in the Fed drug sting, Warren stood by him as long as he could. But the evidence was overwhelming against Gauss because someone in his crew was singing loud to the prosecutors. So Gauss tried to sing his way to a lighter sentence, by fingering Warren as the ring-leader. He also accused Warren of marital infidelities, drug use, gambling. Warren got suspended. The media played the Renegades story big, and they followed it to the top — Warren. They actually went to his house, staked it out, took his picture. But he kept to his story. He rode it out. Months. By the time the investigation was finished, Gauss was bound over for trial, Warren was exon-erated, and the Renegades were banned from the LASD forever. But Warren had that tattoo on his ankle. They all did. Half of them were transferred or took early retirement. Warren had the tattoo removed and he took an IA job nobody wanted. Then, you see what happened. It was like Saul on the road to wherever it was — he started out a badass Renegade and ended up the saint of Internal Affairs. He had this thing for catching bad guys, and he just switched it over to catching bad cops."

"It seems personal," Hood said. "He thinks this department is his. Like if you hurt it, you hurt him."

"Oh, it's personal all right. His wife died of a heart attack about halfway through the investigation. She had a bad ticker but all the stress didn't help. They had a good thing. I saw it. To me, she was the saddest casualty of the whole damned mess, that and the way the public thought we were Nazis. What Warren wants now is that nobody like Roland Gauss ever puts on a sheriff's badge again."

"That's a good cause."

"People like Warren need a cause. They need an enemy with a face. They need a story and a part in it for themselves. Me? Five more years and I'm gone. Montana. Idaho. Typical cop cliché, but that's fine with me. That's if I can talk my wife into it, and survive five more years. Blood pressure too high. Cholesterol too high. Putting on pounds. Tired a lot because I can't sleep at night. They say it's pressure but I don't know. What's pressure? Everyone's got pressure. Being a cop was never more than a job for me. But somehow, that wasn't enough to get me through the years without wearing down. I'm not like Warren. Or you."

Hood and Marlon had had the first part of this conversation a year ago, just before Marlon got Hood onto the Bulldogs. Mar-

273

lon was in Vietnam and Hood was in Iraq so they had things in common. Marlon was a patrol sergeant and Hood did investigations with NCIS. Marlon knew what it was to be ambushed in a jungle, and Hood knew what it was to be ambushed in a desert town. But Hood also knew how it was to be hated by your own side. He felt betrayed and alone. He understood Jim Warren's need to find men he could believe in. Hood had it, too.

"You think Bradley Jones blew Kick away?" Marlon asked.

Hood nodded. "Her birthday was yesterday. I hope I'm wrong."

"Me, too," said Marlon. "I liked Bradley. He'd make a deputy someday."

"I told him that."

"And what's he think?"

"He likes the idea but won't admit it."

"He still running his own little hoodlum crew?"

"I think so."

"Does he still hate you?"

"Mostly."

"He might get over that."

"He sets a course and follows it, just like his mother."

"Stupid. I don't mean she was stupid. You know what I mean."

24

Hood called Erin and told her about Kick.

"Bradley was here all night," she said. "He's still here — out in the barn. He's pulling the engine on the truck."

"I need to talk to him."

"I can't tell you exactly where this place is."

"I know where it is."

"But —"

"Don't worry. I'll see you in less than an hour."

Hood had gotten Bradley's address from police at Cal State Los Angeles, where Bradley had registered but never attended class. Hood confirmed it by tracking one of Bradley's gang — the forger — through Probation to the same address. Hood wasn't surprised to find that he was living in the Antelope Valley. Bradley lived on an unimproved, unmaintained county road, in a house he didn't own, far from L.A.

A few minutes later Hood steered the Camaro down Soledad Canyon Road toward Acton, a town of just a few hundred people spread over a few miles, tidy homes, large parcels, horses, hills and blue sky.

His first turn off of Soledad Canyon was a dirt road, wide and freshly bladed and running north. The second dirt road was narrower and turned to washboard that attacked the stiff suspension of Hood's IROC and threatened to demolish the interior. The third dirt road was narrower still but the washboard ended. He stopped at the chain-link gate, pulled the chain and padlocks off the pipe rail, swung it open, ignored the "NO TRESPASSING" sign and drove through. When he got out to close the gate a soft cloud of dust surrounded him.

Further down, the road improved. There was a pasture and a few head of cattle, and the sage and foxtail brome was dense and healthy from the rain. He passed a small stream and an outcropping of rocks. It looked to Hood like a good place for grinding acorns and chipping arrowheads and keeping watch. At first he thought he saw a ground squirrel sitting atop the highest point, then he realized that it was a surveillance camera.

Hood drove around a long bend, down an

incline, then out into a broad meadow. There were buildings on the far upper slope of the meadow. The meadow was fenced and he could see horses, some grazing, some watching his car. He came to an electric chain-link gate, and a small speaker stand and keypad.

He pressed the call button and waited. A pack of Doberman pinschers and a small Jack Russell terrier barked and growled from the other side of the gate. He pressed call again. Bradley's voice was half-static.

"Beat it, Hood."

"Nice dogs."

"Have a nice day."

"Kick's dead. I can make this official business or not."

"What's the 'not' get me?"

"It allows you to open the gate and talk to me here where you live."

"Otherwise you drag me to the station and hook up the cattle prods? Or do you waterboard now?"

"If you'd like. I want to say hi to Erin and I'll say yes to a cup of coffee."

Hood could hear Bradley talking to someone. He didn't sound happy. Finally the gate opened and the Dobermans charged out and came to Hood's side of the car, snapping, sharp-eared, sleek and muscled. The terrier finally couldn't restrain himself any longer and he sunk his teeth into the leg of the Doberman in front of him. The Dobie wheeled shrieking and the Jack Russell bolted away. But they didn't touch the Camaro. They stayed almost exactly one yard away. When Hood tapped the gas and passed them they spread out on either side of the road and sprinted ahead of him all the way to the house, the terrier lagging far behind.

Hood parked in the circular asphalt driveway in front of the house. It was a sprawling one-story with faded yellow paint and a roof of buckling wood shingles eager to burn. Bright beach towels hung in the windows instead of curtains. There was a deck out front with an awning over it and an older man stood leaning on the railing, looking down at Hood. He was dressed in jeans and flip-flops and a USC sweatshirt. He wore sunglasses. The dogs had lined up along the deck to look down on Hood, too.

He cut the engine and lowered a window.

"You're Hood."

"I know that. Who are you?"

"Bradley told me all about you. This is private property you're on."

"Somebody let me in."

"I own this land and this house. It's paid

for. I'll die here and that's fine with me. You have to die somewhere so it may as well be with your dogs."

"It may be sooner than you think with that roof."

"I got the brush cleared back. Two hundred feet is what they recommend but I did three hundred. I do extra on things I care about."

"You sure talk a lot for a guy with no name."

"Preston."

"Well, Preston, where is he?"

"Come on up. This way."

"You have those dogs under control?"

"You'd know if I didn't."

The deck needed refinishing and creaked underfoot. Two of the dogs smelled Hood's pants and boots and the others panted and watched him. Preston shouldered through the door and Hood followed him in. The living room was beaten leather couches, old concert posters tacked to the walls, and two acoustic guitars gleaming in their stands. In the corner was a baby grand piano, polished and stately.

"Erin's a musician," said Preston. Hood looked at him and saw the odd angle of his head as he spoke. "Come on."

Preston led him through the living room

and down a short hallway. He turned right into a kitchen. It was dark and small and to Hood it looked scantily equipped. Beyond the kitchen was a dining room and at the table sat a chunky fiftyish woman in a blue bathrobe. The Sunday *L.A. Times* was piled on the floor beside her and a stack of advertisements and coupons waited on the table in front of her.

"That's Wanda," said Preston, looking at the woman with that odd angle of head. "I'll bet she's keeping up with world events."

"You're Hood," she said.

"I can't fool anyone," he said, realizing that Preston was blind.

"They're out back wrecking another car," said Wanda.

"Come on," said Preston.

He led Hood outside, around a beaten stucco garage, down a ramp and into a small barnyard. His trail across the earth was narrow and well worn through the weeds. The dogs followed.

Bradley was in the barn, up to his shoulders in the engine of an old white F-150. Clayton, the document forger, stood across from him, also bent into the depths of the engine. Hood nodded to Erin, who was sitting at the end of a picnic bench under one of the barn windows, a small guitar resting on one thigh and an arm draped over the body. Wedged between the bench and her leg was a notebook with a pen on top. Stone, the car thief, sat at the other end reading a thick hardcover book. Between them was a pot of something steaming and one upside-down mug and an ashtray with a cigarette burning in it.

Preston walked over toward the workbench, felt for the chair, then swung it around backwards and sat down facing Bradley's direction. The dogs spread out around him on the cool concrete floor.

"Look what I found," he said.

Bradley straightened and looked at Hood. He flipped a torque wrench full circle and caught it by the handle. "Not hard to find someone trespassing right up to your front door."

Erin waved and smiled feebly but didn't look at Hood. Clayton glanced at him. Stone never looked up from his book.

"So what do you want, Charlie?" asked Bradley. "You may as well just say it here and say it quick. I've got work to do."

"Someone blew Kick away about four hours ago," Hood said, though he knew where all this was going.

The quiet barn got quieter.

"I got a cup for you," said Erin. "Have

some coffee, Charlie."

He walked over and upended the cup and poured. He caught the worry in Erin's eyes as she looked back at the guitar strings. Hood went over to the truck and stood between Bradley and Clayton. The engine head was off and the cylinders were exposed and he could see the burned silver black carbon in them.

"Kick was an unformed child playing games in the land of little error," said Bradley to the engine. Then he looked at Hood. "So I don't feel one bit sorry for him. My only slight regret is that I wasn't the one to blow the life out of him. But that would have taken a risk far greater than Kick's life was worth. As you can probably infer, and as all of these people will tell you, I've been on this property since last night and right here in this barn since before sunrise this morning."

Bradley flipped the wrench again and caught it.

"That's right," said Preston. "I never let him out of my sight."

Bradley dropped his wrench to the floor and it landed with a clang. Clayton dropped his, too. Stone dropped the book to the floor with a flat crack and Erin dropped her notebook and Preston took off his glasses and aimed his dead white eyes at Hood and they broke out laughing.

He smiled and waited for the laughter to trail off. "Well, that's two felons, a blind man, and a woman who loves you."

They all booed him. Erin strummed her guitar loudly, no chords, just dissonance. Hood wasn't sure if she was trying to drown them out or join them.

Then Bradley wiped his hands on a once white T-shirt. "We're just funnin' ya, Hood. Come on, we'll talk."

They walked out and Bradley led the way up a trail from the house to an outcropping of rocks. The day was warming. Hood saw a small patch of California poppies blooming eagerly after the rain, the first he'd seen all year.

"Did you go to the grave yesterday?" Hood asked.

"I drove in from above, up by the mausoleum. I almost came down when I saw your Camaro but I didn't feel like seeing you on my mom's birthday. No offense."

"I wouldn't have wanted to share my mom with you, either."

"I didn't kill him. I wouldn't have waited six months. My decision on that was made a long time ago. He's a Southside Crip with enemies all over the place. It wasn't me. All of those people back there will tell you I was here."

"I can see that. But the description fits you and the timing is right."

"Where?"

"Skid Row."

Bradley shook his head, as if killing anyone on Skid Row would be beneath him.

"How?"

"Shotgun. Black cowboy hat, dark bandana over his face — outlaw style. Jeans and boots. He was tall, white or light Hispanic. Drove a black Silverado."

"Well, you won't find a black Silverado anywhere on this property."

"That's for sure."

"But I do have jeans. And boots. I even got a combat Mossberg in my room, and a finger to pull the trigger with."

"If I have to ask Erin where you were, Bradley, I'll see it if she's lying."

"Go ahead. I *want* you to ask her. You'll see that she's telling the truth, just like the others. Did she give you directions here?"

"I found you through Cal State L.A."

"I didn't attend one class."

"You applied and used this address. It's on the campus police cop-only website."

He studied Hood, then chuckled softly. "I'm thinking of applying to the Sheriff's.

Or maybe LAPD. You still willing to get me in?"

Hood knew where Bradley got his flair for the dramatic, his confidence in the bluff, his belief in the making of luck.

"Talk to me when you're serious, Bradley."

"You going to rat me to LAPD for what I said about Kick? That was all in the past, man."

"They'll make the connection without me."

"I didn't kill him, Charlie. That's the last time I'm going to say it to you."

His eyes on Hood were hard and unwavering. His chin was strong. Conviction? Challenge? Wounded pride? Truth glides through appearances, thought Hood.

"Bradley, you can kill a man and hide behind your friends and get away with it. But you can't get away with it for very long. Friends don't stay friends forever."

"Yes, sir, Mr. Sheriff, by golly."

"Learn from your mother."

"You don't know what I've learned from her."

"She let herself get killed for nothing. You have to understand the connection between what you do and what it leads to. She understood that, but she couldn't control

285

herself. Almost, but not quite. You're going to have to. Bradley, you can do anything in the world you want."

"I'm doing exactly what I want."

"Living with creeps? Dragging Erin through your messes? You don't know what you have because it's all been given to you, and you think you deserve it. You're a spoiled child in the body of a man. Suzanne coddled you. You should have had your ass kicked a long time ago."

"You can try."

"By your age you have to kick your own ass."

"You old guys all say the same thing."

"So will you if you live that long."

"Having fucked my mother gives you no rights with me. None."

"She'd be ashamed of you right now. Her heart was big. She tried to take care of the people who loved her."

Hood turned and walked alone back down the path to the barn. He saw the men and the dogs. Clayton offered him a beer. The Jack Russell followed him. Erin was out on the front deck in the shade, guitar over her knee, red hair hiding her face. The notebook was at her feet and the pen was on it and there was writing on the page in red ink.

She shook back her hair and looked up at Hood. Her beauty came at him sideways and just under what was visible, a body blow.

"Was he here all morning like he says?"

"Every minute of it," she said, and Hood saw that she was lying.

"Did he threaten you?"

"Come on Charlie. He wouldn't do that."

"Talk to me."

"There's nothing to say. Just isn't."

"Write a song about a guy who's willing to sell out his girl so he can get away with murder."

"Sell me out?"

"Obstruction of justice? Perjury? It's jail time, Erin."

She looked up, briefly, wiped a tear on a knuckle, the guitar pick still in her hand. "Hood? Don't. Please get outta here before he walks up. If he sees me crying he'll figure all the wrong things."

"You've got my numbers if you need me."

"I need you to go."

Hood kicked the railing upright, hard. Erin flinched and the terrier launched into a fit of barking. Hood stomped down the steps to his car. He was furious and ashamed of it.

He aimed the IROC down the drive and

goosed the throttle and looked in the rear-view mirror. The little dog receded and blurred in a cloud of dust and Erin watched him drive away.

He used that afternoon to meet with the local cable TV reporter who'd done a segment on the Lancaster LASD substation Toys for Tots campaign of last year. She gave him a DVD copy of the show.

Back in the Hole he played it on the computer and got exactly what he'd hoped for: the voice of Terry Laws.

"Well, it's the least we can do for kids who don't have a leg up in life. It makes us all at LASD really happy to bring a little joy this time of year."

He listened to Laws say those two sentences a dozen times. Then he played the copy of the 911 tape that Warren had procured. But the anonymous call was so distorted, Hood couldn't say with any certainty that it was made by Terry Laws.

So he tried Draper's voice.

"Good. Because I don't want anyone talking trash about my partner."

Again, there was no way to hear much of a similarity. The more he listened the less it sounded like either of them.

He called a spectrograph examiner and

made arrangements to get the recordings to him.

25

Tuesday morning, in Superior Courtroom 8, Ariel Reed led Hood through the events last year that had brought IA to a crooked lieutenant's criminal emporium in Long Beach.

She asked him how he met the informant, Allison Murrieta, and what made him think she could be trusted.

Hood told the truth. His ears rang mildly and he hoped his face wasn't flushing. The fallen lieutenant glumly regarded him, and regularly whispered into his lawyer's ear. There were a few LASD deputies in the room — the accused's loyal supporters — who occasionally smiled at something Hood said. Judge Mabry eyed him with hard curiosity and the jury was a blur to him, thirteen faces that he tried to avoid.

On the cross, the defense did his best to make Hood look like an oversexed bumbler. *And by then you were involved intimately with Ms. Jones, correct?*

Yes.

So you never questioned her motive for alleging that the defendant was selling stolen property?

I knew she wanted to hurt him.

Did it ever occur to you that she was using the lieutenant to deflect your attention from her own criminal activities?

No. She had admitted her own criminal activities.

But Mabry sustained Ariel's several objections, and reminded the defense who was on trial here.

Hood was finished by the noon recess. They ate lunch in the cafeteria.

"You were good," she said.

"I hope we win."

"I'll win. They weren't able to make it a bad arrest and that's their best chance."

They talked small for a while after the meal was done. Two of the defendant's partisan deputies took a table not far away, after giving them bemused stares. One spoke and the other laughed.

Ariel turned to them. "Can I help you?"

They looked away. Ariel took a call, stood, walked to a window and looked out. Hood saw her nodding but not saying much. When she came back her expression was skeptical.

"Let's get some air," she said.

They stood outside the Criminal Courts entrance in the meek downtown sunlight. The cars moved slowly and the pedestrians moved quickly.

"I used to smoke," she said. "I did a lot of it right here."

"I still do, once in a while."

"I can't do things once in a while. It's another character flaw, like the way I split atoms."

"There are plenty of things worse than that."

"Charlie, look at me. Eichrodt passed the evaluation with flying colors. Both memory and speech, dramatically improved. Dr. Rosen is going to recommend that he be sent back here to stand trial for the murders of Lopes and Vasquez. My boss wants me to be a part of that team. I said yes."

"I don't think he killed them."

"He'll have his day."

"Possibly rigged by two sheriff's deputies."

Ariel shook her head and looked out at the street. "Life is all curves, Charlie. It's not straight, like a drag race. Wish somebody would have told me."

She offered a small smile and her hazel eyes pried at him.

"Let's walk down the street and get

lunch," he said.

"We just had lunch."

"Let's get another one."

"Perfect."

It was. Hood hadn't spent a more pleasant hour in the last six months. He actually ate the second lunch, probably due to nerves. She talked on without a comma. Unlike the lawyer he had just seen in court, Ariel the person was self-deprecating, somewhat goofy and quick to smile. She described her line of the Reeds, especially the women, as "a motley crew obsessed with speed" and the men as "pointlessly energetic."

He walked her back to the courthouse and felt the late winter chill settling over the city.

In the parking structure his phone rang. It was a sweet-voiced girl saying she wanted to talk to him about Londell Dwayne.

26

Patrice Kings was a mocha-skinned girl with olive eyes and a steady stare. Her hair was light brown and long. She had on black jeans and red canvas tennies and a suede jacket with a faux fox collar and cuffs. Her bag was big and floppy and studded with rhinestones. She was waiting near the ticket windows in the municipal stadium parking lot, standing beneath the suspended fighter jet, just where she said she'd be.

The light was fading fast and there was an orange band in the western sky. The desert cold settled down from above.

"Can we walk?" she asked. She looked at Hood like she was memorizing him.

"Let's walk."

They were rounding the broad bend of the outfield before she spoke again.

"Londell was with me that night the policeman died."

"I've heard that story before."

"The motel man over in Palmdale can prove it. He would remember us. And another clerk, too, a woman."

Hood buttoned his blazer against the cold, turned up its small collar and jammed his hands into his pants pockets. He had dressed for court. She watched him closely.

"Which motel and what people?"

"The Super Eight. Kevin. Big white fella, young. The woman was Dolores."

"Anybody else?"

"Nobody."

"Just you and Londell?"

"Just me and Londell."

"Tell me about it."

Up ahead he could see the ticket windows and the fighter jet. There were a few cars in the parking lot. The marquee said the next event was a classic car show this weekend, hundreds of cars.

"There isn't much to tell. He's got a girlfriend. He didn't want anyone knowing about me. Yet."

Again she gave Hood the assessing stare. He had seen in some people experience beyond their years, but never in a ratio so wide as in Patrice Kings.

"How old are you?"

"I'll be sixteen."

"When?"

"When I get done being fourteen and fifteen."

"You're fourteen."

"Until September."

"You're fourteen and a half years old."

"I know how old I am."

"Did Londell send you here?"

"Yeah he did. He's scared. He's got Crips on him for stuff, and Eighteenth, too. And the police on him for the murder of that guy that lost Londell's dog. And you know what that means, means they shoot first and ask questions later."

"He's got to turn himself in, Patrice. We can't prove his alibi without him. You talking to me here just isn't good enough."

"I knew that's what you'd say."

"Londell knows it too. You tell him to call me and I'll pick him up and take him to jail. He won't get shot and he won't get hassled. Inside they have it segregated so the Crips and Eighteenth won't jump him."

"He don't trust cops."

"He's trusting me with you. Why did Londell pick me to hear this?"

She looked at Hood hard. "He said you were fly for a white guy and had some humor. And something 'bout your ears."

He almost said that he was the one whose partner Londell was suspected of killing, that he was the witness who could help Londell to a lethal injection. But he guessed if he did, this might be the last communication he'd ever have with Londell Dwayne.

"He didn't kill anybody," said Patrice.

They were back to the ticket windows so they started a second lap.

"Where is he?"

She was studying him again.

"It's the only way to help him," said Hood.

"I know what you think. But he treats me good. With me, he's easy and funny and we don't do drugs. And he doesn't bring any weapons around. Lonnie doesn't like weapons. You know he's always in some kind of trouble but he's gettin' tired of it. He's actually thinking about joining the union down in L.A. They got a ironworkers local taking ex-gangsters, and a bricklayers too. He sounds good in his voice when he talks about it. I can tell he means it. He's not lazy."

They continued around the stadium. When Hood looked over there were tears in her eyes.

"See, Hood, I know him, and Londell can be something. He just needs to believe. Like, he's got all kinds of Detroit Tigers stuff, but he never even seen Detroit. He just likes the way that D looks. He's looking for his own respect, you know? World's been calling him a piece of shit so long he's afraid he'll start believing it. D, man. D. To him it's not Detroit, it's *Dwayne*."

"And you were with him that night?"

"All of it. I'll swear it if you let me, sign a paper."

Hood believed that she was telling the truth about Londell, just like he believed that Erin was lying for Bradley. It's all in what you see, he thought.

"He has to turn himself in."

"Can you help him if he does?"

"He'll get treated like anyone else, Patrice. I can't do favors for him."

He saw her gaze move to the listing old Mercury in the parking lot. She waved. The car started up and reversed out of the space and came toward us. The driver was a young woman wrapped in a Raiders jacket.

"Your sister?"

"Yeah."

"She knows about you and Londell?"

"She's the only one."

Patrice reached into her bag and pulled out a plastic shopping sack that had some weight to it, and handed it to Hood.

"In there I got it written down — the names of the motel guy Kevin and the lady, Dolores, and what time we checked in and what names we used. But the best thing is we were messin' with the digital, you know, and we got some shots with the date and time on 'em. You can change that stuff if you're good with electronics, but we aren't, but we also got shots of the TV in the background because we were making faces like the people in the show, and you can check those shows and the times and you'll see we're telling the truth about where we were. Show those pictures to the motel people. Ask them if we were there. Londell wasn't anywhere near that guy who got dead. The proof's in there. Our future's in there. And we want the camera back."

"None of it means anything without Londell," Hood said.

He held the bag out to her but she turned quickly and ran to the idling car. She got in and slammed the door. As the Merc pulled away Patrice was pointing at him.

He turned to see Londell leaning against one of the counters at the ticket window.

"You passed an audition you didn't even know you were having," he said. "Otherwise you would never a laid eyes on me."

"Well, here you are."

"Yep, here I am. I give up, man. No way I can outrun two crazy girlfriends, a hundred hostile niggas and a million cops. Take me straight to the judge. I'm innocent."

He turned to the wall and put his hands behind his back then spread his legs. "I believe in America. Yes I do."

On the way to jail all he talked about was his pit bull, Delilah, kidnapped by Terry Laws and later lost by him.

"She's up in the hills with the coyotes after her," he said. "I told Laws he was responsible. He said she'd be all right with him. Bullshit, man. A cop named Laws. Now she's gone."

27

The next morning Hood met with three men and a woman who had partnered with Coleman Draper over the past two years. The men all rated him as a competent reservist. They said he was professional, firm but polite with the public, familiar with LASD procedures and equipment. They said they'd ride with him again but would prefer a sworn deputy.

The woman was a thirty-ish deputy named Sherry Seborn. She was attractive and wore no ring, had seven years with the department. She said she drew Draper at a roll call when she started nights just before Christmas last year. She too said that Draper was professional and well mannered with the public. They had pulled over a suspected drunken driver and when he had become belligerent, Draper had talked him down, gotten him cuffed and into the back of the cruiser.

But, as she and Hood sat in a corner of the substation cafeteria, she quietly said she'd rather not ride with Draper. She'd told her superiors not to pair her with him again. She looked out at the bright cool day. A distant passenger jet left a neat contrail in the blue.

"He impressed me at first," she said. "The drunk was getting hotter and Coleman cooled him off. Just talked him right into the cuffs. That was early in the shift. Later, after we'd booked the guy, I asked him about the Eichrodt bust. He said it was a bloody mess and it got him working on his verbal skills. He said he didn't want another battle like that, ever. Told me about his stitches and bruises."

"None of that sounds too bad," Hood said.

"Too good, maybe. That was what I got from Coleman — he was too good."

"There must have been something more than that for you to go to the patrol sergeants about him."

She looked at him and hooked a wave of thick brown hair behind one ear. "I didn't give them a reason. I'm not required to."

"Give me the reason."

She sipped a soft drink and studied him. "I don't love IA."

"I don't either."

"I've seen some good deputies catch some bad stuff from you people."

"I have too. Help me."

She looked outside again, then back at him. "On first break, he made a cell phone call. We were at a coffee pub. He talked while he ordered, talked when he paid, talked when he picked up his coffee and put in the cream and a lid. He was talking to a woman, I could tell. He'd already told me he wasn't married. His voice was smooth and encouraging, with Spanish phrases thrown in. I know Spanish. He said beautiful things to her. A lover. He said he'd be coming home to her soon. Fine. That was more than fine with me.

"But then, later in the shift, he made another call. I was driving, and when I glanced over he was staring through the windshield, very much wrapped up in his conversation, and he didn't even glance over at me. The radio was quiet so what am I supposed to do? I listen. He's talking to the woman again, but his voice is completely different. It's a voice of calm authority, and he's giving her very specific instructions about how to handle a situation at her work. She's bartending or waitressing or something like that, and a guy was coming on to her that night and he was telling her exactly what to say to him and what tone of voice to use when she saw him again. He called her by name — Juliet. And I thought, this guy's a bastard, not because he was telling her what to do and controlling her with his soft fascism, but because she was a *different* woman. It had to be. About the time I realized that, I realized that Coleman was playing to me. He didn't look at me, and he never turned to me, but he was pleased that I was listening. The kicker was, when he finally hung up, he slipped the cell phone back onto his belt and gave me a little smile. The smile said, *No biggie, just you and me, babe.* Then he said: 'Sherry, choose life.' I asked him what that meant and he just shrugged. I said something wiseass. But Draper gave me the creeps. Here's this cute guy, plenty of money is my guess, playing cops and robbers on my shift, cheating on his women and telling me what to choose. What I chose was not to ride with him again."

"Did he call the first woman by name?"

"I didn't hear him do that."

"How did the shift end?"

"Professional. Brief. I clocked out and got to the lockers as soon as I could. I've seen him at roll call since. He smiles but he doesn't engage me in conversation. He's not around as much."

"Did he say anything more about Shay Eichrodt?"

She shook her head.

"Terry Laws?"

"Said he was a good guy, learned a lot from him."

"How about Prestige German Auto?"

"He said it was a cash cow and he didn't even have to get his hands greasy anymore."

"Did he talk about his family?"

"He said his father used to be a reservist down in San Diego County."

"What about a brother and sister?"

"No mention."

"Israel Castro?"

"No."

"What else?"

"Recruitment," said Seborn. "I found that odd. I don't know a deputy alive who looks forward to handing out brochures and applications. He said he loved doing recruitment for the department — schools, job fairs, county fairs, whatever. He said he was always looking for that special person."

"Special how?"

"He didn't say."

"What else? Anything else. The weather, Sherry, I don't care."

She looked out the window then back at Hood. "He talked about Mexico. Said he loved fishing in Baja. Said he went down there every Friday to fish. Said he always took a load of good used clothes and electronics, and canned food down to this charity in Baja. The young people love used Levi jeans, he said. And anything electronic. Said it made him feel good, watching people build their dreams."

"Build a dream."

"Something like that."

"Every Friday?"

"Every Friday. He and Terry Laws."

28

A few minutes later Hood had traded his Camaro to another deputy for a VW Jetta sedan and was driving it to Prestige German Auto. It was located in Venice, just a mile or so from the beach, in a mixed residential/business zone off of Venice Boulevard.

He waited in the lobby for a few minutes while a man cashed out two customers, gave them their keys and receipts, and thanked them sincerely for their business. His shirt was white and clean with an oval patch that said "Heinz."

Hood looked at the premium wheels and tires on display, and the samples of the German strut systems for sale there, and the various aftermarket gadgets for German cars. But mostly he looked at the BMW, Daimler Benz, Porsche, Audi and Volkswagen certificates earned by Prestige German's expert technicians. There were six of them: Klaus Winer, Dieter Brink, Joe Medina, Eric Farrah, Richard Tossey and Heinz Meier. On the counter ahead of him he saw six small trays containing business cards for each.

When it was Hood's turn he asked for an express oil and filter change. Heinz noted that Hood was not a regular customer but he had Hood read the estimate and sign the bottom. The estimate was for $85.

"Expensive," he said.

"It is a twenty-point inspection."

"That's over four dollars a point. I heard you guys are good. The head gasket in this car will need to be replaced soon. If I'm happy with the oil job, I'll make an appointment to bring it in."

"Good, good. Thank you, Mr. —" He looked at the sheet. "Mr. Welborn."

"I'll be here if you have any questions."

Hood handed him the keys and toured the store displays again, then sat in the lounge. There were four other customers watching TV and reading newspapers. There was free coffee and bottled water, and vending machines, and posters of sleek fast German cars on the walls.

When Heinz took the work order back into the repair bay Hood went to the counter and got a card for each mechanic.

Then he went outside and stood for a minute in the small parking lot. The day was cool and damp, with a layer of coastal haze. He walked around the block of mostly small stucco houses and old wooden fences. There was a day spa, a donut shop and a psychic's parlor, open Tuesday-Friday from 11 a.m. to 2 p.m.

When he had almost come back around to the Prestige German lot Hood came to a six-foot textured concrete wall that nearly reached the sidewalk. There was an artsy wooden gate with an oxidized copper mail slot and an intercom. He waited for a break in the traffic on Amalfi, then stood on his toes and looked over. He looked at the small bungalow behind the garage on the Prestige German Auto lot. The shades were drawn and there was no car in the narrow driveway. Draper's home, he thought, as on his application in 2005.

Back in the Prestige German office Hood studied the bill and asked about the brand of filter used.

"It is Volkswagen approved. And yes, the Jetta is leaking oil. It is likely from the head. It will not repair itself, hmmm?"

"I'd like to speak to the owner," I said.

"Mr. Draper is not here. I am the one responsible for operations. There is a problem?"

"No problem at all. I just like to know the people I do business with."

Heinz studied the young man before him, then reached into a tray and gave him one of his cards.

"I am Heinz Meier."

Hood shook his hand, paid him in cash and left.

Back in the hole it took him only one hour to locate the Prestige German Auto mechanic that he was hoping to find.

Eric Farrah had skipped bail on a shoplifting charge then vanished from his job at Valley BMW in Encino eight months ago. He was accused of stealing a box of Fuente cigars valued at two hundred dollars. His failure to appear would cost him five thousand dollars and a heart-to-heart conversation with Charles Robert Hood. He was twenty-two, and looked like a kid that Hood had gone high school with in Bakersfield, a talented bronco rider.

At closing time, Hood tailed Farrah from Prestige German, down Amalfi, to his car. When Farrah heard him approaching he turned and Hood handed him a cigar.

"That's a Fuente like the ones you bagged. I'm a cop. Don't run."

"Fuck. Shit."

"Don't use up all your best dialogue. Give me your car keys."

Farrah glared at Hood, then jammed a hand into the pocket of his grease-stained pants and dropped a heavy set of keys into Hood's palm. Hood hit the unlock on the key fob twice and the doors of Farrah's BMW unlocked with a clunk. Hood opened the passenger-side door and motioned to him. Farrah thought once more about running, Hood guessed, then decided against it and got in.

Hood climbed into the driver's side and started the engine. "No use calling attention to ourselves."

"Man? Who are you? Where's your badge?"

"I'm going to drive around this corner and park."

"Oh, man. This is the genuine shits."

Hood parked one block over under a magnolia tree. He badged Eric Farrah and told him who he was.

"You and I are going to talk, Eric. If you do well, I'm going to get out of this car and walk away and you might not see me again. If you don't, I'm going to drive you to jail. Even if you spring for a good lawyer you'll spend a few weeks in lockup because the judge won't give you bail twice, and you've got failure to appear on top of the shoplifting. You'll be inside even longer if you wait for a public defender, but you'll save money. That's how it works. Either way, you're free to keep that cigar I gave you."

Eric Farrah was a pink-skinned young man with fuzzy white whiskers and expressive blue eyes. His hair was curly and white. "Talk about what?"

"Coleman Draper."

Farrah looked at him, mouth open just a little. First there was doubt on his face. Then relief. Then a crafty smile. "I can do that."

"I thought you could."

"What did he do?"

"That's the last question you're going to ask."

Farrah told Hood that he'd worked for Prestige German for seven months. He'd arranged with buddies at Valley BMW not to rat him out when Heinz called to confirm his good standing as a former employee and skill as a mechanic. After impressing Heinz, he met Coleman Draper the next day. They had coffee in Draper's office, which was down the hallway behind the lobby. He was younger than Farrah had expected. Draper had seemed distracted but interested in him: hometown, schools, travel, plans for his life. They talked briefly about the repair and maintenance of German cars, the concept of customer satisfaction, then about salary and benefits and responsibilities.

"Then out of nowhere he asked me how long I'd been ducking the cops. I said I didn't know what he was talking about, and he said I had fugitive written all over my face. So I told him. He shook his head like he was disappointed. He said never risk jail for cigars. We talked awhile. The office walls had framed photographs by a guy named Helmut. Really horny stuff. Then Mr. Draper just stood up and offered me his hand and said I would start tomorrow. He said if I felt the need to steal cigars again, come talk to him about it. He said if I lifted so much as a spark plug from him he'd have my arms broken. I believed him."

"Have you felt like stealing cigars again?"

"No. I wouldn't have stolen them in the first place except I was drunk. I had the money. A bad day. It just happened."

"How often do you see him?" Hood asked.

"Maybe . . . once a month. It's a minute here, a minute there. He'll come in and hang around and watch us once in a while. Talk a little, maybe take a look at what we're doing. He's an awesome mechanic. He

313

could strip a Porsche down to its chassis and put it back together blindfolded."

"Ever socialize, beers after work, lunch?"

"He took us to lunch at the West Beach for Christmas. The people there knew him. Hostess and waitresses all over him. Total babes. He paid for everything. He mostly listened. The Germans love to talk. I think he's entertained by them. The thing about Mr. Draper is he's never all there. Always has something else on his mind. That doesn't mean he's not paying attention, though. He's just paying attention to more than one thing."

"The other mechanics talk about him. What have you learned?"

"Some of the Germans think he's gay. I don't. Some of the guys think he used to be a crook, and some of them think he used to be a cop. And based on the way he knew I was in trouble, I'd say it's one or the other. He pays us really well, and we get good bennies and time off, but we all understand that if we swipe anything or skim the register, we're in genuine deep shit. Joe saw him at LAX getting out of a Town Car. Klaus saw him in Laguna at a restaurant."

"What restaurant?"

"Klaus never said."

Hood looked out at the Venice street, the

crowded houses and the cracked sidewalk and the power lines sagging above. Juliet, he thought. Laguna hostess or waitress.

"Here's something," said Farrah. "One night last August I got into a fight with my girlfriend and I had to get out of the apartment. We were living on Washington so I walked up and over toward work — just somewhere to go where she wasn't. I bought a sixer and figured I'd use my key and sit in the employee's patio behind the bays. It's just a concrete slab and an umbrella and a picnic table and a piston ashtray. It's got a chain-link fence with the privacy slats in it because the house on the other side is owned by Draper. Two of the slats are torn up near the top and from the table you can see the driveway and garage and front part of the house. So I've got three dead soldiers and here comes a car up the driveway to Mr. Draper's house. It's around ten. And I know I'm not really supposed to be there, but I've left the patio lights off so I just sit still in the dark and watch through the hole. It's Mr. Draper's M5 — 2000, black on black, Dinan chip, five hundred plus horses and you can hear every one of them. Then right behind it comes this red F-250 extended cab, with a camper shell and a heavy-duty tow package. Mr. Draper gets out of his car, and this big muscle dude gets out of the truck. They don't talk. Mr. Draper opens the Beemer trunk and Muscle Beach opens the lift gate and the tailgate on the Ford. They take two rolling luggage bags out of the M5 trunk, and two more out of the back, and slide them into the bed of the truck. They're big bags and they look about medium weight from the way they handle them. Then Mr. Draper opens his garage and he brings out three clear plastic tubs. It's fishing gear — big shiny reels and tackle and short, thick rods. Mr. Draper and Muscle Beach, they've got this efficiency thing going. They don't say anything. They move quickly but they're not in a hurry. It looks like they've done it before, and it's something important. They don't act like two buddies going fishing. They don't exactly look it, either. Because it's a warm night and they're dressed casual, jeans and sport shirts, and they're both packing pistols in cop-style hip holsters, up high on the belt like detectives. Like you are."

"What night of the week?"

"Friday. My payday. But Margo's always tired from working at Von's all week and I want to party. So we fight instead. We have bad luck on Fridays. That's when I stole the cigars."

Fridays, Hood thought. Build a dream. Take a drive with four suitcases full of something you wear a gun to protect. Fishing gear? Levi's for the poor?

He asked Farrah how much money Prestige German took in each week, and he said around twenty grand. That came to an annual gross of over a million dollars. In addition to Heinz, the manager, and five full-time mechanics, there was a part-time bookkeeper, a window washing service and an old janitor that Draper kept on though he didn't actually do much. Farrah told me he made $29.50 an hour now, up from the $25 hourly he made during his first six months. That was five bucks an hour more than Valley Beemer paid him, and the raises here at Prestige, according to Heinz, could come fast and generously.

"As long as you work you ass off and treat the customers like kings," said Farrah. "I got no trouble doing that. I'm good with cars. I like people okay. It's Heinz's job to write the business. He likes to make customers feel cheap if they don't do what he says is necessary. He says most west side L.A. people don't want to look cheap. A tune on a Benz S class is eight hundred, and a replacement headlight is six-fifty, so they never look cheap to me. Hell, if you jump-start an S class convertible you can fry the computer for the convertible top — thirty six hundred bucks, right there. Happens all the time."

Hood watched a couple of teenaged boys saunter toward them on the sidewalk — baggy Dickies and Raiders jackets and bright white athletic shoes. They gave Hood the look and he stared back and they looked away.

"Farrah," he said. "Here's the deal. If you tell Draper we talked you'll be in jail yesterday. This is a fact."

"Don't."

"It's up to you."

"I don't owe him. I owe me."

"Most of the jerks in jail think that way, too. So maybe I should drag you down there now. Then I'd be sure you're not going to talk to your boss."

"Not necessary. You made me a deal, man. You gave your word."

"When was the last time you saw him?"

"Last month. He was coming home after a run. It was early in the morning."

Hood wrote his number on a sheet of notepad paper and set it on center console.

"I can help people who help me," he said.

"Make the cigar problem go away?"

"I doubt it. There's other things."

"Name one."

"Give me a reason to."

He got out and crossed the street toward Prestige German.

29

Hood made Laguna by late afternoon. In the public library he copied the restaurant listings from the local phone book then walked back across Coast Highway to the Hotel Laguna.

He ate outside on the deck. It was slow so he took a table by the railing where he had once sat with Allison Murrieta. He pictured her sitting across from him. He thought that memories are a blessing and a burden. The sun sat on the ocean like a fat red hen then sank in the night.

In candlelight Hood started at the top of the alphabet and called down the list, asking if Juliet was working. He found no Juliet at all until his twelfth try, at a restaurant called Del Mar. She was seating customers at the moment. Hood thanked the man and rang off.

He sat in the bar of the Del Mar and watched the black Pacific through the window and Juliet as she came and went from the hostess stand in the foyer. She was on the tall side, and lovely. Her smile was measured but her hair was blond and uncomposed. She wore a black backless dress and heels. She had an easy way with the guests, and some of them she greeted by name.

During a slow period she came over and asked the bartender for a soda with lime.

"I like Laguna when it's slow like this," Hood said.

"Do you live here?"

"I just visit."

"I love it here anytime. I think it's the best city in the whole world to live. I'm a Lagunatic."

"I live in L.A. It's got lots to love, too, but lots not to."

"I like the art museums and Spago."

"I went to the drag races at Pomona last week. That was great fun."

She looked at him with mild doubt. She sipped her soda from two thin red straws. "We don't have drag races here. We have drag queens."

"That's funny."

"I'm Juliet."

"I'm Rick."

"What do you do?"

"Security."

"Like TSA?"

"Commercial-industrial, mostly. Copyright and patent protection, things like that."

"The Chinese don't honor them, do they?"

"Not always."

"I took a class in Szechwan cooking once. Oops, duty calls. Nice talking to you."

She touched his coat sleeve and got back to her stand before the next party of four came in with a gust of cool March breeze.

Hood stayed a little longer then left, nodding to her on his way out. He sat in the Camaro across Coast Highway and waited. She came out at ten o'clock, wrapped in a black leather coat, with a red scarf around her neck and a red tote over her shoulder. Instead of the heels she wore white athletic shoes and she headed south on PCH at a good clip. Hood got out of the car and followed behind her down the opposite side. There were enough people walking that he didn't stand out. Her hair bounced and shined in the streetlight and shop lights. She took long strides and never once looked back. At the Laguna Royale she veered across a walkway and into the lobby. She walked past the wall of mail slots, pushed a white card into another door, then pulled it open with both hands and disappeared.

He waited for a few minutes, then walked across Coast Highway and went into the lobby. He found mail slots for a J. Brown, a J. Astrella and a J. Clayborn.

He hiked back up Coast Highway to his car, keeping his head down and his eyes open for a black 2000 M5. He drove the Camaro back down and found a parking place across from the Royale. It was a good place to keep an eye on the parking entrance. An hour later, just before midnight, he saw a black M5 signal a turn into the Royale. In the streetlight he saw a swatch of white hair and a snapshot of Draper's face as the car made the turn then bounced down the ramp toward the garage.

Hood sat in his car for an hour, listening to the radio. He was too far out of jurisdiction to get the L.A. Sheriff's band so he listened to the news. No sign of Draper or Juliet.

It was also too late to call Jim Warren but he did anyway. Warren sounded slow and lucid as he always did. Hood asked him for a GPS transponder to put on Coleman Draper's civilian car, and a portable receiver to track it with. Hood knew he would have needed a court order to attach such a device to a suspect's car. But he also knew that IA had powers beyond the law, even beyond the U.S. Constitution. A cop under suspicion of IA has no Fifth Amendment right — he must answer even the most self-incriminating questions or possibly lose his job, benefits, reputation and future in law enforcement. He must surrender his shield and gun upon the demand of a superior. His work and pay can be suspended during an investigation. He never knows when he'll be called to testify against himself or another officer and he has no right to an attorney unless he is ordered to stand trial.

Hood feared and disliked IA for all of this, as did most cops, but he was willing to make an exception for Coleman Draper.

So he laid out for Warren the basics of what he knew: that Vasquez and Lopes had been pulled over that night but didn't live to tell about it; that Laws, and likely Draper, had begun to receive large amounts of money shortly after Vasquez and Lopes lost their lives; that every Friday night since then, Laws and Draper had done a job that earned them roughly seven thousand dollars apiece. Next, Hood also laid out what he suspected: that Laws and Draper had framed Shay Eichrodt and beaten him senseless to cover themselves.

"You think they murdered the couriers

and took over their route," said Warren.

"That's what I think."

"Where does Londell Dwayne come into play?"

"I don't know yet."

There was a long pause.

"I'll see what I can do," said Warren.

30

In the morning Hood stood outside the interview room and watched through a one-way window as Bentley and Orr questioned Londell Dwayne.

Dwayne sat cuffed at a steel table, ankle irons secured to rings in the floor, dressed in the yellow jumpsuit issued to accused violent felons. He was dull-eyed and tired.

Bentley sat across from him in a crisply laundered white dress shirt, no tie. He wore a silver cross on a chain around his thick black neck. There was a folder on the table in front of him, and a digital recorder next to that.

In one corner of the room stood a tripod with a video camera that could be turned off by an interviewer for "off the record" statements. Hood knew that these statements would be videotaped by the two hidden cameras, one positioned in another corner and the other hidden behind a false heat vent behind Dwayne.

Orr paced.

Dwayne sat back and dropped his cuffed hands to his lap.

"I'm not going to record now," said Bentley. "I'm hoping we can have an honest talk here. Just man-to-man, you and me, nice and easy."

"Talk away," said Londell.

"You are in a whole bunch of trouble," said Bentley.

"I got the alibi."

"You think you do. Londell, you are under arrest on suspicion of assaulting two peace officers. That would be the Mace. Figure one year in jail. You are under arrest on suspicion of possessing a machine gun. That would be the M249 SAW that I personally saw hidden under your mattress in your apartment. Another year in prison and a ten-thousand-dollar fine. You are under investigation for the statutory rape of a fourteen-year-old girl. One more year in prison. And guess what?"

Dwayne glared at him. "What?"

"That's the *good* news."

"That's mostly all bullshit. I peppered the cops because I was being wrongly pursued. I never even seen a real machine gun in my life. I have never touched a real machine

327

gun. And I definitely never raped Patrice. I made love to her. You know the difference between rape and making love, don't you?"

"That's also called illegal intercourse. She has to be eighteen, Londell. Everybody knows that. Tell me you didn't know that."

Dwayne shook his head tiredly, but said nothing.

"And that is the least of your problems, because what I want to talk to you about is the murder of Deputy Terry Laws."

"Talk all you want. I wasn't there."

"That's not what his partner says. He was right there, sitting next to Laws in the squad car. He says you were the shooter."

"I can't help what his partner says."

"But he knows you, Londell — it was your buddy, Hood."

Londell's glassy stare followed Orr as he paced. "Hood? If it was Hood, then he knows it *wasn't* me."

"You're the one who's blind, Londell. You can't even see the depth of the shit you're in."

"*Hood* said it was me?"

Hood saw the disbelief on Londell's face. Dwayne shook his head and made a face like he'd just swallowed something nauseating.

Bentley sat back and crossed his big arms.

"Londell, there are two ways for you to play this. One is you keep lying and covering up and we bury you with the eyewitness, and with additional evidence. We'll get to that evidence in a minute. The other is you help us and we help you. You tell me what happened, the straight truth of it, and I help you get a fair trial — or maybe no trial at all. I'm sure you had your reasons. They're probably reasons I can understand. Maybe it came down to your dog — Delilah. I know all about what happened to Delilah. Laws took her and lost her, or sold her, or worse. I got a dog too, man, and I'd kick the ass of any man that would hurt that animal. But Londell, you are looking at the death penalty here. You gunned down a cop right in front of another cop. California Penal Code One-Ninety was *written* for guys like you."

Londell slumped down in the steel chair. "Why Hood want to mess me up?" he asked quietly. He shook his head, looking in Bentley's direction. "I didn't kill that cop and I ain't going to no lethal injection. That's my final answer."

"That's exactly where you'll go if you don't come clean and tell us what happened."

Londell sat up straight and leaned toward

329

Bentley. He seemed suddenly light and energized. "I know more than you do. You're the fool here, not me."

"Tell me what you know."

"Here it is: I was with Patrice when the deputy got shot up. We have two motel people can tell you that. We got pictures we took with the date right on them. That's proof for any jury in the world. You can take me to the court but I'll win. I'll win because I can prove I wasn't even there. It's so simple even you can understand it, Bentley."

Bentley stood and sighed. Orr stopped his pacing in front of Londell and looked down at him.

"The motel people aren't sure," said Bentley quietly. "I showed them your mugs and they weren't sure. Witnesses who aren't sure don't get far in court."

"That's a lie. How can they not be sure?"

"Why would they lie?"

Londell sat back again, hard, and the dull patina returned to his eyes. "We got the pictures we took."

"Anybody can change a time and date stamp, Londell. You know that."

"This is ceasing to be funny. We got Will Smith on the TV, right in the background. We were trying to make faces like him. That proves what night it was when the pictures were taken, proves we were there, proves I didn't mess with the time and date."

Bentley put both hands on the table and leaned over toward Londell. "I took the camera to the affiliate that shows *Fresh Prince.* The episode on your camera isn't the episode they aired that night."

"Bullshit, man! It's the one where the girl's father parachutes out of the airplane and leaves Will Smith but Will Smith can't fly. Then Will Smith finds the other chute and jumps and they land in the same tree!"

"The network didn't air that show the night Terry Laws died. They aired it the night *before.* I think you changed the date and time, Londell. That's what the TV station thinks, and that's what I think."

Londell leaned forward now, put his forehead on his cuffed hands. After a moment he sat back up.

Hood was surprised that Bentley and Orr were making up so many lies. They'd already told him that the motel employees ID'd Londell and Patrice with near certainty, and that the *Fresh Prince* episode had indeed been aired that night throughout Southern California. But Hood also knew that creative interrogations are one way that cops get confessions from the guilty — they simply give up. And the innocent? Well, some of them give up, too. Hood didn't think Londell would. At least not now.

"What about the machine gun we found, Londell?"

Londell sat up again. He looked hard at Bentley, who was still looming over him from across the table. He looked at Orr, who was leaning against one wall, arms crossed. He looked at the big mirror that hid Hood.

"If you tell me you found a *machine gun* that belongs to me I'm gonna explode right up through this ceiling and fly all the way to the moon and live forever in total freedom away from lying-ass criminals like you."

"Blast off," said Bentley. "Be sure to send me a postcard."

"I can't talk to you. I want a lawyer. Actually, with the lies you telling, I need a hundred of them."

"Londell, you say you didn't kill Terry Laws? Well, if you're telling the truth, the last thing you need is a lawyer. You know why? Because if you get a lawyer he's gonna make a deal with us and that deal is going to send you to prison for a long, long time. He'll think he's doing you a favor. He'll think he's doing his job. You hide behind a lawyer now, and you're meat, nothing but young black meat."

"I had a twenty-five-caliber pistol I never shot. Bought it legal and you guys took it and I haven't seen it since. I don't even know how to *use* a machine gun. What do I want with a machine gun?"

"It was in your apartment."

"I've been framed. You guys framed me. I want those hundred lawyers right now."

"You sure about that? It's your right, Londell. I'm just telling you, once you get the lawyers involved it's a loser for you."

Orr had left the interview room and now stood with Hood, looking through the one-way glass.

"You're hitting him hard," Hood said. "He's not budging."

"He's a tough little shit."

"He's either innocent or the best liar I've ever seen."

"I keep thinking about that machine gun in his bed frame," said Orr. "But he puts up a good fight, doesn't he? Looks to me like's he's more pissed because we're lying than because he's been caught. This ought to be good. Watch."

As if on cue, Bentley sat across from Londell again. He stared at him for a long beat, a bug-eyed Sonny Liston kind of stare, half death and half abyss.

Londell stared back, tired but contemptuous of the liars he was dealing with.

Bentley opened the folder and spun an eight-and-a-half-by-eleven-inch photograph across the table like a playing card.

"Tell us about this."

Londell squared the picture before him with a finger, and looked down at it. "That's a machine gun in a bed."

"And guess where that bed is?"

"I don't know but I can tell you where it isn't. It isn't my bed. That isn't my apartment. And that isn't my machine gun."

"Guess again."

Hood watched as Bentley set a series of three more photos in front of Londell. Even from outside the room Hood could see that they were establishing shots — a wide-angle shot of Dwayne's bedroom, and the hallway leading to the living room, the living room with the door open to the flat Palmdale desert.

Londell lunged across the table at Bentley. But the ankle irons held and Bentley casually backed his head out of range like a superior boxer. Londell landed hard on the steel, cuffed wrists outstretched, one side of his face down, ankles still anchored to the floor rings. He was breathing hard. He looked up at Bentley with a wild eye, or it might have been at Hood.

"Why you treat a brutha like this? Why you hate me? You try to execute the *wrong man*. You just need a handy nigga to lynch and I'm it. Your soul is dead, man. Fuck you, Bentley."

Londell retracted himself across the table and back into the chair.

Bentley watched him for a moment, then he rapped on the door and the guard let him out. He joined Orr and Hood and for a moment they all looked down at Londell Dwayne slumped in his chair. He looked up and flipped them off with both cuffed hands.

"All we really have is the SAW," said Bentley. "And you as a witness, Charlie. And the transport deputies telling us how Londell mad-dogged Terry Laws for taking Delilah away from him."

"I can't make a positive ID," Hood said. "I can't ID anybody with a bandana over their head and sunglasses on, at night, in a hail of machine gun bullets."

"That's certainly what his defense would argue."

"It would be the truth."

"Yeah, Charlie, I can see the difficulty. They're going to arraign him on the assault, gun and sex charges tomorrow. Judge won't set a bail Londell can make. That keeps him nice and close while we make the case for killing Terry."

They watched Londell for another moment. Then Bentley turned to Hood. "What's your gut say, Charlie?"

"It wasn't him."

"Why?"

"You know the gut," he said. "It feels what it feels but it doesn't say much."

Hood watched two big deputies come into the interrogation room, cuff Dwayne and unlock his ankle irons, then guide him out the door.

As Hood walked across the parking lot in the late morning sun he got a call from the spectrographic voice analyst. He said the 911 recording was made outside in a high wind, or maybe with the caller's head sticking out an open window in a moving vehicle. He'd cleaned it as best he could but the recording was compromised. The anonymous call about a shooting and Eichrodt's fleeing red truck could have come from either Terry Laws or Coleman Draper or hundreds of millions of other men.

31

I order two good cognacs and look down at Sunset Boulevard. It's after midnight and the clubs are still an hour from letting out. The L.A. air is a soft mixture of restaurant and car exhaust and bottled scents with their hint of human rut, all rising up from the strip. I draw it into my lungs before lighting another cigar.

The boy takes his snifter and swirls the liquor and looks out over the city. I clearly remember when I was just a little younger than he is — not that long ago, really — and the terrible sense of liberation I experienced after the tragic death of my family. I was utterly alone, except for a few friends, and my dogs. My world became a different place.

"I know where this story is going," he says.

"You think you know."

"Laws is doomed by his conscience."

"But doomed to what? Things change. You

will see. Within just a few weeks, I began to see a change in Terry."

"He regrets his erratic behavior."

"No. It's better than that. He doesn't even *see* it. Listen, a month later we're making another run, and Terry asks me to stop off in Puerto Nuevo, the lobster village south of TJ."

"I've taken Erin there."

"Well, Terry says there's something he wants to show me in Puerto Nuevo. He says he's been driving past it his whole life but has never really seen it. But because of something that happened to him a few days ago, he says he sees it now. *Gets* it, is what he says."

"You're leaving something out."

"Patience. I can't reveal the future without a present to rest it on, right? Okay, so I'm driving Terry's red pickup truck. We've just crossed the border into Tijuana. Now it's time for Mexican Customs. A chipper bunch, I can tell you. We've got $385,000 and all the usual fishing stuff in the back, protected only by a camper shell and our badges and our weapons and ability to use them. And here's Terry, sitting next to me, badgering me about Puerto Nuevo.

"I've got no interest in Puerto Nuevo. For me, the purpose of this trip is not tourism.

All I want to see is El Dorado, get my cut and get home. The truth is that Terry has pissed me off — his drinking, his mood swings, his blather, his new babe, his so-called ideas. But we make it past Mexican Customs. I look at the rearview mirror and watch the Customs booth recede and the officials approach the next vehicle. When I look over at Laws, Terry is staring out the window with an odd smile on his face. He hasn't had a drink since we left L.A. He hadn't even joined Avalos for his usual pre-journey shot of tequila. Terry was usually drunk by now, and starting in on his second flask. What was up?

"We park outside a very small church on a dirt road in Puerto Nuevo. It was chilly and foggy for June. I smell the ocean, which is just a few yards away, and I also smell the lobsters boiling in the dozens of Puerto Nuevo restaurants up and down the village streets. As a teenager I'd come down here scores of times with Israel and other friends, for drinking and eating the lobsters then sleeping it all off in TJ.

— This is it, said Laws.

— It's a church.

— Come in. I haven't been in here since I was a boy. I want to ask you something.

"So I follow him in. Churches have always

disturbed me. They make me feel unimportant. I sense the atrocities committed in the name of God through the ages but even that can't cheer me up that night with Terry. The church is tiny and simple, no vestibule, just a few rows of pews and a raised altar with a small stained-glass window behind it. The cross is smallish and smooth. There are candles and plastic flowers and paintings of saints on heavily lacquered boards hung along the walls. It's cool and it smells to me like incense and mildew. Laws walks toward the altar then stops and turns to me, smiling. His bigness is exaggerated by the smallness of the church. He looks almost gigantic in there.

— Laurel and I are going to be married the last Saturday in August.

— Of this year?

— Yes, Coleman. Nine weeks from now. And I want you to be my best man.

— Well, okay. That's great, Terry. I'm sure she's a fantastic woman and you deserve her.

— I remember this place from when I was a boy. Dad brought us down here a couple of times to see the blowhole and eat lobster and buy tourist stuff. And I remember standing in this little church. Right here, where we are now. And I remember feeling something here. It was something that moved in my heart, like a tickle, like speeding along a rolling highway when you're a kid and your dad or mom is driving — you know that tickle in your guts?

— To me it was sexual.

— Well . . . anyway, I never had that feeling again for about thirty years. Until last Sunday when I took Laurel to church.

"And, of course, I understand: Terry's beatific stare, his booze-free smuggling, his impending marriage, his renewed interest in this church. I felt like I was standing at the base of a mountain that was about to collapse. Dread? Terror? I'm not sure there's a word to describe a catastrophe that hasn't happened yet but assuredly will.

— You found Jesus.

— He found me. Coleman, I never knew how bad I needed to be found. It's like the feeling I had in this church thirty years ago, but ten times as strong. Fifty times.

— I'm very happy for you and Laurel, Terry. And for you and Jesus. But we should get back to the truck. Mexico is not a place to leave our kind of luggage unattended.

— I'm glad you'll be there with me, man. Laurel is going to be stoked, too.

"I clap Laws on the shoulder and force a smile. I look into his joyful eyes. But I'm doing a lousy job of hiding my worry. I'm happy that Laws has found a fortune, and a woman with unbelievable legs who wants to marry him, and found Jesus, too. But I can't avoid this weighted black thought that Terry is becoming a dangerous partner. I feel this heavy blackness in the same place that Terry feels the tickle of God.

"That night at Herredia's, just after dinner is served, Terry asks Herredia, old Felipe and me to bow our heads in prayer. Terry thanks the Lord for this great bounty and for the great friendships that have sprung up between us. He asks that the food be blessed for His service, and he concludes grace in the name of Jesus Christ, our savior, amen. Then, all through the meal he talks about his personal relationship with Jesus and he inquires directly into the health of each man's soul. He says he will gladly witness to the Lord for us when we are ready. He refers to Laurel several times as the woman who has saved him through Christ. When dinner is over I look at Herredia. *El Tigre* has the same dark glower that he had the very first night we met him, you know, where he's deciding not whether to kill someone, but how."

"You guys are in trouble."

"But listen. The next day we take Herredia's fishing boat out of Ensenada and speed southwest. It's a twin-engine Bertram fifty-eight-footer with outriggers and bait tanks — tournament rigged and ready. The engines have just a few dozen hours, Herredia tells us, but that was about all he said. He's angry and it shows.

"And my other problem is I don't fish. Never did it as a boy, never did it as a man. I don't care about fish unless it's on a menu. But, as you remember, I'd sold Terry and myself to *El Tigre* with gifts of fishing gear, some of which I'd personally endorsed. You know, the international brotherhood of anglers. So, when I begin to see that Herredia will want to take us fishing someday, I go out a couple of times on a half-day boat out of Long Beach, try to learn something about it.

"Now I have to call upon all of my acting skills to play the part of a seasoned saltwater angler. The postures and language of the sport come easily to me, but it takes more than 'tude and lingo to select, tie on and work a lure well enough to fool a wild animal. I concentrate on the fishing like I've never concentrated on anything in my life, except maybe seducing women, and I stay within my capabilities and I start catching some smaller fish. I can't believe it! Herredia, of course, he sees that I'm not really very good but that's perfect for him — he ridicules me and puts me in my place, does the whole macho trip you'd expect from a guy like that. But the fish quit biting my lures, and I start to feel the first shivers of panic at being unmasked. What if Herredia sees how deeply I'd been lying when I gave him all the fishing tackle? My guts start to ache. I start messing up my casts, getting tangles and knots. My confidence vanishes. I dig a hook into my damned thumb and pry it out and try to fish through the pain, but I still can't get so much as a sardine to bite. Even way down in the water, the fish sense my incompetence. I catch Herredia staring at my middle section and I wonder if he's thinking shotgun or the fillet knife I saw Felipe sharpening early that morning. I'm fucked.

"Then? Well, then Terry Laws starts doing something that Terry Laws turns out to be very, very good at. He fishes. Terry is fast and fluent with the knots, he can cast hundreds of feet of line with the flick of a wrist, he's a wizard with the squid jigs, and when it comes time to set a hook his big arms pull the rod back smoothly and quickly and not a single fish — not even a dorado weighing thirty pounds — broke his line or rejected his hook. He's all *over* the Bertram. Every time I look up, there's Terry, hooked up, rod bent, line screaming out as a big fish takes it to the depths. Then he's hustling along the high gunwale, trying to keep his line from tangling with the others and his fish from getting under the boat, sliding on the wet deck, slipping, righting himself. I know that if Terry goes over he'll probably drown before we get him back up, but this fact doesn't deter Laws one bit.

"So of course it's Terry's troll line that gets hit. He runs to the stern and grabs the rod and sets the hook and settles into the fighting chair. He braces his legs and draws back the rod into an acute bend, then bows to the fish, reels in a few feet of line, and pulls up tight to it again. I'm cheering while Laws fights this animal. After twenty minutes he's sweating hard and his total line gain can't be more than fifty yards. But after half an hour the fish starts to give up line and Terry reels his heart out and then, about seventy-five yards off the port side, the striped marlin launches itself skyward and his flanks buckle and flex in the sunlight and he crashes back into the ocean in a silver explosion. Fifteen minutes later Felipe gaffs the fish and drags it onto the deck where it flops and hammers and tries to get that sword into somebody, the comb on its back raising and lowering, gills gaping slower and shallower. When the fish is dead Terry hefts it in his arms for pictures, taken by Herredia himself. I've never seen him so just plain happy. The marlin weighs in at one hundred and seventy-nine pounds."

"So Terry saves himself by fishing?"

"Don't interrupt. That night back at El Dorado, Terry breaks his own alcohol ban and downs three double tequilas before dinner. He sways as we take our seats in the dining room, tries to blame it on the rolling of the boat. The women dine with us that night, a rarity in Herredia's domain. They're tastefully and expensively dressed and Terry compliments each one on her appearance. He says that Jesus loved prostitutes because they knew shame.

"After dinner, in the billiards room, we shoot no-slop eight-ball and we drink more. The stereo's on and two of the women dance while the other two watch *Under the Tuscan Sun.* Terry pours a large glass of single malt and sits in a big leather armchair. It's an old chair, seasoned by decades of use — Herredia's use, of course — and Terry just plops right down in it and begins regaling the room with stories of the fishing day. He has to speak loudly to get above the stereo and the video. He talks about the faith necessary to believe that a fish will strike your lure. How it's like making a woman fall in love with you. His next topic is what it's like to kill a man, what it does to a soul. Ten minutes later his glass shatters on the tile after leaving a trail of liquid down his shirt and pants and Herredia's good chair. He's snoring.

"Oh yeah, I love the way this is shaping up. Herredia is leaning over the table to calculate a bank shot angle, and at the sound of the glass shattering he straightens and walks around the table to me. He taps my chest with the point of his cue stick, and it leaves a faint cloud of blue powder on my shirt. But his look surprises me. It isn't the glower of boxed fury like the night before, but the soulful, sad expression that he had worn when he proposed the assassination of Hector and Camilla Avalos.

— It is over, he says quietly.

— Yes.

— Very dangerous.

— Carlos, you are correct in everything, but I ask you to give him one more chance.

— One more chance to do what?

— He's not like this at home. But when he gets down here, he feels safe and brave and lucky. He thinks this is where he can

347

fight his demons.

— Demons always win. He should not go where they are.

— I can guide him away from them.

— You said this before.

— Give the child a chance to be a man. Do it for our friendship.

— Coleman, you are not a fool are you?

— No, sir.

— He was weak when you first came here. His hands were shaking when he tried to zip open the luggage on that very first night. Now, all of him is shaking, not only his hands.

— You have my word. If I can't get him to right himself, I know what has to be done.

— Consider: the desert all around us is waiting. He caught the best fish today. He is happy.

"I look over at the dancing women and the unconscious Terry and old Felipe sitting by the door with the shotgun leaned against the wall next to him. *El Tigre* has a stricken look, a look that tells me he already regrets what he's about to do.

— He is yours.

— Thank you.

"I got Terry up early the next morning. I expected something — the sudden appearance of men I didn't know, the racking of a

348

slide, the metallic whisper of a blade clearing leather. But I made my muscles move and I loaded the car and I got Terry into the passenger seat and I drove away. We left El Dorado in the still darkness. There's nothing darker than a Baja California night."

The boy is nodding. His self-confidence is impossible to empty, even to diminish for more than just a moment.

"So this is also a tale of the foolishness of *El Tigre*," he says.

I lean forward toward him. "I would lower the volume of my voice if I were you."

He snorts, but blushes. I love this boy.

"We've come to the part of the story where chaos has turned to opportunity, and opportunity has turned back into chaos. We've come to the part of the story where Terry Laws discovers the character of his own soul."

"I'll miss the drugs, sex and rock and roll."

"There will still be plenty of that. Another cognac?"

"I'm blitzed."

"Then I'll continue the story on another night. It deserves more than a drunk audience. And of course, I want to talk to you about Kick."

The boy looks at me as sharply as he can.

His eyes are fine but I know his thoughts are out of focus. He has impressive powers of concentration and tolerance to alcohol but there are limits to every power on Earth.

"Okay," he says. "Kick. That story deserve more than a drunk teller."

"I look forward to meeting your woman."

"Yes."

"For anything good to happen to us, she has to know that she was here, with us, from the very beginning. She must be part of our foundation. We've talked about this."

"See you then."

32

Shay Eichrodt held out his big hands and Hood fastened the cuffs, but not too tight. He wore an orange jail jumpsuit rather than his light blue mental hospital jumpsuit. He had let his hair grow to a stubble but his face was clean shaven and still very pale.

Dr. Rosen guided him by one arm and Hood took the other. When they stepped outside Eichrodt came to a stop and looked at the sky and the leafless trees and the efficient, unimaginative buildings of Atascadero State Hospital.

"Mmm."

"This way, Shay," said Rosen.

Hood introduced Eichrodt and Rosen to Ariel Reed, and explained again to Eichrodt that she was one of the Los Angeles District Attorney prosecutors who had seen to his commitment at Atascadero.

He towered over her as he offered her both hands. She stepped into his shadow and shook them.

"Longer hair," he said.

"Oh. Yes, I'm growing it."

"Me too."

Hood explained to him once again that Ariel would be riding back to jail in L.A. with them, if he was still willing. Hood reminded him of his rights under *Miranda* and told him that Ariel's purpose was to listen to his story and advise the District Attorney's office on how to proceed. This was considered an informal interview; as spelled out in the affidavit, Eichrodt would say nothing under oath, nothing said could be used against him in court. Hood told him he could change his mind now about having a DA present, or change it at any point during the trip.

"You need to read and sign this," said Hood.

He held out a clipboard and Eichrodt took it in both hands, turned his back to the sun and read it. It took him almost five minutes. When he was done he nodded and took Hood's pen and wrote his name at the bottom of the second page, above "Defendant."

They drove down the highway through grasslands green from rain and stands of oaks. The trees along the road cut the sunlight into slats. In the rearview Hood saw Eichrodt staring out, hardly blinking. A deer watched. Hood glanced at Ariel and she was looking out, too, the bars of sunshine passing across her and moving back to Eichrodt.

Eichrodt told his version of the arrest. His memories seemed clear, even though his language at times came slowly and he would have to wait for the arrival of some words. He used slang and profanities that he hadn't used the last time Hood talked to him.

Eichrodt said that he was returning home to Palmdale from a bar in Victorville. He was working nights. He'd get off at midnight, close the Hangar at two a.m., drink and do occasional drugs with the bartender and assorted friends until three or four, then drive home. Same damned bar every night, same damned people. The Hangar was a dive but the beer was cheap. He was in fact high on alcohol, methamphetamine and PCP when they pulled him over. The deputies were a little blond creep and a fag muscleman. He showed them his license and got out of the truck like they said. The muscleman told him to turn and face the truck and put his hands behind his back and that's what he did. The muscleman cuffed him. Eichrodt was looking down at the dusty red paint of his truck, he said, when

353

the first of the baton blows caught him between his shoulder blades. He turned and charged the deputy, using his head as a battering ram. Both deputies used their clubs.

Eichrodt looked out the window while he talked. Hood saw that he was only partially concentrating on the story. Another part of his attention was out in the rolling central California hills.

Eichrodt said that at first, they tried to take him down with leg and body shots but he wouldn't go down. The meth made him fast and the PCP killed the pain and he believed that he would somehow win the fight and get away. He caught the muscleman once in the forehead, hard, but that was the only good shot he landed. The fight lasted several minutes and he was panting like a dog. His eyes ran with blood and it was hard to see. He estimated that he was hit thirty to forty times, approximately ten when he was on his hands and knees and too damned wore out to protect himself. He said cops don't usually hit the head because it's bloody and too easy to really mess a guy up, but these fuckers hit his head a lot. There was blood on both deputies' shoes and on the pants of the muscleman. Some of his teeth were on the ground. By then the handcuffs had cut into his wrists.

The next thing he remembered was waking up in a hospital. Bunch of people taking pictures of him, flashes pissing him off. This memory came to him only recently, he said. Later there was a pretty nurse named Becka who had freckles and green eyes. His stitches hurt and smelled bad. Then came the long days in the hospital bed. His stitches didn't hurt anymore but they sure did itch. Then came surgery to reduce the swelling in his brain, the groggy weeks of not understanding what had happened or what was happening.

After that were the long confusing hours in court. All he understood about it was that his ass was in a sling and he couldn't remember a fuckin' thing. The worst part was remembering, then not having words to describe the memory, then having the memory go away again. He said that memory is the only thing that means squat, without it we'd all be just rocks.

Eichrodt told them that after court he wanted to die, and at the mental hospital he hung himself with a strip of bedsheet but the ceiling sprinkler came off from his weight and he stood there in the middle of his room with the noose around his neck and the water coming down, freezing his ass off instead of being dead. But a few days from then he started feeling a little better, and the medications began to free his memory but he thought that the cold water had something to do with it and son of a bitch if Dr. Rosen hadn't told him that an early American mental therapy was dunking the maniacs in cold water hoping to shock them out of being nuts but it didn't do nothing but half freeze them. He said Dr. Rosen was a genius.

Hood drove and listened and said nothing. Ariel turned in her seat so she could maintain eye contact with Eichrodt, and she made notes.

She asked if the deputies had their guns out when they approached his car.

He said they did not.

She looked at Hood, then back at Eichrodt and asked him if they said anything to him.

He said nothing but license and registration and step out of the car please. During the whole time they were whackin' on him all they did was grunt, like it was just a job they had to get through.

She asked about the white van, Lopes and Vasquez.

He said they kept asking him that in court. And he kept trying to remember and maybe talked himself into remembering something

356

that never happened. Because if you can forget something that did happen you could just as easy remember something that didn't, right? But now he knew he never saw any white van or any dead men or any money. He said he didn't see one god-damned interesting thing that whole night until the cop's lights showed up in his rear-view mirror and he pulled over and the little blond and the muscleman got out. And if he really had taken all this money and put it in his truck, then the deputies must have found it and turned it in, right? Right? So what was the big deal?

They drove for a while in silence.

"Man," said Eichrodt. "Did you see that hawk back there?"

"It was a red-shouldered," said Ariel.

"Had something in his claws."

"Looked like a gopher," said Ariel.

"To me it looked like a hot dog but I doubt it." He watched the bird sail over a hillside. "Thanks for driving. I'm gonna take a . . . ah fuck, you know a . . ."

"Nap," said Ariel.

"You read my smashed-up mind."

He leaned his big head back on the rest and fell asleep.

A few minutes later Ariel handed Hood a sheet of paper from her notepad. It said:

Does he remember the truth, or just how to lie?

Hood shrugged and she wrote again.

I don't believe what I just heard. I believe every word of it.

Hood nodded and steered the car south down Highway 101. They stopped in Carpinteria for lunch and got an outside table in the cool afternoon, where the orange giant wouldn't get stared at by customers. Eichrodt concentrated on his food and ate slowly. When the sun came out from behind the clouds Eichrodt faced it and close his eyes.

"I never got my ass kicked that bad," he said. "Makes me feel old. I don't need that kinda shit. You going to send me to prison?"

A moment of silence.

"Shay," said Ariel. "I don't know what we're going to do with you."

He nodded and smiled, his eccentrically white false teeth gleaming and perfect.

"I like it longer," he said, pointing at her hair with a fried filet of cod.

"Thanks, Shay. Finish your lunch."

He nodded and gave her an arch stare.

After delivering Eichrodt to the County Jail that evening Hood and Ariel had dinner at the Pacific Dining Car and drinks at the

Edison. This would have cost Hood the days' pay but Ariel insisted on paying half, and she talked her way into a good table at the Edison on what turned out to be a very busy night.

She sipped an appletini and stared off into the crowd but she didn't seem to focus on anything.

"You did a good thing today, Charlie. We'll reconsider the case against Eichrodt. With Laws dead and Draper under suspicion we might have to delay or dismiss. That could lead us to charges against Draper. With the kind of detail Eichrodt was giving us today, I think a jury would believe him. I did. Mostly."

"Good you asked him whether Laws and Draper had their guns out on the approach," Hood said. "That's important."

"It sure got my attention. If the deputies really believed they'd pulled over a double murderer with a truck full of drug money, they'd have had their guns out and ready. That's when I thought — this guy might be telling the truth."

"And Rosen can lay down a medical foundation for the recovery," Hood said. "He's musty and kind and believable."

It was Hood's turn to stare off at the people in the bar, and consider what he was doing. Six months ago he had helped to bust a fellow deputy, and failed to help a reckless woman stay alive. He had voluntarily left L.A. for the Antelope Valley, where he had hoped for quieter days and time to reflect. But now he was IA and deep into a cold case involving murdered drug couriers, suspect deputies, mysterious piles of money and a machine-gunned partner. Hood felt like a wrecking ball.

"What?" said Ariel.

"I used to like being a deputy."

"You still should. You're a good one."

Hood wondered if that could be true. "In Anbar I got myself hated for chasing some soldiers who murdered a family for no good reason. There were some bad reasons. Now, back here, I spend half my time ruining the lives of my own men. Ariel, I signed up to throw the *bad* guys in jail."

"But they come in all shapes and sizes. And, sometimes, uniforms."

"I don't feel sorry for them. Or for myself. What I'm saying is I want to be part of a team I believe in. I want it real clear — us and them. *Us* and *them.* I want to believe in us. I want to be on our side. Simple."

"Simple hardly ever works." She leaned forward and tapped her glass to Hood's. "Charlie, if I could pick one guy they could clone into thousands of cops and deputies, it would be you. You're honest and smart and you give a damn. There isn't much more."

"A thousand Hoods. Scary."

"But we only get one of you. And to be honest, I'm very happy to be the woman sitting across from you in this bar. Glad to be in the same molecule with you, Hood — one little atom to another."

She gave him her small, thrifty smile and he saw the glimmer in her eyes. He looked into them. What he saw thrilled him: someone singular, irreplaceable, beautiful.

"You're going to make me blubber," he said.

"We have napkins."

Hood smiled back and sipped his drink. An old man came across the room toward them. He walked slowly with an ornately carved cane. His hair was white and neat and his eyes were clear. His suit was expensive and well tailored. When he got to their table he stopped and put both hands on the cane and looked down at Ariel, then at Hood.

"It is good to see two young people who are happy," he said. "Enjoy every sandwich." He nodded and slowly walked away.

"What a nice thing to say," said Ariel. She

flushed and the color was still on her fair cheeks. Her dark hair shined and she looked brilliant.

"Charlie, you know I love to drive. Name something you like to do."

"I drive a lot, too. Not racing. Just driving and watching out the windows. I drive hours and hours and hours for work, then I drive more. Then I dream about driving. Then I wake up and drive again."

"Why?"

"I'm looking for something that got away."

"What is it?"

"I'm not sure."

"Where did it get away from?"

"Inside. I actually felt it go. So I weighed myself and I was a pound and a half lighter. But you know how bathroom scales are."

"You're pulling my leg."

"No, I'm really not."

She studied Hood with her level gaze, her legal assessment look. Then she pulled her chair closer and put her hand inside his jacket and over his heart.

"Something's left in there, Charlie. You didn't get completely cleaned out."

Hood lowered his face to hers, touched her temple with his nose, breathed in. She turned and brushed his lips with hers.

"Let's drive," he said.

Hood drove the Camaro over to Sunset, then headed up into the Hollywood Hills. He passed the turnout where Allison Murrieta had taken him last summer, and he tried to postpone the memory of her for just a moment but this was a new thing for him and he felt disloyal. He found another overlook, a little farther up. He parked the car and left the engine idling and the defroster on low. Below them the dark flanks of the hillsides cut shapes in the city lights, and above them a cloud drifted, quiet as a ghost, over the moon. The stars glimmered in the sharp March night.

"Let's continue that kiss, Hood."

They continued it. Even with the defroster on, the windows fogged up and Hood had to turn the air conditioner on also to get them clear again. He pawed blindly at the controls with one outstretched arm, the other still wrapped around Ariel, their lips locked in a passion for the ages. He felt like a teenager.

Much later Hood drove back down out of the hills to Ariel's car, still in a downtown lot near the Edison. He stood by her El Camino as she let herself in.

"Come to my place," he said.

"Could you replace a hot outlaw with an atom-splitting lawyer?"

"You can't replace anybody with any-body."

"Not tonight."

"Does someone else have that honor?"

"Once upon a time."

"He was lucky."

"He's no longer with us. Or, is he?"

"I understand that question. I'm sorry."

"That's enough. That's adequate. That was a good kiss."

33

That Friday night Hood followed Draper's M5 three or four cars back from Venice to Cudahy, then dropped even farther behind when the streets narrowed. The windows of the BMW were tinted dark, and the most Hood could see of the driver was a profile and a flash of blond as he made a turn. Hood knew Cudahy as a rough little city, a backwater of gangs and drug trafficking and bureaucratic corruption, once patrolled by LASD, now patrolled by a police department with a poor reputation.

He also knew that one of Cudahy's criminal fixtures, a heavy named Hector Avalos, was found shot to death last week just a few miles from here, dumped on a side street in South Gate. But Hood knew that Avalos was a Cudahy homie all the way, had done his time in County and Corcoran, and was widely suspected of running narcotics out of this complex. Hood had heard the rumors of dogfighting. Avalos was tight with the city government. There was a big funeral for him but from what Hood had heard, nobody from city hall showed up.

From a curbside two blocks away he saw men emerge from the shadows and escort Draper's car off the street and into what looked like a large warehouse. Hood heard the boom of the rolling metal door when it closed. The men were gone. He drove around the block once and parked out of sight down the dark avenue, and waited.

The laptop on the seat beside him in the Camaro had a large monitor with a brilliant picture. The color maps of the locator program had five levels, from a one-block close-up to a five-hundred-square-mile overview. In any setting, Draper's car was marked by a flashing red X. If his car moved so did the arrow, at a proportionally corresponding rate. The nearest address and cross-streets were listed in a window on the right of the screen, when applicable. When Draper had hit sixty on a Cudahy boulevard the window was a blur of letters and numbers, like a slot machine in mid-whirl. The locator program even had a beeper so Hood could estimate distances by the frequency of the tone.

An hour and a half later the black M5

came rumbling out of the warehouse and bounced onto the street. Hood let Draper get around the first corner, then pulled away from the curb.

Southbound traffic was light until they hit Santa Ana, where a new-car transport trailer had jackknifed and closed all lanes of Interstate 5. New Toyotas were littered across the asphalt, some on their sides, some upside down, all with the protective white tape still wrapped around them. Hood winced at the sight of the battered new cars. The heavy traffic was detoured off at Seventeenth Street, then through Santa Ana and Tustin and finally back onto the interstate again at Red Hill. It took forty minutes.

In San Clemente Draper exited suddenly at Palizada. Hood wondered if he suspected he was being followed, but he couldn't see how or why. Hood stayed well behind the Beemer. Draper drove directly to a fast-food place, pulled into the drive-through line, ordered, paid, got his bags and was back on the freeway in less than ten minutes.

An hour after that he pulled into the passenger vehicle entry lane to Mexico at the border crossing in San Ysidro.

Hood glassed Draper's car from a parking lot of a Mexican insurance office. His Steiner Night Hunter binoculars brought him in very close to the M5, and the special lens coatings allowed in a remarkable amount of light. There were four cars in front of Draper. When it came his turn Hood could see him handing identification to the Customs man. Soldiers walked around the M5, inspecting it with a lazy curiosity. Then the official handed back Draper's ID and waved him through.

The flashing red X vanished, as Hood had known it would. The virtual world ends at the border — Mexico is as free from the digital net as the U.S. is clutched by it. Which left Hood with the task of following someone who didn't want to be followed. He knew that Draper would spot him.

So he put down the binoculars and sat in the lot for a while, then drove to a market and loaded up on food and drinks with lots of caffeine in them, and a cooler and ice to keep them. He bought a plastic beverage bottle in case he got stuck away from a bathroom for too long a time. He found a restaurant lot and parked away from the building, facing the incoming border traffic. He was only about one hundred yards from the U.S. Customs booths.

He ate and drank and listened to the radio. He turned on the beeper full volume, walked around the car a few times, then dozed and ate and drank more. It was midnight then it was two then it was two-ten. He moved to another lot with a worse view. He dozed and waited for the beeper to sound.

It went off just after three-thirty. Hood followed the black M5 through San Ysidro and onto the northbound 5, headed for L.A. He stayed six or seven cars back and both cars made good time in the light predawn traffic.

Then Draper cut northeast on the 57, took it all the way up to the 210 and exited in Azusa. He drove up Azusa Avenue to where it changed to San Gabriel Canyon, and rounded the bend. The road was almost deserted so Hood pulled over and watched the screen. Draper exited San Gabriel Canyon at Mirador, drove three short blocks and stopped moving at 122 Clearwater. Hood waited ten minutes for the red X to start up again but it didn't.

Hood drove to Mirador and started across a bridge over the San Gabriel River. The river was whitecapped and high from the recent rain and he rolled down his windows to hear it. When he reached the peak of the bridge at the halfway point he saw the community guardhouse on the far side, still faintly lit in the dawn. Behind it he saw the nice new houses, gated and huddled up against the steep San Gabriel Mountains. As he approached he saw that the entrance barrier was down and the booth light was on and a guard was inside, hunched in a heavy black jacket. Hood stopped in the pull-out short of the booth, U-turned and headed back across the river.

Back in the hole at the prison, Hood did a title search of 122 Clearwater in Azusa and came up with the Ronald Draper Trust. He thought about that for a minute, then did title searches on units 18, 29 and 45 at the Laguna Royale.

And just as he had figured, one of them was owned by the Roxanne Draper Trust.

Both properties had been purchased in the last year and a half. Hood called the county to confirm what he suspected: Coleman Draper was the sole trustee for both trusts.

Because it was Saturday, it took Hood a long time to track down an official with the Azusa Water District, but when he finally found someone she was able to tell him that the water bills for 122 Clearwater were paid by Alexia Rivas. Another half hour of phone calls got him a Laguna-Moulton Water District assistant manager who said that water service charges to unit 18 of the Laguna Royale were paid by Juliet Brown.

Hood met Jim Warren at a Palmdale bar one hour later. It was strictly a drinker's place: a TV, a country-only jukebox, a shrunken old bartender wearing jeans, a red cowboy shirt, and a belt with a buckle the size of his head. There was a pool table in the middle of the room but no players.

They carried their drinks to an empty booth in the back. In the dim overhead light Warren looked old and weathered.

Hood told him about Draper's run to Mexico and back. He told him about the Friday nights that Terry Laws had invariably taken off work since the murders of Vasquez and Lopes, and the Friday night fishing trips that Draper had talked about with Deputy Sherry Seborn. Hood told him about the valuable properties in Laguna and Azusa that Draper had bought in the last year and a half.

Warren sipped his beer. "Did you see any containers in Draper's car?"

"I never got close enough."

"So he could have been fishing down there."

"Could have been."

"Charlie, if we show ourselves at the

wrong time, it's over. If we move and he's not carrying the money, the whole thing dries up and blows away."

Hood thought about the four-plus hour drive he'd recently made from Venice to Cudahy to the border, following the flashing red X on the screen of the laptop.

"What are the chances he made you, Charlie?"

"I only got close enough once to see his face clearly. He was looking ahead so he didn't see me. The rest of the time I was far enough away to use the binoculars. It was busy everywhere and I never pressed him."

"You're positive it was him?"

"Positive."

"Did he use any unusual routes, stop and wait, backtrack, anything evasive?"

"One stop for food in San Clemente. The rest was a straight shot."

Hood pictured Draper's M5 idling at the border crossing, the casual way he handed his ID — his shield, no doubt — to the authorities on both his way in and his way out.

"We could tip Customs and let them do their thing at the border," said Warren. "If he's transporting cash, then down he goes. If he's not, a border stop might just seem to him like bad luck. A random check — no harm done — and we're a hundred and thirty miles north, minding our own business."

"He wouldn't believe it was random," Hood said.

Warren nodded and sat back and looked over at the bartender, planted in front of the TV. One of the patrons set his glass down hard and the barkeep moved toward him without turning his gaze from the set.

"Follow him again this Friday," said Warren. "If we can establish a pattern we can find a way to make it work for us."

"I'll need a plainwrap that doesn't look like one of ours," said Hood. "The Camaro is too conspicuous for two runs in a row."

"Rent something. Charge it to the IA number I gave you. How do you like the Hole?"

"It's cold and miserable, sir."

"I used to ice fish on Porters Lake, Pennsylvania, when I was a kid. It was similar."

"I used to ride a bike through the Bakersfield, California, oil patch on winter afternoons. Not similar."

For a minute they sat in silence. The drinkers at the bar were quiet and Hood could hear the mumble of the TV.

"What went wrong with the Renegades, sir?"

373

Warren looked across the booth at Hood. Hood had always liked the history in the faces of old men and he saw now that Warren had much of it.

"The Renegades were a false good idea. On paper we made sense — we were principled and tough and effective, and we kept each other sane. But the world isn't run by ideas. It's run by human nature. I didn't know that then."

"Human nature as in Roland Gauss?"

"And men like him. They find each other. To some of us the oath we took and the tattoos on our ankles were a bond of honor. To them it was an excuse. A joke."

"I see Roland Gauss in Laws and Draper," Hood said.

"I do, too." Warren leaned toward him and spoke softly. "You've got to shadow Draper one more time, Charlie. I know you want to take him down now, but follow him south again. We have to know him. And when we know him we'll see a way. I want him. And when we truly have him, I want his people in Cudahy. And when we have them, I want his people in Mexico. I want to lay waste to them all. They're sucking the blood of this country through a golden straw."

Sunshine flooded through the door, was suspended, then gone. A middle-aged

374

couple walked to the bar in a hail of hellos and shoulder slaps, and the bartender poured their drinks without them ordering.

"Reed and the defense rested yesterday," said Warren. "I was there for the closing arguments. She was terrific. The jury was instructed and now it's up to them. Ariel and I had a cup of coffee after. She sends her regards."

Hood thought of Ariel summing up, artfully swaying her jury, locking her cage around the accused, a cage that he had helped make.

"I won't ever get used to putting my own guys away," said Hood.

"I haven't."

"It's the worst job a cop can have."

"No. It's worse watching one get away with it."

Warren folded his big gnarled hands on the table and looked at Hood. "Play it very cool on Friday with Draper. If he does anything erratic or unusual, hit the brakes and come home. You're way out of jurisdiction. I've cleared you with San Diego Sheriff's but they won't be in a hurry to help you out. Don't be a cowboy. That's one thing about IA, Hood — most of the time you're alone."

Hood understood going it alone from Anbar, from wondering if the bullet that caught him would come from an Iraqi or from one of his own. He believed that the most terrible thing in the world was to be hated by your own people.

34

That afternoon Draper put on his reservist's uniform and drove to Cal State Los Angeles to participate in the fourteenth annual "Career Crusade."

He walked past exhibits set up by the various municipalities, corporations, trade unions and employment services. The city of Los Angeles had a large tent, as did Santa Monica and Long Beach. The *Los Angeles Times* had a good sized tent also, and hundreds of newspapers for giveaway. The Retail Clerks Union exhibit was bustling. There was even a booth for the Musicians' Local, featuring a motley bunch of apparent musical artists, and one magnificently lovely young redhead who tracked him from behind her sunglasses as he walked by and nodded at her. Draper had never thought of musicians as organized labor.

In the LASD tent he shook hands with Sergeants Beverly Cresta and Mike Grgich, and several uniformed deputies. A newish cruiser was parked in the shade, freshly washed and waxed, doors open and windows down. Cresta had put together a bulletin board with pictures and articles about the Sheriff's Department, and a divisional breakdown with lists of various job descriptions and salary ranges. Grgich sat beside a large monitor that played a Sheriff's Academy promotional video on a loop. Grgich was stout and muscular and reminded Draper of his old partner, but when Draper shook his hand he felt the very distinct aura of contempt coming off the man. It was a common reaction to reservists.

He took a seat behind a folding table littered with brochures and promotional LASD decals and applications fastened to clipboards. The day was cool but the sun was bright so he put on his shades and tried to look friendly and welcoming. Draper had personally recruited four people to his department. Two were now deputies, one was enrolled in the Academy, one had washed out last winter. None of the three was particularly promising to Draper — they were straight, dull and uninterested in bettering themselves outside the rules of the department. Perfect law enforcers. But who knew? If he kept talking to the young men and women of L.A., he was bound to find a person with the same ambition, courage and dedication to self that had gotten him to where he was today.

Draper understood that one person was only one person, and could only accomplish so much. But two people were much more than just twice as many. Two were a force, and could easily become three and four or five, and a force could do things that one man could only imagine. The bigger your force was, the better, up to a point, of course.

He let the sun warm his face and thought of the Renegades, and the small steps they had taken a decade ago, before they were turned against each other and busted and outlawed. He understood that an ankle tattoo could mean much more than just membership in a clan within the department — it could mean power, breadth and capacity. Draper knew he could lead the New Renegades, if he could only find them. He had had a start with Terry, and now he was ready to pick up where he and Terry had left off.

A stoop-shouldered young man with a cadaverous complexion examined a "Physical Requirements" pamphlet, set it back on the table and tapped it thoughtfully, then walked away.

A big-bodied blond woman came up to Draper. "What's the starting pay?"

"Four thousand and eighty-three dollars a month for a sworn deputy," he said. "Support staff and technical start around two thousand."

"So you don't get rich working for the sheriffs."

"Who told you you'd get rich?"

"I want riches."

"Why?"

"I believe I deserve them."

"You deserve nothing."

Draper saw Grgich look his way.

"What I mean," he said, "is that few people get rich working for other people. And there are other rewards in law enforcement."

She shrugged and walked off.

Emblematic, he thought. There was no shortage of desire for riches out there, but so few people had the intelligence to find a way to accumulate wealth, and fewer still had the drive and energy to make a profitable idea real.

"So, what's the starting pay?"

The question was delivered to mock the pugnacious tone that the big woman had used, but it was a man's voice. Draper recognized it. He looked up at the boy. He was tall and built well, wore his black hair long and a neat goatee. The pretty red-haired musician was with him. She wore a long black coat, jeans that were worn thin at her thighs and red cowboy boots. She studied Draper from behind her sunglasses.

"Well it hasn't gone up in the last thirty seconds," said Draper, with a smile.

"Four grand to risk your life every day?"

"And guess what? If you don't get fired, you get raises. Are you a student?" asked Draper.

"Was. I can't sit still all day and not learn one thing I don't already know."

"So you know it all?"

The boy looked hard at him. "I know more than some bored reservist like you."

Draper stared at him but the kid wouldn't look away. Instead he either smiled or smirked — it was hard to tell. Draper was aware of Grgich's interest and chose to ignore him.

"Try me," said the boy.

"Come *on,*" said the musician.

"No," said the boy. "Ask me something and see if I know the answer. It's got to be something *you* know the answer to, not some bullshit fantasy question like a second-grader would come up with."

Draper sat back and crossed his arms. He sensed Grgich's critical attention but didn't care. Last night he had played solitaire with a deck of cards before going to bed. "What famous king is represented by the king of hearts?"

"Charlemagne. The king of diamonds is Julius Caesar, Alexander the Great is the king of clubs, and the king of spades is David."

"Where is the first historical reference to a place called California?"

"A Spanish novel written in 1500. Montalvo. My mother was a history teacher, so you're shit out of luck on stuff like that."

"He's not lying," said the redhead.

Draper laughed. "Okay, okay. A way to measure time that is based on the motion of Earth?"

"Sidereal time. Nobody uses it but astronomers."

"Then what is an astronomical unit?"

"The Earth's average distance from the sun — ninety-two million, nine hundred and sixty thousand miles."

"Frontolysis."

"The breakup of a storm front. Frontogenesis is the formation of one."

"The Mojave green rattlesnake has what type of venom?"

"A unique mix of hemotoxic and neuro-toxic. It's the only *crotalid* that has such a venom."

"He used to collect snakes and lizard when he was a boy," said the musician. "Made up a whole list of the Latin names."

"What are you," Draper smiled, "his acolyte? You follow this kid around and wor-ship him?"

"Mostly it's he who worships me."

Grgich laughed aloud, and scooted his chair a small bit closer to Draper.

Draper watched the girl smile and won-dered again what her eyes looked like behind the sunglasses. Then, as if on cue, she propped them up on her head and looked down at him with lovely blue eyes. He searched them for weakness while he smiled back.

"You should obviously know the average number of hairs on a redhead's head," said Draper.

"Ninety thousand," said the boy. "Blondes have the densest growth, with one hundred and twenty thousand. I read that magazine article, too. But I wondered how they did the counts."

"Quit showing off, you dolts," said the girl. She had a smoky voice and a creamy complexion and a strong neck. "You're supposed to be recruiting us. So, do you like being a deputy?"

"I love it," said Draper.

"What about the danger and low pay?"

"There's less danger and more money than you think. Do you like being a musician? What instrument do you play?"

"Guitar, piano and harp."

"Harp. Like an angel?"

"I've never seen an angel play one."

He stood and offered his hand to the boy. "I'm Coleman Draper."

"Bradley Jones. This is Erin McKenna."

"Last question for you, boy genius," said Draper. "Are you even slightly interested in a career with the LASD?"

"I'm slightly interested in just about everything."

"We should talk."

"We are talking."

"After this thing."

Bradley Jones checked his watch. "We'll be back."

They were back at sundown. Draper was collecting things from the table and putting them into one of Sergeant Grgich's boxes. Grgich ignored him and made a show of stepping in front of Draper to shake hands with Bradley and Erin and make conversation in an overly loud voice.

Draper drove them to a bar out on Garvey in Monterey Park. It wasn't a deputy's hangout and it wasn't quite a dive but Draper noted Bradley's unimpressed expression as they walked past the drinkers at the bar and got a table in the back.

The waitress was older and she sized up Bradley for an ID check but Draper vouched for the age of both his guests. She took their order then went to another table. Draper watched Bradley watch her go. Erin glanced at both men and Draper held her eye. He was still looking for the weakness in her.

They sat in silence for a moment. Draper looked at the two youngsters before him — Erin looked a couple of years older but she couldn't have been much past twenty-one or twenty-two — and even at his own age of twenty-nine he felt drawn to their youth and potential.

"Find us some music, would you?" asked Bradley.

"Sure," said Erin. "I'll do that for you."

"I love you but I don't deserve you."

Draper heard no sarcasm in Bradley's voice, no condescension or hidden meaning. Draper recognized the words as something he would say to Alexia or Juliet. They were the kind of words he had spoken all his life, the most important words on earth: the ones that people wanted to hear.

"I've got something cooking, honey," said Erin. "I'll be right there at the bar."

She kissed Bradley's cheek and stood and Draper watched her walk to the bar and glide onto a stool and swing her purse onto the bar top. She had left her long black coat over the chair next to Bradley so Draper got a better look at her shape. She was painfully beautiful and the sight of her sitting alone at a bar on a Saturday afternoon amazed him.

"Fantastic," he said.

"Told you. I really *don't* deserve her."

"No. Clearly not." Draper laughed and drank. Erin went to the jukebox then back to her stool. She dug a pen from her purse and took a bar napkin from the stack, and Draper watched her scribble something down on it. A moment later the Stones were happily yapping away about making sweet love while the rain came down. Two bikers clomped in and sat down the bar from Erin. One was tall and one was wide. Bradley stared at them and the wide one stared back.

"She's writing music right now?" asked Draper.

"She's always writing music. She writes

almost everything the Cheater Slicks play."

"I'm very impressed."

"I knew you would be."

Draper clinked his glass with Bradley's, then set it down and positioned it perfectly in the center of the cardboard coaster. He watched the bikers move down the bar and sit on either side of Erin, and Bradley watched them, too. Draper spoke loudly now, playing to Erin.

"I guess what I'm saying, Bradley, is that the LASD is a great place to launch from. It would give you an advantage that civilians don't have. It would be your base and your force. From there you could engage the world. You can become a bureaucrat and rise up through the ranks. You can go into private or corporate security. You can position yourself for election to public office. On an everyday, practical level, you would be armed. The law would be on your side, as you go about your day. You could move directly and efficiently toward getting what you want."

Bradley said nothing. He had locked eyes with the wide biker, who had swiveled away from the bar and leaned his back against it. The tall one had his shaggy head pressed in close to Erin and Draper could hear the low-pitched gravelly sound of his voice in some kind of narrative — a joke, he thought, or maybe a story about life on a chopper. Draper saw that the two men were rough and experienced, not weekend bikers or mere aficionados of the Harley-Davidson brand.

"If you want riches you take them," said Draper.

"My mother said it's not take what you get, but get what you take."

"She was wise and beautiful."

"She's dead."

"Those two men aren't going to go away."

"I can see that."

"This uniform is provoking them. They know that Erin is with one of us and they're hoping it's me."

"No. The thick one knows she's with me."

"I'll bring her back over and we'll avoid trouble."

"No."

Draper heard the louder, more guttural deliverance of a punch line from the tall man, and saw Erin turn away from him and looked back at Bradley. She looked annoyed. She pulled open her purse and threw in her pen. Wide, still looking at Bradley, hiked up his balls.

"Christ," said Draper.

Bradley stood and walked over and

stopped short. Draper got up and followed. Erin tried to rotate on her stool but Tall was leaning in tight on one side and Wide was leaning back staunch on the other and she didn't have the strength to move their shoulders.

"Let her out," said Bradley.

"She likes it here," said Wide.

"And we like her here," said Tall. "But she don't have a sense of humor. Be honest, boy, do you fuck her enough?"

"Plenty, guys, plenty," she said, and tried to shoulder past Tall but she couldn't move him. Her purse slid off her lap to the floor.

Bradley took a step forward and knelt and picked it up and stood there with the strap in his hand. Then Wide slid off the stool and stood. He was taller than Draper had thought. He poked Bradley with a finger.

"I like your girlfriend," said Wide.

"I love her. And I don't like you."

Erin had moved into the space vacated by Wide. Draper reached out and took her hand and ushered her back to the table.

"Enough, you idiots," he said. Then, to the bartender, who had just picked up a cell phone, "Everything's cool. Buy them a round of doubles."

Wide poked Bradley in the chest again and Bradley let the purse fall and took the man's hand in a casual motion and bent the wrist down with his thumbs and turned the hand sharply. Wide screamed and went to one knee and Bradley turned the man's wrist further and Wide grabbed wildly with his free hand but Bradley stepped away and lifted and turned harder and Draper heard the bone snap and the anguished, breath-sucked scream. Tall stepped forward and threw a punch that caught Bradley on the head but he was already leaning away from it. When Tall followed with a big right roundhouse Bradley stepped inside and blocked it, popped him in the forehead with an elbow, clawed one eye with the fingers of the same hand, then pivoted and drove the butt of his open left palm up into Tall's nose. There was a bloody explosion and Tall pitched backwards and Bradley threw himself high into the air and caught the man in the rib cage with a bone-crushing kick. Tall collapsed to the floor like a dropped blanket.

It took about ten seconds.

Draper threw Erin's coat over one arm and pointed her toward the exit.

Then he pulled Bradley back by the collar of his shirt and looked briefly down at Tall, who was curled on his side, panting and bleeding. Wide was still on one knee, white-faced and clammy, his left wrist cradled in his right hand but twisted freakishly askew.

Bradley shook Draper off and took two quick steps to Wide but he didn't throw or kick. He just stared down at the guy for a long moment, then turned back to Draper.

"If we stay I'll get mad."

"We should go."

Draper pulled him toward Erin and gave her the coat, then went to the bar and offered sincere apologies to the barman and the waitress. He dug five hundreds from his wallet and set them by the drink garnishes and stir sticks.

"I'll be back in an hour to make sure everything is all right."

"That's okay, Coleman," said the bartender.

"Who's that kid?" asked the waitress.

"Just some brat who wants into the Sheriff's."

"You going to take him?"

"What do you think?"

"I'd take him. Be easier than fighting him."

Draper went over to the bikers. Tall had progressed to his hands and knees. There was a puddle of blood under his bowed head and a long drip leading down to it from his nose. Wide now sat on a bar stool with a nauseated expression on his face and his mangled wrist already beginning to bloat.

"I'll be back in a few minutes," Draper said. "If you assholes are still here I'm going to arrest you and take you to jail."

"I'm going to kill that kid someday," said Wide.

"Bring help."

Draper drove them back to the Cal State parking lot and followed Erin's directions to their car. It was a classic Cyclone GT that Draper had admired the first time he'd met Bradley, a long few weeks ago. Draper opened the door for Erin and closed it after helping her get the tail of her long black coat properly arranged inside.

"Can I borrow your boyfriend for a minute?" he asked.

"Sure. But don't let him beat up anybody else."

"Just a minute for some deputy-to-deputy talk. Ninety seconds, max."

They walked down the rows of parking spaces, mostly empty now after the Career Crusade.

"Don't tell Hood about today."

"I haven't told him about anything."

"There's more to the story of Terry Laws."

"I know that."

"Soon. Bradley, if you were the one who canceled Kick, congratulations. It's what I would have done. I hope the little shit got to enjoy the feeling of the number six before he died. I admired everything about your mother, except that she took up with Hood."

Bradley studied Draper's face. "I didn't care much for that, either."

"And one more thing. As you've seen, to get what you want out of life, you will have to lie to Erin successfully. Other than that, you can build the life she wants. You can take her straight to her dreams. And of course to your own."

"You're like the devil in a uniform," said Bradley.

"Most people don't notice devils."

"Most people are fools."

"Let's prove that together someday."

They were almost to the car. Draper could see Erin looking through a side window at them. He knew that she would be Bradley's downfall, unless he was an extraordinary boy indeed. It was the way of the world.

Bradley got in and started up the Cyclone and screamed off with a fishtail and a billow of tire smoke. Draper shook his head and smiled as he got into his car. He had been young once, too, just about Bradley's age when he had given up the dusty roads of Jacumba for the glittering promise of L.A.

In some ways Bradley reminded him of himself. In others he saw that Bradley was far behind him. Bradley had bravado and intelligence. He was hugely selfish, and had an outlaw pedigree. Draper wondered if, because of their similarities, Bradley might someday try to see him for who he really was. Draper had spent his entire life staying close enough to people to influence them but far enough away to remain unknown. Father and mother? Brother and sister? Yes, and okay and fine — he had loved them in the conventional ways. But he could not let them see him truly. Few had seen Coleman Draper and none for very long. But he thought that Bradley Jones could be different.

35

"Hector's arena on fight night? Pure insanity. Gangsters everywhere, and not only Mexican. Every Eighteenth click for miles around is there. Cadres of Crips and Bloods and Gangster Disciples. I see stone-faced *Eme* captains and smiling MS-13 killers and Aryan Brothers and Nazi Lowriders and Asian gangs. And not just gangs — the arena is filled with unaffiliated freelance horribles of every size, shape and color. Talk about a good place for people-watching.

"There are athletes I recognize from the papers — football players, boxers, a recent NBA draftee. Some spectators have brought dates. Every imaginable drug is being used right out in the open, washed down with every imaginable drink, topped off by joints and bongs and pipe loads and tobacco. The smoke hangs in a cloud high up in the ceiling. I figure that if any ten of these people had been gathered in any other place on

Earth, there would be multiple homicides and epic mayhem. But fight night is different. It's a boiling cauldron of L.A. bad guys out for good clean fun. No business is done. All are equal. Affiliations mean nothing. Everyone there is having a great time.

— Look at these fucking people, says Laws.

— That's the only thing they're *not* doing.

— Yet. Let's get the money and get out of here.

— Hector wants us to stay.

— I'm not staying. You can.

— We're a team.

— We're way outnumbered, partner.

"So we climb the stairs to the luxury box as usual. We go in. Rocky and three of his shotgunners stand guard at the windows while Camilla locks the sliding glass door and Hector begins pouring shots of something from a dark blue bottle with no label on it.

"They want to party and Terry and I just want to get the money and get the hell out of there. But the luggage is right where it's supposed to be, and the unloading and weighing and vacuum sealing and repacking go smoothly. Four hundred and eight thousand dollars — an all-time high. Avalos predicts that Herredia will give us all a bonus, yes, yes, yes, a bonus *grande!* He's drunk as I've ever seen him, and still lucid.

"I stand behind the sliding glass door and look down on the action. I wonder if God feels this way, gazing upon Earth. What a world: a brindle pit bull is tearing into a smaller, black dog, and the two factions of the crowd are bellowing against each other as if their lives are in the balance. High up in the bleachers someone collapses and they load his limp body down the crowd but nobody bothers to stand, they just slide him along hand to hand like a big bag of beans. When he gets to the bottom a couple of young *vatos* drag him into a walkway between the bleachers then hustle back to their seats.

"Now the brindle has the black dog by the throat and the smaller dog is tight to the brindle's leg but both animals are so exhausted they can only lie there, breathing hard. Did you know that dogs in combat sometimes sleep for several minutes right in the middle of a fight, an instinctive symbiosis before mustering their energies again to kill each other? Well, they do. Then the black dog lets go of the leg and the brindle is able to stand and bore its bloody head into the throat of the smaller dog. And then he starts that savage shaking that pit bulls do. I have to squint it's so hard to watch, being a dog man myself. I whistle something. The crowd is screaming for death but the black dog's owner finally throws in a white rag, then two men wearing elbow-high welder's gloves jump the pit walls and force apart the dogs.

"Laws pulls two of the rolling suitcases to the sliding glass door, then comes back with two more. Below, the black-dog faction is booing and the brindle faction has gone bonkers, throwing their drinks and cheering. Some approximation of a doctor makes a show of examining the limp black dog with a flashlight. He wears welder's gloves, too.

— There's no way, says Laws.

— No way what?

— No way to see this and not die.

— Ignore it.

— That's what I mean. You have to be dead to ignore it.

— Steady, Terry. Five minutes and we're out of here.

"Rocky and his three men escort us down the steps. It's much louder outside of the private box, and a wild musky smell cuts through the drug and tobacco smoke. The whole arena feels ready to ignite. Single file, Terry and I each push one suitcase and pull another, all of which bounce precariously down the steps until the rollers hit the floor. They draw plenty of looks but nobody is inclined to contest four stubby combat shotguns holding eight rounds each.

"Suddenly Laws veers off to the fight pit. He parks the suitcases upright and hops into the ring, and I think for sure this is the beginning of the end."

"You've said that before," says Bradley. "Laws has gotten you to the brink at least twice before, with Herredia."

"I didn't know what a brink was until now. I stop and watch Terry. I figure he's going to strangle or maybe even shoot the dog handlers or the doctor. His big body blots out the sight of them. I can't really see what he's doing. I let go of one suitcase and rest my hand on the pistol under my sport coat. The shotgunners, who are supposed to be protecting the money, all lower their weapons at Terry.

"But the crowd sees what I can't see, and it goes quiet for a long beat. Then, all of a sudden there's a drunken roar. And when Terry climbs back out of the pit, he's got the defeated black dog in his arms and a martyr's calm on his face. The dog is wrapped in a Mexican blanket. The ring doctor jumps the wall and stuffs a handful of something in Terry's jacket pocket and

Terry says something to him and the doctor says something back. But Terry doesn't even break stride. Rocky takes one of Terry's suitcases and one of his gunmen takes the other, and the six of us and one mostly dead dog proceed to the exit. We proceed to the exit!

"I steer my VW Touareg south on Interstate Five. In the rearview I see Terry back in the second row of seats, holding the animal on his lap. The car smells of blood and fear, and Laws is talking to the dog in a low voice, telling it that things will be okay, you're going to be just fine, hang in there *amigo*.

— The doctor said his name is Blanco, says Laws.

— He's black, not white.

— That doctor helped us out. He really did. There's scissors and butterfly stitches here, and a bunch of antibacterial ointment and swabs and gauze and a roll of white tape. Laurel will love this innocent warrior.

— He's probably going to die, Terry. You have to figure he's going to die.

— Don't tell me what to figure, Coleman. There are figurers greater than you.

— I'm saying the dog can die.

— Blanco will not die.

— Keep the blood off the leather, Terry.

— It's all in the blanket. Good dog. Good Blanco. You hang in there, my friend.

"The dog is still alive two hours later when we come into San Ysidro and join the line of traffic heading for the border. Laws and I both know that getting an American dog in and out of Mexico is much harder than smuggling large sums of drug money, so we take Blanco to a twenty-four-hour emergency veterinary clinic. Laws badges the employees and pretty much tells the truth about Blanco and what happened to him. He gives them his credit card and agrees to an estimated twelve hundred bucks for treatment and boarding charges, just for the night. The young vet says that Blanco's chances are "fair." Terry tells the doctor that the dog will live. I'll tell you, something in the tone of Terry's voice really got my attention. I'd never heard that tone from him. The young doctor, he turns kind of pale, and he nods and looks away."

I watch Bradley Jones as he puts the flame to a fresh cigar.

"So," he says. "Laws has found his heart and lost his mind."

"Approximately."

"Near the dirt road that cuts off from Mexican Highway Three, I hit the brights and look for the small pile of stones that marks the turnoff. Terry still has the dog on his lap and that almost sad, almost content look on his face, like he's bound for heaven or something.

— It's important that Herredia has confidence in us, I say.

— What's that supposed to mean?

— There was the falling-in-the-swimming-pool incident. Then the passing-out-in-his-chair incident. He worries about your religious conversion, Terry. He worries that it will interfere with our work.

"Laws goes quiet while I guide the SUV off the asphalt and bounce it across the shoulder to the dirt road that leads to El Dorado. Dust rises in the headlights and the beams straighten into the desert.

— You told me all that before, Coleman.

— Stay focused, Terry. Stay calm. Choose life.

— I've murdered for profit. I've been forgiven by God. I see no contradiction in that. I see no reason why God should interfere with our work.

— God is not our employer. Herredia is.

— Then I will render unto *El Tigre*.

— Terry, keep your God and your jokes to yourself. You should know that by now. I can't cover for you much longer.

402

— Don't worry. Be happy.

— I worry and I am not happy.

— Blanco is going to be fine.

I order a bottle of good Brunello and we choose two more cigars. The night is still young and the Sunset Strip is just now beginning to find its mood. When I first moved from Jacumba I rented a place on Horn, just a few blocks from here, but I could only afford to keep it for two months. I had a business to build. But I found myself a Sunset girl, and we had more than our share of moments. Excessive women are easy to identify — they have a visible aura, as excessive men have known for centuries.

I taste the wine and nod, and the waitress pours.

"So, we make El Dorado shortly after midnight. We're escorted in, as usual. It's a moonless night and I can feel tension in the air. A helicopter circles steadily high above. Laws is a bloody spectacle, but luckily, he always traveled with a change of clothes. He excuses himself to change. The American women are not to be seen, and Herredia is preoccupied. Felipe keeps his one good eye extra close on me.

"But the unpacking and weighing go smoothly. Felipe weighs and repackages our share. Laws doesn't say much, and neither does Herredia. We eat a light meal, and six hours later we're back at the animal hospital.

— Blanco is doing very well, says the vet. He's stabilized and resting. I think he's going to be okay.

—What did I tell you? asked Laws.

"The doctor nods and looks at Blanco asleep in the crate. Laws signs off on the fourteen-hundred-dollar charge and carries the crate to the Touareg. I get the bag of pills and ointments and I see the vet's relieved expression as we walk out.

"San Ysidro is hazy and slow in the winter dawn. I look out the window and see something beautiful in this place. And a feeling tries to come to me that I haven't felt in a while — not since Terry had made a fool of himself after the fishing trip. The feeling is that everything is going to be okay. *Okay.* What a sound that word has, when you hear it clearly and you believe it. I look over at Terry and of course he's got Blanco on his lap and a peaceful gaze on his face as he looks down on the thing. Madonna and child, whatever, I think, whatever happens next is going to be okay. And as soon as you tell yourself that everything's going to be okay, that's when the gods choose to demolish your hopes, right? So get a load of this.

Here's what Terry says next.

— Do you ever feel like confessing to all this? Just putting it all down, in words or on a tape in your own voice? Not necessarily so anybody could hear it. Just to relieve your soul.

— No, Terry. I've never, ever thought that. Not even for one second.

"The adrenaline hits me like lightning. I truly cannot believe what Terry is saying, though I hear it very clearly. *A confession!*

— You haven't done that, have you, Terry? Made a tape, or written something down?

— Maybe.

— You either have or you haven't.

— I haven't. I was kidding.

— But Terry, if you were going to confess, how would you do it?

— DVD. That way it's me, my voice, my face. My whole visible and audible being. And there wouldn't be any doubt that I was coerced or framed. It would be the truth. I'd start with Eichrodt and work my way forward."

— And what about me, Terry?

— What about you? You're my partner, and we did most of this together. I'd take half the blame for Vasquez and Lopes. Just because I didn't have the balls to shoot him doesn't mean I'm less guilty than you. But

I'd have to include you. This is about truth. You have to put in the whole truth or it's just another facet of a lie. Right? See what I'm saying?"

I pour another glass of wine for each of us. Bradley is studying me with new eyes because he now sees that I had a reason to kill Terry Laws. But he knows I did not kill Terry, because I am not Londell Dwayne, or whoever Hood saw that night. So Bradley is wondering, as is all of L.A., who killed Laws? And why? Of course, I know the answer to both of those questions. And I'll tell them to Bradley when I think he's ready to crash through the next wall of truth.

36

"Four nights later, a Tuesday, we're patrolling the desert out of Lancaster substation. It's cold. I'm still stunned by Terry's idea of confessing. These are the most dangerous words he's ever spoken to me. He's my friend and I'm the only thing standing between him and Herredia. But now I see that I might not be able to save Terry from himself. I feel as if I've had a judgeship forced upon me, that Herredia's prosperity and Laws's life and my own future have been melted into heavy slag and poured into my lap.

"I look out at the new strip mall and the off-brand gas station and the young black dude in the lowered red Nissan with the brindle pit bull in the front seat beside him sticking its thick blunt snout into the wind.

— That's Londell Dwayne, says Laws.

— It's not Londell's car.

— I didn't know he had a dog.

— He probably just stole them both.

— That's what I was thinking.

"So we follow the red Nissan for two blocks up Twentieth Street then flash him and hit the siren once and the Nissan cuts across the dusty shoulder and comes to a stop. Laws is out first. He marches to the driver's side of the Nissan. He's not moving with his usual hulking amble, but a purposeful stride. I walk around the back of Londell's car to the passenger side, rest the big four-battery flashlight on my shoulder and aim the beam through the front side window. No passengers except the dog. There are two unopened twelvers of Rainier on the backseat. No other cargo or obvious contraband. Just Londell Dwayne, looking up as he talks to Laws, and the dog looking at me through the glass. It's bigger than the brindle that tore up Blanco at Hector's last Friday night. It looks healthy and groomed but parts of its ears are missing and there are old scars on both sides of its muzzle. I turn off the flashlight and watch Laws over the roof of the car.

— Nice ride, Londell. Where did you steal it?

— This car is a loaner, my man. Lattie's friend's brother.

— Let's see the paper and your license.

"I watch Londell dig out a wallet and hand his license to Laws. Then he reaches across to the glove box and I pop the holster strap and set my hand on the butt of my gun. The pit bull shifts its front feet and what's left of its ears seem to stiffen. Londell looks up at me with his usual sleepy wiseass expression, then opens the glove box and fishes around for the registration slip, and hands it over to Terry.

— Tell me about Lattie's friend, says Laws.

— His name is Keeshawn and he's a good dude. Keeshawn's visiting from L.A. He lent me this ride so I could get us some beer. You will find that exhibit in the seat behind me, not getting colder, by the way.

— Whose dog is this?

— My dog, rescued from bad people and now living the good life in beautiful Antelope Valley.

— What's the dog's name?"

— She a bitch, not a dog. And her name is Delilah.

— So that makes you Samson?

— That is not the connotation. She's beautiful and desired by other pit bulls. It's got nothing to do with me.

— Step out of the car, Londell.

— Yes, sir, Mr. Lawman.

"I watch Londell climb out of the little

car, and I see that the dog is eager to follow him, but she holds herself in check. She leans toward the now empty driver's seat, tail wagging hopefully. The door slams and the dog climbs into the driver's seat and watches her master. I wait until Laws has Dwayne up against the car before I walk back to our unit and call in the plates. I watch Laws and Dwayne bathed in the cruiser headlights. Their figures are exaggerated by the lights and the shadows cast beyond them. They look like stage actors illuminated from below. Dwayne is slender and of medium height, but he looks huge in the bright lights.

"I see Laws, steadying Dwayne's back with one hand and running his other hand down Londell's rib cage. Then Terry switches hands and sides. He reaches around under Dwayne's sweatshirt, at the waistband of his baggies. Then all of a sudden, Laws hops back with a gun in his raised right hand, then hops back again, quickly out of range in case Dwayne turns and lunges for it.

— Londell? Homes! What is *this?*

— That's my hundred percent legal, twenty-five-caliber semiautomatic self-defender I got at a gun show at the fairgrounds.

— But you concealed it. That's against the law. Makes me think you might want to use it on my partner or me.

"The plate check comes through, so I hook the radio handset back in its cradle, and walk back to the Nissan.

— Hot ride, I say.

— No! You cannot make a case against Keeshawn owning this car! It cannot be!

"Laws hands the gun to me. Then he cuffs and Mirandizes Londell, and spins him roughly around. The sudden movement sends the dog growling. It's a scary sound. I can see her breath against the window glass. Her jaw muscles ripple into chevrons and her ears go flat to her head.

—You fight that dog, Londell? asks Terry.

— No way! She's my beauty girl. She's no fighter.

— I think you're lying. I think you fight her to make money. Look, she's chewed up.

— She's chewed up because she used to fight. She never been in a fight ring since I got her. Never.

— I'll bet you breed her for it, too. To make more dogs you can fight with, make more money.

— If I ever made one dollar off Delilah I request that you show it to me.

— I got a fighting dog at home, says Terry.

411

I rescued him from the pit. I've seen people shot and stabbed but you know what? Most every one of them either asked for it or deserved it. But that little dog of mine, just about ripped apart? He didn't ask for any part of it.

— You arrest me, what's going to happen to my dog?

— You don't deserve that dog.

— Deputy, things regarding Delilah can seriously piss me off. She's the one part of me you shouldn't mess with.

— I'll take care of her.

— No, man! No you won't! You think she's a fighter and she isn't. You leave Delilah alone.

— Or what, Londell?

— Or I'll smoke your white ass.

— You just threatened a police officer, Londell.

— I sure *did,* Deputy Lawman.

"Laws yanks Dwayne away from the Nissan and toward the cruiser. Skinny Londell looks like a straw man in Laws's grip. Delilah bares her teeth and her lips quiver and her only sound now is a soft, guttural rumble. I hold open the left rear cruiser door and Laws shoves Londell in. Dwayne can't move his arms so he pitches forward and hits his head on the steel protection screen. When he rights himself and looks at us, I see on his face a powerful desire for violence. It surprises me. I can see that whatever Dwayne is thinking, he would *do* it. He had fully given himself over to the idea of it.

"The jail transport unit shows up ten minutes later and two deputies move Londell out of the cruiser and into the transport van. And while he makes that walk, Dwayne gives Laws a long killah stare. He's got a deputy clamped to each arm. He's singing something to himself and shuffling his feet and weaving and bobbing his shoulders like a boxer entering the ring but his hands are still pinned tight behind his back and his black eyes never leave Terry. I was impressed by this. Very impressed."

"But why?" asks Bradley. "There's nothing impressive about being mad."

"Because I've never been truly angry at anybody in my life. Not angry enough to do what Londell wanted to do. To me, anger had always seemed a primitive and distracting emotion. But to witness it untethered and wild, as in Londell, gave me a new respect for its power. And all of this anger, *because of a dog!*"

"I understand the anger," says Bradley. "It's a simple reaction. Like ripples in a

413

pond when you throw in a rock."

"Then you probably believe that Londell murdered Terry."

"Of course he did. The description in the papers was Londell. Right down to the Tigers hoodie. He had motive, motive enough to impress you."

I smile and relight my cigar and signal the waitress. I order a bottle of Napa Valley Claret that I've had before.

"Of course, Animal Services arrives and they can't figure out how to get a furious pit bull out of a car. Delilah is snarling and snapping at them — dogs *know* the true enemy when they see him. There's a black dog catcher and a white one. They have a noose and a tranquilizer gun. White says if one of them cracks a door and tries to lower a window for the noose or the gun, the dog is going to chew his arm off. Black says if they break a window the dog's going to run away and get hit by a car or bite someone, or maybe both. White says they could tow the car to impound and take it in the high bay and close the bay doors then break the window and the dog couldn't run off.

— I'll take care of the dog, says Laws.

— How? asks Black.

— You guys just piss her off. Beat it. I'll take care of this animal.

— We've got a job to do here, says White. We're trained to do it.

— Clear out, ordered Laws. Do it now.

"When those clowns are gone, we go get Terry's truck at headquarters and then head back to Londell's Nissan. The dog is sitting in the driver's seat, watching us. We stand a few feet away and wait a while; Terry says Delilah needs a few minutes to get used to us. Then Terry goes to the car and reaches for the driver's door. The dog hops over the center console and settles neatly in the passenger seat, and Terry gets in.

"He shuts the door and starts talking in a deep and calm voice. I can't hear the words. Terry talks on and on, like he's telling the dog the details of a baseball game or the Dow Jones. A moment later he gets out of the car, steps back and kneels down and claps his hands once softly. Then Laws says, *Come on, honey,* and he claps his hands again and Delilah bows her head and wags her tail and climbs into the driver's seat, then, very ladylike, she steps down into the dirt and goes to Terry. He doesn't touch her. He stands and walks to his truck with the dog following, and he opens the passenger seat like she's his date, and he taps on the front seat and Delilah jumps in. Terry comes over to the unit and stands with me, and the dog watches him. A few minutes later our tow truck angles off the road and stops. The driver gets out to size up the Nissan.

— What are you going to do with the dog, Terry?

— Take her home.

— She should be at the pound.

— She's better off with me.

— What if something happens to her on your watch? Londell threatened you. He's crazy enough to do something.

— Don't worry about Londell. He'll appreciate this when he cools down.

— If he cools down.

"We lean against our prowl car and watch the tow truck driver hoist the Nissan onto the ramp, then raise the ramp and the car onto the back of the truck. Finally the heavy contraption roars slowly onto Twentieth Street and we're alone on the dark edge of town.

— I did it and it's over and I feel better, says Terry.

— You did *what?*

— I told the truth. All of it.

— This talk of confession doesn't amuse me, Terry. It goddamned bothers me is what it does.

— I walked out into the hills a few nights

416

ago and I told the sky, Coleman. That's all. It needed to be said.

— Did you record it?

— No.

— Was Laurel with you?

— Of course not.

— Was anyone?

— Yeah. God himself was there. His Son was there and the Holy Ghost, too. It's okay, Coleman. The truth has been told. The past has no power over me now. I'm free.

— Terry.

— What?

— Nothing.

— I'll never do anything like that again.

"For a while we stay there, leaning against the cruiser, me with my arms crossed and Laws with his hands folded together in front of him. We both look up at the stars.

— Shift is about over, Terry.

— See you back at the station, Cole.

"I watch Laws's truck bounce onto Twentieth Street. I feel betrayed and alone and empty. I walk into the desert a few hundred yards, out where the streetlights and strip mall lights mean almost nothing, and I wonder how one man can look at the sky and stars and see God, and another sees only sky and stars.

"Who was the fool there — Terry or me?

Both of us? All I could really say was that I had badly misread Laws. The same square-jawed decency that had made it possible for Terry to carry on a secret criminal life had grown into weakness, shame, guilt, and a craving for penance and forgiveness. Terry's weakness had led him to God instead of the devil. This had surprised me. I had been wrong."

"Three hours later, son of a bitch if Terry doesn't call, just as I'm turning onto Laguna Canyon Road. I know why he's calling even before he speaks. I know what he's going to say.

— She got away, says Laws.

— Of course she did, Terry. That's what scared dogs do.

— We were fine all the way to my house. I parked in the driveway. Blanco was barking from inside. Delilah heard it and she bristled up like she was being dropped into the pit. She went for my arm. It really hurts. Deep punctures and the skin is light purple and green already. I got her off and she hit the ground running. Way into the hills. Laurel got a dish towel around my arm and I got my flashlight and went after Delilah. It's black up there, man. I couldn't find her. I heard the coyotes yapping. That's going to be one helluva fight if they attack her."

— Use lots of rubbing alcohol, Terry. Really get it clean.

— Laurel scrubbed it out like a stained coffee cup. Goddamn, it hurts.

— Okay, Terry, don't worry. We're going to figure it out.

— I'm not worried about Dwayne. But I am worried about Delilah.

— Don't worry about Dwayne or Delilah.

— And Coleman, what I said? About what I did in the hills a few nights ago? I'll never do anything like that again.

— You've told me twice that you won't do it again. Why *twice,* Terry?

— It helps me believe in myself.

"So, Bradley, there I am, talking to a partner who must repeat himself in order to believe in himself. This is the partner I've chosen. I feel as if I have a thousand pounds of rusted iron inside me. For a moment I think about cashing out, just selling the properties and disappearing to Fort Lauderdale or Dallas or Boulder. But you know something? I'm a native son, born in this great state, and I didn't want to surrender my turf to Terry Laws or *El* fucking *Tigre* or anybody else. I belong here. Here is where I'm going to live and die.

— Take care of your arm, Terry.

— I'm thinking I might have to miss El Do this Friday. Because of the bite. And miss some patrol shifts for a while.

— Come back when you're ready. I can cover you south of the border.

— Can you cover me for two or maybe three Fridays?

— Okay.

— And all the rest of them, after that? You wouldn't have to split anything with me ever again! No. I'm kidding. That's some other guy talking. You know the real me. You know what I'm made of, Cole.

—Yes, I do.

37

Friday evening — time to go fishing, time to build a dream — was cool and eager to be dark. A cold Aleutian storm was set to hit by midnight and the air felt brittle.

Hood followed Draper's M5 east on Venice Boulevard to the 10 to the 5 to the 710, the same route as before into the heart of Cudahy and Hector Avalos's former kingdom.

Again he parked well away from the warehouse. He settled into the seat of his rented Charger and watched the stationary, unflashing red X on the laptop map. Evening turned to night without a sunset, just a failure of light behind the advancing clouds.

Ninety minutes after he parked the X started flashing again and a moment later Draper's car crossed the avenue a block ahead. Hood waited, then followed him to Interstate 5, the same way he'd gone before.

The Friday night traffic was light into

Orange County. There was no accident this time, so they sailed through Santa Ana and down into Irvine and past Laguna, invisibly linked. Draper exited on Palizada in San Clemente, just as he had the last time, and he drove through the same fast-food place, and for all Hood knew he got the same thing to eat.

On the dark, fast run through Camp Pendleton Hood settled in five cars behind him, then fell back a few, then moved over and closer for a few miles. He watched the red X. He looked out at the Pacific to his right, black and shiny as obsidian. He thought of Ariel Reed.

Then, with a bright shower of sparks the M5 veered sharply out of the fast lane, cut across three more lanes and barreled onto the shoulder.

Hood sped past and worked his way to the right shoulder a mile south of where the M5 had pulled off. He checked the screen. The X wasn't flashing or moving. Through the back window of the Charger he could see the M5, flashers on, parked on the shoulder a mile behind, near the top of a slight rise.

Hood's first thought was a blowout and the exposed wheel sparking on the freeway. But the M5 hadn't hobbled off. It looked fine, except for the sparks spraying out from beneath the back end. His second thought was road debris — a muffler or hubcap or body trim or something metallic that had fallen from another vehicle and caught underneath the car. And if Draper gets under the car to look for damage or dislodge something caught there, Hood thought, he could see the transponder.

He got out of the car and stood looking back up the freeway. The cars and trucks roared past in an endless speeding river. He got the Night Hunter binoculars from the front seat and steadied them on the roof of the Charger. At first he didn't see Draper, just the M5. Then Draper rose into view near the driver's side of his car, annoyedly brushing off one shoulder of his leather bomber's jacket. He walked around to the other side and dropped out of sight again. A moment later he stood, holding what looked like a long strip of body molding. It was bent and dented and shiny. Hood watched him chuck it onto the shoulder and smack his hands together and climb back into the car.

Then Draper's emergency lights went off and the M5 moved forward on the shoulder, signaling a merge into the right lane. Hood pulled into the slow lane and puttered along at about fifty for a minute or so, keeping an eye on the X and the rearview. The X gained on him and Draper raced past in the middle lane, sparkless and fast, apparently making up for lost time.

Next came an uneventful thirty minutes at seventy miles an hour that took them down into San Diego and toward the border. The X blinked comfortingly. Hood's guess was that Draper hadn't found the tracking device. Working in the dark under a low-slung car, there was a very good chance that he'd missed it. Hood thought it was possible that Draper *had* found it, and had the presence of mind to leave it on and act normal while he hatched a plan.

The rain started at the San Diego city limit. It was light and uneven and the roadside trees shined and swayed in the breeze.

Suddenly, Draper broke pattern and swung off the 5 and onto Interstate 8, heading east. Hood followed, past the college and La Mesa and El Cajon and Alpine. As he left the sprawl of cities the darkness of the land met the darkness of the sky and the traffic thinned and he fell farther back. He called Warren to tell him about Draper's car hitting the debris, and his abrupt change of route. Warren said it was pouring rain in

L.A., high wind, flights grounded at LAX and wrecks all over the place.

"Stay back and don't pressure him," said Warren. "The center of this storm is headed your way. Be cool."

"Always cool."

"I mean it, Charlie. If you get out of cell range you're on your own. If Draper saw the transponder you're the hunter and the hunted."

Hood followed Draper into Cleveland National Forest, hills black, rain steady. An occasional light twinkled far out in some valley or high up on a hill, but they were tiny in the vast darkness. Hood thought that Draper was heading for the border crossing at Tecate. Then he thought Draper was going to Jacumba — home turf. Hood stayed a mile behind, with three vehicles steadily between them. To his right trucks groaned up the grade while on his left a yellow Corvette passed him, easily going a hundred, and Hood thought of Allison Murrieta, who was driving a yellow Z06 the night he pulled her over for speeding and changed their lives and a lot of other people's lives forever. Again Hood wondered if he had been one block south, or maybe back at the donut shop getting coffee, or if he'd pulled a different beat that night, he might never have laid eyes on her and who knew, maybe she'd still be alive.

A mile before the McCain Valley Road turnoff Draper signaled and moved into the exit lane. The rain was heavier and it was harder to see his lights. Hood couldn't follow him without announcing myself so he stayed where he was and drove past the exit and when he was out of sight he braked and pulled onto the center divider and made a wide, slow U-turn. He parked, turned off the lights and watched the blinking red X. Draper was heading southeast on old Highway 80 toward Jacumba, the last American outpost on the screen, bordered on the south by black, blank Mexico.

Hood wondered if Draper had planned all along to cross in Jacumba tonight, illegally. Draper would know the back ways in and out. He'd know them very well.

Or, he might have stopped there just to gas his car, or drive by his old home, or the restaurant his family used to own, then back onto the interstate to cross legally at Tecate or Calexico.

But maybe he knew he was being followed and he was about to destroy the transponder, vanish into the topography of his boyhood, cache his treasure, and make his way back home to L.A. in a day or a week or a

426

month or never.

The red X moved slowly toward Jacumba. Hood looked in the direction of the town, just a faint nest of light cradled in the dark border hills.

He checked his cell phone but there was no service this far out. The rain drummed on the roof of the car. Hood knew that if Draper had found the transponder, the game was over. But if he hadn't found it, then Hood was still a secret shadow. Draper wasn't driving like a man on the run. Hood wondered if he was making too much of a piece of highway debris caught up in a rear end strut.

The X made Jacumba in five minutes. Hood watched it turn onto Railroad. At the Calipatria intersection it stopped. He remembered Amigos Restaurant, once owned by the Draper family. Four minutes later the X began moving again. This time it backtracked to Railroad, then went north toward Draper's boyhood home, now owned by his friend Israel Castro.

Hood sat there for thirty minutes, watching the red X. It neither blinked nor moved. Unable to resist a better look, he swung onto the interstate, then took McCain Valley Road to old Highway 80. As the interstate receded in his rearview mirror, the dim and scattered lights of Jacumba waited ahead.

Then he was there. He drove slowly past Amigos Restaurant, circled and drove by again. An older couple hustled out into the parking lot with newspapers over their heads. A younger couple with an umbrella went in. A young man in a white straw cowboy hat stood smoking outside the front door. The rain came off the awning in slanting silver and the Amigos sign wobbled in the wind. The bar looked busy. Behind the glass brick windows Hood saw the silhouettes of patrons, and a string of what looked like Christmas lights blinking above them.

He drove to Draper's old home and parked down the street in the darkness. Home was where people went. There were lights on in the house and in the garage. Ten minutes later the garage door went up. The M5 was there, alongside a black Durango. Draper and another man stood behind the BMW, looking into the open trunk. Hood recognized Israel Castro from a newspaper picture of him addressing the El Centro Rotary Club. They were talking, apparently, about what was inside. Draper had missed the transponder, thought Hood: I've got you.

Draper had put on a dark baseball cap.

From where Hood sat he could hear nothing but the sound of the rain on the roof of the Charger. Then Draper closed the trunk and got into the car. He backed out and the garage door closed on his friend and the Durango.

Draper backed up all the way through the chain-link gate, which opened automatically. Hood could hear the rumble of the M5 and see the dust swirling about his taillights as Draper slowly picked his way back to Railroad.

But, watching the red X, Hood saw that instead of going north toward town, Draper was taking Railroad south toward the border. He gave Draper a few minutes to get well ahead, then he started up the Charger and followed. He wondered again if he was following or being led.

Soon the few and scattered lights of the city were behind him. According to his GPS locator the M5 was a mile ahead, but he could see nothing of it — no taillights, no shine of paint or reflection of glass — only the tire tracks left in the soft mud of the road. He turned off his headlights and found his way in the faint light. Then he felt the car bump and the rough road become smooth, and he felt asphalt beneath his tires. Hood looked at the locator map and saw that they were now in a place where the roads had no names, paved or not.

Near the top of a minor rise he stopped, got out and pulled on a blanket-lined canvas coat and an old oilcloth cowboy hat for the rain. He walked to the crest and glassed a wide valley. The scrub was dark and the boulders were pale and dulled by the rain. But the field glasses took advantage of the slight ambient light, giving Hood a decent view. Raindrops rapped against his hat. He saw the M5 creeping along below, no headlights for Draper now, either, just red taillights and the running lights moving through the rough country. The car made a wide curve to the right and disappeared.

A few minutes later Hood stopped where he had last seen the M5. The flashing red light issued from half a mile away but from here Draper's car was invisible. The great black mystery of Mexico filled the bottom third of the monitor. Again Hood got out, quietly nudging the door closed with his hip. From behind a boulder he glassed the scene below.

A metal building stood at the bottom of a wide swale. It looked like an airplane hangar, or a machine shop, with a big rolling door large enough for cars and trucks. From where Hood rested on the boulder he could hear the sound of a generator, and the rain drumming on the roof. The building was unlit until the M5 pulled up. Then it was flooded in hard, bright light.

Draper let himself into the building through a side door. Lights went on inside. A moment later Hood heard the hum of a motor and the rattle of the metal door rolling up. Draper stood for a moment in the doorway, lit from inside. Hood could see a dusty old car behind him, and a black dune buggy with fat tires, and a couple of small dirt bikes. Slowly Hood lowered the binoculars and set them on the boulder in front of him and waited to see what Draper would do.

Draper pulled the M5 in and parked it beside the dune buggy. Then he got out and opened the trunk again with the key fob and he pulled out two suitcases.

He's going to make the run through the hills tonight, thought Hood. No checkpoints, no Customs. Just friendly faces and familiar trails on a rainy night, and Mexico only a mile away.

Suddenly, light hit the boulder in front of Hood. He could see the grains in the rock.

"Do not turn. If you see my face you die. Raise your hands slowly."

Hood didn't know the voice. It was a

man's voice, calm and certain. He raised his hands. Far below he could see Draper looking up at him.

"I'm a Los Angeles Sheriff deputy," said Hood. "I've got ID in my wallet. Think about what you're doing."

"Do not move."

Hood heard footsteps coming fast, then felt a gun barrel against his back. The man roughly popped the snap and pulled the .45 from his belt holster and Hood heard it land on the ground behind him. Draper was leaning against the trunk of the M5, still watching.

When the man behind him bent to run a hand down his calf, Hood lifted the binoculars by their strap, turned fast and whipped them down on the man's head as hard as he could. The heavy glasses hit like a mule kick. The man went over in a heap. Hood pulled the gun from his limp hand and turned off the hiker's headlight. Then he rolled the guy onto his face and cuffed him with a plastic restraint. Hood was expecting Israel Castro, but this man was older — forties, dark hair and a dark mustache. Behind the Charger, Hood saw a small dune buggy, black and chromeless, made for running almost invisibly on dark nights like this.

When he looked back down at the metal

building Draper was gone and the power door was rolling closed.

38

Hood's prisoner was out cold. The cut on his scalp was bleeding, but not hard. Hood used the hiker's headlight to find his gun, then he slid the gunman's forty-caliber into his jacket pocket.

He locked the Charger and began the descent, stepping sideways down the embankment. There was prickly pear and cholla cactus, and the rocks were loose and slick from the rain.

By the time he made the building the rolling door had clanged into place and the lights had gone off. There was still a slit of light from inside, visible at the bottom of the rolling door, and the rough sound of the generator burning gas to make electricity.

He drew his gun and put his hand on the doorknob. He took a deep breath, then threw open the door and rushed inside, weapon up. Close to the M5 he ducked down and scanned the concrete floor for feet. Just a dusty car and a black dune buggy and two small BMX bikes with dirt-covered tires and exhaust pipes.

Draper was gone and so was the luggage. The rain hit the metal roof. The generator labored patiently in one corner. Gun still up, Hood went through a door and into a smaller room. There was a desk and chair, and a couch. Shop lamps burned overhead. No windows. On the floor between the couch and the desk was a woven Mexican blanket with pictures of jumping swordfish on it. He knelt to catch the light better and saw the muddy footprints on the floor. The blanket was bunched carelessly.

Hood went to a window and looked out and saw nothing. Then he came back to the rug and kicked it into a pile in front of the desk. Beneath it was a sheet of plywood fitted into the concrete floor. It was about a yard square, with a black enameled handle screwed onto each side. He chose a side and lifted, then pulled away the plywood.

Below him was a cavern approximately ten feet square. A ladder down. There, another generator along one wall, vented with metal flex tube through the ceiling of the tunnel. Two red gasoline containers. And a light-bulb hanging by a wire that ran down a tunnel, overhead and out of sight. The tunnel walls were framed with two-by-fours, and the bottom planked with two-by-sixes.

His training told him to stop right here, retreat and come back in daylight, with help. But that was a long wait, a cold trail, and hours for Draper to disappear, hide evidence, reappear. Standing on the ladder and reaching up, he moved the rug over the opening as best he could, then pulled the wooden door fully into place. It thumped solidly shut. A wiggle of fear came up Hood's back and crawled across his scalp.

When he got down into the cavern he strapped the hiker's headlight on and walked into the tunnel.

Smuggler's tunnels are not long. A tunnel is a slow and difficult thing to make, and once located by an enemy, they are pure liability. Two hundred feet is average. Hood knew the Mexican border was close, but he didn't know how close.

The light was good and the tunnel was straight for twenty steps. It went right. The overhead lights were twenty feet apart. It was cold and Hood heard the patient drip of water. Between the walkway slats he saw the oily blue reflection of light on pooled liquid.

The tunnel went on. Twice more it made

a right turn of thirty degrees. On his fiftieth step Hood stopped and listened. Still, the drip and the distant groan of the generator. The lights flickered off, came back on.

Hood felt the proximate terror of being underground. He was mildly claustrophobic and he felt the first flicker of panic deep inside him, sharp and small, a spark made by flint. He ignored it.

At step one hundred he stopped again. He believed that he was halfway through but this was only a sense in a place that confounded sense. On his one hundred and ninetieth step Hood found himself in a small room. There was a generator here, too, but it was not on. There was a ladder.

He climbed to the top and waited for a long minute. He found it hard to believe that he was a man of sound judgment. There was no light around the edges of the hatch. He heard nothing. He sensed open space on the other side of the wood but again, this was only a feeling.

Hood tested the plywood with the finger-tips of both hands. It rocked slightly.

The hatch opened on hinges to an interior darkness: no stars, no breeze, no rain. In he climbed, closing the hatch and turning on the headlight. He was in a very small room. There were brooms and buckets and a fire extinguisher and two toolboxes and stacks of toilet tissue. He looked down at the wooden door through which he had come, and saw the big red-and-white plate with the graphic bolt of electricity and the electrocuted cartoon man tilting off his feet and the word *Peligroso!*

He pushed open the closet door to rows of student desks. Beyond them was a table and a blackboard stand. There was a Mexican flag in a stand in one corner and a Baja California flag in another. Between them was a sliding glass door through which he saw nothing but darkness. Rain on the roof. Through the dripping windows on his left Hood saw only night, and through the ones on his right flickered the lights of the village of Jacume.

The suitcases from Draper's car — side by side and handles down — stood by the door on the other side of the classroom.

Hood turned off his light and stood still for a moment. He tried to see through the windows but only saw darkness and rain. There was just enough light to pick his way past the rows of desks to the luggage.

The suitcases were heavy. He rolled one onto its back and unzipped it. He turned on the light again and saw newspapers and rocks the size of softballs inside the bag. No cash. The other was packed with the same thing. The papers were the *Los Angeles Times* and *San Diego Union Tribune,* recent dates. The rocks were the ones you'd find all over the vast borderlands between California and Mexico. He turned off the light again and squatted on his haunches beside the suitcases.

Hood realized that Draper had seen the transponder way back in Orange County. Some quick thinking and a call to Israel Castro was all it had taken to turn his luck. Hood figured the money was now headed back to Tijuana from Jacumba in the black Durango, driven by Castro. They'd made the luggage switch in Israel Castro's garage. Draper had drawn him into the labyrinth of Jacumba, then lost him like a fox playing a hound. Hood saw that the man with the gun was supposed to deliver him to Draper, or a shallow grave in a big desert. The cost of huge error began to settle on him.

An engine started outside and headlights suddenly splashed against a window. He saw the big SUV, tucked back in the darkness until now, lumbering toward the classroom through the rain. Then two more sets of headlights blazed to life from the darkness on the other side of the building, and the vehicles converged through the night.

Hood scrambled back to the closet and flung open the hatch and started down the ladder. But even before he reached the bottom he heard the footsteps pounding through the tunnel toward him, closing fast. He reached out and yanked the electrical line from the tunnel frame. The line slapped down and fixtures sparked and the circuit shorted and there was nothing but blackness and the cursing of men less than a hundred feet away.

He struggled out and let the plywood drop into place and closed the closet door. He stood in the classroom and surveyed his few options. The only door was at the front of the room and Hood was at the back. Through the windows on his right he saw the dark SUV hunker to a stop and the doors fly open. To his left, the two other vehicles slid to a stop.

Hood saw his chance. He pulled the heavy oilcloth hat down hard, holstered his gun and zipped the canvas jacket to his chin. Then he jammed his fists deep down into the pockets and ran toward the slider. He tried to think of a prayer but couldn't.

Outside someone racked a shotgun. The front door shuddered from a kick. Hood hunched his shoulders and launched himself headfirst through the glass.

It was cheap and thin, and Hood broke through with a shower of shards. He slipped and faltered but stayed up, then took off running for the darkness where he could not be seen. He fell down a steep embankment and rolled, hitting rocks and branches, then sprawled into a bed of rusted cans and bottles and litter at the bottom of the barranca. He was breathing hard as he pulled a long triangle of window glass from his cheek. Then he was upright and climbing the bank on the other side. He heard voices behind him and he saw men and the shapes of men in the headlights of an SUV barreling in his direction.

Hood topped the ridge, then jumped down and cut toward Jacume. There was a narrow pathway to follow — a game trail, or maybe a motorcycle path through the dense brush. But almost instantly he heard the rumble of the SUV close behind him and he saw the headlights strafe the ground ahead. He scrambled down into another barranca leading into further darkness. He was no longer sure what country he was in. The flashlight beams crisscrossed around him like the strands of a spider's web. He clawed up a hill.

The first gunshot cracked and the bullet hit the ground in front of him. Then another. The SUV groaned closer through the brush and the flashlight beams closed in.

The gunfire came fast and brief, as in the alleys of Anbar, and a bullet hit him down low on the side of his back. It felt like he'd been kicked by a horse. He fell forward and got to his knees in the mud. It didn't hurt but he felt a terrible, terrible disappointment. He drew his gun and turned and fired off three shots at the vehicle windshield. The glass shattered and dropped like a blanket of diamonds. The SUV veered wildly and flipped.

Hood stood and ran but he could gain no speed. His heavy canvas jacket was soaked by rain, and his oilcloth hat seemed to weigh thirty pounds, and his side suddenly felt like a red-hot poker had gone through it. His hand came away from it black with blood. He was short of breath and suddenly, extremely tired.

He made it up a hill to an outcropping of rocks. He crawled into them and found good cover and a place to brace his gun. He thought of the hundreds of westerns he'd seen and the hundreds of boulders that men had died behind. He thought about not making thirty years old. And he thought this was a rough place we live in, where a bunch of bad guys could run down one decent cop and murder him right under God's nose. It wasn't even personal.

He looked out at the flashlights flickerng toward him, then at the SUV, overturned on a hillside with the headlights still on and its wheels still turning. The men converged with short, purposeful steps. Hood could see mist in the light beams. He knew they didn't know exactly where he was, only that he was close and armed. He was irrationally happy that they didn't have dogs. He steadied the handle of the forty-five on the rough boulder and waited for someone to come into range. He thought of Ariel Reed, and Allison Murrieta, his mom and dad, his brothers and sisters. With awful surprise, he realized that his life had been short.

Then the world in front of him went white. The men froze in a bright blizzard and their flashlight beams vanished, and the SUV was blanched by snow. A wind came up behind Hood and he thought, Oh, so this is how it happens: the light comes and brings the wind, and the wind lifts you out of your body and you become the wind, rising up through the rain and into the kingdom of air and sky.

Hood realized another thing: there's this tremendous roar. It comes suddenly and it's really loud, then it gets even louder. It's rhythmic and monstrous and powerful. Your enemies scatter.

And then the roar lowers from the sky and pivots to the ground on runners. It's an official machine, God's own, an emblem on the side, spilling out angels with guns.

So you push yourself up and stumble or roll or crawl or all three down the hill to greet them.

39

He spent three days at a hospital in San Diego. He ate a lot of food and took a lot of blood. Warren showed up the first day and debriefed him for his warrant request. He recorded the interview and took notes, and left immediately.

Ariel visited, looking concerned and beautiful. She had won her case. Two weeks until sentencing. In a separate matter, the district attorney himself was deciding the fate of Shay Eichrodt. Ariel told Hood she had recommended that the charges against him be dropped. She'd also had the blower on her dragster reworked, and bought a new set of slicks. She couldn't wait to get behind the wheel again.

Marlon shuffled in, told Hood that he looked like a dweeb and to hurry up and get out of this place. He told Hood to call for backup next time, rather than being an idiot. He also said that Laurel Laws had been calling LASD, to speak to Hood — something about a dog. Hood called her right after Marlon left, and sure enough, Londell Dwayne's dog had returned to their home three weeks after disappearing into the hills. Laurel wanted Hood to come get her, and deliver her back to Londell.

Warren showed up again the hour before he was discharged, and told Hood that he'd be riding home with him.

When they started out Highway 163 the day was clear and cool and the jets zoomed low in and out of Miramar. Hood had a gauze pad taped to his side to drain the gunshot wound — a jagged, unstitched, wildly painful hole from back to front. The flesh around it was black that faded to purple then blue. Hood had three stitches in his right cheek from the glass. He had a plastic hospital bag with more gauze and tape in it, and Betadine, a large bottle of antibiotics and a small one of Vicodin. Warren said that he was a poster cop for lucky.

"The judge issued," he said. "We've got an arrest warrant for Coleman Draper, on suspicion of transporting cash from the sale of narcotics to Mexico."

"But let me guess. You can't find him."

"We staked out his home and business in

Venice. He hasn't shown in three days."

Hood thought of the Laguna and the Azusa properties that Draper owned, and of Juliet Brown and Alexia Rivas. "I've got some ideas where he might be."

"The next time your ideas are dangerous, Hood, wait for backup."

"I thought it was then or never."

"Bullshit. That was a Renegades thing to do. Trust me, Hood — life is much better when you're alive."

"I can't argue that."

"I'm teaming you up with Stekol. You two have one assignment — bring in Draper."

Hood knew that Brian Stekol was the bald black man in the sharp suit who was driving Warren's car the night Terry Laws had died. And that Stekol was a Distinguished Marksman on the LASD shooting team, and a black belt in Judo.

"Whose whirlybird came to my rescue, Lieutenant?"

"A joint task force."

"Which one?"

"Nobody will say because they poached on Mexican soil in order to salvage you."

"Why do that for me?"

"They thought you were an Arellano Cartel captain, being chased down by Herredia's bad guys. The task force had

447

heard about a hot new tunnel — probably the one you found. If they'd have known who you really were, this would be a Mexican morgue and you'd be dead."

Hood thought about this unsettling truth as they headed north for L.A.

Warren said that the joint task force had made no arrests the night of Charlie's shooting, and had not questioned a single suspect. Not Draper, not Castro, not anyone. They had all scattered into the boulders and barrancas and tunnels on the Mexican side — the forbidden zone. The overturned SUV had Mexican plates and had been stolen off a street in La Jolla two years ago.

Warren's real news was that Londell Dwayne had been released on bail the day before. His alibi with Patrice at the Palmdale motel had checked out and the murder rap for Terry Laws had been dropped. He was still up for the Mace and the machine gun and unlawful sex with a minor, but he'd come up with enough cash for the bond.

Hood dozed in the sun coming through the window. His pants got wet and he dug into his bag of tricks and changed the bandage. He had a brief glimpse of old age. It seemed better than the alternative. It was painful when he reached behind him to press the new dressing against his skin. A bullet hole is an ugly thing.

"I want that son of a bitch," he said. "Draper."

"If we share with the DEA they'll nail his ass at the border if he tries it again."

"No. *I* want him. For us."

"That's interagency rivalry, Hood. It's selfish and counterproductive"

"I know what it is. But the Feds don't care about Eichrodt and Vasquez and Lopes."

"I want him for us, too," said Warren.

"Damn this thing hurts."

"Get some rest. Take a few days off."

Hood got up early and drove around the city. The late winter light was beautiful in Silver Lake, and the Sunset Strip seemed docile in the early morning, and even the dark corridors of downtown had a wholeness he had never seen. He had breakfast then drove up to Terry Laws's ranch.

Delilah was a brindle pit bull, a former warrior by the look of her. She greeted Hood with a placid stare from the kitchen floor, where she lay beside Terry's dog, Blanco.

"At first they wanted to kill each other, then they sniffed around and got friendly," said Laurel. "Now I can't keep them apart. Dogs need dogs."

Hood held out one hand and the dogs came over and he bribed them with treats from a pet store. He bribed them more. He slipped a light nylon lead over Delilah's head and wasn't surprised that she barreled along beside him to the Camaro.

"Thanks for taking care of this," said Laurel. "Terry loved dogs."

"You're welcome."

"You going to be okay? Marlon told me."

"Healing up already."

She shook her head. "You guys don't get paid enough. I mean that with all respect."

"Then I take it that way."

With Delilah on the passenger seat beside him, Hood headed north for Lancaster. Gradually the green of L.A. flattened into desert, and Hood saw the yuccas and sage, and the poppies beginning to bloom on the shoulders of the highway. He saw the subdivisions, some populated and some still being built, stretching for miles across the beautiful, affordable desert. He drove past the substation and the park. He realized he wanted to see all the things that he would miss if he had died back in Mexico.

Londell met him in the Subway parking lot. Hood got out of his car and brought Delilah but he had to let go of the leash when she spotted Londell. Londell ran toward her and swept her right off her feet. Hood had the thought that Londell ran differently than the shooter who had killed Terry. Londell looked like the shooter, but he didn't move like him.

"Thanks."

"Glad I could help."

Londell kissed the dog on the nose and swung her around like a dance partner, then set her down. "I didn't kill that muscleman."

"I guess I should thank you."

"And I'm gonna beat that machine gun rap," he said. "I have no idea how it got there. I got no idea how to even use it. None of my prints are on it. No prints at all — wiped clean, right? My belief is the shooter framed me."

"That's not as ridiculous as it sounds."

"It's not ridiculous at all. What's ridiculous is how beautiful Delilah is. Don't she make you happy, just looking at her?"

"Well, she's a good dog, Londell. Didn't give me any trouble at all."

"See you around the 'hood, Hood. Me and Patrice are going to get married soon as it's legal. I'll be a union man by then."

That evening after dark Hood and Stekol got a beat-up Taurus from the motor pool and drove to the Laguna Royale. They made

451

Laguna in a little over an hour. They followed a resident into the parking lot and cruised the place but there was no M5 in sight.

But Juliet was working at Del Mar again.

"Hello, Rick."

"I changed it to Charlie. But this really is Brian."

She looked at them with accustomed doubt. She wore a black sleeveless dress and a string of pearls. "Still in security, or did you change your business, too?"

"It's similar to security."

"I hear a lot of lines." She shook her head and escorted them to the bar.

"You're moving kind of slow tonight, Charlie-Rick."

"Dinged myself."

"I'm reluctant to ask how."

"Coleman knows."

Hood opened his badge wallet and let her read the shield. She studied him more closely now. "Is he dead?"

"I doubt it."

"You're like him."

"Not really."

"I can't talk until later."

"Is he coming in tonight, Juliet? I need to know."

"There's a chance. He usually calls."

452

"You tell me when he does. No reason for a scene here at work."

"You're like him."

After Juliet's work they sat at a corner table in the Marine Room. It was late and the evening was cool and downtown Laguna was quiet. Juliet had put on a black faux fox-collar coat that Hood found to be striking.

He told her they were IA, and what that meant within their department, and some of what he knew about Reserve LASD Deputy Coleman Draper. He told her about Draper's home and business in Venice, his probable connection to the deaths of two men in Los Angeles County, his apparent affiliations with recently murdered Hector Avalos, and with Carlos Herredia's Tijuana cartel. He told her that Draper was manipulative and potentially violent. He didn't tell her about Alexia Rivas or the warrant for Draper's arrest.

She looked at him and Stekol with genuine bewilderment but said nothing when Hood was finished. She sipped her wine and stared out the window.

Then she turned back to them with a skeptical rebuke on her face. "What do you mean by Coleman's 'probable connection' to the deaths of two men? Did you see him kill them?"

"No."

"Did anyone?"

"We have evidence. We have no witness."

"It's very hard for me to imagine him doing such a thing. What do you mean, 'affiliation'? Did you see Coleman with known criminals?"

"In the vicinity of. Coming from and going to."

"Then he could be undercover, working for a different law enforcement organization than yours. Maybe a state one, or even federal."

Hood guessed that Coleman himself had planted this seed. "He isn't working for another department, Juliet. He and his partner framed and beat a man almost to death to cover up a double murder that they committed. It was one of the most brutal things I've ever seen done."

"And you know this as a fact?"

"I have some of it from the man himself. The rest is half-buried but I'm digging it up."

"How can a man that brutal be tender?"

"To get what he wants."

"I've known him for a year and you for ten minutes. You arrive and accuse him of

454

things but he's not here to defend himself. You come here and give me vapors, smoke. I want facts."

Stekol leaned toward her with a glitter of cuff links, impressive in his suit. "Do you know Alexia Rivas?" he asked.

"No. Why?"

"She's a young woman your boyfriend lives with when he's not living with you. This is a fact."

She winced and colored and looked out the window again.

"He owns a home in Azusa, same as he owns your condo," said Hood. "Alexia pays the bills, same as you do here in Laguna. Apparently they have a young daughter."

"Would you lie to me to get what you want?

"I won't lie to you," he said.

"I know cops do that all the time."

"Less than you think."

She took a long sip of the wine, then another, then set the glass back on the table.

"Okay," she said. "Then I won't lie to you. I've never been sure if Coleman is what he said he was. Once I saw a gun. I think he wanted me to see it. He told me he was part of a federal law enforcement organization that required secrecy of fact. *Secrecy of fact.* He said nothing about any other kind of business, or another home. Of course, I knew he had to live somewhere when he wasn't living with me. Our foundation is that I ask no questions about his work. That was our first rule. That was *our* secrecy of fact. And I'll tell you right now that he showed no inclination to violence with me, ever. He was . . . is . . . very empathetic to me. He listens closely and he understands. He is a gentleman. He asks. He doesn't take. He's courteous and generous. He's passionate. His attention is absolute. He lost his entire family to a fire when he was fifteen years old. Sometimes — often — when we're not talking or touching or doing something together, he's quite simply not there. I think he's back with his family."

Hood thought for a moment about how a person can be one way to some people and the complete opposite to others. Nature. Training. Necessity. Juliet was not a fool, but she had been fooled by Coleman Draper.

"Juliet," he said. "Coleman Draper is alone in his own world. The rest of us are only in it to be used. He would explain himself to you with different words. But that's what he does."

She took another long draw on the wine, then held up her glass and rocked it at the waitress.

"When was the last time you saw him?" Hood asked.

"He was home last Tuesday and Wednesday."

"Do you know when he'll come home to you again?"

"There is no plan. There is never a plan."

"That just changed," Hood said. "We're going to make a plan to arrest him. He's dangerous — to you, to everyone. You do the right thing and nobody else will get hurt. Will you help us do that?"

"You strip my illusions and break my heart, then demand civic responsibility?"

"That's right," said Stekol with a smile. "Same thing that happens to us cops every day we show up for work."

The waitress set a glass of wine on the table. Juliet looked at it but didn't drink. "I wondered if he had other women. I convinced myself that it didn't matter. Coleman and I are an arrangement. But I didn't simply fall into it. I jumped. I closed my eyes and jumped."

"You don't owe him anything," said Hood.

"I still don't believe that I've been making love to a murderer. I truly felt it in him at times — love."

"You're not the only one he fooled, Ms.

Brown," said Stekol. "He fooled our whole force. There's hundreds and hundreds of us."

"Can you help us?" Hood asked.

"I will help you."

"No," he said. "*Can* you? Can you fool him? Can you lie to him convincingly? He'll be alert to anything different because now he knows that we know."

She took another long sip of the wine. "I've never been a good liar."

"I'm going to make it easy. If he tells you he's coming, call me before he gets there. If he arrives unannounced, wait until it's safe to call me. Wait an hour. Wait a day."

"And act as if everything is the same."

"He already knows that nothing is the same. So you can't give him any reason to suspect you. If you can't do this, Juliet, say no. It's dangerous — it can come down to a word, a moment, a look. I won't ask you to and you don't have to."

Juliet looked at the men. Having interviewed so many suspects and dealt with so many crooks, Hood had a good sense for the lie. But he also had a good sense for the truth, and some people are not capable of duplicity.

"We never talked," said Stekol. "Erase us from your mind. And put Coleman back in.

Put him back in just like he was before — cute and full of love for you and so intuitive when it comes to your feelings."

"Don't mock me."

"No mockery at all," he said. "If a woman was as good to me as Coleman is to you, I'd be with her every minute I could."

She swirled her wine and frowned down into it. "How sure are you about what he's done?"

"I took a bullet in the back four nights ago because of him," said Hood. "That's how sure I am."

"But what if you're wrong?"

"Then he'll walk and sue us and I'll still have a nice scar to talk about. And you and Coleman can stay together and be happy and look back on what fools we cops were."

"I don't think that that is impossible."

"He betrayed you," said Stekol.

She finished her wine and set down the glass. She didn't look at either of them. "I can do it."

Stekol glanced at Hood. His expression said: *But* will *you?*

40

Draper walked into his Laguna Beach condominium a week later, tan and fit. He set his bags in the entryway but kept the box tucked under his arm. He looked through the sliding glass door at the pale moonlit cove and the glimmering black Pacific and thought of the sliding glass door through which Hood had escaped in Jacume. And he thought of the bad luck of having a U.S. task force apparently mistake his pursuit of lowly deputy Charlie Hood for an upper level cartel disturbance. Because of that, Hood was still alive, and the tunnel was useless, and extra law enforcement attention was now focused on Jacumba and Jacume, and Draper would never work again as a reserve deputy, at least for the LASD. It was a small consolation that he still had his shield and service sidearm.

He heard the faint sound of the TV from

the bedroom, and saw the subtle shift in the light as it played into the hall.

"Coleman?"

Draper stood in the bedroom doorway. "Who else lets himself in here at night?"

"So many. But you're the one I miss."

Draper was not used to sincere greetings from Juliet, even humorous ones. This was an Alexia greeting. It put him on alert though he was tired of being alert.

She was sitting up in bed, surrounded by pillows, a glass of wine on her nightstand. She had on red satin pajamas and a black silk robe with a multicolored dragon on it. She tapped the sheet beside her and he came in and sat there. He handed her the long gold box.

"Things did not go well."

"I tried your number."

"I have a new one."

She opened the box and smiled and touched a blossom. "Beautiful."

He leaned in over the roses and kissed her, just barely touching. He inhaled her breath and gently bit her lip. He took a deep breath of clean cool Laguna air and cut roses and slowly blew it back into her. Her hand was warm on his cheek.

"Disaster, Juliet."

"Did anyone die?"

"Not that kind. The kind that will multiply and complicate, like a tumor."

"I'm very sorry, Coleman. But you look good. Did you draw an assignment in Maui?"

He smiled. They had a standing joke that if secretive, world-hopping Coleman were to travel to Maui for work, he would have to take her. She loved the Grand Wailea. In fact he had fled to Honolulu on forged ID and spent six days lost among the tourists in Waikiki. She parted the lapel of his sport coat just a little, confirming the gun.

"Juliet, I wish it had been Maui."

"Let's just go there on our own."

He looked at her. He instinctively distrusted her eagerness. He had not chosen her for eagerness, but for her stubborn reticence, her pride, her belief that she could fight distance with distance.

He got off the bed and went to the kitchen and poured himself a glass of the wine. The bottle was half-full but there was an empty in the wastebasket under the sink and when he touched the opening his finger and thumb came back wet. She drank more when stressed. So far tonight: emotional, eager, stressed. He looked out at the aimless heave of ocean, and the cracking little waves racing up the sand. He thought that everything might really be okay. Juliet might just be happy to see him, and stressed by work, or by her inability to conceive children, or by life itself. Or not at all. Maybe he was reacting poorly.

He still felt some of the raw surprise and insult he had felt upon seeing the GPS transmitter clamped to the chassis of the M5. But it was more than surprise and insult. It was a total questioning of self. Of his intelligence, his abilities, his preparedness and his luck.

Hood: whistle-blowing, skirt-chasing, slow-to-draw, Bakersfield hick Charlie Hood. When Draper had seen the transmitter, and later the image of Hood himself sitting in the black Charger in Jacumba — caught by a security camera hidden in a tree and transmitted to one of the monitors inside Israel's home — Draper had for the first time in his life felt enmity toward a fellow human. It was a new emotion for him, or at least a sharpening of older ones, and very different in its magnitude. For the first time in his life he truly wanted to kill somebody, rather than simply seeing that it was the easiest and most practical thing to do. Other people had come between him and his desires, but Hood had thrown himself between them. Hood had *seen* him.

She came into the kitchen with her wine-glass and hugged him lightly then went into the living room and turned on the gas fireplace. The flame popped to life behind the ceramic logs. Juliet sat on the leather love seat and crossed her legs under a throw blanket. She looked at the flames.

"Come sit with me," she said. "We can see a beach without tourists and a flame without fire. I'll rub your back."

Draper joined her, set his wineglass on the end table and leaned forward, elbows on knees. He felt her hands on his clenched neck and knotted shoulders. She was empathetic, her strong fingers drawn straight to the trouble spots and the bundled tension. He'd been riding in the SUV that turned over, and he'd wrenched his neck and shoulder. The driver had taken one of Hood's bullets through his hand and gotten safety glass shards in his face.

Draper took a deep breath and let it out. Juliet's thumbs found two mounds of pain on either side of an upper vertebra and she methodically kneaded them away. She was better tonight than usual. Another concern. By the time she finished half an hour later and led him to their bed, Draper was sure that something had happened and he was reasonably sure what it was.

She made love to him with less self-absorption than usual, now more generous and attuned to him. When they were finally finished he held her face against his beating heart and he smelled her tears before he felt them on his skin.

"Talk to me, Juliet."

She sobbed instead.

"When something hurts you it hurts me," he said. "We can't have a beach without tourists and a flame without fire and tears without a reason, all in one night, can we?"

"I've been trying to tell you something."

"I know. What is it?"

"They asked me to betray you. Hood and Stekol."

He felt the adrenaline hit. It wasn't there and then it was. He felt his body fortify itself and his vision take on a new sharpness as he looked to his holster lying on the floor beside his shoes.

"And what did you say?"

"I said yes. I said I would call when you came."

He said nothing while he dressed and slid on the shoulder rig and put on his coat over it. He stood to the side of the bedroom window and looked through the edge of the drawn blinds without touching them. More condos. A street lamp. A peek of Pacific

465

Coast Highway. Headlights and taillights and the glittering parade of chrome, glass and paint.

"Are they watching us now?"

"No. I'm supposed to call."

"How do you know they're not watching us, Juliet? Why would you say that to me?"

"I can't be sure. You have to trust me. I told them I would call, Coleman. I deceived them. But I need to ask you a question."

Draper was glad for the darkness of the room because she couldn't see him. What he had wanted to do to Hood he now wanted to do to Juliet, but the desire was urgent, and here she was, not five feet away, utterly defenseless.

His voice was a mamba in dry grass. *"Ask."*

"Did you kill the men they say you killed?"

He walked to the bed and looked down at her. He lay beside her and again held her head against his heart. He stroked her hair and took the back of her slender neck in his strong right hand, and he pressed his body down the length of hers. "I did not. Before you and the god of beaches, flame, and tears, I swear to you that I've never killed anyone in my life."

"I would know it if you did."

"You would know it if I did."

"I told them you didn't."

"You told the truth."

"They told me about Alexia."

"Alexia is married to my cousin. They rent my property in a town called Azusa. She's not their business, or your worry, Juliet."

She moved her face away from his in order to see him but he knew she would not see him truly enough. Her eyes were wet stones in the darkness.

"I told them we're an arrangement but that's not true any more. I love you, Coleman. With all of my big unruly mess of a heart, I love you."

"I love you, Juliet. I'll call you and tell you what to say to them. I'll tell you what to do."

"I need that now."

Draper glided off the bed and looked again through the crack alongside the blinds then he went to the living room. There was nothing in the bags to incriminate him, nothing that he needed.

The best way out, in case they were watching, was through the sliding glass door, down to the beach, south across the cove and over the rocks, then through the side streets to Coast Highway. A cab would get him up to Newport and he could figure things from there.

He went back into the bedroom and

kissed Juliet on the cheek and told her he loved her again. Her fingers trailed off his face.

Then he unlocked and opened the slider and slipped out and carefully pushed it closed. He was thankful that he could do this instead of jumping through it headfirst like Hood.

He leaned back and skied down the embankment, his shoes filling with beach sand, and when he hit the firmer floor of the cove he kept to the shadows of the rocks and loped south.

41

Saturday night was starless and damp, a night for secrets and consequence.

Draper steered the Touareg south on I-5, past the power plant and on to Pendleton. He looked to the place he had pulled over to retrieve the piece of chrome trim caught under the chassis of the M5, and reminded himself that this had been a curse that he could still turn into a blessing.

"So, this is all we do?" asked Bradley. "We drive a few hours and I make five grand?"

"This is all we do."

"Rocky doesn't trust me."

"You'll have to do better with Herredia."

"He's not famous for trusting. I heard he used a cartel rival for chum on one of his fishing trips. He personally cut up the pieces."

Draper heard no worry in the boy's voice. Bradley looked out at the ocean, slid his automatic from the deep pocket of his duster, considered it, then put it back. Next he brought out a pack of chewing gum, gave a stick to Draper and took one for himself.

"I saw the flash of green once," the boy said absently. "Right there, off Trestles. I was sitting on my board outside, waiting for the set. It was November and when the sun went behind the water there was a green rectangle and it sat on the sky then it was gone."

"I watched three sunsets in a row from Mallory Dock in Key West," said Draper. "I never saw any flash of green or anything else."

But it was dark now, the sun hours down, and Draper aimed his thumb toward the box in the backseat. "What's your gift for *El Tigre?*"

"You'll see. A lot more impressive than your collection of fishing trinkets."

Draper enjoyed the boy's truculence and was annoyed by it, too. Earlier, when Bradley had loaded his box into the backseat, Draper had seen that it was heavy. The boy handled it with care. It was a square pasteboard box, big enough for a computer or a small TV perhaps, sealed with clear packing tape.

"So," said Bradley. "Where we picked up the luggage and weighed the money, that's not the usual place, right?"

"Why do you think that?"

"There was an air of uncertainty."

"It was more than uncertainty."

"But I'm right. That's not where it usually happens. I understand that Hector Avalos was Herredia's L.A. man. But Hector bought it, and the money wasn't in Cudahy. So I'm thinking Rocky is the man now. And you."

"Things change, Bradley. Routine is death."

"For Avalos it was."

"You should watch, shut your mouth. Learn."

"Yep. For five grand a week, I can do that."

Bradley was quiet for a while. Draper saw the lights of Oceanside to the south. At the border, Draper didn't recognize the American Customs man, who quickly waved him through. Saturday shift, he thought, not the Friday night people he was used to.

The desultory Mexicans were new to him, too. They looked at his ID and LASD shield and asked him to roll down the windows of the SUV, and in the white glare of the floodlights they perused the plastic tubs of fishing gear, the loose rods, Bradley's pasteboard box, and the rolling luggage in the back.

When Draper had passed through Tijuana and got onto the toll road he felt the familiar relaxing of his body, the comfort of American law surrendering to the darker, more flexible liberties of Mexico.

In the dusty driveway of the compound Old Felipe pointed his shotgun at Bradley while a *compañero* patted him down. Draper studied Felipe's puzzled expression as he sized up the boy. Bradley chattered away in Spanish. Draper saw the other gunmen, more than usual, stationed in the shadows. He knew that word of his troubles in Jacumba had traveled south on Herredia's network. And that news of a new partner nominated to replace Terry Laws had been dispatched by Rocky through his *Eme* confederates. Draper had asked Rocky for positive spin. Draper was bullish that Bradley would pass his audition. Rocky had clearly disliked the boy, but the decision was Herredia's. Draper remembered what *El Tigre* had once said about Laws: *The desert is made for secrets.* Draper hoped to hear none of that tonight, fully understanding that he was the executor of the fate of Bradley Jones.

They entered Herredia's inner sanctum. First went Felipe, then Draper, then Bradley, bearing his gift box, then a big man and a skinny man who went to the back corners of the room. Two more men wheeled in the luggage and went outside and closed the door behind them but Draper didn't hear them walk away. He looked back at Felipe in his usual seat by the door, the combat shotgun across his lap, his hand on the grip and his weathered brown index finger tapping the trigger guard.

Herredia sat at his big iron desk. The huge Desert Eagle revolver lay in front of him. He didn't rise to greet Draper, or smile, or even acknowledge him. All of his dark attention went to Bradley. Draper saw something ancient in Herredia's stare, and he thought of lions eating cubs, and Pharaoh and Moses, and wondered if he'd need to shove Bradley off in a bulrush basket.

"What are you?" asked Herredia.

"An outlaw, sir, by birth and profession."

"What is loyalty?"

"The greatest gift that can be offered or received."

"Who has your loyalty?"

"Those loyal to me."

"Take one step forward and set down the box. At your feet."

Bradley stepped toward Herredia, squatted and lowered the box to the floor, then straightened and folded his hands contritely behind his back.

"How important is your life to you?" asked Herredia.

"Pretty damned. This is all we get, as far as I can see. I'll negotiate the afterlife when I see that I have one."

"Did you kill the man who shot your mother?"

"Yes."

"How many others?"

"None, sir."

"Did this make you proud or ashamed? Did it draw you toward God or the devil?"

"Proud. The devil. Of course."

Herredia idly picked up the gun and set it back down on the desk, pointed at Bradley. He never took his eyes off of him. "Why do you say of course?"

"I thought you would understand, sir."

"You presume to understand what I understand?"

"I don't mind the company of the devil, Mr. Herredia. I'm just a thief. If you feel closer to God, then I apologize to you and to Him. Very sincerely."

Herredia looked at Draper for the first time. Draper saw no recognition in the black eyes. Then they were back on Bradley.

"How old are you?" asked Herredia.

"Eighteen."

"Your driver's license says seventeen."

"I round up on the little things. But I always count the big things with extreme care and accuracy."

"Such as in the luggage."

"Yes."

"Open the box slowly. Felipe has a knife."

But Bradley flicked his wrist and a switchblade appeared and the blade clicked open. Draper saw the ripple of surprise in Herredia's face. Bradley knelt and swept the knife across the taped seams — middle and both sides. He closed the knife with a one-handed flourish and dropped it into a pocket. He pulled out a red, green and white beach towel from one end, uncoiling it from within. Then another. The Mexican colors, thought Draper: cagey.

Bradley dropped the second beach towel to the floor and looked down into the box. All Draper could see was what looked like a glass bottle of water. There was something dark inside but the light reflected off the surface of the liquid and Draper could not make out what he was seeing.

Then Bradley reached down into the box and hefted out the bottle by its bottom. He held it outward toward Herredia.

Draper saw the head bobbing in the liquid

and the long black hair floating just off the bottom. The head was pale. He couldn't see the eyes or the expression of the face.

"This is the head of Joaquin Murrieta," said Bradley. "He was my great-great-great-great-great-great-great-grandfather. He is the same Joaquin Murrieta that you've read about — the legendary horse thief, marksman, gambler, seducer and generous benefactor of the poor."

"Set him on my desk."

Bradley stepped forward and set the jar in front of Herredia.

Draper watched *El Patrón* peer into the jar. The head tilted and wavered slowly in the liquid, as if it were carrying on a conversation.

"His head was supposed to be lost in the San Francisco earthquake of 1906," said Herredia.

"It was stolen the day before by his great-grandson, Ramon. It was passed down to my mother, the outlaw Allison Murrieta."

"But where is the hand of Three-Fingered Jack?"

"It was never in the same jar with Joaquin. That was an error of history. There were many errors about Joaquin."

"Fantastico," said Herredia. "Felipe."

The old man came forward and leaned

his craggy face to the jar. His voice was a whisper: *"Murrieta!"*

With this, Bradley turned and looked at Draper, whose attention went back and forth between the head in the jar and the wide-eyed delight of Carlos Herredia.

Then Bradley turned back to *El Patrón.* His voice was clear and calm. "I can't let you have him, sir. He's family. I wanted him to meet you. I want you to understand that I am who you need."

Herredia frowned and snarled something to the men in the corners. They burst past Draper and closed in on Bradley, a pistol held to each of his temples as they wrenched back his arms and pushed him up hard against the iron desk.

"He is not a gift?" asked Herredia.

"I am your gift."

Herredia stood and lifted his tremendous handgun and pushed the end of the barrel into Bradley's chest.

Draper estimated the line of fire through Bradley's heart and took a small step to his left.

"You bring me Murrieta then try to take him away from me?"

"I am Murrieta. You, of all the men on Earth, understand that."

Herredia spit out a command and the men

477

forced Bradley to his knees. Draper watched Herredia lean across the desk, brace himself on his left hand, and touch the barrel of the gun to Bradley's forehead. Draper squinted at the dire tableaux.

Bradley said nothing. He didn't bow his head. From where he was standing, Draper couldn't see the expression on the boy's face but he could see Herredia's menace and when the hammer of the revolver locked back into place, the sound seemed to come from every corner of the room — from above and below, ahead and behind, from left and right.

"I do not like you," said Herredia.

"I was hoping you would, sir."

"You are not trembling. You look up at me with fear but without terror. Where is your terror?"

"I have faith in you instead."

"Where did you get this faith in me?"

"From Draper. He's a good judge of men, and he fears and loves you. As do I."

Herredia looked at him and Draper held his gaze. Herredia straightened and set his gun back on the desk.

"Of what real use to you is this head?" he asked.

"It's a family thing, sir. Like an old Christmas ornament passed down through generations. Or a cane carved by an ancestor. Or the metal shaving mirror that my great-great-grandfather brought home with him from World War I."

Herredia gestured and sat back down and the gunmen lifted Bradley to his feet.

"Gracias, hombres," said Bradley. He took a deep breath and let it out slowly, then straightened his back and shook his head as if to clear it.

Herredia looked him up and down, and smiled. "What is this? What has the new Murrieta done to himself?"

"I was hoping you'd overlook it."

"I overlook nothing."

Draper saw the sparkle of liquid on Bradley's left boot, and the small pool of liquid on the floor.

"Actually," said Bradley. "I felt a wee bit of terror."

"Bravo, Jones," said Herredia. "You are maybe a little less crazy than I thought you were. Coleman, take him to his room while we weigh the money. You will stay here tonight."

Draper felt a flood of goodwill sweep into his heart. He couldn't remember the last time that things had seemed so possible.

Bradley bowed deeply to Herredia, turned and followed Draper out.

Late the next morning Draper flashed his ID and shield to the U.S. agents manning the booth and they waved the Touareg through with only a cursory second look.

Picking up Interstate 5 north, Draper's head pounded smartly from the night before. Herredia had insisted on a bacchanalia just like in the old days with Terry. He enjoyed impressing Bradley with his power and wealth and his taste in wine, women and guns. Draper looked over at Bradley, slumped, head bobbing, a weathered Stetson pulled down low, sunglasses slipping down his nose. The kid could party, no doubt about that.

"How does it feel to have five grand in your pocket, tax free?" asked Draper.

"I can't feel my pocket."

"Every week, month after month, year after year."

"I'm not going to drink like that once a week."

"Learn to control yourself."

"I did exactly what I wanted to do."

Draper sped north through National City, looked out at the great ships docked there, the massive warriors of the U.S. Navy in for repair and maintenance.

"It's a great gig, Coleman. I wonder why you decided to cut me in."

"This isn't a job for one man."

"There are plenty of other men. Why me?"

"Because we're similar."

"Yeah. Two arms, two legs and a hangover."

"And because I see and understand you. I endorse your handling of Kick. Two can accomplish what one can only dream of. We have a future."

Draper was aware of Bradley studying him over the sunglasses.

"You think you understand me," said Bradley.

Draper said nothing but he knew he understood Bradley better than Bradley understood himself. Bradley was still a child. He believed that he deserved everything he had: his good mind and strong body and sharp eyes, Erin, his friends, his luck. But Draper saw foolishness in him, too, and he believed that Bradley would never discover his true self until much of what he had was taken away. Draper could help with that, especially with Erin, when the time was right — a bright moment in the future, something to look forward to, a diamond in a dark mine.

But as the miles slipped behind him Draper's thoughts darkened to Hood and the awful predicament that the young deputy had forced him into. Since the Jacumba disaster, Draper had all but surrendered his two fine homes, his two lovely women, his little girl, his auto repair business, and his reservist's position in the LASD. They were all too hot to touch. He was nothing more than a fugitive. Using false ID, he'd rented a Culver City apartment from a landlord happy to accept cash from a man who wanted no receipt. He felt displaced, bullied, humiliated. He refused to run: this was his home, his land, his people. He had to get his things back. Maybe not the sheriff's reserve badge, but everything else. *Everything else.* But now, all he could do was lie low. Luckily he had large stockpiles of cash, and his precious weekly gig for Rocky and Herredia, constantly bringing in more and more cash.

He felt a growing anger at Hood, who had brought all of this down on him.

"I need your help with something," he said.

"I'm not going to loan you my five grand."

"I want you to set up a meeting with Hood."

Draper looked at Bradley and saw the

gears working in the boy's mind, trying to engage.

"Why?"

"I need to see him. But if he knows I'll be there he'll bring the cavalry. If he thinks it's only you, he'll come alone. Somewhere unremarkable. Somewhere public. The boardwalk in Venice, say. You don't even need to show up. Better if you don't."

In the boy's dark eyes Draper saw the glimmer of something seen and grasped, if not yet completely understood.

"Hood," Bradley said quietly.

"Look what he did to your mother," said Draper. "Look what he's done to me. He's the only one who has actually seen me. He's the only witness against me. And he'll damage you too if he can, Bradley. He eats away at things."

Bradley said nothing for two miles. Then he turned and studied the cardboard box containing the head of his notorious ancestor, lovingly repackaged for transport by Felipe back at El Dorado. Looking then at Draper, Bradley's expression was unknowable.

"I'll think about that," Bradley said. Five minutes later his hat was on his lap and his head was lolling back against the window.

42

A week later Hood drove to Venice Beach to meet Bradley for breakfast. Hood was surprised the boy wanted to see him. It was early enough to get a good parking place near Ocean Front. Hood waited in front of the bookstore, looking at the covers. It was the first day of spring but the morning was gray and cool and the sidewalk was slick and the beach sand was darkened with drizzle.

It was too early for the bodybuilders at Muscle Beach, and too early for the bookstore to be open, but the sidewalk was busy with joggers and boarders and bladers and cyclists.

Hood could tell that Bradley had something on his mind yesterday when he called to set up breakfast. He was pretty sure he knew what it was.

A couple of days earlier, Erin had called him to say that she'd gotten a recording contract with a good indie label. Not much money, but a start. She was crazy happy. They'd celebrated the next night at the Bordello, drank a "whole truckload" of champagne, and at six in the morning, while watching the sun rise over Vasquez Rocks, Bradley had asked her to marry him. He'd actually bought her a diamond ring — big rock, gold. Must have cost five grand, she guessed. Bradley had told her that the diamond would outlive them both but their love would outlast even the diamond. She accepted immediately. She said she'd never felt so free and powerful and blessed in her life. She also told Hood to act surprised if Bradley called: she couldn't keep from telling him herself ASAP, but she didn't want to steal Bradley's thunder.

After twenty minutes there was still no Bradley so Hood walked south toward the pier. He watched the fishermen for a while, saw the bait dropping into the dark green ocean and the mackerel slapping in a red bucket. He called Bradley but got no answer, so he headed back to his car.

Ocean Front was busier now, the sidewalk bustling and the vendors setting up. A platoon of pretty girls bladed past him, hair flying. A couple glided by on a bicycle built for two. A bunch of joggers hurried by, tight and colorful, like a school of fish.

Hood looked out toward the glassy dark Pacific and saw Bradley traipsing across the sand toward him. Bradley had on bomber's jacket and a trucker's cap and his long black hair was flying in the wind beneath the cap.

Then, fifty feet ahead on the boardwalk, out where the bicycle built for two vanished into a throng of power walkers, Hood saw Londell Dwayne coming his direction. He wore his black Detroit Tigers hoodie and a black knit cap down over his ears, and sunglasses. His hands were in the sweatshirt pocket.

Hood wondered at his unusual gait — not the lanky, cool-ass shuffle that was Londell — but a purposeful march. Londell was a man on a mission.

Hood wondered why Delilah wasn't with him.

And why Londell was whistling.

He wondered why Dwayne's face remained steadily fixed in his direction. Hood could tell that the man was concentrating on only one thing: him.

Hood looked quickly at Bradley, hands in his coat pockets now, still trudging through the sand toward him, eighty feet away.

A skater weaved between Londell and Hood. By the time she passed out of his field of vision Londell had dropped his gloved left hand from the hoodie pocket. The right hand remained hidden. He was still fixated on Hood, who elbowed back his coat and popped the holster snap and rested his hand on the grip of his weapon.

Londell was thirty feet away when a pair of joggers angled between them. In their wake Hood saw Dwayne bring out the pistol. Hood heard someone yell, "He's got a gun!" and then everyone was screaming and running, the air stiff with chaos.

Bodies flew past at all angles, as if launched by an explosion. A small boy wearing ear buds and playing a harmonica walked between Hood and Londell, oblivious to what was happening. Hood grabbed him by his collar and pulled him to the ground. He heard the sizzling buzz of a bullet going past his face. But his line of fire was suddenly clear and to him the world stopped for one full second while he shot Londell twice dead center. Dwayne crashed through the display window of a swimwear store and sprawled through the mannequins as the glass rained down on him. Hood could hear the screams of the people all around but all he saw was Londell, gun still in hand, covered by the shards of glass. With his weapon in a two-hand grip, Hood ran to

487

the window and reached in and pulled away Londell's gun.

Hood's two shots had hit six inches apart, one just above the heart and one just under. Londell was breathing fast and shallow and blood ran from his mouth and nose and pooled near the base of his throat. Hood looked behind him toward the beach but Bradley was gone.

Then Hood looked back at Londell and that was when he finally, truly saw the man. He could hardly believe his eyes. Hood lifted Dwayne's cap back, which freed the pale blond forelock to wave in the ocean breeze.

Hood pulled off the sunglasses and looked into pale gray eyes. He ran a fingernail down the man's cheek and saw the path it made through the black makeup.

"I'm not afraid," Draper whispered. "Never was. Not now."

"Maybe you should have been."

Draper looked at him and blew between his lips like he was trying to whistle.

"You and Terry shot Lopes and Vasquez, beat Eichrodt so hard he lost his mind."

Draper coughed blood and nodded. "I'm dying."

"You took out Terry when his conscience got too heavy. And you let me live so I could

ID Londell."

"Never afraid. Not once. Not now."

"You set the Jacumba fire, didn't you?"

Draper's hand lifted and paused uncertainly in midair. It looked like he was offering something to Hood. Hood grabbed it and pried out a small automatic and a switchblade. The gun was upside down in Draper's fist and the blade was still closed. They fell to the glass, followed by Draper's hand. Then a rattle shook his throat and his face softened and the life drifted from his eyes.

Hood heard a siren. The morning light was choked off by the crowd behind him. The boy with the ear buds and the harmonica squeezed in close beside Hood then turned and played to his audience.

43

Three days later Hood was called into Undersheriff John Robles's office. Lieutenant Warren was there, and the coroner, Larry Pace.

Hood sat.

"We'll get right down to it, Charlie," said Robles. He was a short, stocky man with a head of silver hair and a wide, dashing mustache. "Your report on the Draper shooting said you fired twice. The techs recovered two casings that came from your service weapon, and two bullets — one from Draper's body and one from a wall in the building. But Larry did the autopsy and there were three bullet holes in Draper's body. So we've got a math problem. Any ideas?"

Hood's idea was Bradley. Hood had wondered a dozen times about him: why he was there, what he was planning, what he actually did. Hood never saw or heard another gun go off — not unusual during simultaneous fire. He understood that Bradley had set him up for Draper with his invitation to breakfast, but after that, things got iffy. How and where did Bradley and Draper meet? Did Bradley not understand that Draper would try to kill him? Did Bradley then try to save Hood? Did Bradley know full well what Draper was planning, and only change his mind about his own allegiance at the last moment?

So Hood told them about his arrangement to meet Bradley, and seeing him crossing the sand. He told them that Bradley was Allison Murrieta's son, and that he had kept in loose touch with the boy since her death. Hood said that he and Bradley had a distrustful, competitive, uncertain relationship. Hood told them that Bradley was smart and strong and he admitted to liking and feeling some responsibility for him.

The men traded looks.

"LAPD questioned Jones in the Skid Row shooting," said Warren. "Kick — the gangster who shot his mother. They made no arrest. What's your take on that, Charlie?"

"He denies it. He has a decent alibi."

"*Your* take, I said."

"I think he did it."

"Well," said Robles. "I guess we should

talk to young Bradley Jones."

Two days later Bradley strolled into the room wearing new Lucchese boots and a leather duster. He was ten minutes late. He nodded at Hood and introduced himself to Warren, Robles and Pace, shaking hands. He took off the long jacket and tossed it onto a sofa. Then he sat in the hot seat directly across the desk from the undersheriff. He crossed his legs and leaned back.

"Well, I've gone straight to the top," he said, looking at the undersheriff. "Almost."

"Tell us about Kick," said Robles.

"I'll tell you the same thing I told the L.A. cops. I was home when he bought it. I was sixty miles away. I've got five witnesses to that fact. Logically, the L.A. cops are looking elsewhere for the shooter. It was gang-related, my guess. Kick killed my mother and I'm glad he's dead and that's the end of it."

"We'd like the names and numbers for your five friends," said Robles.

"Bit out of jurisdiction, aren't you?"

"Tell us about Draper."

"Now *that's* an interesting story. He tried to recruit me for LASD at a career fair at Cal State L.A. a couple of weeks ago. He recognized me from what happened to my mom. I told him I wasn't interested in law enforcement and he said he wasn't strictly talking about law enforcement. We had some drinks later. He told me to apply with you guys. He said with him as a reservist and me as a deputy, we could do some good things together. No specifics. At the end of it, he told me that he and Hood were tight, but not to tell Hood that we'd talked. I figured he wanted to recruit me all himself, with no help from another deputy. Later, after some trouble he had in Mexico, Draper asked me if I could set up a meeting with Charlie. Charlie was acting wrong, Draper said, and Charlie couldn't know Draper would be there. A public place, he said — the boardwalk in Venice. I agreed but I didn't like it. I don't love you, Hood, but I don't wish you any serious harm. So I thought I should attend that meeting, just in case. In case of what, I wasn't sure. I had no idea what was going on when the black dude drew on Charlie and Charlie blew him away. It wasn't until the next day I found out it was goddamned Draper."

"Did you fire?"

"Fire what? I wasn't even armed."

"Why'd you split?"

"I could see that Charlie was okay. I knew the cops would be there soon. I don't mind a reasonable amount of trouble but I don't see any reason to run straight into it."

"Draper was hit three times," said Pace.

"Good shooting, Charlie," said Bradley.

"He only fired twice," said Robles.

"*Very* good shooting, Charlie."

In the silence, Bradley looked at Hood, then to Warren and Pace, then across the desk to the undersheriff. He smiled, then he laughed. "No," he said. "No, guys. Sorry. It wasn't me."

"Then who was it?" asked Warren.

Bradley looked at each of the men again. "Well, the obvious call is that Charlie thought he fired twice but let loose three. You carry an autoloader, Hood. I'll bet you whittled that trigger down real light, too. Easy to pop off rounds in the heat of combat."

Hood had wondered the same thing himself. It was possible. It was also true a person who has fired a gun at another person knows exactly how many times he pulled the trigger. You remember it. You hear it and you see it, over and over.

Bradley looked at him. "Then be logical about it. How many casings did you pick up, Charlie?"

"Just the two I fired," he said.

"What caliber was the phantom bullet?"

he asked.

There was a moment of silence then. "We couldn't come up with it," said Robles. "It went through Draper and the store, out a back window and into the neighborhood."

Bradley looked at each of them, then laughed again. "How do you guys expect me to explain a bullet you can't even find?"

"There was a third entry wound up closer to the neck," said Pace. "My ballistics guys said the exit path lined up with the hole in the window."

"And two witnesses said a guy in a bomber jacket and a cap was there when Draper went down."

Bradley shook his head. He took a deep breath. "So, did Bomber Jacket fire a gun or didn't he?"

"They weren't sure. Confusion. Fear."

"So, the witnesses have no idea who fired a bullet you don't have. Gentlemen, I need direction at this point. What do you want from me?"

Then Bradley stood and hooked his thumbs into his jeans pockets and looked at each of the men again. "One of the reasons I came down here was to answer your questions, just casual, like Charlie said it would be. I don't mean to be a wiseass but when I get falsely accused of shooting somebody, I feel the need to state my defense clearly.

"But I also came down here because I wanted to tell you a couple of things. One, Coleman Draper was doing some side work that was bringing him ten, twelve, fourteen grand a week. A *week.* It involved some Mexican heavies in the Tijuana Cartel and some *Eme* connects here in L.A. Two, something went wrong with the deal, then Terry Laws was murdered. Draper never told me that Laws was part of it but I think he was. I think Draper and Laws were in it together. And Draper killed Terry, but I don't know why."

Glances all around, then Robles sat back in his wheeled leather chair. "Tell me, did Draper indicate that his status as a reserve was a part of this profitable side job?"

"When he recruited me he said the badge and gun would open doors for me that I hadn't even known were there. He implied that he wasn't talking about legitimate doors within law enforcement, sir."

"Why do you think Laws was involved?"

"Draper talked about him a lot. You know how he sounded when he talked about Terry Laws? Regretful. Like he regretted what had happened to Terry but it was somehow necessary. I got the very strange feeling that he was recruiting me to the department to somehow replace Terry. That may be way off. But it's the feeling I got from Draper."

In the silence that followed Hood formed a deeper appreciation of Bradley Jones's intelligence and bearing, and a deeper suspicion of his stories.

"Gentlemen, I want to tell you one more thing. I could never tell Coleman Draper this because I never fully trusted him. But I can tell this to all of you — I want to join this department. I want to be one of you. I've got about a year before I can apply and I'll spend that time in college, and in the Sheriff's Cadets Program. I've got twenty-ten vision, I can run the sixty fast as anyone in your department, I can press my weight, and I've got an IQ high enough to embarrass me but it doesn't. It's all yours. Put me to the test."

Another silence. Then Robles leaned forward and shook his head. "It's not up to any of us whether you make it into the Academy or not. It's strictly merit."

"Fine," said Bradley. "I understand that. But I want you to understand this: I want what you have. I'm engaged to a beautiful woman I don't deserve. I'm going to give her the life *she* deserves. I'm going to give her love and loyalty and a family. I know some of you think I took vengeance on

Kick, but I didn't and I've proven it. So far as this idea of someone other than Hood shooting Coleman Draper, well, you got the wrong guy. I can't explain it and I'm not going to try."

Bradley lifted his leather duster from the sofa and swung it on and walked out.

44

Hood drove up the highway in the morning, headed north through the Antelope Valley California Poppy Preserve. The wet winter was a week over and the hills were carpeted with flowers, miles and miles of them, eye-shudderingly bright, rippling in the breeze.

Ariel Reed sat beside him in the Camaro, fiddling with the CD player. She had listened to one of Erin McKenna's nightclub recordings twice by then, and Hood was betting that she was going to play it again. He had seen that Ariel tended to do things over and over. Sure enough, the first song pounded to life again as they sped through the flowers.

Later they parked and Hood got the basket and blanket from the trunk. They hiked up over a rise, then down into a swale and along a dry creek bed and into a valley formed by two long hills, the flanks of which shivered with orange poppies.

They walked until the road was far behind them. A sudden surprising silence rose up to meet them. Hood felt small but not unimportant. He spread the blanket on a flowerless spot and they sat under a sky so blue it stretched credibility.

Hood poured two powerful margaritas over ice. They toasted and Ariel drained hers in one swallow, set the glass back in the basket, then kicked off her sandals. She lay back and hiked up her dress to get the sun on her legs. She spread one arm out on the blanket and shaded her eyes with the other.

"I feel like a lizard."

"In a yellow dress."

"In nature, color has a purpose. I might attract a mate."

"You have."

"Can you do some push-ups for me?"

Instead of push-ups Hood took off his shirt and lay faceup beside her, but not too close. He rested the margarita glass squarely over his navel. He thought of Bradley, and the choices facing him in the next few years, and which way he would go. He wondered if the Bulldogs might take him back, or if he should stay with Warren in IA. Then he drifted. It was easy to drift. No feeling like the sun on your skin, he thought. Even through his eyelids it was bright.

Hood thought briefly of the dogs he had when he was a boy. Then of riding horses and playing tennis. All of this past seemed to play forward logically and in a necessary way, as a prelude to the here and now. To him, these were good memories of good things. He turned his head and peeked at Ariel sprawled carelessly on the blanket nearby. He couldn't believe his good fortune in getting her out here, though all he'd had to do was ask. She told him once that she was wound as tight as a golf ball and Hood had seen this to be true. Her brain fired so fast her mouth had trouble keeping up. He had hardly understood her when she told him that the DA had dropped the charges on Eichrodt — all he heard was a jumble of words. But now, that version of Ariel was gone, replaced by someone unwound and happily reptilian.

"I know you're looking at me," she says.

"Hard not to."

"Quiet is an actual thing, not an absence."

"Another margarita and you could become one with it."

"I have no sunscreen on. My skin is a different kind of warm. My vision is hopping with little dark flecks that seem to move on their own."

"My sister called them eye skippers. Like a water skipper but —"

"Give me a kiss like that one up in the hills."

Hood downed the drink and tossed the glass and rose to one elbow. He looked into her eyes to see a gloriously alien creature. The bullet wound hurt but his heart felt whole. The blanket was big enough to keep them in and the world out.

ACKNOWLEDGMENTS

I sincerely thank the team at Trident Media, agents supreme, the best allies a writer can have. Huge thanks also to Gary Shimer for the cars, Dave Bridgman for the guns, Sherry Merryman for the research and Gary Backe for the Antelope Valley. You rock my Casbah, every one of you.

T. Jefferson Parker

ABOUT THE AUTHOR

T. Jefferson Parker is the bestselling author of fifteen previous novels, including *The Fallen, Storm Runners,* and *L.A. Outlaws.* Alongside Dick Francis and James Lee Burke, Parker is one of only three writers to be awarded the Edgar Award for Best Novel more than once. Parker lives with his family in Southern California.

The employees of Thorndike Press hope you have enjoyed this Large Print book. All our Thorndike and Wheeler Large Print titles are designed for easy reading, and all our books are made to last. Other Thorndike Press Large Print books are available at your library, through selected bookstores, or directly from us.

For information about titles, please call:
(800) 223-1244

or visit our Web site at:
http://gale.cengage.com/thorndike

To share your comments, please write:
Publisher
Thorndike Press
295 Kennedy Memorial Drive
Waterville, ME 04901